Books by Jaclyn Kot

The Between Life and Death Series

Between Life and Death (Book 1)

Between Sun and Moon (Book 2)

Between the Moon and Her Night (Book 2.5)

Between Soul and Vessel (Book 3)

THE HEART IS
BREAKING

BETWEEN SOUL & VESSEL

JACLYN KOT

Between Soul and Vessel
Jaclyn Kot
Copyright ©2025 by Jaclyn Kot

Editing by Jessica McKelden
Proofreading by Alexa at The Fiction Fix and Vanessa
at Veerie Edits
Cover design by Gigi Creatives
Formatting by Imagine Ink Designs
Map by New Ink Book Services
Chapter art by Steven Rice

Intended for Mature Audiences

CONTENT
WARNING

This book is a dark fantasy romance that contains
content that could be triggering.
Please visit www.jaclynkotbooks.com for more
information.

*To you, the warrior, the woman, fighting battles no
one can see.
You are strong. Your voice matters.
YOU matter.*
<3

Chapter 1

Sage

I drifted on the current of nothing.

The vessel that housed my soul was weightlessly suspended in the air. It was as if someone had severed the cord that connected me to my body—but there was something about this place of nothing. Something I couldn't quite put my finger on. A finger I did not need. Nor a hand, nor an arm. Because in the realm of nothing, I didn't need my body.

. . . I didn't need anything.

My eyelids were closed, and yet I could see.

In particular, I could see what was above me—

A plethora of stalactites reached down from the rocky ceiling. The uneven, icicle-like structures were luminescent, glowing a brilliant, effervescent blue on the roof of the cave's mouth. The color pulsed, growing brighter and then dimmer, as if it were breathing. As if it were alive.

I recalled that feeling. I had been alive once.

But when or how, I could not recall.

I admired the sparkling, brilliant, breathing formations.

How lovely. How true.

How true?

It made no sense and yet, it made perfect sense.

I would stay here for the remainder of eternity, drifting on the river of nothing.

Please do not leave me, Little Goddess! a male roared inside my head.

But the owner of the voice I could not place.

Hands that were tipped with vicious claws fished me out of the waterless river. They hoisted me onto the rocky bank and began to drag me along. My soul peered at them, taking in the strange, beautiful, enchanting creatures, their skin forged of charcoal gray and intricate white markings. They were tall and lean, their faces long and finely tailored and so heartbreakingly beautiful. Both of them had large, ethereal wings, tucked neatly in. And their eyes—housed beneath hairless brows—were completely black.

"It's a pretty one," said an ethereal voice, beautiful and soft and . . . male.

"Indeed. The empress did a good job upon its creation," said the other one. The sound was equally lovely, but this one was higher pitched. Female, perhaps?

"Yes, she did," agreed the male as they continued to drag me forward. If they found my body heavy, they didn't let on. In fact, by the way they walked, one would think they were hauling something as light as a pillow behind them.

Weave her another fate! a masculine voice demanded—

the same one I had heard before.

"Where do you think she will send it to next?" asked the female as she glanced down at me. Her hairless brows lowered, her expression changing to confusion.

"I dare not make a guess. The empress knows things we never will," replied the male in his soothing voice. He dropped my arm, and it slapped against the rocky floor—the sound echoing. "Put her on the table and I'll prepare for the extraction." His clawed toes scratched against the ground as he walked away.

"Nemtuk," the female said as she quickly dropped my hand.

"You know I can't let you perform the extraction," the male—Nemtuk—said. "Not after what happened last time. You nearly destroyed that poor soul."

"No, that's not it. I think it's watching us," the female said, her eyes fixed on mine.

"Impossible," Nemtuk scoffed. "They do not possess the ability to be conscious here."

"I'm serious. Come over here and look," she said.

"Fine. Fine," he sighed. His nails clicked against the ground, growing louder as he approached. Clawed fingers clamped onto my cheeks, moving my head from side to side as he gazed into my blank, lifeless face. He let out a shriek and dropped my head. "We must take it to the empress at once!"

All around us, minuscule water droplets were suspended in the air, blanketing it in a heavy layer of fog so thick I did not know how the strange, beautiful creatures were able to fly through it. Yet, they did, as if they had some inner compass guiding them. Light fought its way through the mist, bouncing off the frozen crystals, making them glitter.

It was beautiful.

If I had breath to take, I imagined it would have been stolen.

Nemtuk carried me in his unusually long, lithe arms, his wings stretched out behind him. They were a shade darker than his charcoal skin, almost black but not quite. My gaze drifted to the end of his left wing. There, the air worked away at one loose feather, as if it were chiseling it out, desperate to take it. I had been watching it for the duration of our flight, a time I had no means of measuring.

Did time even exist here? Or was that back . . .

Back where?

My thoughts stumbled, tripped, and fell, straight down a black hole of nothingness. There was a lapse, something I was missing or forgetting. But when I tried to reach for it, it was fleeting.

I returned my attention to the feather, watching it tick back and forth. Back and forth. Back and forth. I wondered when it would give up its fight and just let go.

Nemtuk cleared his throat. "Imari."

"Hmm?" she answered, her face fixed ahead.

"I must admit . . ." There was a small bit of hesitancy, as if he didn't want to reveal the next part. Slowly, he continued,

"The closer we get to the Celestial Opal Palace, the more anxious I become."

"I can understand why. If I was your gender, I would probably feel the same way." She let out a breath through her narrow nostrils—more slits than circles. "But you must remember, Empress Avena's laws do not extend to our kind. We are her most prized creation. You have nothing to worry about."

"I suppose you are right," Nemtuk agreed, albeit his teeth weathering against his bottom lip spoke otherwise. Charcoal skin crinkled between his hairless brows as he stole a quick glance at me. When our eyes met, he swiftly looked away.

Attention returning to the wiggling feather, I noticed the stubborn current had made some progress, as I could now see a bit of the quill. At any moment, the wind would have its way and finally pluck the silky, shiny plume free—stealing it away like a thief in the night.

When it finally did, I expected to feel some satisfaction at seeing the lone feather fly into the air, something I had been heavily invested in, but as I watched it fade into the distance, there wasn't a sliver of feeling to be found.

Chapter 2

Von

Find her.

With every strike of my phantom heart, that message rang out. Again, and again. A steady, constant thrum pushing adrenaline into my bloodless veins. Pushing me into madness as I grappled with reality. I had lost her. My mate. My Sage.

But I *would* get her back.

It was a vow I had roared for all to hear, to the heavens, to the Creator above. I didn't care what it would take. Rivers of blood, piles of bones, souls upon souls—whatever the cost, I would pay it for her, without hesitation.

I knew she might hate me for what I was willing to do in her name, but that's why she had always been the hero, and I the villain.

With my shadows clawing at the air behind me, I stormed into a cell at the very back of my dungeon, in the underbelly of my obsidian castle. The air was thick, riddled with the stench of rot, shit, and piss.

In the dim blue firelight provided by the braziers placed outside the cells, my eyes locked on the redheaded ass-licker. Before he could loosen his brown-tipped tongue, the iron of my fist smashed into his jaw, sending him careening to the floor.

I barely recognized my own voice, more demented creature than immortal, as I demanded, "Where is Soren?"

"Aggressive," Folkoln said as he strolled around me, watching Arkyn as he rolled onto his side, choking and sputtering. "But tell me, brother, if you snap his jaw off, how will he tell you the information you seek?"

Ignoring him, I grabbed hold of Arkyn's collar and lifted him from the cell floor. I shoved him against the wall, teeth gnashing as I reiterated, "Where *is* he?"

"I told you before, he's probably at the castle," he sputtered, his hands grabbing hold of my wrists, squirming like a maggot covered in its own filth as he tried to fight my unbreakable hold.

"He's not." I squeezed my fist, cinching the cloth tighter, allowing him a fraction of the air he needed to properly breathe. I could have easily snatched the air from his lungs without lifting a finger, but right now, more than ever, I needed to use my hands. I needed to feel the crux of pain as I split my knuckles open, needed to feel every bit of it so I could stay grounded in my cause.

A flutter of wings sounded, followed by light footsteps.

"I found him, my king," Fallon's voice came from the cell door.

My eyes remained on Arkyn. "Where?"

"In Belamour."

I shoved Arkyn into the wall, the volcanic glass spiderwebbing with deep fissures. Releasing him from my chokehold, he slid to the floor, gulping down mouthfuls of air.

Turning, I faced Fallon.

Her eyes stretched wide, the air in the back of her throat catching. I was no stranger to the look she gave me, my immortal ears familiar with the whisper of a breath faltering. It was the same response everyone else seemed to emit whenever they saw me, now more than ever—

Fear.

After the Three Spinners agreed to help me get Sage back, I had just barely wrangled my beast form into submission, but he had not left me unmarked. My eyes were stained an inky, otherworldly black. My ears, sharpened into points, like two daggers, remained, as well as the menacing horns. My skin was stained with bolts of onyx as if I was the conduit between the heavens and the earth, struck by the electricity produced from warring clouds.

In truth, when I caught my reflection in the mirror, I no longer recognized myself, but that disconnect was not because of my appearance. It was deeper than flesh and bone, and it went directly to the core of my being.

If I ever had any humanity in me, it had been destroyed when she died.

When I lost Sage the first time, when our babe died with her, I fell into the abyss of darkness. There, in the swirling pit of emptiness, I was forged into the hunter, my task at the forefront of my mind—tracking down the immortal who murdered my mate and my child. I had vowed to make Nicholas suffer, ten-fold the amount he had inflicted upon her.

And that was exactly what I had done, before I ended his miserable life.

Now, I was being forged into that same creature, but this time, it was different. Although the years were long, I had hope back then. I'd known Sage would reincarnate, and eventually, we would be reunited.

But now I knew the truth. She would not.

And it changed everything.

It had changed me.

It had made me . . . whatever I was now.

"Show me," I said to Fallon.

"Alright." She nodded, her form shifting into a raven.

"Lock the cell," I directed Folkoln, his reply lost as my umbra swept around me, taking me to the Living Realm.

The Jewel of Edenvale was going to shit, and it was going to shit fast.

For hundreds of years, Belamour had been a sanctuary for the wealthy and the upper class due to its proximity to the castle, which had traditionally housed a great deal of the monarchy's army. But when news had spread of Aurelius's and the mortal king's deaths, Edenvale had been thrust into chaos, fumbling to decide on a new heir—the mortal king's young son or his estranged nephew. As the idiots of the court argued over which one to choose, mortals did as they always did when they had no authority to answer to—they began to pillage, turning their sights on the richest city in Edenvale first.

In less than a few weeks, a good portion of the opulent, indulgent city was left in ruin. The once polished, brick-paved streets were full of mud and excrement. The stained-glass windows were shattered, the stores gutted and ransacked, though some establishments and houses had been left untouched, Sage's and my manor included.

When my winds had whispered to me about what was happening in Belamour, I'd come here and placed wards around the gothic manor I had built for Sage—ensuring it would not be harmed. During the too-short time we spent together, the memories of that place were something I cherished, and I would do everything to guard it, to ensure it would still be standing when I finally brought her home.

Fallon flew beside me as I walked, her wings held straight out as she drifted on a pocket of air. Bits of ash rained down on us. A crackling, popping fire chewed at a building to my right. People dashed toward it, carrying buckets of water as they attempted to quench the ravenous flames.

The boisterous laughter of a drunk, copulating pair caught my attention—the man's dirty, unwashed ass on full display as he jerked into the woman, his trousers slung down by his feet. I did not see how she could find any pleasure, all things considered, but she had her head tossed back and was moaning in ecstasy.

Mortals.

What a peculiar bunch.

Fallon tucked her wings in as she descended to the ground, shifting into her human form at the same time. She nodded toward an inn a few buildings down. "That's it."

Like the majority of the buildings on this street, the inn looked to have seen much better days. The windows were boarded up with slats of wood, and the door looked like it was one swift kick away from falling off its hinges.

As we walked up to it, I looked up at the cracked wood sign swinging above the entrance.

The Little French Cat Inn.

I quirked a brow at the strange name, repeating my earlier sentiments—

Mortals.

When we walked inside, the scent of ale and damp wood was strong. People sat at their tables, hunched over their drinks as they spoke to one another. Their conversations fell short as they turned toward me, horror spreading from face to face, passing like a torch. I scanned each one. Not a single, sniveling Soren to be found.

"Where did you see him?" I asked Fallon.

"He was over there, sitting at the bar," she replied, nodding in the indicated direction.

"Well, he's not there now," I observed before I started to walk between the tables, my bootheels sticking to the ale-covered floors.

Fallon scurried behind me. "My king, where are you

going?"

I eyed the face of the weathered innkeeper. "To have a little conversation."

As I approached the man, he reared back into the cupboard behind him, causing the bottles and cups to chatter. I slid onto a wooden stool and dropped my elbow to the bar top with a loud *thunk*. The man nearly jumped out of his swiftly paling skin.

"C-c-c-an I get you something?" he stammered.

"The hospitality," I said with a saccharine grin, one that quickly fell from my lips. "I'm looking for a boy around eighteen years of age. Dirty blond hair. Brown eyes." I raised my hand to just below my shoulder. "About this tall." I wiggled my fingers. "Missing a few of these."

The innkeeper glanced at the stairwell.

That one look told me all I needed to know.

"Room." It wasn't a question, so I didn't ask it like one.

He swallowed harshly, his Adam's apple performing a desperate bob, as if it were attempting to squirm out of him, something I imagined his soul wanted to do as well.

"The king asked you a question," Fallon grated. "I suggest you answer it."

"You best listen to her. I'm a desperate soul, and you know what they say about desperate souls, don't you?" I paused for a moment, my gaze shifting lazily from one side of the room to the other. "They'll burn it all to the ground to get what they want."

"Second floor. Room twenty-four," he squeaked, clenching the countertop behind him.

I tapped the counter twice, my rings clattering against the stone top. "Thank you, boss."

My shadows swept around me, taking me to the second floor.

I walked by the first three rooms, stopping when I found the one I was looking for. My knuckles drummed gently against the door as I purred, "Housekeeping."

I could hear the little worm's heart pounding on the other side.

My hand lowered to the handle, but it wouldn't twist. I rolled my eyes. Mortals and their fickle locks. A blast of my angry winds sent the door flying open, smashing it into oblivion against the wall on the other side of the room.

Soren was in a crouched position, a blade in his good hand. "Don't come any closer," he sputtered, voice trembling.

Fallon's footsteps sounded as she came running behind me.

"Took you long enough," I teased her under my breath.

"I mean it," Soren warned, the blood chased from his skin, turning it ashen.

A flick of my eyes summoned a blast of air to smash into Soren's hand, knocking the weapon onto the floor. His face snapped to the side, his body tense as he decided what to do—make a run for the weapon or try something else.

Unfortunately for him, I was in no mood to play.

Harnessing the darkness, I flashed from where I stood and resurfaced behind him. My hand wrapped around his throat as I said, "You're coming with me."

Chapter 3

Von

"Out of the way, child," Ezra bellowed at one of the kitchen staff as she carried a pot over to the sink, dumping out the bubbling, hissing contents. A billow of steam rolled toward the ceiling, followed by something pungent, something that smelled like ammonia.

She sighed in relief. "That was a close one."

With my fist balled up in the back of Soren's tunic, I steered him through my fading shadows into the kitchen, back at my castle in the Spirit Realm. I had given the cavernous room to Ezra so she could work on her magic potions—one of which she promised would help me get Sage back.

I shoved the sniveling worm ahead, my fist releasing from his shirt. It was just enough force to make him stumble but not enough to make him fall to the floor.

My brow raised. There was a large, dark splotch between his legs. I glanced down at my thigh, noting a trace of dampness on the black leather. I groaned as realization dawned. The pungent smell was not from Ezra's pot—it was Soren's piss.

He'd *pissed* on me.

"Fucking mortals," I grumbled as I waved my hand over my leg, dissolving the urine. I looked at Soren's trousers, my magic cleaning that mess as well.

I *didn't* do it for him.

The last thing I wanted to smell was his piss. I imagined the rest of the staff would agree.

Soren looked down, stunned to find his pants were dry.

Ezra turned around, her milky-white orbs looking past me. "You found him, I see." She cracked a smile, entertained by her own overused joke.

"When do we start?" I asked, eyeing a staff worker dumping a copious amount of salt into a boiling pot. Salt was something Ezra had requested a lot of lately, so much so that I was having it delivered to the castle in wagon loads. I didn't ask questions, nor did I care. If salt was the answer to me getting Sage back, I'd harvest every crystal, until the realms had no more to give.

"In due time," Ezra answered as a girl handed her a wood cane. Swollen and stiff knuckles wrapped around the handle. "Soren, dear, can I get you something to eat?"

"W-w-where am I?" he stammered, looking around.

"You are in the Spirit Realm," Ezra answered.

"Am I dead?" he asked, two fingers and three nubs raking back his blond hair, as if getting that mop out of his eyes would help him see. A laughable notion—the boy was as blind as they came.

"Unfortunately, not yet. Although, I will thoroughly enjoy it when your time comes," I said, my voice making him bristle.

He turned around and began to back away from me. "I a-a-always knew th-th-that something was-was off about you."

"I am what I am, but at least I am not a spineless traitor." My tone was menacing. "Not only did you cross Sage's unconscious mind barrier, but you used it to manipulate her into thinking Ezra's life was at stake. Because you did that, my hand was forced into making a deal to protect her, one that meant I could not save her when she needed me the most."

"Save her?" Soren asked. "From what?"

So then, the boy didn't know.

"She is dead." The words were like ash on my tongue. My chest grew still, the oxygen evaporating from my lungs.

His eyes widened. "That's why I don't feel the connection to her mind anymore," he spoke to himself. "But wait . . . doesn't that mean she's here?"

"No," I said. "When mortals die in the Three Realms, they come to the Spirit Realm, but when immortals die, their souls cease to exist here."

"So . . . she's really *dead*." Soren choked out the last word. His expression folded in on itself as tears filled his eyes. They began to leak down his face as he fell to his knees. "It's all my fault."

Tap. Tap. Tap.

Ezra's cane sounded against the floor as she moved to Soren's side. She patted his head in a bid to comfort him.

"Although your actions played a hand in the events that led to her death, they are not entirely to blame. Sage chose her own path, and she sacrificed herself to save countless others. Now it is our turn to save her."

Soren looked up at Ezra, his voice breaking as he asked, "How are you going to do that?"

My muscles stiffened. Soren was one of the last people I wanted Ezra divulging our plan to, especially while it was in its infancy.

Continuing to stroke his head, she replied, "With your help."

The tightness in my muscles eased.

"How am I going to help?" Soren asked.

"I'll get to that, but first, let's get you something to eat and a nice hot cup of tea," Ezra said. She pursed her lips in thought. "Although, we might have to go to another kitchen to find you something . . . edible."

"Ezra," I cut in, voice flatter than a slab of stone. Colder, too. "I'd like to speak to you. Outside."

"Alright," she said, the rhythmic tapping of her cane following me out of the room.

When we were out of earshot, I turned to her and snarled, "Soren is a traitor, and he should be treated as such."

"Soren is a scared little boy who wants what everyone else wants—to live," she countered, her hands resting on the top of her cane.

"Then he really should have made better choices," I stated, my tone menacing.

"He was dealt a poor hand, and he made his decisions

based on it."

"That does not excuse what he has done."

"No, it doesn't." She paused. "But he does genuinely care for Sage, and that is something we will use to our advantage. Besides, for what we are going to ask him to do . . . he is going to need his strength. A full belly will help him with that."

I raised one brow in challenge. "Who said anything about *asking*?"

Ezra sighed, licked her cracked lips, and then said, her voice soft, "I understand your anger toward him—"

"Clearly you do not," I interjected, my teeth clenched. "Have you forgotten what he's done? That useless mortal is part of why Sage is no longer here. I will show him all the grace he showed her when he wove his lies into her mind, making her believe he held a knife to your throat, all so he could save himself."

"I have not forgotten, no." She took a breath. "But a wise god once told me people are more amenable when they believe they have a choice, even if they do not." Beneath her milky-white orbs, I could see the razor-sharp mind at work. "I wonder, where is that god now?"

I chuckled at that. "You would try to turn my own words against me in order to manipulate me?" I asked, somewhat amused.

"I wouldn't dare," Ezra lied with a coy smile.

"Mhm," I responded, looking past her, through the doorway, and into the kitchen at the boy who had pissed himself mere moments ago. Perhaps Ezra was right. Perhaps force wasn't the answer . . . at least, for the time being. "Fine, we'll do it your way."

"I was hoping you'd say that."

"But the second—"

"I know, I know," she interjected. "*Then* we'll try it your way."

I nodded, forcing a breath into my heated lungs. I watched the boy and muttered, "I do not trust him."

"Nor do I," she agreed. "But for this to work, we *need* him."

A muscle ticked in my jaw. I hated that truth. Hated all of this.

But if this was what it took to have Sage back in my arms, I would endure.

Speaking of—

"The mixtures you have been preparing, how are things going?" I asked, crossing my arms over my chest.

"They are getting closer," she answered. "But I'm going to need those tears from a Lost Soul, as we discussed before."

"I'll get them."

"Good. You concentrate on getting those, and I'll focus on my part."

I nodded. "Alright."

Her cane guided her as she walked back into the kitchen, her voice filling with false pleasantries as she said to Soren, "Now, about that cup of tea."

Chapter 4

Sage

Beams of light shot down from the heavens. They were like the blade of a mighty sword, piercing the fog, forcing it to fall to its knees, to surrender to the light's mighty ruler—

The sun.

Moonbeam, a regal voice whispered in my ear, the word echoing through the blank expanse of my thoughts.

I was puzzled at that. Moonbeam? There was something familiar about the word, something I couldn't quite—

"It's been a while since I've seen the Capital," Imari said, her hair dancing behind her, caught on the melody of the whistling wind as she flew.

The wind. Something twisted inside me. Something strange.

"Same," Nemtuk responded, swallowing harshly.

I looked over his shoulder, marveling at the

mountainous female statues that began to emerge all around us. They were towering, glorious sculptures that stood in splendor, gilded in divine femininity, from their curvaceous frames to their long, flowing hair. They were so incredibly lifelike, it almost looked like the bottom of their gowns were waving in the wind. In one hand, they bore a sword, raising it in victory. In the other, they held a severed head—all of which were . . . *male*.

"It is a testament to the empress's might," Imari observed, conjuring a small nod from Nemtuk as he stared at the stone giants, his eyes impossibly wide.

Down below, extravagant streets framed by opulent temples stretched on for miles. The temples glistened in the sun's caress, their glass-like exteriors varying in design and colors from one to the next. Some of the structures had fluted columns stretching from base to ceiling, and others had ornate spires that pierced the sky.

They were all so different.

But it was what they were made from that linked them all together—

Crystals. Some were citrine in color while others appeared to have been forged from rose quartz or amethyst. Some were darker, as if their walls had been filled with wisps of twirling smoke.

"What do you think the goddesses do in those temples all day?" Imari asked, her voice dropping just above a whisper.

Nemtuk pondered her question for a moment. "Probably boss their slaves around." A small smile brimmed on his gray lips, showing off his sharp, pointed teeth. "Go get me another glass of wine," he said, his voice shifting to a snobbish tone. "I've only six hundred cups today and I am in dire need of another. Hurry now."

Imari chuckled then sighed. "Must be nice."

"I imagine it is," he said, the smile fading from his lips as he looked skyward.

"You have nothing to fear," Imari reminded him.

"You're right," he breathed, giving a small, firm nod.

"Come on," she directed as her wings clapped downward, the tips almost touching as she left the current she had been riding and began to fly higher.

Nemtuk followed behind her.

When the world faded below, a new one began to emerge.

Nestled in the embrace of the heavens was a floating mass of land, the bottom full of colossal formations that looked as if they were mountains flipped upside down. The mountains were imperfect, broken, and jagged—like they were missing parts of themselves. It was as if they had been rooted to the ground hundreds of feet below and brutally torn from it in a fit of rage.

Once we reached the other side, it was like seeing the other half of a coin. The craggy stone shot up into mountains in the middle of the island, a sea of cerulean surrounding it. The shimmering waters were calm and serene, gently brushing against the lip of the landmass but never tumbling over. Raised above the sea were dozens of pathways, all of them stretched from the edge of the island to the very middle—to celestial buildings that surrounded an unfathomably opulent palace, forged from opal stone. Light refracted off the glistening walls, the pastel colors dancing and shimmering as we flew closer. It was something out of a fairy tale, it's grandeur beyond comprehension.

We landed at the foot of the grand palace's crystal doors, and like the rest of the impressive structure, they towered before us. Above them, ancient symbols were carved into stone—a language, one I could not read, at least, not at first. But the longer I studied the strange markings, the less foreign they became.

The Celestial Opal Palace, home of the Great Empress Avena, Protector of all Femalekind.

Movement captured my attention, pulling it back down to the doors. On them, two carvings appeared, depicting a smiling female and a towering, beautiful male—the most gorgeous one I had ever seen, a truth I was certain of. Crowns, crafted from bones and burning with a dark, shadowy flame, floated above their heads. The male wrapped his strong, powerful arms around her as he softly kissed her neck. She guided his ringed fingers to her rounded belly, filled with the gift of life. Roses bloomed around them, intricately linked by winding vines.

They were happy . . .

So very happy.

A feeling, one I had no name for, kicked at my numbness—like a fist knocking against a door. Although it might have been closed, I could hear it as it pounded away, screaming to be let in.

"It's eyes are leaking," Nemtuk said in astonishment, his voice plucking me from my thoughts.

Imari came closer, peering down at me. "Have you ever seen this before?"

"Never," Nemtuk answered with a slow shake of his head. "The connection between soul and vessel is severed, and yet, somehow, they are still tethered." With a curled, claw-tipped finger, he dabbed at my face, sweeping up the tear. He studied it.

"It's rather peculiar," Imari said, her attention shifting to the door. "Do you think it showed her something?"

"It very well could have." Nemtuk nodded before his expression turned sheepish. Subtly, he probed, "Do you see anything?"

"I do," Imari answered. "I see myself, standing in front of an applauding crowd, accepting a blessing from Empress Avena." A smile caressed the corners of her heart-shaped mouth. She looked at Nemtuk. "What do *you* see?"

His eyes drifted to the door, and his expression turned sheepish. "I'd rather not say."

"You see me, don't you?" she teased, letting out a soft laugh.

"I do not," he blurted out.

"Welcome to Avolonia. The *Doors of the Heart's Desire* are quite something, are they not?" asked a female voice as she strode *through* the closed doors. She was small in stature, but the way she carried herself, the certainty in her step, the upward tip of her jaw, spoke otherwise. She wore a silk robe, dyed the same color as the sky above. A leather belt wrapped around her petite waist, and from it hung a small cloth pouch and a rabbit's foot. A strip of white paint ran across her face, passing over her wine-colored eyes. Her hair fell in gentle waves.

At her approach, Imari and Nemtuk bowed their heads, but it was Imari who said, "Yes, Priestess Avriel."

The priestess's eyes slid to mine, her brows raising ever so slightly. "You have traveled all this way to deliver just *one* soul? How come?"

"Because, it seems to be, well . . ." Imari paused for a brief moment. She leaned in and whispered, "Awake."

The priestess shook her head. "That can't be."

"I would not lie to you," Imari spoke swiftly. "Please, take a look."

Hesitant at first, Priestess Avriel looked from Imari to Nemtuk, who still had his head bowed, then back to me. She took one step closer, eyes roving over my limp carcass as if I were some strange, dangerous specimen.

Then, she peered deeply *into* me.

Suddenly, she let out a gasp. "The soul *is* awake! Come. Quickly." Avriel turned swiftly, her heels clicking loudly as she charged toward the entrance.

Imari took my vessel from Nemtuk. In a silent goodbye, the two exchanged looks rather than words. Imari turned and carried me toward the doors—the man and pregnant woman still present.

Inside the palace, the soft, melodic tune of a harp echoed off the cavernous walls, accompanied by a beautiful female voice that harmonized with the enchanting instrument. Statues, similar to the ones I had seen before but much smaller, were carved into the walls. Females, a medley of ages and species, lined the hallways, their whispered conversations stalling as we passed by them. One with the face of a cat caught my attention. She stopped licking her paw as her slit pupils fell on me. Her ears shifted backwards, her eyes widening.

"Open," Avriel commanded as we approached another set of doors.

Two charcoal-skinned women, dressed in sleek, white robes tucked beneath silver armor, nodded in response. With a wave of their claw-tipped fingers, blue magic swirled into the air, curling around the cylindrical handles and pulling the doors open.

When Imari stepped through them, the world exploded in brilliant light. It shone through the thin vaulted ceilings, through the opal structure, sparking pure magic before my very eyes. A ballet of greens, pinks, purples, and reds. It was like the Northern Lights had been brought inside, the colors dancing with one another as if they were alive.

Elegant tapestries hung from the ceiling. A woman who possessed beauty unlike I had ever seen before was featured in each one. Her hair was spun of gold, her eyes the color of freshly bloomed lilacs, her skin a rich ivory encased in a golden glow. Although she was the focal point, the story told in each tapestry was different. Some spoke of reverence, while others told of great victories. At the far end of the room was a dais. Upon it sat a mountainous throne forged from the same dazzling gemstone as the rest of the palace—

An opal throne.

The throne was enchanting, but the giant who sat upon it was beyond compare.

She was *stunning*.

An intricate, ornate crown, forged of crystals, sat upon her gently floating blonde hair. Her body was a rich landscape made of feminine curves, the dips and valleys outlined in the colors of a dawning sun. That same glow encased the exquisite gown she wore, surrounding her completely in the light of divinity. The wispy, pastel-green fabric of her sleeves draped downward, spilling past the throne onto the polished floors.

She was no mere woman, nor was she just a goddess. She was the mother, the ruler, the beginning and the end, all of which had been featured in the tapestries that surrounded this incredible room.

She was—

"Empress Avena," Priestess Avriel said with great reverence as she and Imari dropped to bended knee, just before the dais.

A dozen shirtless, masked men lounged around the empress's throne—their bodies chiseled with muscle, their sleek skin glistening with oil. Some of them were giants, just like the empress. Some held gold platters, trays chock-full of food—fruits, breads, cheeses, and various meats. Two held wine jugs. The other ones simply stood there, their masked faces fixed on us. The masks looked like they were made of iron, each one different—some had been inspired by the faces of animals, while others looked more demonic with wicked horns.

Horns.

The empress had a pair as well, but hers were antlers. They were beautiful. Majestic. The ivory bone elegantly curled up and out, stretching into multiple polished points, like branches of a tree. Intricate gold chains draped from them, linked to teardrop-shaped diamonds.

The giant's gaze roved from the priestess to Imari and then to me. Her eyes flared wide, and the huge goblet slid from her hand. It struck the stone floor, the sound louder than thunder. Wine sprayed out everywhere, dousing one man's leg and foot in dark-red liquid.

He didn't move an inch.

He didn't even look.

He just remained there, perfectly still.

Slowly, the empress stood, her attention fixed on me, while mine was drawn to her wrist. On it, a thick cuff crafted from gold and decorated with an ancient dialect—the words worn by the caress of time. Although it was lovely looking, something about it felt . . . off. The empress's hand stretched toward the arm of her throne, her fingers not quite touching, but ready to grab hold in case she needed it for balance.

"I knew this day would come, I just never imagined it would take so long." Her voice was like velvet—smooth, rich, and alluring. "But now that it has, it is almost hard to believe," she remarked to herself. "I have so many, *many* questions."

Silence swallowed whatever time passed next.

No one dared make a sound.

She glanced to one of the masked men, gesturing to the spilled wine, and said, "Clean this up."

"Yes, Your Majesty," he spoke in his deep timbre— warm and enchanting. He was muscular and tanned, his hair blond and curly. With a wave of his hand, a bucket and a mop appeared beside him, sudsy water sloshing over the brim. With a swirl of his finger, the mop lifted from the bucket and began to scrub the floors.

The empress turned her attention back on us. She began her descent down the stairs, her gown trailing behind her. As she moved toward us, her body became smaller, stopping when she was about six feet tall. Reaching us, she commanded in her regal, enchanting tone, "You may rise."

Swiftly, Imari and the priestess stood.

The empress looked at Imari. "How did you find her? Were you alerted to her passing into this realm?"

Imari shook her head. "I'm afraid not, Your Majesty. Somehow, this soul must have slipped through the screening system. I did not realize *she* was of importance to you. Otherwise, I would have flown much fas—"

"Silence," the empress cut her off. "All that matters is that you found her and brought her here. For that, you will be rewarded."

"Thank you, Your Majesty," Imari said, bowing.

The empress gave a regal nod of her head, before her eyes shifted to mine. "She is conscious," she said, although, unlike the others, she did not seem surprised.

"Yes. That is why we knew to bring her to you," Imari said. "We knew she was different."

"She is," the empress assented.

"Who was she?" Priestess Avriel asked, taking a step forward.

"The question is not who was she, but rather, who has she become? It is a question we must gain an answer to, swiftly. There is one person who can help us with that. Follow me," the empress said before she started for the doors.

Chapter 5

Avriel

The rabbit's foot, hanging from my belt, bounced rhythmically as Imari and I followed Empress Avena. Gently, my fingers clasped around it, my thumb stroking the soft, white fur.

It reminded me of *him*. Instantly, the tension in my shoulders eased.

I had served Empress Avena for the majority of my life, and I had gone to the Creator's Tower, nestled in the northern part of the palace, thousands of times before.

Still, I *hated* going there. Detested it with every fiber of my being.

Not that I showed it.

The men in this castle were forced to wear physical masks, but as for us women, ours were invisible, carefully honed from years of hiding our true thoughts and feelings about the world we lived in.

I braced myself as we turned to our left and walked down the last, long hallway, leading up to the monstrous tower.

The tower received its name from Emperor Alaric. He was a primordial god, the creator of everything. In this very tower, he would spend countless hours plucking the stars from the sky, shattering them apart, and creating souls. He made their vessels too, forging life on his great, mighty anvil. Emperor Alaric had made nearly every species known to femalekind—mortals and immortals, animals and mythical creatures—even *dragons*, which no longer existed. Well, at least, not living ones. Dragons had all been destroyed during the War of the Creators, which led to Emperor Alaric's defeat, dethroning, and ultimately, his death.

His wife, Empress Avena, had been the one to take his life.

After, she had the tower completely gutted, destroying everything and anyone she deemed to be of no value to her. She had kept the emperor's journals, his anvil, and his hammer, which she'd used to forge her own creations, infusing a different truth into those she made—infusing them all with lies, that she was the original creator, that Alaric was the imposter.

And they all believed her, especially the Ashamori, her most loyal subjects—which was what Imari was.

I couldn't blame them. I, too, had also once believed her. I'd even gone against my own mother when she tried to tell me otherwise.

The truth of the past was an easy thing to corrupt, especially when anyone who opposed it had their tongue permanently silenced.

A memory pried loose, and my mother's sad, smiling face flashed before my eyes, right before her soul was torn from her chest and crushed by the hand of the very female who walked in front of me.

"This way," the empress said as she turned to her right.

I took a breath, knowing I was going to need it, as I followed her inside the tower.

Dozens of mezzanines were stacked over top of one another, circling the exterior of the tower, open in the very middle, all the way to the roof. Hundreds of feet above, hung from the ceiling, was the remains of a dragon, its magically preserved body on display instead of being given back to the soil, where it could decompose and finally rest in peace. Dozens of stygian forgemasters were at work, experimenting and testing, breaking and—according to them—fixing. Animals howled in their cages while hammers clamored and chisels picked. A horrific female scream sounded from somewhere up above, followed by a whirring noise that made my blood run cold.

"What is this place?" Imari whispered to me, her eyes shifting this way and that.

Where morality comes to die, I wanted to say, but instead, I replied, "The Creator's Tower is a place for education, where new species are created and great mysteries are solved. It is overseen by the top stygian forgemaster—"

"Victor," the empress said by way of greeting as the man himself approached us.

The centuries had not been kind to him. His shoulders were permanently curved from a lifetime of standing over top of his . . . *creations* as he worked on them. His eyes bulged from their sockets, the whites littered with broken blood vessels. His skin was paler than the dead, which was rather fitting, considering a lot of the things he worked on ended up that way.

Something that could also be said for the empress.

Although Victor and Empress Avena had been able to create some species, they couldn't create like Emperor Alaric could. They had tried and tried to remake dragons, the emperor's greatest creation, but they failed time after time. In their desperation, they had resorted to horrific measures, which was why this place had become what it was.

I often wondered if Emperor Alaric had rolled over in his grave knowing what had become of his beloved tower. Could he hear the desperate cries of those tormented inside this terrible place?

I could.

Every night when I laid my head down to sleep, they were all I heard. Even though my room was on the opposite side of the palace, my mind had recorded the sounds, playing them over and over again.

"Your Majesty," Victor said, voice hoarse. He cleared the phlegm from his throat, making an awful sound. Due to his lifetime of service, Victor was one of the only males in this realm allowed to go without a mask when in public. He also didn't have to bow to the empress. It was considered highly disrespectful not to bow to our sovereign, yet the empress didn't seem to mind. Had it been anyone else, she would have had their head.

But Victor got special treatment.

I had once heard a rumor he had been quite handsome in his younger years—however, I believed the nature of his work had drained him of any beauty, inside and out.

Still, I put a fake smile on my face as his slimy eyes slid to mine, his smiled widening as he said, "Priestess Avriel." I swore I could hear his back popping as he forced his shoulders back, trying to stand taller.

"Forgemaster," I greeted him, tipping my head in respect. It made me want to vomit.

The sound of something buzzing, and the desperate roar of an animal from somewhere up above, sent my nerves on edge.

"To what do I owe the honor?" he said, his slimy tongue pressing against the corner of his parted lips, moving up and down. Up and down. Up and down. The act, accompanied by the way he was looking at me, made me want to crawl out of my skin.

Still, I hid my true nature, my invisible mask permanently in place. "I'm here with the empress," I said, giving him a soft, fake smile.

"Always such a *good girl*," he rasped, his words sliding over my skin, painting them in his nauseating filth.

The need to run and find a scalding-hot tub to douse

myself in and a wool brush to scrub my skin raw with became exceedingly strong, but I steeled myself.

The empress gestured to the female in Imari's arms. "Do you recognize her?"

He stepped closer, surveying the white-haired female. His hand wrapped around the bottom half of her face, shifting her head from side to side. "Oh yes," he cooed with a raspy chuckle, his eyes glinting, as if a shiny new toy had been gifted to him.

My fingers twitched at my side, desperate to reach for the rabbit's foot. I didn't know the female, but I felt for her in that moment, watching as he put his grimy, horrible hand over her face, as if he had a right to.

He looked at the empress, his eyes gleaming with excitement. "If she is here, Nockrythiam might follow."

"Nockrythiam?" I asked, feeling as if the wind had been knocked out of me. There wasn't a soul alive who hadn't heard that legendary name, regardless of how hard the empress tried to erase it. He was the greatest fighter in all of the lands, the bringer of death, and the last defender of Emperor Alaric. The Ender of Realms.

I glanced at the vessel . . . How was she connected to him? It was a question I was determined to find the answer to.

"Let us hope that she succeeded at her task," the empress said, ignoring me. "Nockrythiam is the key."

"Indeed, he is," Victor agreed, pulling his hand from her face. "Shall we find out what happened?"

"Yes. How long will it take?" the empress asked,

resting a hand in the crook of her hip.

He surveyed the condition of the vessel, before he said, "It shouldn't take much more than a few hours to repair the damage, but as for the soul—"

"I'll see to that," the empress cut in, raising her hand, the one with the gold cuff on it—something she *never* went without. "It will be much faster that way."

Victor eyed the jewelry, then replied, "Very well."

He and the empress began to walk toward a secluded room. Imari and I followed behind them.

Long legs speeding up, Imari caught up to Victor. "I can help."

"And you are?" Victor asked without so much as glancing her way.

"Imari, sir. I work at station 104 along the Miyakai River and—"

"Thank you, Imari," Empress Avena cut her off. "But I have another task for you, which I will explain later."

We filtered inside the room, brightly lit. Inside, there were trays and walls full of various tools and instruments. The look of them made my blood run cold. In the middle of the room, an altar made from stone. It looked hard and unforgiving. Cold. It fit the rest of this place.

"Lay her there," Victor directed Imari, gesturing to the altar before he walked towards a desk. Slung over the chair was a blacksmith's apron. He grabbed it and began to put it on.

Imari laid the female down on the altar and then took a step back.

"You can wait outside," the empress directed Imari before her eyes shifted to mine. "I want an emergency council meeting arranged three hours from now."

I glanced at the white-haired female, a gnawing feeling in my stomach. Although she was a perfect stranger, leaving her with Victor just didn't sit right with me. But just as I always did, I bowed my head to the empress and said, "Yes, Your Majesty."

I could feel Victor's eyes on me, watching as I walked out the door.

The second I was outside, my twitching fingers grabbed hold of the rabbit's foot, and I left the tower as swiftly as possible.

Chapter 6

Sage

"She looks like him," Empress Avena said, her voice a soft whisper as her fingertips passed over my face, mapping the architecture of my bones. "It's the nose."

I couldn't feel any of it.

"What do you plan to do with her . . . after?" Victor rasped, his words rattling from deep within his chest. He was bent over my vessel, a chisel in one hand and a small hammer in the other. He tapped it along my skin, working on the tattered flesh and gaping wound in my chest, caused from . . .

I searched for an answer but found none.

"I suppose that depends on her memories. If she succeeded at her task, then I will reward her. However, if she failed, I will have her soul crushed, once and for all," the empress said as she brushed a strand of hair behind my ear.

"You delude yourself with false hope," Victor said as he

turned toward a tray, his ichor-covered fingers passing over top of the different tools. "I do not need to look at her memories to know how things must have played out with Nockrythiam, *all* factors considered." Selecting a chisel with a smaller point, he went back to work. *Tap. Tap. Tap.*

The empress looked up at Victor, her eyes full of fire, her features twisting in anger. She hissed, "I do not delude myself at all. *I* set all the pieces perfectly. *I* was the one who infiltrated the minds of the Spinners, whispering to them that a new king was coming. *I* was the one who had Nockrythiam dethroned, handing his two favorite realms over to the New Gods we created. And then I sent *her*. I placed Aurelius's heart in her chest, knowing the organ would sway her every thought. I pitted her and Nockrythiam against one another. I did *everything* right to ensure that she would succeed at her task. That she would kill Nockrythiam and send his soul back to me."

"You do not need to remind me. I was there through it all. But have you forgotten, Avena? Despite all of the things you did to ensure success, she *still* had a child with him," Victor countered.

Something tugged at the inside of my vessel, the slightest feeling. Like the tick of a finger. But it was gone as fast as it came.

"That doesn't mean anything." The empress glanced down at me. "He could have easily forced her. Nockrythiam was a ruthless beast after all."

"Oh, I doubt that," Victor disagreed, looking up from his work. His tongue pressed into the corner of his mouth, rubbing against it. "She probably couldn't keep her legs closed."

The empress's nostrils flared, but she said nothing. "How much longer?"

"She's done," Victor answered as he tossed his tools onto his tray.

"Good," the empress stated. Bolts of lightning burst from the corners of her eyes, streaking outwards, sparking then vanishing. She plunged her hand into my chest, her fingers rooting around, searching for something.

From inside my frozen vessel, there came a sound—a scraping of metal on metal. Like coins grinding against one another inside a cloth purse.

She pulled her hand from my chest and flattened her palm, studying the strange bits of broken, silver shards. She raised them to her mouth, her eyes glowing even brighter. Her lips pressed together, and she blew on them—the swirls of air visible.

The shattered remnants began to glow. Then, they began to move.

They rose from her palm, swirling and twirling, dancing with one another as they began to line themselves up. It was like watching a circular jigsaw puzzle put itself back together, the strange pieces trying to fit in this spot then that, until finally, they sealed together, creating a perfectly round, silver ball.

The empress shifted her glowing, sparking, electric eyes to mine, and then she shoved her hand back into my lifeless body.

At first, I felt nothing.

And then, I felt *everything*.

A drum began to beat inside me, growing louder and stronger, forcing ichor to pass through my shattered veins, healing them with each strike. My lungs, once tattered and torn but now healed, instinctually looked for oxygen, but there was none to be found. Desperation clutched at me. I felt like a drowning person on the verge of losing consciousness. Panicking, I tried to breathe in, but instead of air, it felt like I filled my lungs with water. It was heavy, so heavy, and it dragged me under until blackness swept over me.

Was this the end?

A bloodcurdling scream tore its way out of me, and my eyelids sprung open. I jerked upright and began to vomit over the side of the altar. The retching did not cease as my body expelled a briny, watery substance.

A cool hand slid over my heated skin, rubbing my back in gentle movements. "That's it. Let it all out," the empress spoke softly, her voice melodic.

A string of saliva dribbled down my chin, stretching at the command of gravity's pull, until it snapped and dripped into the clear vomit below. When the violent clenching of my stomach began to subside, I rolled over, my body shaking and dappled with beads of sweat. Panting, I looked up into the eyes of the empress.

"Now, shall we see if you completed your task?" she asked, her voice calm and serene, like the glass top of a lake, untouched by wind. She pinched at something in the middle of my forehead, pulling a strange material from my body, like a layer of organza that had been tightly wrapped around me.

Memories stampeded into my thoughts, shoving me backwards, back to *him*.

Polished floors emerged beneath me, glistening with bits of broken chandelier. The underlayers of my decadent gown sounded against one another as we swayed back and forth to the enchanting, dark melody—a symphony of death.

I looked up into the eyes of my soul's other half. My mate. My love.

My safe haven.

Amazing, isn't it? he mused, the heat of his breath caressing the shell of my ear. *How responsive you are to my touch.* He spun me away from him, our hands disconnecting. A cavernous mouth, forged of shadows and obsidian, stretched wide and swallowed him whole.

"Von!" I cried out, reaching for him as he disappeared along with the rest of the ballroom.

I'm right here, he spoke from behind me.

His voice calmed my frantic heart.

Walls and floors, forged from black glass, stretched before me. I turned to him, tears brimming in the corners of my eyes. He held my gaze, surveying my tears before his attention drifted to my hand, his beautiful face fracturing with concern.

I looked down, finding a thin linen tenderly wrapped around my finger.

Goddess, please, I can scent your ichor. It is a fresh

wound. Let me see it, he said, his voice almost . . . pleading. He held out a tattooed hand, and I almost went to put mine in his, but I stopped.

"Von, this is a memory," I said, looking around us, trying to find a way out. The obsidian walls began to breathe, pulsing in and out, in and out. Then, they started to move. My eyes stretched wide—they were closing in on us!

Panicked, I turned to Von. "We need to get out of here."

It needs to be set, he said, his attention locked on my broken finger. *I promise to be as gentle as I possibly can.* Carefully, he grasped the end of my crooked finger. When his lips came crashing down on mine, my world was enraptured in his dark flames. My finger made a loud noise as the bone was snapped back into place.

That sound repeated, growing louder and louder as it began to shift from a clicking into—

The headboard tapped against the wall in slow, rhythmic movements as I lay beneath my mate, my legs wrapped around him, our bodies connected as he drove into me with delicious, long, sensual strokes. With each one, he etched his name into my bones, carving himself into me with heartbreaking gentleness.

Tonight, he had taken his time with me, his lips leaving no part of my body untouched.

Tonight, he had worshipped me, treating me as if I were a sacred temple.

And tonight? Tonight, I wanted *all* of him.

Are you sure? Von asked, forest-green eyes locked with mine. His wild black mane tumbled over his broad, inky shoulders, spilling around me. A slender braid, the one that had my feather tied into the end, swayed with each rhythmic thrust.

"I am. I want this," I reassured him, my hands grazing down the length of his powerful, masculine arms, the muscles taut as I melted beneath him. My body was soft and pliable, molding to his hardness.

A smile, brighter than I had ever seen before, crested on his full, beautiful lips. *I want this as well,* he pledged softly, his hand drifting between my breasts, lowering down my torso to the flat of my stomach. His large hand spanned over my abdomen. *You are going to make such an incredible mother.*

It's a shame you won't ever become one, snarled a heavily accented voice—

Nicholas.

The bed dissolved beneath me, and I began to fall.

Sage! Von yelled in desperation as he reached for me and I for him.

A hand, forged from bone-breaking strength, clamped around my wrist, pulling it down, pulling me onto another bed, but this one was not wrapped in black silk. No, it was made of lies and deceit and pain—so much pain. Aurelius's body shoved against mine as he drilled his fingers into my jaw, forcing it to open. Leaning forward, he filled my mouth with his ichor, and then he clamped his hand over my lips, making me swallow the taste of him down.

Welcome back, Aurelia, he said as his forceful knees wedged my compliant legs apart. He pressed himself into me, stealing everything I thought I knew about myself in one painful thrust. Without permission. Without consent.

Tears welled in my eyes.

Make it stop. Make it stop.

"Make it fucking stop!" a voice screamed. My voice.

Something hard pressed into my hand—

A blade.

The Blade of Moram.

It was enough. It would free me from him. From this.

I turned it on him—on me. I would sacrifice it all to make *this* stop.

Please do not leave me again, Little Goddess, Von yelled from somewhere in the distance. His voice was a powerful tidal wave, breaching my shores and flooding me with emotion.

"Von," I cried out as the blade dissolved from my hand.

Aurelius's body split in two, falling to the sides like two pieces of cloth. A scream tore out of me as Nicholas emerged in the middle, his hand shooting out for me.

Von's not coming to save you this time, Nicholas sneered as he grabbed my wrist and tossed me over his shoulder.

"Nicholas, wait," I pleaded as he walked us out of the bedroom and into a courtyard, toward a tree with crisp, snow-white leaves.

The hairs on the back of my neck raised.

I could *feel* myself being pulled toward it.

"No!" I sobbed.

It couldn't end like this.

I never got the chance to tell Von about our—

"And so, I have my answer," the empress snarled through clenched teeth, her voice unceremoniously dragging me back to the present.

I was lying on a cold, hard slab of stone, in a strange room, filled with horrifying tools and eerie objects.

The empress looked down at me, her voice filled with disappointment. "You have failed at your task, child, which means you are no longer of use to me. Your soul will be destroyed among the sands, your existence erased forevermore."

Child. The word slammed into me.

I looked down at my torso, at the hardened plains of my stomach, my trembling fingers snaking their way across my empty abdomen.

Empty.

My heart fractured, the hairline crack snaking its way through the middle. Then, it shattered. Into thousands of tiny, tiny, tiny pieces. So small, even time itself could not make them fit like they had before.

I was forever changed. Forever *broken*.

A deep, low-pitched sound grew from the back of my throat, growing and growing until it turned into a screaming sob. I collapsed onto my side, wrapping my arms around my naked frame as I curled into myself.

Voices blurred over top of me, the sounds fading in and out, warring with the ringing in my ears, warring with my mangled mental state as I sobbed for the loss of our child. Any concern for my own safety was forgotten as I fell into the depths of this cold and bitter truth.

Von and I had been so close to having the family we dreamed of. We had been *so close,* and Nicholas had robbed us of it. Of our child. Of our future. Of *everything*.

Another scream tore out of me, my cheeks scalding hot against my river of tears.

Hands grabbed hold of me, forcing me onto my back.

I didn't fight them. Why would I?

What did I have left to fight for?

I felt a prick of pain in my arm, and I turned my head to the side.

Through bloodshot eyes, I saw a blurry figure standing beside me. In their hand was a strange cylindrical glass device with a sewing needle pressed into the end. The sewing needle was stuck in my arm. Their thumb pushed on the end and whatever liquid was inside the glass began to disappear.

Slowly, warmth began to spread over my body, like a comforting blanket slowly being pulled over top of me. It chased away the pain, the torture. And filled me with a sense of . . . peace.

Willfully, I handed myself over.

Chapter 7

Avriel

In the empress's grand council chambers, murals dominated the dome-shaped ceiling—telling the story of how the empress won the War of the Creators. During the day, light spilled through the arched windows, lighting the murals, and quite literally making them come alive.

When I was a young girl, I had spent hours in this room as my mother prepared for the meetings. While she worked, I would stare up at the ceiling and watch the paintings as they moved, mesmerized by them—and the empress herself, for her bravery and her strength. How proudly she had fought to make a better world for femalekind.

Or at least, at the time, that's what I had believed.

Back then, I made a vow to myself that someday, I would serve the empress, and so, I became a priestess. After my mother's death, her job was shifted onto my shoulders, as was the customs of these lands. So now, apart from being a priestess, I also served as the empress's secretary.

Why the empress hadn't executed me, alongside my mother, was a question I had asked myself more than once. Perhaps it was because she was egotistical, and she didn't perceive me as a threat. Or perhaps she was trying to prove something to herself, that the actions of the parent didn't determine the level of loyalty from the child. Perhaps I was an experiment, one she could easily end the second she grew bored.

Pulling my attention from the ceiling, I glanced around the room, full of light conversations. I had managed to gather eighteen of the twenty council members, which I felt was rather good, considering the limited time I'd had to summon them all.

Seventeen members sat at the round table, placed directly in the middle of the room. The last one, Mercia, the Goddess of Animals, sat on the windowsill, her eyes set on the cardinal flying outside. She lifted her hand from the fluffy cat nestled in her lap and placed it against the glass. The bird flitted around in excitement, its beautiful red feathers glistening in the sunlight.

As I had never been granted a seat at the table or really allowed to stay in the majority of the meetings, I stood at the back of the room in the shadow of a towering column.

To my right, the double doors swung open.

A chorus of wood screeching against stone sounded as the council members shoved their chairs back and quickly stood. They bowed to the empress as she walked into the room, her pace swift, her heels thunderous. Her expression was far from composed—she didn't bother to hide her frustration, wearing her anger as if it were her crowning glory.

"Everyone sit," she snarled out as she took her seat, the chair magically sliding in, caught on the breath of her immense power.

Immediately, the council members followed suit; even Mercia swiftly left her perch and sat at the table, positioning the cat back on her lap. The fluffy feline let out a small, barely audible meow before she settled in.

The empress's gaze narrowed on the cat, before it flicked up to Mercia's. "Must you always bring your animals with you?"

"Apologies, Your Majesty. I can send her back," Mercia said, lowering her head in respect.

The empress loosed a breath. Waving her hand in dismissal, she stated, "It's fine."

Next to stride into the room was a guard, carrying the white-haired female from before.

Upon seeing her, a few of the council members let out an audible gasp.

They must recognize her, I thought to myself.

I scanned their faces, noting which ones clearly did, spotting a common factor—all three of them had been council members since the War of the Creators. Considering that the white-haired female was somehow linked to Nockrythiam and he'd existed during that time as well, it made sense.

Still, their reaction left me even more curious about her.

Her vessel looked much better than when Imari had first brought her here, the wound in her chest completely healed over. Her eyes were closed, her breathing slow and rhythmic, the color of her skin warmed by her thrumming veins. Clearly, the connection between soul and vessel had been restored, yet she was completely unconscious.

I didn't doubt she had been given a sedative of some sort.

Again, I wondered who she was.

It was a question I suspected would be answered very shortly. I could only hope the empress would forget I lingered here.

But the empress, who had the eyes of a hawk, spied me and said, "You may leave."

"Yes, Your Majesty," I answered. I bowed to her then started toward the door.

"Actually, priestess," she said, calling after me.

I paused mid-step and turned toward her. "Yes?" I asked, a mustard seed of hope remaining.

"Would you tell Shadow that I will need those swords finished by next week?" she asked.

"Of course, Your Majesty. I'll see to it now," I said, bowing once more before I took my leave.

When I stepped into the hallway, the doors swung shut behind me, reminding me I still had not earned the trust of the empress. However, considering I was the daughter of a traitor, that was to be expected. It just meant I needed to work harder to convince her otherwise.

And then, when the empress's back was exposed, I'd get revenge for my mother.

I didn't know how I was going to do it, but I'd find a way.

Chapter 8

Shadow

"Fuck," I growled, tossing my hammer into the wood bucket sitting beside my anvil. Grabbing the red-hot blade, I shoved it back into the ravenous forge. Along with it, some of the meat seared off from my right hand.

The smell of burning flesh permeated the air.

I rolled my hand over, observing the damage I'd inflicted. Bits of iron bone peeked through burnt skin. Tipping my masked face to the ceiling, I rolled my neck back, stretching out my taut muscles. A breath of air passed my lips as I leaned into the sweet sensation of pain.

It was one of very few things in this world that felt good.

"Shadow, your hand," a worried voice said, followed by rushed footsteps. "Let me see it." Small, feminine hands, half the size of my own, cradled mine—her skin so soft. So delicate.

"It's fine," I answered, although I didn't pull my hand away, quite liking the feel of her touch.

Avriel shot me an incredulous look. "It does not look fine." Letting my hand go, she reached for the small cloth pouch hanging on her belt, right beside the rabbit's foot I had given her for her birthday last year. She loosened the tie and stuck two fingers and a thumb inside.

I leaned in, pretending to get a better look at what she was doing—although I already knew. We'd done this countless times before. In truth, I just wanted to be closer to her. I breathed her in, savoring her citrusy, herbal scent. Lemons, bergamot, and rosemary.

If this world was a free one where I could openly speak my mind, and someone was to ask me what my favorite scent was, I'd point to her. If they asked me what my favorite color was, I'd say her eyes. Favorite anything? Easy answer—her.

But this world was not free, nor was I, so I could never tell anyone that.

Not even her, despite how badly I longed to.

"Hold still," she scolded me as she sprinkled the silver powder over my injuries.

Upon contact, it began to melt. Then, it began to bubble, emitting small hisses before it disappeared. Small threads, the color of my tanned skin, began to shoot from one side of the wound to the other, stitching the burns back together, until my hand was as good as new. The process was painless, no more than a tickle.

She looked up at me and asked, "Better?"

"Better," I said, stealing a glance at her heart-shaped mouth. I bet she had the softest lips.

"Good." She flashed me a smile, the small gap between her teeth ever present. When I was a young, foolish boy, I would tease her about it, but now, I found it endearing.

I smiled back at her, the gesture hidden beneath my mask.

Our gazes caught, hooked for a moment too long before we both forced ourselves to look away. I turned to my forge while she tied her pouch shut.

Holding on to the seesaw-style lever, I pressed down and then brought it back up, repeating the motion. This filled one of the bellows with air while the other emptied, feeding oxygen to the fire. The flames grew brighter, feasting on what it was being given. With each push and each pull, the heat from the forge wafted toward me, lapping at my skin, causing beads of sweat to brim. That was precisely why I didn't bother wearing a shirt when I was blacksmithing. By the time I was done, it would be drenched in sweat. My pants already felt bad enough, glued to me like a second skin, but considering the door to this room seemed to constantly have people coming and going, I wasn't about to walk around ass naked.

Avriel joined me, taking up residence at my side. How I wished I could extend the space to her forever, hand her the deed to it and put a ring on her finger, just like people used to do centuries ago.

But that was a wish that could never be, and I damn

well knew it.

She inspected the lever, her attention drifting to the bellows, then, "Don't you find this a bit . . . archaic?"

"My forge?"

"Yes." She nodded. "There are more modern ones. Some don't even have a lever or bellows, for that matter."

"I've seen them at the blacksmith shops in the Capital. They run on magic." My hand slid from the lever, and I walked over to the small table, grabbing a sheepskin glove. I slipped my hand inside, picked up a pair of tongs, and walked back to the forge.

"They do. They seem to be more efficient."

I quirked a brow, pinning her with my gaze. "Are you saying I'm not efficient?"

Her mouth popped open before she swiftly shook her head. "No, mortals on a Sunday, no. I didn't mean it like that. I just meant it might be a better use of your time. Er—" She let out a frustrated sigh. "I'm sticking my foot in it, aren't I?"

I chuckled. "Little bit."

Returning my attention to the forge, I pinched the end of the blade with the tongs and pulled it out. It was the perfect shade of orange. Taking it over to my anvil, I laid it on the flat, picked up my hammer, and began to shape it.

Tang. Tang. Tang.

The sound of metal forging metal stalled our conversation, but when the blade needed to be reheated, I placed it back into the fire, and Avriel picked up where we'd left off.

"I didn't mean any offense."

"I know you didn't," I replied as I began to pump the lever.

"I just know how much you enjoy blacksmithing, and I thought you might like trying out something new. Her Majesty would probably gift you a new forge if you asked her."

My arm went still. A second passed, or maybe it was two. Muscles firing, I pressed down on the wood handle, continuing what I was doing. "The empress has already given me so much. I could not ask her for more." The words felt bitter on my tongue. When no reply came, I glanced to my right, saying, "You've gone quiet on me now. What is it?"

"Nothing." She stepped closer to the forge and peered down at the heating blade.

The rhythmic squeak in my handle, the gusts of air from the bellows, and the crackling of the fire occupied the silence as I waited for her to say something more. But, as usual, she offered nothing.

"Come here," I directed softly, taking a step back as I gestured for her to stand in front of me.

She shot me a suspicious look before she complied.

My fingers roamed down the length of her arm, never touching her until they reached her hand. Gently, I took it and guided it to the handle. "Magic makes things simpler, yes, but when things become too easy, there is little satisfaction in it. When there is no satisfaction or pride, it cheapens the work." I guided her hand on the downstroke, and the forge came to life. Her scent bloomed around me once more, the proximity of her body so close to mine, it was torturous.

How badly I wished to close the distance between us.

"What are we doing?" she asked, her voice all breathy.

I knew the meaning behind her words was deeper. I could tell her the truth, that we were playing a very, very dangerous game, but if I did, that would acknowledge that there was something between us, and for her sake, I couldn't do that. So I kept my answer at surface level. "I'm going to teach you how to forge a lump of metal into a blade."

And so, for the next three hours, that's exactly what we did. I taught her how to load the forge with the right amount of charcoal, how to ensure the blade was hot enough to work with, as well as other basics like the proper way to hold the hammer. Sometimes, my hands had a mind of their own and they'd caress her arm, something I'd catch too late. Sometimes, she would stop hammering and peer down at my traitorous, wandering hand that had *somehow* made it to her waist on its own accord. Swiftly, I'd remove it.

"What did you call the last step again?" Avriel asked. She was standing over by a barrel filled with oil. Sometimes I used water or brine, but for the type of metal we were working with, oil was the best choice.

"Quenching the blade. It's the most crucial step," I told her as I pulled the red-hot blade from the fire, showing it to her. "Do you see the color of the metal?"

She stepped closer to me, surveyed it, and said, "Mhm, it's a bright cherry red."

"Right. The color signals that it is at the correct temperature, and it is ready to be quenched." I walked over to the barrel, taking the blade with me. Avriel followed. "When Aryx first taught me how to forge, he would have me periodically test the blade with a magnet, prior to quenching."

Avriel joined me at the barrel. "Why a magnet?"

"When metal attains a high enough temperature, it becomes non-magnetic. It's called the Curie point. Once it reaches that, you know the blade is ready to be quenched. It's more of a surefire way to know the blade is ready, rather than judging by the color, which can vary for a number of reasons."

"So then why don't you still use the magnet method?" she asked.

"I'm no longer a novice," I purred, drawing out the words so she could taste the double entendre. I gave her a playful wink, before I plunged the blade into the oil. Smoke erupted, curling its way toward the ceiling. Avriel let out a gasp of surprise as she watched with big eyes.

Later on, when the blade was cool, Avriel and I sat on a wooden bench. Moonlight spilled through the window, highlighting the beautiful copper hues in her hair—like the leaves in fall. Yes, another favorite of mine.

"Do you see any cracks?" I asked, watching her as she turned the dagger over in her hands.

"No," she replied.

"Run your fingers along the flat. Do you feel anything?"

She did as I asked, her fingertips whispering across the steel. Something so delicate and something so deadly. It had my mind spinning one too many ideas.

Looking up at me, she answered, "It's smooth."

"Indeed. Next time you come, I'll show you how to make a handle for it."

"I'd like that," she said, our gazes catching.

A ribbon of her hair fell in front of her face, and before I could stop myself, I was reaching for it. Gently, I tucked it behind her ear.

The door to my shop swung open, and I swiftly pulled my hand back, looking toward the entrance, where a masked male stood. He was almost as tall as my six-foot-five frame, a forest of curly blond hair piled on top of his head.

"The empress has requested us for Thursday night's *festivities*," said Aryx, the God of Love—my mentor and closest friend. His eyes shifted between Avriel and me—drawing conclusions that could have us all condemned to have our souls crushed. "Ah, apologies. I didn't mean to . . . interrupt."

Avriel jerked upright. "Nonsense. You aren't interrupting anything."

"I'll go," Aryx interjected while nodding, his metal mask glinting in the firelight as he performed the small action.

"No, no, it's fine," Avriel stated. She handed me the blade. "Thank you for showing me how you make these. It's a beautiful piece. Oh, and by the way, the empress needs those swords made by next week." Long gone was the softness in her voice; now it sounded formal, like she was talking to a stranger.

I hated it.

Suddenly, the door closed, leaving both Avriel and I gawking at it.

"Shit," she hissed under her breath.

I couldn't help but smirk as I teased her, "Priestess, I thought you weren't allowed to swear?"

"He just saw you tucking my hair behind my ear," she seethed, her eyes as wide as the empress's polished saucers.

"I'm not sure if he saw that, but if he did, Aryx won't tell anyone," I reassured her. "Breathe, Avriel. We're fine."

She took a breath, her chest rising. At the end of her exhale, she said, "I hope you're right."

Chapter 9

Von

The aroma of various herbs and potions, accompanied by an overpowering brine, infiltrated my nostrils as I walked into the infirmary, located in my castle's northwest tower.

Almost all the beds were filled with freshly departed souls, some still wet from being pulled out of the Da'Nu. Those were the ones who mourned uncontrollably, while the others who had been here longer, who'd had more time to process that they were, in fact, dead, sat in their beds, sipping a cup of tea or eating a bowl of soup.

Soultenders, healers tasked with caring for the souls as they transitioned from their mortal lives into their eternal ones, bustled back and forth, moving from bed to bed. Their dark robes dusted the glass floors as they walked, their shoes crunching the salty remnants that had yet to be swept up. Despite being a river, the Da'Nu had high levels of sodium chloride, so naturally, those who came out of it were covered in it.

Salt. I seemed to be surrounded by it lately. If it wasn't because of Ezra and her concoctions, it was because of the river and the souls pulled from it.

Down the middle of the lengthy room, there was a long string of tables that housed various-sized glass containers, chock-full of numerous herbs, spices, and medicinal mixtures. A hand-carved wooden spoon was placed in each one. Reactive metals like aluminum and copper were not to touch the ingredients, because not only did it alter the taste, it could neutralize the healing properties.

Standing at one of the tables was the Goddess of Companionship. Her hands, etched in intricate white flames, gestured as she spoke to one of the soultenders.

The cloaked woman nodded, before she reached down and picked up a small jar from the table. She handed it to Zahra, clasping her hand warmly.

"Thank you," Zahra said to her.

"Of course, goddess," the soultender answered, her voice young and airy. She turned to me, my gaze mapping the discolored skin on her face—a pitted landscape full of scar tissue, her top lip and the tip of her nose chewed away. To anyone else, they would see a normal girl, but I saw the truth of how she'd died.

"My king," she said to me, bowing in respect before she made her way over to the bedside of a slumbering man.

I nodded in reply, then turned to Zahra. "How is she today?" I asked, my eyes meeting hers.

The whites of her eyes were bloodshot, the flames in

them dimmer than normal. That told me all I needed to know.

"Not good," Zahra breathed, those two words full of worry. We began to walk toward a corridor, leading to the private rooms. "She refuses sleep, food. Not even the comforts of being reunited with her parents or those before them bring her solace."

My brows furrowed. "Transitioning can take time," I reminded her.

Zahra's voice grew quiet. "And if she doesn't? Then what will you do?"

"Zahra," I sighed. "I can't think of that right now." And truly, I couldn't. I couldn't think of losing another person I cared about, not right now.

She let out a breath. "Apologies. I know you are hurting deeply, despite your hardened exterior."

"It's alright," I stated, offering no more.

We walked the remainder of the way in silence, listening to the bloodcurdling cry, followed by bouts of sobbing coming from the closed door we approached. I opened it, allowing Zahra to enter first.

The small, private room consisted of a bed, a few chairs, and a tiny kitchen area. Lit sconces lined the walls, bathing the room in cool, blue light. Kaleb, who was seated in one of the chairs, jerked his head up, his weary eyes meeting mine. His hand was linked with the woman's who was lying on the bed—

Harper.

A lump formed in my throat as I walked over to her

side. It had been a few days since I saw her last, and she looked just as tormented as she had then. Her skin was pebbled with sweat, her hair matted in clumps, the skin sunken under her eyes.

"Von," she sobbed, her hand slipping from Kaleb's.

"I'm here," I said as I walked toward her bedside while Zahra made her way to the small kitchen space. I sat down, the bed groaning under my weight, and I took Harper in my arms, wrapping her tightly in my embrace.

"I need to go back to the Living Realm. Lyra and Ryker—" Her voice cracked. "They need me." Desperately, her fingers clenched my tunic, and she buried her face into my chest. Another sob wrenched its way out of her.

Zahra, who was heating a teapot with the caress of her flame, glanced at me—her worry ever present.

I let out an exhale, then said to Harper as my hand rubbed her back, "You will be reunited with them again, but you need to complete the transition first."

"I cannot accept this is my fate. I will not accept it. Lyra needs my protection."

"She has Ryker and Graiyson," I softly reminded her.

"I will check on her for you," Kaleb added. "I will check on them all."

I looked at him over the top of Harper's head, silently thanking him.

He just barely acknowledged my gratitude, the nod of his head mechanical.

I understood.

Losing Sage had broken us both.

"Harper, dear, do you think you could try to drink some of this?" Zahra asked as she held a cup and saucer in front of Harper. "It will help."

Slowly, Harper lifted her head, her hands unweaving from my tunic as she considered Zahra's offer.

It was easy to tell they were related. The two shared a great deal of similarities, from their appearances to their personalities. The five-times-great apple had not fallen far from the tree.

Harper's eyes flashed black, a look of pure hatred and disgust twisting her face into something demonic. She shoved the cup off the saucer and it fell to the floor, the cup shattering upon impact, the herbal drink puddling around the broken remnants. "How many times do I have to tell you?" Harper snarled, her voice no longer hers. "I do not want anything *you* have to offer! You think to trick me with your fake smile, but I know what you are trying to do." Her head turned to mine, her expression murderous. "You are all trying to trap me here. That's the reason you won't let Sage see me, isn't it?" She shoved against my chest. "Isn't it!"

Worry wrapped like bars around my chest, constricting my breath, but I kept my voice calm as I said, "Harper—"

"No!" she roared. Her attention snapped to the door. "Sage! Sage! I'm here! They are keeping me in here!"

Swiftly, Kaleb reached across the bed and grabbed Harper's hand. Like a fire wicked out of oxygen, she immediately stopped shouting.

I didn't know if it was Kaleb's connection to Sage or what, but he seemed to help Harper battle her demons. When

66

he wasn't near, she became worse. So now, he spent a lot of time in this room, just looking after her. Because that's the type of person he was.

The blackness fled from Harper's eyes and her expression softened. She looked from me to Zahra. "Zahra . . . Von . . . I . . . I'm so sorry." She looked down at the bed, the cloth shredded. "What is happening to me?"

"You are just transitioning." I held her gaze. "And you are going to be okay."

But for the first time since I'd retrieved Harper's soul from the Da'Nu, after she had died from her injuries she had received during the battle that took place in the Cursed Lands, I wasn't so sure. Seconds ago, when I saw the color fade from her eyes, replaced by a blackness that rivaled my own, heard her voice change into something that sounded nothing like hers, I knew that time was running out for her.

Which meant I needed to act swiftly.

Bits of flame rained down from the red sky, scorching the rocky, barren ground. Not even weeds survived in these desolate wastelands, forged from eroded slopes and jagged, looming mountains. The acrid scent of rotting flesh hung so thick it was like a dense fog coating the air. It was a sure sign I had entered the land of nightmares and horrors—

The Eighth Tier.

I had made it to house the most depraved and maniacal

of souls—the sick and twisted who would have taken pleasure in being eternally burned in the level above. It housed a myriad of sinister, bloodthirsty monsters.

Come to think of it, it would have made a great home for Saphira.

Shadows swirled beside me, producing one angry-looking immortal.

"What are you doing here?" Zahra whisper-yelled at me, her eyes darting from side to side.

"I could ask the same of you," I replied, my boot crunching a petrified bone in half as I strode forward.

"I'm here to make sure the monsters of this place don't spit-roast you alive," she hissed, her long legs doing their best to keep up with mine.

"We all have to eat," I quipped flatly.

She didn't look impressed.

Another swirl of black marred the air to my left. Dameon stepped out from it.

"I had no choice in the matter," he said with a sigh.

I understood. Mated males were territorial creatures, and we all had that same unrelenting need to protect our females—which was one of the two reasons why I was here.

"It's fine," I sighed as we continued ahead.

Zahra sidestepped a luminescent, bubbling puddle. A rotting hand, full of maggots, shot out from it, reaching for her ankle. Before it could grab hold, Dameon's flame sword found purchase, slicing it clean off. The creature let out a high-pitched, garbled scream as it pulled its bleeding nub under the surface. The severed hand bounced against the ground, flopping around like a fish out of water as purple blood poured out of the end.

"Are you alright?" Dameon asked, moving to her side.

"I am," Zahra reassured him.

"Waaaaait!" cried out a strange voice from a chasm not far from us.

A leg slung out of the deep fissure, tossed up on the side. Then, an arm, then, another. Another leg. Lastly, a head emerged. It had the eyes and mouth of a mortal but the nose and ears of a rabbit. The naked creature bunny-hopped toward us—aggressively sized cock and balls unceremoniously on full, *bouncing* display.

I quirked a curious brow—how didn't the creature get ground rash?

Dameon flung his hand to the side, his flame sword at the ready.

The man-rabbit stopped, covered his face, and hissed, "It's too bright! Too bright! My vision givers! My vision givers!"

I looked at Dameon, pressing my hand downwards.

He gave me an *I-better-not-regret-this* look before he dissolved his sword.

"Speak your purpose, creature," I said, my voice firm.

He lowered his hands and slowly began to approach me. "I only want to eat it. Nothing more. Nothing less. Just a little nibble here. Just a little nibble there."

"Eat what?" Zahra asked.

The creature pointed to the twitching hand.

"I'm going to be sick," she said, covering her mouth.

The man-rabbit rattled out a laugh. "Silly goddess. Have you never tasted such a delicacy before? The maggots make the Puddle Dweller hands *so juicy!*" He threw his hands into the air, emphasizing the final word.

"That'll do it," Zahra gagged, and she turned away.

The creature held up his grimy little fingers, wiggling them in anticipation. When he went to dive on the hand, I brought my combat boot down on it.

"No, no, no," the creature cried out as he tried to pry the hand from underneath my boot. "You're squishing it! You're squishing it!"

I bent forward, an empty grin twisting my lips. "How would you like to make a deal?"

Chapter 10

Von

A heavy mist rolled off the murky bog. It swirled around my ankles, tempting my shadows. I paid it little mind, my attention stuck on the eerily calm waters. Yes, this was the place. Although I hadn't been to these lands in decades, if not centuries, I was the maker of them and I knew them well.

"I didn't agree to this!" the man-rabbit screamed—his writhing body shadow-chained to a boulder.

"Technically, he didn't," Zahra said under her breath, her arms threaded over her chest. The white flames inked into her skin glowed in the darkness of this place—a sure sign her powers were at the ready, should they be needed.

"Semantics," I replied, my gaze swinging from Zahra to Dameon. "I suppose it is a good thing you two came after all. Who wants to do the honors?"

"The honors of what?" the creature squeaked.

My attention flicked toward him, conjuring an apple which my shadows swiftly wedged in his mouth.

"Mm-mm, mmmph," he complained in muffled grunts.

Dameon chuckled while Zahra, the bleeding heart said, "Is that necessary?"

"Probably not." I shrugged. "But you gave me the idea with the whole spit-roast thing." The corner of my mouth twisted upwards. "And I couldn't help myself."

"Of course not," she sighed as she took a step toward the creature, a dagger forged from white flame emerging from her palm.

The creature's eyes went wide. "Mmm-mm!"

"I'm not going to hurt you," she reassured him.

Dameon stepped to his mate's side, his hand slipping around hers. "Let me do this," he said as he gently slid the dagger from her hand. "Your ichor is too precious to spill."

"Charmer," she spoke softly.

He smirked, released her hand, then wrapped his around the blade. Fist clenched, he pulled the blade out, forging a deep cut in his skin. Before it could heal, he smeared his ichor over the creature's chest.

"Mmmm-mmm!" the man-rabbit protested, his small body fighting against my unbreakable chains.

When Dameon was finished, he took a step back and asked me, "Do you think that'll be enough?"

"Lost Souls can smell a drop of immortal ichor from hundreds of miles away. It will be enough." I patted Dameon's shoulder then walked up to the little beast. My fingers snatched the apple from his mouth. I rolled it over, studying the side where the creature's mouth had been—the crisp, red flesh had turned brown and mushy. A small crack formed, and dozens of worms began to tumble out.

"You trickster. You-you fraudster. You swindler!" he snarled the words at me.

"I've been called worse," I said as I discarded the apple and began to walk away, Dameon and Zahra following in tow.

"Come back! Come back!" the man-rabbit screamed at us.

When we were twenty paces away, the land on a slight incline from where we'd laid our trap, my shadows swept around us, making us undetectable.

"Blasted immortals!" the beastly thing snarled. "Never to be trusted!" He slammed his head against the rock before he screamed at the top of his rotten lungs, "Somebody help me!"

"I'm curious," Dameon whisper-spoke to me, his face fixed ahead. "How were you going to do this on your own?"

I knew what he meant. Ichor was an important part of the equation, and my veins could not produce a single drop without Sage. But Lost Souls craved one thing more than immortal blood—they were cannibals, hungering for those who were like them, broken and tormented. Lost. When Sage died, that's exactly what I'd become.

Eyes fixed ahead, I answered, "I had planned to go into the bog and use myself as bait."

"Even for you, that would have been dangerous," Dameon remarked.

"It would have been, yes. So when the wee beast with the third leg showed up, I realized this was a better plan."

Dameon chuckled at that. "He's rather . . . *gifted*, isn't he?"

"Impressively so," I agreed.

"Are we seriously discussing his cock?" Zahra interjected.

"Yeah," Dameon said at the same time I said, "We are."

She stared at us, shook her head, and looked back at the creature.

A few seconds passed.

Then, Zahra muttered under her breath, "You think he gets ground rash on that thing?"

A low laugh rumbled past Dameon's lips while I cracked a desolate grin.

Without Sage, I was an empty vessel.

In the distance, the water began to bubble.

A crown of sleek, black hair broke the surface, rising just enough so that a pair of black eyes could look out. Those dark, ominous eyes were filled with a great void—an emptiness beyond compare. They shifted, narrowing in on the creature.

"Oh no. Please. No. No. *No!*" the small beast screamed, trying to fight against his restraints.

The head lifted out of the water, revealing a feminine face—once full of beauty, but her pale, opaque skin, which showed the tainted, black veins beneath, had robbed her of her looks. Networking her torment, they spiderwebbed under her skin. She glided forward, taking her time as she closed in on her prey. Reaching the shore, she stood. Wet, faded fabric clung to her body, the tattered ends breaking off into bits of string that clung to her bony legs covered in black scabs. Her ribs poked through the cotton dress, making it seem as if she hadn't eaten anything in weeks.

The three of us did not speak a single word, our attention fixed on the unsettling truth now standing before us, of what Harper might become. Granite packed my stomach. A sinking feeling—one I knew weighed on all of us.

The closer she got to the man-rabbit, the more he screamed. When she was an arm's reach away from him, her attention fell to his chest. She slid one finger over it, gathering up the ichor. She brought it to her nose and then to her mouth. A serpentine tongue slid from her lips, flicking over her gilded finger.

"Mmmm, the ichor of the gods," she said, her voice haunting. She dipped her head and began to lick the creature's sternum.

I stepped out from my shadows, revealing myself.

Her head swung my way and her eyes grew wide. Her rusty jaw unhinged, dropping all the way to her chest, and she let out a screech so horrible, it was like shards of glass piercing my eardrums.

"Fuck!" Dameon roared as he and Zahra both covered their ears. I did the same.

I needed to stop her horrendous screaming, but how? Pulling the oxygen from her frozen lungs would do nothing—she didn't breathe.

In a blur of movement, she stood in front of me, a wicked grin spreading across her maniacally twisted lips. Her hand shot out.

I tried to catch her arm, but my hand passed straight through it.

Like daggers, her fingernails drove into my neck.

A black fog rolled out of her screaming mouth. It clawed at the air, consuming everything around me. It swept into my nostrils, filled my lungs, and stole my eyesight. It pooled into my ears, removing the sound of her screaming and replaced it with—

"Von?" asked an *unmistakable* voice.

The fog started to clear, my vision returning, revealing *her.*

Azure eyes met mine.

I nearly fell to my knees.

Sage.

We were standing in our child's nursery. Rocking chair, crib, dresser, baby blankets, and tiny, tiny clothes . . . it was all there.

Sage had her hand placed on her stomach, a small bump present. The word *queen* was tattooed on her hand, right below her knuckles. In place of a wedding ring, *Von* was stitched with black ink into her skin. I looked down at my own hand, finding her name swirled in elegant lettering on my ring finger.

Moonlight cast through the window, caressing the white, silky strands of her hair, making it shimmer. She wore a black robe, the sleeves and hem adorned with lace. Her breasts were fuller than I recalled them being. Pairing that with the subtle curve of her belly made me wonder . . .

Could it be?

I breathed in, inhaling her citrusy, sea-breeze scent . . . *No, she wasn't pregnant.*

She came over to me, her hands settling against my chest. She nodded to the crib, then whispered to me, "I just put her down for a nap."

I looked at the crib, the one I had spent hours carving by hand. I could hear the sound of her tiny heart beating—a small, rhythmic drum. It was strong.

No. This was wrong.

"Hey," Sage spoke quietly as she reached for me, her fingers soft against my cheek. Gently, she guided my face to hers. "I know I haven't been myself lately. It's just . . . all of this is so new to me. I don't know if I'm doing this right or . . ." Her white lashes lowered, tears brimming in her eyes. "If I'm failing her."

Seeing her like that . . . it broke something in me. I couldn't stand to see her doubt herself—she was an incredible mother to our—

This isn't real! the beast within me snarled.

Fuck off, I told it as I pulled Sage into my arms. Her body was warm, brimming with life.

Gently, I clasped her chin, directing her gaze to mine as I said, "She is lucky to have you. As am I."

And then I kissed her.

Her arms wove around my neck, her body pressed up against mine as she handed herself over to me. When she broke the kiss, I nearly snarled, but she placed a finger against my lips, and with a naughty little grin, she whispered, "Let's take this to our room."

I nipped at her fingers, and she tried to stifle her giggle, not wanting to wake our little princess. Deciding that I didn't want to risk waking her either, I plucked Sage from the ground, and in a blink, we were in our private chamber.

I carried her over to our bed and gently laid her down on the black silk. It contrasted against her ivory skin, making her stand out, like a silvery moon nestled among the dark night sky.

Creator above, she was a vision.

Magically, the sash of her robe undid itself, and the silk parted, revealing her beautiful, sexy body to me. She was a precious gift in fervent need of my attention. My devotion.

I knelt between her parted thighs, drawing my fingers up them as I took my time admiring the changes to her body. Her breasts were indeed much, much fuller—brimming with milk for our daughter. And then there was her stomach and that darling little bump, thankfully still present. I quite liked seeing it, through every stage of her pregnancy.

There, she had created life.

And although I had given her the seed, it was she who had spent nine months growing and tending to it. It was she who'd suffered the late nights, the morning sickness, the discomforts of growing another. It was she who'd screamed with the cry of a warrior as she gave birth to our daughter. A memory played out in my mind, of how strong she had been on the day of her birth. The way her hand had crushed mine with her immortal strength. The way she had cried when she first held her in her arms.

The way we both did.

"You females are a wonder," I said, marveling at her. "All that you went through in order to create our daughter." Slowly, I shook my head. "I am in awe of you."

"It was worth it, and I would happily do it again." She smiled at me. "Actually, I will, as soon as my monthly cycle returns."

"My love . . ." I raised a brow. "Don't you think it's a bit soon?"

"Have you looked at yourself?" she asked, raking her heated gaze down my body. "When I see you, all I can think of is making babies."

A throaty laugh rolled from my lips. "Although I enjoy the act, more than anything, you do know we can have sex that does not lead to children, yes?"

Sage went silent, and the lightness in the air dissipated.

My smile faded. "Did I say something wrong?"

The silence lingered.

"Little Goddess."

Her chest rose as she drew a deep breath. When it fell, she said, "Despite the morning sickness, I liked being pregnant. I enjoyed the nights when you would place your head against my belly and talk to her." She looked down, her fingers spreading across her stomach. "I enjoyed having a part of you always with me."

"I will always be with you," I promised her.

Will you really, though? challenged the beast within.

I ignored him, my attention fixed on my mate.

Although I did not doubt Sage was genuine in what she had just told me, I knew the bond could amplify things, making baby fever more like an obsession. Because of our past, I wanted to ensure that Sage wanted more children because *she* wanted them, not because the bond was swaying her to have more or because she was the Goddess of Life and it was genetically what she had been created to do. So I said, "How about, when your cycle returns, we revisit this topic. But until then"—I gave her a devilish grin—"we can practice."

She tilted her head from side to side, mulling things over. "I think I can agree to that." Sitting up, her arms enveloped my neck and she kissed me deeply. Within seconds, my clothes were gone, and I had myself sheathed within her.

"Von!" she cried out, her legs wrapping around me.

My hips stilled, giving her time to adjust. "That is the sweetest sound," I murmured.

"What?"

"My name on your lips."

"Then I will say it over and over and over again until you are sick of it."

"That is a day, my love, that will never come," I promised her, sealing my words with a branding kiss, searing my vow into her lips.

Slowly, I worked myself into her before I struck a sensual pace.

Abs contracting, I rolled my hips, giving her body

those long, deep strokes I knew she craved. The kind that made her feel like I was weaving my black magic into her. The kind that evicted her soul from her body as she came undone.

I knew what my mate needed from me, and I was more than happy to give it to her.

Wherever she wanted—*thrust*—whenever she wanted—*thrust*.

"Von!" screamed a panicked voice, echoing around me.

"Zahra?" I jerked my head up, trying to understand where it had come from. My body went rigid. "Did you hear that?" I asked Sage, looking back down at her, mortified to find that hairline cracks were beginning to form all over her body. "No!" I yelled, my hands moving to each one, desperately trying to heal her.

"It's okay," she said, her fingers reaching for my face, tears brimming. "You have to let go of this dream so that you can save me." Her hand fell over her abdomen. "Save *us*."

Crisp, white light burst through the cracks that had formed in her skin. When she shattered, the flash of light emitted was so bright it blinded me. Desperately, I felt for her, but I could no longer feel the velvety softness of her skin; all I could feel was rock-hard soil.

Slowly, my vision returned.

I was kneeling . . . on the ground.

The Lost Soul was on the run, heading back toward the bog. A flaming serpent, conjured by Zahra, swirled around us, the head latching on to the tail and cutting her off.

I shot to my feet.

Wasting no time, Dameon forged a lariat made of flame. Over his head, he circled the rope in a smooth motion before he let it go. The loop soared into the air, toward the female. It fell over top of her and Dameon pulled it tight, jerking her backwards. She stumbled, hissing and screaming as she tried to fight her way out of the rope. Despite it being forged from fire, the flames did not burn her, but they did restrain her.

"Welcome back," Dameon grunted at me.

I could have told him I was happy to be back, but frankly, that would have been a lie.

Was I so desperate for Sage that I would willfully hand myself over to a fake vision of her? As I walked up to the Lost Soul, the answer stared me in the face.

I grabbed the flaming rope, cinched around her concave waist, jerking her toward me. "Here is how this is going to go. I have questions—questions you are going to answer. The sooner you do, the sooner you can go back to your cozy little bog life. Pretty simple, yes?"

"What about me?" squeaked the creature, still strapped to the rock. I had all but forgotten about him.

I turned to Dameon, a toying smirk on my lips. "What should we do with him?"

Dameon gave a one-shoulder shrug. "Make him suffer for being such bad bait."

"Please, no, no!" he began to plead.

"Relax, we're only fucking with you. You can go free." Fulfilling my end of the bargain, I conjured the hand from before, tossed it at his feet, and dissolved the chains. The man-rabbit lunged at the hand and began to chow down.

Zahra gagged.

I turned back to the Lost Soul, who was snarling at me. "Now, about those questions. Oh, and—" I fished out the glass vial that Ezra had given me from my pocket. "I'm going to need one more thing."

Chapter 11
Sage

"*That is the sweetest sound,*" Von murmured, his eyes meeting mine. They were the color of lush, vibrant leaves and mossy ground. His eyes were a forest, one I could stay lost in for the rest of my life.

My breath caught in my throat. "*What?*"

He smiled. "*My name on your lips.*"

"*Then I will say it over and over and over again until you are sick of it.*"

"*That is a day, my love, that will never come,*" he vowed, and my heart nearly burst as his rapturous mouth met mine.

I sank into that moment of pure bliss, our bodies joined as one, as Von and I gave ourselves to one another.

In that moment, there was only love and passion and something so heartbreakingly beautiful. The way Von loved me was beyond compare. There was no limit to it. No *boundaries. Only open, strong arms, all the forehead kisses a good girl could want, and one Spirit Realm of a hard, steely cock.*

Speaking of . . .

With that lethal weapon of his, he thrust inside of me, the strokes long and deep and sensual. They set every nerve ending within me on fire, taking me to oblivion.

Von's body grew still. His muscles turned even harder, and he jerked his head up. "Did you hear that?" he asked.

I didn't but . . .

Something was wrong. With me.

Like the prairie ground in the summer, starved from months of having no rain, my skin began to crack apart. At first, the fissures were small, but then, they started to grow bigger, until my body was full of them.

And Von, my mate, my love, my everything—he looked so desperate. So tormented. So completely and irrevocably destroyed.

"No!" he roared, his hands sliding over my skin, trying to keep me from shattering.

It broke me to see him like that.

My lips moved on their own accord. "It's okay," I told him, my voice soft. My vision began to blur. "You have to let go of this dream so that you can save me." I placed my hand over my stomach. "Save us."

I awoke to the sounds of someone coughing, hushed conversations, and sputtering sobs. The last sound, I realized, was coming from me. I forced a breath of air into my trembling frame, silencing my desperate cries. Slowly, my eyes flickered open, and my blurred surroundings began to sharpen.

Opal bars surrounded me, shooting all the way up to the ceiling, sectioning me off from the vast, dimly lit dungeon. A small bowl of water, which reminded me of a dog's dish, sat in front of me, right beside the doorway that led into my cell. Surrounding me were dozens of cells similar to mine, some with a bench, some with a tiny single bed, and some with nothing.

The majority of the prisoners wore sacks over their heads, a braided rope wrapped around their necks, keeping the abrasive-looking fabric in place. Small eyeholes were cut into the cloth. Nearly all of the prisoners looked to be men—judging by their builds—although due to the lack of light, it was hard to tell for sure.

However, there was one other female prisoner, her cell across from mine. She held her hand up against her mouth as she coughed and coughed and *coughed*, the sound echoing loudly off the stone walls.

"Would you quit your hacking?" mumbled the prisoner in the cell next to hers, his voice barely audible through the thick fabric. He was curled up on a bench. "I'm trying to sleep here."

"Can't help it," she wheezed, her lungs rattling in her chest before she started to cough some more. "I'll be dead come Saturday's games, anyway."

Games? I wondered.

"Same," said another, then another, and another. Others nodded, a solemn look filling their eyes.

I realized the majority of them were going to die this weekend. I didn't know what they had done to deserve such a fate.

A small voice inside of me whispered, *Nothing. They didn't do anything to deserve this. You can save them.*

I ignored it.

There was a time when I'd once thought myself a savior, a defender of innocent life, but I hadn't even been able to protect myself.

I couldn't even protect our *child*.

I rolled over, turning toward the wall. I realized that my bottom felt wet, and so did the floor. Cheek sliding against stone, I looked down—I had been dressed in a plain, cotton shift. Down below, the fabric was wet, clinging to my body. My legs slid against the cold and unforgiving floor as I pulled them up toward my chest, my arms wrapping around my knees.

And so, there I lay, the Goddess of Life, covered in my own urine.

I wasn't a savior. I wasn't a fighter. I wasn't a warrior.

I was nothing.

The Goddess of Nothing.

Footsteps sounded in the distance, growing nearer until they stopped outside of my cell.

"Open it," said a female voice—one I had heard before

but couldn't quite put a name to.

"Alright," replied another.

Keys jangled at the entrance. Hinges squealed as the door swung open. I didn't bother to look.

"Set it over there," the first voice directed.

"Of course, Priestess Avriel," replied another woman, her voice gruff.

Priestess Avriel. That's who the first voice belonged to. I remembered it from when I was first brought to the palace. I also recalled the way she had looked at me, the pity and sadness in her eyes as the creepy male known as Victor placed his hand over my face. I was thankful I hadn't been able to feel his touch at the time.

Brief footsteps sounded by my feet. A guard placed a tray down. On it was a steaming turkey leg, a slightly burnt bun, and a cup.

"I know it's not exactly the most exciting meal, but at least it's something," the priestess said from behind me. "I've brought you a few other small comforts as well."

I glanced over my shoulder, watching as a few maids filtered into the cell, placing a bedroll on the floor. On top of it were extra blankets and a change of clothes. Another maid came in and she placed a basin of water with a washcloth beside the bedroll.

"The maids can help you wash up if you would like," she said, her voice soft. "Unless you'd prefer to do that yourself."

"Why help me?" I rasped, my throat barbed with thistles.

"As a priestess, it is part of my duty to look after any females who find themselves in the empress's dungeon," she said.

Slowly, I got up, rotating so my back rested against the wall. I glanced over at the food, eyeing it suspiciously.

"It's not poisoned, if that's what you are wondering," she stated, her hands clasped in front of her. To the left of them, I spotted a rabbit's foot hanging from her belt. I didn't know why, but I felt a strange bit of warmth resonating from it.

"Why should I trust you?" I asked weakly.

"You have no reason to," she acknowledged as she stood up. Her hands twisted together, and she raised her left shoulder, performing a small shrug. "But if I were to poison you, it would be a kinder way to die than what awaits you in the arena."

The empress's words replayed in my mind. *You have failed at your task, child, which means you are no longer of use to me. Your soul will be destroyed among the sands, your existence erased forevermore.*

Games. Arena. Sands. Existence erased.

It all clicked.

I rested the back of my head against the wall, staring up at the ceiling, full of shifting pastel colors. "So then I, too, am to die, yet again."

"Leave us," Priestess Avriel said to the others.

They did as she asked, and the door closed shut behind them.

"I'm going to complete my rounds. Holler if you need

anything," replied the one woman dressed in expensive-looking armor.

"Thank you," the priestess responded as the guard walked away. She moved closer to me, stepping around the small wet spot on the floor. She crouched down beside me, glancing from left to right before she whispered, "Time is of the essence. Tell me how you know Nockrythiam, and I might be able to help you."

Help.

I had been like her once, eager to help.

Where had it gotten me in the end?

Here, in a foreign land, sentenced to be executed. No mate. No child. No family.

I had nothing now.

She waved her hand, and on a gust of air, the tray of food slid closer to us. "If small steps are what you need, then we can start here." She picked up the cup and offered it to me.

"You can command wind," I said, unable to help thinking of Von. Longing filled me as I hesitantly took the cup. I brought it to my lips and drank down some of the water. It was cool and crisp, and it felt heavenly on my poor throat. I drank some more.

"Yes, it is the main source of my power," she answered. "I heard Nockrythiam was also quite good at commanding it."

"Unlike any other," I stated, lowering the cup. I glanced to the turkey leg, the skin crisp and brown. I bet it tasted good.

She picked up the plate and handed it to me. "Go on. Eat. You are going to need all the strength you can get if you are to outlast a soul crusher."

I took it, my cold fingers savoring the warmth. "Soul crusher?" I asked, taking a small bite. The meat was savory, warm, and delicious. I felt a tiny bit lighter than before.

"Soul crushers are warriors who fight in the arena. They are tasked with . . . well, as the name implies, crushing souls. A vessel can be reborn, remade, but a soul, once crushed, cannot. It is ultimately the end."

I thought back to the way my soul had been decimated when the empress pulled it from my chest.

"I don't understand. My soul was shattered and the empress repaired it. Is that different?"

"It is." She nodded. "Soul crushers wear a special gauntlet known as a soulius. When a soul is crushed with it, there is no coming back from such a fate."

My appetite faded, and I lowered the drumstick.

So this was to be the *true* end of me.

I had been ready to accept such a fate not so long ago, when I used the Blade of Moram to kill Aurelius, knowing that it would kill me as well. I had been willing to sacrifice myself for the ones I loved. And in some ways, I had done it for me too—so I could be free of Aurelius.

But that was my choice. One I had made peace with.

Now, here I was once again, chained to a reality I could not free myself from . . .

My fingers drifted over the cloth above my abdomen. It took everything within me not to unravel into a mess of great, gasping sobs.

"Were you . . . with child?" she asked, her voice soft.

"I was." Those two words were so incredibly bitter on my tongue. Like acid, chewing into my taste buds. I discarded the half-eaten drumstick on the plate.

"What happened?"

"I was murdered." My thumb brushed over my stomach as I looked down, then up at her. "We both were."

Her expression filled with sadness. "My condolences."

I didn't respond.

Really, what could anyone say to that? Condolences wouldn't change the past, but perhaps a bit of truth could alter the future.

"You asked how I know Nockrythiam," I started. "He's the father of the child I lost . . . He is my mate."

Her mouth fell open like a window with a broken latch.

"Holy shit," the priestess whispered to herself.

Chapter 12

Von

"Did you get it?" Ezra asked, her cane tapping against the kitchen floor as she walked over to me, her curved shoulders ticking from side to side, emphasizing the weakness in her bones. Ezra was a peculiar immortal; why she chose to age and die and be reborn from the soil, when she could live for eternity in her prime, was beyond me.

Then again, *a lot* of things Ezra did were beyond me. Beyond us all.

"I did," I answered as I produced a small glass vial. In it, tears—provided from the Lost Soul. "Are you sure this will be enough?"

Ezra snatched the vial. She brought it to her ear, silent for a moment before she grinned and said, "Yes, this will be enough."

"What will they do?" I inquired, walking behind her as she returned to her bubbling pot. The girl stirring it stepped out of the way.

"I'm not completely sure," Ezra replied as she popped the cork and dumped the tears into the hissing concoction. When she was done, she tossed the vial over her right shoulder, the glass shattering on the ground. "For good luck," she muttered to herself.

I looked at the broken vial, blinking at it and the legendary level of mass fuckery Ezra had obtained. Feeling the very last of my nerves beginning to fray, I grated, "What do you mean you're *not really sure?*"

"I mean exactly that. I'm not really sure, but I have a hunch. A hunch that this is necessary." She turned to the girl. "Make sure you keep stirring it. We don't want the bottom to burn."

"Alright," the girl said with a nod. She picked up the wooden ladle and returned to her task.

Ezra faced me, her clouded eyes shooting straight past. "Yes."

I quirked a brow. "Yes, what?"

"Yes," she stated again. Then, she gave me a toothy, knowing grin. "To the two questions you've been asking yourself since you returned."

"I'm going to need more than that, Ezra," I sighed, mentally preparing for another helping of nonsense, but what else could be expected from the old rock worshipper?

Instead, I got the opposite as she replied, "The Lost Soul might be right about what she told you. If she had been able to see her husband after she passed, it might have helped her to transition. I know this can be very risky and have adverse effects, but at this point, I fear Harper is treading in dangerous waters. So yes, to answer your question, I think you should trust the Lost Soul and bring Ryker and Lyra here to see her." She paused. "Put it like this—what do you have to lose?"

Ezra had a point.

I thought it over for a while, weighing each side—risk versus reward. After some time had passed, I let out a breath, then said, "Alright. I'll have Folkoln go get them."

"Let us hope that it works," Ezra added.

All I could do was nod.

"Now, about that second question of yours. Lost Souls are misunderstood creatures. They are conduits, speaking between worlds, even connecting the living to the dead. You see, they act as a channel and connect souls, even ones that have been extinguished. They then use that connection and exploit it, sometimes trapping their victims forever." Her voice softened. "The reason why *it felt so real* was because it was Sage's dream pairing with yours. It was really her."

My eyes widened.

For a brief moment, Sage and I . . . we had been *connected*.

Her dream and mine—husband and wife, our precious daughter, slumbering soundly in the room next to us. A family. Together. Bonded.

The future we should have had.

I let out a shaky, deep breath as I tipped my head toward the ceiling, carving every precious second of our shared dream into my mind, holding on to it as if it were my last. Every touch. Every glance. Every kiss. Every second of it. From beginning to end.

The only problem?

It was a dream, and it wasn't real.

It *wasn't* real.

The pain was, though.

A dagger to my chest, carving out my heart, splitting my rib cage open and tearing *her* from me. It hit me with the weight of a crumbling mountain, nearly wiping my legs out from underneath me. I had to put my hand against the wall just to stabilize myself as I grappled with my reality—

Sage wasn't here.

And neither was our child.

I looked down at my ink-marked skin, my gaze shifting over the ones I had made with her. I would hold on to my tattoos with everything I had as I stumbled through the darkness, searching for her light.

Chapter 13

Shadow

"**Y**ou are lucky it was me who walked in on you two the other night," Aryx muttered as we made our way toward the empress's private atrium.

I side-eyed him. "I don't know what you're talking about."

"Uh-huh," he drawled.

Two females walked by us, their eyes fixed straight ahead.

When they were out of earshot, I spoke in a hushed tone, "There is nothing between me and the priestess, nor will there ever be."

"And it better stay that way, for her sake, as well as your own," he warned just before we walked through the red, silk drapery that hung from the arched entrance.

Raucous female laughter and sensual music greeted us as we stepped inside the dim, candlelit room. Incense burned, filling the air with the scent of jasmine. It was the empress's favorite scent, one I could trace back as far as my memory could reach, back to when I was a young immortal. She always had it burning during events like these or in her private chambers, saying it evoked feelings of passion and joy.

But to me?

It reminded me of repression. Of late nights and unwanted touches.

I *hated* the scent of jasmine.

In the middle of the atrium was a circular pool of water, an opening in the ceiling directly above it, the same size and shape as the pool below. When rain poured from the heavens, it would fill the basin. Females, most of whom were scantily dressed, stood around the room, goblets in hand.

At the far end, there was a stage that reached the height of my waist. A canopy bed, large enough to fit four of me— and I was no small male—was placed on top of it. The drapes were pulled to the sides, revealing the immortal resting on it—

The empress.

Small, delicate chains draped from her neck toward her breasts, pooling at her sex. The dress, if it could even be called that, was a masterpiece, designed to keep one's gaze roving all over her, taking in all of her body. Judging by the way the small crowd snuck little looks at her, it was working.

The empress cooled herself with a handheld fan. When

her eyes met mine, a smile curved her painted lips. She snapped the fan closed, directed it toward me, and said proudly, "Everyone, feast your eyes upon *my* undefeated champion, Shadow the Soul Slayer."

Heads swiveled my way, followed by swift clapping. Some women cupped their hands over their mouths, whispering to those standing beside them. Despite their lowered voices, it was easy to hear what they were saying—

"I heard he's crushed one thousand souls."

"Surely, it must be more than that."

"Who cares how many. Look at *all* those rippling muscles."

Aryx chuckled, having heard that one too.

I remained stoic, letting them gaze upon my flesh, slick with oil—as per the empress's request. She liked her possessions to be glistening and shiny, just like the sparkling diamonds hanging from her antlers. A tool to impress. That was all we were.

Unlike the females and the clothes they had painstakingly picked out for tonight's festivities, I had not been afforded the choice.

In public, my muscles were always to be on display, and so my attire was rather simple. A pair of sandals, a bit of canvas loincloth—held in place by my belt—and my mask. The belt was crafted from a wide band of metal-reinforced leather. Engraved into the front was a meticulous piece of artwork showing me surrounded by three opponents in the arena. That was the battle where I had won my title as champion, dethroning the one before me. It was a gift from the empress, one I forced myself to wear for her.

After the empress introduced Aryx—followed by another round of applause—she commanded us to walk into the pool. As we moved toward it, hands reached for us, but their fingers never made contact.

"Remember, my dears, you may look tonight, but no one is to touch, *unless* you are given my blessing," the empress reminded them, her tone sharper than a shard of glass.

Cool water sloshed over my feet, drifting up to my ankles as I walked into the basin, taking my position on one side while Aryx moved to the other. Two masked men came forward. One handed Aryx twin blades while the other gave me a sword and a round shield.

The crowd let out an excited gasp as I swung the weapon, feeling its weight, testing its balance.

Something was off about it.

I peered down the length of the blade, spotting the issue a third of the way down. It had been overworked in that spot, causing the metal to be thinner there. Because of that flaw, it was not a well-balanced weapon, something I would have to compensate for.

"Tonight, I give you a private battle between two of my soul crushers from my harem so that you may see with your own eyes the brutality of the male gender and what I faced when I raised arms against them and the emperor." She paused for emphasis, surveying the room, ensuring every ear was leant to her. "The loser of tonight's battle will be gifted to one of you for the night—" She gestured to the audience.

"To touch, *to ride*, whatever you wish. All because I am a gracious empress."

Giddy with excitement, the females cheered. This was one of the main reasons they had come—to see what it would be like to lie with one of us, to experience the touch of a man and find out what we hid beneath our loincloth, something that seemed to be of great curiosity to them.

When it came to these private events, council members and priestesses were allowed to attend whenever they liked, but for the general public, those who were invited would only be invited once. To the females, it was like winning the lottery. The event of a lifetime. But to me, I saw it for what it was. It was a means of manipulation, a way for the empress to control the masses. She always invited younger females, using this event to indoctrinate them. To show them how horrible us males were and why we had to be kept on a tight leash.

She used her *control over us* as a means of keeping her *control over them*, and it had worked for centuries.

But the excited ladies didn't know that they would never be given the chance to lie with me because the empress would never allow it.

The horrors beneath my mask were proof of that.

My hand tightened, and the metal handle groaned under my grasp.

Overtop of the clapping, the empress looked at us, a smug expression on her face as she said, "Begin."

Aryx moved with the speed and the precision of a lethal arrow, shooting straight for me.

I raised my shield to answer the call of his swords as they came down over top of it. *Thunk. Thunk.*

I pulled back, my sword catching his twin blades just in time. I shoved my shield at him, but he jumped back, narrowly escaping my attempt to knock him off his feet.

He charged again, and I dropped down, missing the bite of his blade by a hairsbreadth as it sailed over top of my head. At the same time, the tip of my sword slid across his skin, splitting it open. It wasn't a deep cut, but it still earned a collective gasp from the audience.

Aryx heeded the wound no mind as he said, "That was a good move. Who was the brilliant bastard who taught you it?"

I cracked a grin. "You speak too highly of yourself." I raised the tip of my sword, pointing at him as a sign I was ready to go at it again, and he charged at me.

Someone was playing offense tonight.

Our swords clashed in a fury of silver streaks as we moved around the pool.

He fired low, and I spotted an opportunity. Muscles firing, I drove my shield down, pinning his blade against the pool floor, causing an explosion of water.

Using his free hand, Aryx sent his knuckles colliding into the side of my face, snapping my head to the right. The edges of my mask cut into my cheek and my teeth rattled in my skull. I leaned into the screaming ache, enjoying the blistering-white pain. The immortal's fist, backed by the strength of his sword's handle, was like taking a cannonball to the face.

Stars peppered my vision. I shook my head, trying to clear them.

"That all you got, you old fossil?" I teased, feeling the warmth of my ichor as it raced like a river down my face, dripping onto my chest.

Aryx chuckled at that.

"They fight like animals," a female said, her voice filled with amusement.

"Truly sadistic beasts," cooed another. "Can you imagine when the realm was full of them?"

"What a horrible time that must have been," stated someone else.

The empress's laughter rang out.

Aryx and I charged at each other again, colliding in the middle in a spray of water and steel. Each time our swords met, it elicited an excited response from the audience. We went at it for a while, putting on a good show. To us, this was no different than a sparring session, something we had done thousands of times, but to them—the females—we were unhinged monsters, lapping at the chance to destroy one another.

I swung my sword, striking from the left, and he parried my attack. I did it again and again, until my hand was flying, firing shots this way and that. One nicked him in the side, and he winced. I took that opportunity to fire my foot into his torso, kicking him out of the pool.

The audience let out shocked screams, racing out of the way as Aryx smashed into a pillar.

I charged after him, arm whipping back, readying to

strike, then swung at him, but he ducked at the last second. My blade chewed into the stone just above his head, slicing off a few of his curly blond strands. They tumbled onto the flat of the blade. I nodded in approval—the blade might be unbalanced, but it was plenty sharp.

"Arghh!" Aryx growled as he forced his blade ahead, aiming for my leg. I swept my shield to the right into his extended arm and knocked his sword free. It went skittering out across the floor.

I flipped my shield to the side and rammed it into his chest, locking him against the pillar.

My hand shot out, grabbing his sword before he could use it on me. The metal chewed like teeth, biting deeply into my skin. Warm liquid seeped through my fingers as I tore the blade from Aryx's hand and tossed it to the ground.

The audience went wild.

Releasing my shield, Aryx gasped for air as he crumpled to the ground.

"Bravo, bravo," the empress said as she stood up, clapping along with everyone else. "The God of Love will be making one of you very happy tonight."

I went over to Aryx, braced his forearm, and helped him up.

He patted my arm. "You fought well."

"You held up longer than I thought you would," I acknowledged with a smirk, and although he wasn't able to see it, he could hear it in my words.

"Fuck you," he said with a laugh, wincing as he ran his hand over the damage I'd done to his ribs, a wound that was already starting to heal.

Servants walked up to us, exchanging weapons for towels.

As I began to dry myself, I felt compelled to glance at the far side of the room. There, sneaking through a back doorway into the atrium, was a priestess who was very, *very* late tonight.

My heart drummed heavily in my chest—Avriel.

Her sparkling wine-colored eyes met mine, and she offered me the smallest and briefest of smiles before she forced herself to look away.

I was thankful for my mask, because I couldn't help but return her smile. Not wanting to put her in danger, I retreated my attention back to the servant who had been speaking to me, although I missed the first half of what they said. *Private chambers* was all I caught.

But I didn't need to hear any more.

I knew the routine.

After every fight, the empress would always request that I return to her chambers. Those *visits*—something Aryx had warned me about—started when I was a young immortal, just a boy by human standards.

I stole one last glance at Avriel and etched her face into my mind, just as I had done hundreds of times before, holding on to her image as I left the atrium and prepared for the next task.

It was the one I hated most.

Chapter 14

Shadow

Jasmine clogged my nostrils, reaching like hands down my throat, filling my lungs with its nauseating scent. I stood in the empress's private chambers, beside a crackling fireplace, doing everything within my power not to toss myself into the flames.

Burning for the rest of eternity would be better than *this*.

I glanced at the sprawling canopy bed, the posts wrapped in silver-dusted filigree. Furs were draped over it—they looked so soft, so luxurious, but I knew that was a lie. The screams of a young boy sounded in my ears, and I forced myself to look away. I hated that bed. I hated this room. I hated *her*—

The empress strode toward me, her hips swaying from side to side like a feline on the prowl, her sights set on me. "Do you like what you see?" she asked. The chains draped down her body swayed from side to side, catching on the firelight as she moved.

"You are the epitome of my desire," I lied, my voice a sensual purr despite the granite I felt weighing down my chest. With each passing second, the flames looked more and more inviting.

"Such pretty, pretty words," she said with a breathy, playful laugh. She waved her hand, and in a swirl of soft light, a goblet appeared in it, which she raised to her mouth. As she drank, her lilac orbs watched me over the rim of the glass. Lowering it to her side, she nodded toward me. "Take off the mask. Let me see the *real* you."

I reached behind my head, unfastened the clasp, and took it off, tossing it onto the sofa.

Cool air swept across my skin. It felt so good just to be . . . free.

To not feel the hard, unforgiving mask clamped against my face. It was the only positive about coming here. The empress would often ask us to remove our masks, something we were only allowed to do when given her permission or if we needed to shave or wash our face or eat. With the iron mask no longer on, virgin powers filled my person—ones I knew next to nothing about, regardless of how badly I longed to.

But the rules were clear—unless you were female, a stygian forgemaster, or an Ashamori, magic was forbidden.

"How does that feel?" she asked, swirling her goblet.

"It feels incredible." I gave her an honest answer, probably one of the only truthful things I would say tonight.

"Are you going to thank me?"

Thank her . . . Thanking her would be like thanking someone who had their foot on your throat and took it off for a brief moment, allowing you a few gulps of air.

She was the *reason* my nearly eradicated gender was forced to cover our faces.

I ignored centuries of pent-up anger and said, "Thank you."

"You're always such a good boy," she cooed softly as she stepped into me. Reaching up, she traced the macabre scars that marred my face, put there by her own hand. "You are hauntingly beautiful, my champion. You have the bone structure of an angel, but the scars of a demon." She paused briefly, a hint of longing seeping into her voice. "If only I had been the one to create you. I would have placed my soul on my anvil, cracked it in half, and placed it right . . ." Her hand slid from my face, over my chin, down my neck, stopping at my chest. "Here."

"You are the beautiful one, Your Majesty," I said, the compliment poison on my tongue.

There was *nothing* beautiful about her.

"Avena," she corrected. "When will you call me by my name?"

"When I no longer respect you," I told her, adding to my pile of lies.

"A day that will never come," she spoke confidently as she started toward the sofa. "Come. Sit with me."

Obliging her request, I followed her.

The leather-wrapped cushion sighed under my weight as I sat down.

She placed the mask on the table and turned toward me, her blonde hair spilling over her shoulders. Propping her elbow on the back of the sofa, she used her hand to rest her chin. "The ladies were impressed by you tonight," she said. "Not that that should come as a surprise." She took another sip of her drink. "In fact, one of them made a bold request."

"Oh?" I asked.

One second, she was reaching forward, sliding her cup onto the coffee table, and in the next, she was in my lap, her legs spread on either side of mine. She draped her arms over my shoulders. Leaning forward, she whispered in my ear, "She asked me how much it would cost her to ride you."

Her tongue ran over the shell of my ear, the heat of her breath scalding against my skin. Unbearable. Yet, I sat there, pretending I liked it.

She pulled back, her eyes flashing with malevolence. "Do you want to know what I said to her?"

"Yes," I replied, playing along.

"I told her that if she ever asked me anything like that again, she'd find a sword in her belly, not your cock." Bolts of lightning sparked from the corners of her eyes, her immense power flashing throughout the room.

Instantly, the fire went out, as if it were scared to burn in her presence.

Her power recoiled and her expression softened. She held my face, bringing her mouth a breath from mine. "You are the one thing that I will never share with anyone. You belong to me, Shadow." With a kiss, she seared her claim against my lips.

I closed my eyes, thinking of Avriel. I pretended it was her heart-shaped mouth I was kissing. I started off gentle, slowly building in speed, until it became rapturous.

"Mmmmmm," the empress hummed in approval, taking me out of my fantasy—

No, it's Avriel, I lied to myself until I believed it was the truth.

Until it really was just . . . us.

Avriel's body began to move against mine, her hips grinding her sex against my stiffening cock. My fingers ran up the length of her side, over her shoulder, bunching in her hair. Gently, I pulled her head back, exposing her beautiful neck to me. I licked and nipped my way down it, gently scraping my teeth along the sensitive flesh.

The empress moaned.

It's Avriel! I roared inside my head, trying so fucking desperately to hold on to the lie.

"Open your eyes," the empress rasped the command. "Look at me."

Unwillingly, I forced them open, looking up at her as I kissed her neck. My teeth throbbed—not because I wanted to drink from her, but because I wanted to plunge them into her throat and rip it out.

"Always my good boy," she purred. Her words made me want to throw up. "Now, it's time for your reward."

In a flash, we were both on her bed, the fur against my back and her on top of me—our clothes gone, swept away by her ribbons of light. Her sex rested against mine. Her arousal leaked onto the base of my length, which was beginning to go soft—not enough that she would notice, but enough that I knew I needed to do something before she did.

The empress did not take kindly to males who couldn't stay erect in her presence, her ego would not have it. Her rules were simple—no erection? No cock. No head. No soul.

Eager to keep all of those things, I began to stroke my length.

She ran her hand over my arm, her greedy eyes feasting on the sight before her. "You are so muscular," she said, her hand moving to my length, slowly taking over. "*So* masculine." She hoisted herself onto her knees, aligning my crown with her entrance.

She moaned in delight as she lowered herself onto my shaft, seating herself to the hilt.

Then, she began to ride me.

And like the broken animal I was, I let her.

Later on, when I was back in my private chamber, I stood in the bathroom, snorting water up into my nose, trying to rinse out that fucking scent of jasmine.

It was everywhere.

She was everywhere.

Her hands wouldn't stop roaming over my skin, wouldn't stop touching me.

I grabbed the wet cloth and began to vigorously scrub, chasing after her hands and everywhere they had touched.

It wasn't enough. I tossed the cloth onto the countertop

and went back into my room, rushing over to my forge.

"Where is it?" I snarled, my hands smacking at hers, trying to get them off me. I looked through my tools, searching and searching. No, it wasn't here. I went over to a bucket, grabbed the handle, and dumped the contents out. I knelt on the floor, looking through the various tools.

A breath of relief found my aching lungs as I spotted the wad of steel wool. I grabbed it and swiftly began to rub the abrasive metal against my skin, chewing through the layers of my flesh.

"Fuck," I heard someone say from behind me, followed by fast footsteps.

Aryx crouched in front of me, his hand clenched around mine, the other grabbing the side of my face, forcing me to look at him. "She's not here," he growled. "Do you hear me? She's *not* fucking here."

I blinked, the haze slowly clearing. I looked down at my tattered skin, raw and full of abrasions, completely covered in my ichor.

Finally . . .

I couldn't see her hands anymore.

Chapter 15

Avriel

It was well past midnight and the festivities in the atrium were still going strong, even though the empress had left over an hour ago, Shadow before her. Their destination was the same—her private chambers.

My stomach churned. I wanted to vomit, and it wasn't just because he was with her. It was because I *knew* what happened in that room.

The *whole* Mother Realm knew.

In the arena, the men in the empress's harem were soul crushers, but in the palace, they were concubines—slaves to her desire, her lust, her greed. Forced to do whatever she wanted, no matter how degrading or painful.

No matter how badly it broke them.

Beyond her chamber's opal doors, the word *no* did not exist.

Sometimes the empress requested to see more than one

at a time, but when it came to Shadow, it was always *just* him. Out of all her concubines, he was her favorite, someone she would never share, even though she pretended she would.

But I remembered that night all too well, when Shadow had lost the fight and had been shipped off to a private room with a young lady, chosen by the empress. The second they'd left, the empress had grown irritated, her nails carving up the arm of her throne. She had lasted maybe ten minutes before she left the festivities and charged after them. The girl was never seen again, and Shadow had been taken back to her chambers, where he'd been forced to stay for weeks. One night, I'd grown so concerned for him that I'd created a distraction, telling the guards that there was a disturbance further down the hallway. When they left, I pressed my ear to the door, listening for any signs of life, but what I heard was so much worse—

Agonizing *screams*, coming from Shadow.

As he'd cried out in pain, the empress had growled at him about daring to let the female kiss his face. As she'd scolded him, I could hear the slicing of something, like a knife carving steak. It made me sick to my stomach, and I had to cover my mouth to stifle my sobs.

His horrifying screams were etched into my mind.

Right beside my mother's.

Both of them had suffered at the hands of the empress, and no one was willing to do anything about it. They all just turned a blind eye.

But I wouldn't.

I would do something.

I didn't know what or how or when.

But the one thing I'd come to realize the second I left Sage's cell—she was going to help me achieve my goal. I couldn't explain it, but it was a feeling, deep down in my gut, and I was going to lean into it.

Which meant I needed to figure out how I was going to buy her more time when she was scheduled to die this Saturday. Mentally, I rolled up my sleeves and got to work—

I walked up to a trio of goddesses standing around a tall table.

One of them was Mercia, a tired-looking parrot perched on her shoulder. She clasped her hands together, laughing as the goddess across from her, Oraina, told her ridiculous tale about the time she'd ended up stuck in a giant spiderweb—one I had heard many times. Eirwen stood between them, a drink in her manicured hand. She was the Goddess of Winter, her stark black hair as dark as night, her bright-red lips a nod to February, and her skin a snowy-white, like the month of January. She just happened to be one of the goddesses who had gasped during the council meeting earlier that week, when Sage had been brought into the room.

I wanted to find out what she knew, but I was going to have to do it carefully. Otherwise, I might risk arousing suspicion.

"Mind if I join?" I asked, my tone sweeter than sugar.

"Of course, Avriel dear," Oraina replied, waving me in.

"Want some?" Mercia asked, picking up the wine jug from the table, swishing it from side to side in invitation.

"I have a bit of a headache today," I lied. "I'll stick with water tonight."

"Understandable," she said, lowering the jug, and then waved over a servant who carried a tray full of goblets. "Are any of these just water?" she asked the servant.

"This one is," the meek female replied, pinching the stem of a gold-rimmed goblet and giving it to her.

"Wonderful," Mercia replied, long, elegant fingers clasping it. She turned my way and handed me the goblet. "Here you are."

"Thank you," I said, accepting it, the stem cool against my fingers.

The servant bowed and then swiftly returned to where she had been standing before.

"That was quite some fight earlier, wasn't it?" I started, hoping to ease into things.

"Was it ever," Mercia agreed. "Talk about muscles!" She shimmied her shoulders, stirring the parrot from its dozing state.

The parrot popped its head up and exclaimed, "Muscles, muscles, muscles! Talk about muscles!"

Mercia chuckled as she petted the colorful bird, stroking her beautiful feathers.

I took a small sip from my goblet, swallowed the cool water, and said, "Will any of you be attending the games on Saturday?"

"If it was here, then I would, but I couldn't care less to

go to Lorphiah. The amphitheaters there are so horribly old—full of dust and cockroaches." Oraina grimaced. "No thank you."

"Agreed. They really need to tear them down and rebuild," Mercia added on. "I don't know why they haven't yet."

Oraina concurred, "I don't know why either."

I looked at Eirwen. "What about you? Will you be going?"

"I'm thinking about it," she answered, giving me nothing more.

Even though no one asked, I still said, "I'll probably go. It's Nockrythiam's *mate*, after all. It seems like a pretty monumental soul to be crushed. History in the making and all that."

"I just hope crushing her soul doesn't come around to bite us all in the ass," Oraina stated with a degree of concern as she drained the remnants of the jug into her goblet, filling it to the brim.

I held my breath, hoping someone would respond so I didn't have to. I didn't want to insert myself too much.

I waited a few seconds more.

Still, nothing.

They all appeared to be lost in their own private thoughts.

Damn it.

I looked at Oraina and asked in a light, conversational tone, "What do you mean by that?"

Oraina shrugged. "I don't know. It just sort of feels like

. . ." She trailed off.

"Bad karma?" Mercia asked.

"Yes, that's exactly it," Oraina answered with a nod.

My lips thinned—that was not the answer I was expecting. I decided to push a little more. "I get what you are saying, but I don't think it's karma, it's something *more* than that." My eyes flicked to Eirwen, handing the conversation to her.

But in typical Eirwen fashion, she said nothing.

So, I continued, "I think it's because she's Nockrythiam's mate. If he were ever to return and find out her soul had been crushed, who knows what he would do." I had zero knowledge when it came to fishing, but I knew enough about it to know that was the hook. Now I just needed one of them to take the bait I was about to dangle before them. "Besides that, there *could* be people out there who are still loyal to Nockrythiam."

Oraina disagreed, "Nockrythiam's followers either died during the War of the Creators or they ended up wherever he did. I don't think we have to fear retaliation from anyone."

"That's not true," Eirwen cut in, lowering her goblet onto the table. It didn't make nary a sound, her movement always so controlled and precise.

"Which part?" Oraina asked, raising a single brow.

"The vuleeries are still here," Eirwen answered, tipping her chin up ever so slightly.

Mercia shivered. "I forgot about those dreadful creatures."

"They are rather ruthless, definitely not something you want to cross paths with." Eirwen paused, her eyes flicking back and forth, as if she were remembering something. Then, "In the past, there was only one person who they showed allegiance to . . . Nockrythiam."

Finally, we're getting somewhere, I thought to myself.

"So, by extension, do you think the vuleeries would be loyal to Nockrythiam's mate?" Oraina inquired curiously.

I could have kissed her, but I kept my mask in place, acting nonchalant.

Eirwen gave a sophisticated shrug. "Hard to say, but it could be a possibility."

"Wait . . . if it's a possibility, why would the empress send Nockrythiam's mate to the arena to have her soul publicly crushed? The vuleeries will show up there after the games, and they'll surely discover her body. If they are loyal to Nockrythiam, wouldn't that be bad?" Mercia asked.

"Again, it's hard to say. Typically, it's only the young vuleeries who go to pick the bones after the games. Most of them probably don't even know who Nockrythiam is. Although, it is a risky move on the empress's part." Eirwen glared at us all. "Don't you dare tell her I said that. You all know she'd have my head."

"I won't say anything," Mercia promised.

Oraina and I chimed in with similar sentiments.

I spoke with them for a while longer before I excused myself.

I *knew* what I had to do, but I had limited time to do it.

My skirts swished across the floor as I walked at a very quick pace up to Sage's cell. As it was well past two o'clock in the morning, most of the prisoners were asleep. It wasn't uncommon for priestesses to spend time in the dungeon, however, it was a bit odd for one of us to be coming at such a late hour. Which meant I had to get what I needed swiftly and get out. The last thing I wanted was to arouse suspicions.

Sage peeked at me from underneath her covers.

"I need a strand of your hair," I whispered, reaching through the bars.

"Why?" she asked groggily as she slowly started to prop herself up on her elbow.

"Long story, and I'm working on very little time." I jiggled my hand. "Hair. Now."

Sage eyed me suspiciously before she plucked a white strand and handed it over. I unfurled a handkerchief and placed it inside, swiftly folding it up.

"Wait," she whispered, her voice almost pleading.

"There's no time," I said then raced back to my private chambers.

The flame of a flickering candle cast long shadows across my desk as I worked.

I dipped the end of the quill into the bottle of ink and then began to write my urgent message on a small slip of paper, my fingers pressing down on the ends to keep it from curling.

When I was done, I took turns blowing and waving my hand over the ink in a bid to dry it. When it looked dry, I performed a small test by dabbing my thumb on the paper. Removing it, I turned my hand over and inspected my thumb—it was clean. Deciding that was good enough, I swiftly rolled up the paper.

Turning my attention to the handkerchief, which was sitting beside the bottle of ink, I unfolded it. I plucked the white hair, and with careful fingers, I wound it around the roll of paper, tying it gently.

Rushing to the window, I undid the brass latch and shoved it open. A burst of night air passed by me, toying with the blank papers on my desk while teasing the flame of the candle.

Chanting in the language of my mother's people, I tossed the small scroll out the window. My breath caught as it tumbled, heading for the ground. I chanted harder, pouring every ounce of my power into my words, into my magic.

A second before the paper hit the ground, the wind listened. It swept it back up into the air, sending it hurtling off into the distance. Relief filled me, but my job was far from done. My message had a long way to travel, and it was my power that was necessary to get it to where it needed to go. So, I chanted.

And chanted.

I chanted through the remainder of the night, until the sun had risen and there was nothing more I could give. Until my body was spent of energy and power. Until my muscles had gone numb and my tongue felt like it was made of lead.

Legs giving out, I crumpled to the floor in a heap of exhaustion.

Please work were the last two words that crossed my mind before I lost consciousness.

Chapter 16

Sage

Dust sputtered out from the ceiling, plummeting around me each time the roaring crowd above cheered in victory. The building shook so violently, I wondered if it all might come crashing down.

I sat on the sandy ground, my wrists in shackles, chained to the wall behind me.

Directly across from me was a looming iron gate, stained with blood and ichor. To my right, there were more prisoners, each one of them shackled, their faces covered.

Metal screeched against metal as the iron gate in front of me swung open. Two armor-clad guards stepped inside— their gauntlets clasped around a man's wrists as they dragged his corpse behind them. Matted, brown hair, stained with ichor and pebbled with sand, hung over his downturned head. His legs, full of lacerations and vicious, deep wounds, dragged behind him, a gilded river of his life's essence trailing after him, marring the sands.

My eyes widened at the corners—a grotesque, fist-sized hole was in the center of his back, going all the way through to the other side. The flesh was tattered, gaping. Gory.

"Always start the pile back here. By the end of the day, there will be hundreds of bodies, so it's important to give yourself enough room for them all," directed the shorter guard, her voice authoritative. Confident. "Also, always remove face coverings from the corpses. We use them for the other prisoners. As this one's face covering didn't make it through the fight, we don't have to worry about it, but for the ones that do, we'll create a separate pile."

"Understood," the other one answered swiftly as they discarded the body. She seemed eager to please. A new trainee, no doubt.

"When the event is over, the vuleeries will come for the corpses." The shorter guard's tone became grave. "Ensure you do not get in their way. Some do not differentiate between living and dead."

"I've heard quite a few . . . unpleasant stories about them. I will make sure to keep my distance."

"Good." The guard grinned at her. "You are going to do just fine here."

Cheering erupted and another plume of dust fell from the floor above. I closed my eyes, waiting for it to be over. The hairs on the back of my neck bristled, as I heard hundreds, if not thousands, of voices begin to chant one word over and over again—

Crush. Crush. Crush.

The guards made their way back to the iron gate, peering outside.

The intense chanting halted.

A moment of silence, followed by a painful cry and a mighty roar.

Then, chaos erupted, and the audience began to scream and yell in victory, stirring the floorboards to cough out another round of dirt and dust. The entire place rumbled, the people's combined voices louder than thunder.

"We don't collect this body, right?" asked the trainee.

"Correct," replied the other guard. "There are three other collection rooms. We alternate with them."

"Alright." The trainee turned around, her gaze falling on me. She leaned into the other guard and whispered, "Umm, boss, there is a female here."

"Yes, there is. I know it's a bit uncommon to see, but it does happen every once in a while. You'll get used to it," the guard answered as she, too, turned to face me. "This one has come with a special request from Empress Avena."

The trainee gaped. "Truly, Her Majesty?"

"Indeed. I would not lie about such a thing."

"For the empress to send her . . . well, she must be of great importance," the trainee remarked.

"Perhaps at one point. But considering she is here, sentenced to have her soul crushed, I'd say that she has lost her favor with the empress."

A guard emerged on the other side of the gate. She jerked her chin toward me. "She's up next."

"We'll bring her out," the higher-ranking guard replied.

The female on the outside tapped the gate then walked away.

Both guards made their way over to me, the trainee a bit more hesitant, her pace slightly slower.

Attached to the higher-ranking guard's belt was a ring full of silver keys. She fiddled with them, looking for the right one. When she found it, she picked up my wrist, slid the key into the lock, and turned it to the side. The shackle landed on the ground with a heavy *thump*. She did the same with the other shackle. Her eyes fell to mine, and she spoke with the smallest hint of compassion, "A word of advice—it will be less painful and over much quicker if you don't fight."

Then, she and the trainee yanked me up onto my feet.

Wait, a small voice whispered inside of me, beseeching me to say the word out loud, but I could not. My tongue was as useless as the rest of me.

They started to drag me toward the gate. I didn't fight them.

Please wait, that inner voice said again.

But why? I asked it.

I had no child. No mate. No home.

I had *nothing*.

So why should I fight?

Bright, blinding light bored holes into my eyes as I was thrown out onto the scalding-hot, bloodstained sands. The iron gate screeched as it swung closed, locking me in the arena.

Drums began to beat, followed by the powerful blast of horns, so strong they courted shivers down the length of my spine. All around me, people began to cheer, their combined voices deafening.

I looked up at the vast crowd, my gaze sliding from one female face to the next. Most of the audience was made up of women, but every once in a while, I'd spot someone who had their face completely covered—just like the prisoners down below.

The audience grew quiet, their attention shifting.

I followed their lead.

Hoisted up high, in a private balcony, was a group of women, all dressed in expensive-looking clothes. The one in the middle, a blonde, stood up from her chair. She straightened her slinky, silk garb before she strode up to the front of the balcony.

She raised her slender arms, adorned in gold bangles. "Good citizens of Lorphiah. The female you see before you has been condemned to have her soul crushed." She pulled her hand down, clenching her fist closed, her theatrics stirring more cheering from the crowd. "It is my honor to present a soul crusher from my house, the noble and revered House of Cinphius, the greatest ludus in Lorphiah, to carry out this execution. In honor of the empress, I give you Norvenia, the scourge of the bloody south. Behold, your soul crusher—" She gestured to a gate, six times the size of the one I had been shoved out of.

Metal groaned, and slowly, it began to lift.

Boom. Boom. Boom.

The ground trembled beneath me as a horned giant stepped out from the gate, dressed in armor. A skeleton of some monstrous beast curved around her shoulders, its sharp spikes sticking straight up. Its skull hung over her breastplate—empty eye sockets forever keeping watch. She thrust her gauntlet into the air, and the crowd exploded with excitement. The gauntlet looked like it was made of massive scales, the fingers tipped with sharp, deadly claws. Whatever creature it had come from had to be huge.

Immediately, I knew that was the soulius Avriel had spoken of.

The giant pointed her brutal ax at me and let out a *bloodcurdling* roar. If a cave that feasted on horror could scream, that was exactly what it would have sounded like. And although it made the hairs on the back of my neck stand, the instincts that kept me alive, those natural fight-or-flight responses, were drowned out by my grief.

I would do as the guard suggested . . . I wouldn't fight.

And maybe, just maybe, when I reached the shores of oblivion, I would be reunited with my child.

Chapter 17

Von

Folkoln, Ezra, Kaleb, Soren the worm, and I were in one of my private offices, made up of mahogany shelves full of ancient tomes and relics. A large, ravenous fireplace was surrounded by a sitting area comprised of four wingback chairs and an exceptionally long settee—the length customized to fit my vast height. A handmade rug anchored the furniture, providing warmth against the cold, obsidian floors.

The rug, among many other improvements, had been one of Sage's ideas when she lived here. That short span of time made up the happiest days of my eternal life.

Happy.

The word was a foreign one now.

Soren was seated at one end of the settee. Ezra was in the middle, Kaleb on the other end. His knee hadn't stopped ticking since he sat down. His fists were clenched, and I was somewhat surprised he hadn't pummeled Soren yet. For Sage's sake, I knew he hadn't.

Folkoln stood by the fireplace, an elbow placed on the stone mantle, hand propping his head up.

"I'm supposed to drink this?" Soren asked hesitantly as he peered down at the cup in his hands. Inside of it was a bubbling, slimy liquid that smelled worse than the shit-filled streets of Norwood.

"You sure are," Folkoln crooned.

Soren swallowed harshly. "Can I ask . . . why?"

"Because you broke Sage's unconscious mind barrier, you two are linked, but you can't contact her because she has passed. With the aid of my elixir, it will restore your connection temporarily, even through death," Ezra answered, her hands resting on the curved handle of her cane.

"So I'll be speaking to her ghost?" Soren asked, complexion paling.

"In some sense, yes. In others, no," Ezra replied, tipping her head from side to side as if it were a balance, weighing her response.

Now I understood why she'd wanted the Lost Soul's tears—because a Lost Soul could link the living with the dead. I looked at Ezra, my expression flat as I said, "I take it you had *more* than just a hunch about what the tears of the Lost Soul would do."

Ezra gave me a wink. "Sometimes you need a taste of your own medicine, Von."

"The tears of what now?" Soren squeaked, voice trembling. I eyed the cushion he sat on, wondering if I should have put a piss-pad down.

"I don't believe anyone gave you permission to speak, fingerless," Folkoln drawled.

"Folkoln," Ezra scolded.

"Yes, love?" he teased, biting his lower lip.

Ezra shook her head and let out a huff. "Remind me why you are needed here?"

"Would all of you just shut up?" Kaleb snarled. He looked at Ezra, then Folkoln, before his gaze landed on the window. "Sage is out there. Wherever *there* is. She needs us, and all we are doing right now is wasting time." He looked at Soren. "Find your fucking balls, Soren, drink the damn liquid, and help me get my sister back."

Soren looked down at the cup and studied it, the teeny-tiny cogs in his peanut-sized brain turning—looking for an escape plan, no doubt.

Enough was enough.

My voice cut through the silence. "You have two options here, Soren, do not think you have a third. You can drink it on your own or I'll shove it down your fucking throat, cup and all."

Folkoln chuckled.

Soren nodded so fast it was almost comical, and perhaps if I wasn't in such a sour mood, it would have been. Eyes darting back to the cup, he raised it to his mouth and drank. Gagging, he lowered it and exclaimed, "Creator above, this is awful!"

"Funny, it didn't smell that bad to me," Ezra said, a bony, crooked finger reaching up to tap her chin. "I wonder if it was the—" She cut herself off. "Never mind."

"Does he need to drink all of it?" Folkoln asked, enjoying every second of this.

Ezra lowered her hand back to her cane and nodded. "That would be best."

"You heard them," I told Soren.

He blew air through his lips, then, like a good mutt, he forced himself to swallow the rest, face contorting in anguish. When he was done, he slammed the cup down on the end table, sputtering and choking and trying not to vomit. After he regained control of himself, he raised the neckline of his shirt to wipe at his mouth.

Then, we waited. And waited.

After a while, Soren looked at Ezra. "Nothing is—"

His mouth slammed shut, his head snapped back, and light shot from his eyes, beaming up at the ceiling. A scream, horrific and unnatural, shredded through his throat with such force that blood bubbled from his mouth.

"What's happening?" I asked Ezra, striding forward.

"He's going to die! Fuck! He's our only way to contact Sage!" Kaleb exclaimed, jumping up. He ran his hands through his hair, his body tense. Wide-eyed, he looked at Ezra then me. "What do we do?"

"He's not strong enough." Ezra placed her hand on Soren's arm, whispering in a language I had not heard for many centuries. "Vee norhvic mor leann." She repeated the words, over and over again.

"What is she saying?" Kaleb asked me with urgency.

But it was Folkoln who replied, "She's lending him her

strength."

Brightness shone from Ezra's eyes, blinding my own.

She continued to chant. Each time she said the words, her voice weakened.

"It's not enough," I said, moving toward them.

"Von, wait!" Folkoln growled.

But it was too late because I grabbed Soren's arm and began chanting with Ezra. "Vee norhvic more leann. Vee norhvic mor leann."

White-hot heat scorched into my hand, like a brand upon my skin. It sunk into my palm, carving its way through my arm, up into my chest. There, pain exploded. My teeth gnashed as the force of it brought me to my knees.

"Fuck's sake," Folkoln growled. His hand fell on my shoulder, and he started to chant along with us.

The world around me blinked out and a new one took its place. I was surrounded by a roaring crowd, full of females, in some decrepit-looking arena.

But all of it faded away the moment I saw *her*.

Crumpled upon bloodstained sands was my mate. My Sage. My everything.

She looked like a ghost of her former self, her expression vacant, like she had already checked out. She was dressed in rags, hair matted and clumped. She looked thin. I ached to take her in my arms, to bring her back here, to cook for her, to brush her hair . . .

But I couldn't do any of that.

Weary blue eyes lifted to mine. Tears gathering, she whispered in disbelief—

Chapter 18

Sage

"Von?" I breathed his name, my body trembling like a frostbitten leaf, shaken from its branch and captured by his wind.

Real or not real?

Could I believe what my eyes were telling me? Was he truly standing before me?

I wanted to believe it, even if it was just a beautiful, dark lie.

He looked *different*. His eyes were an endless onyx, his skin etched with bolts of black—had he gotten more tattoos? And he had . . . horns. They were sinister things, and yet, they sort of suited him.

My beloved Death knelt before me.

"Little Goddess," he said, gentle hands clasping my cheeks, thumbs brushing away my tears. His masculine scent washed over me, and I breathed him in. I realized in that moment that I wasn't just grieving the loss of our child, I was grieving the loss of him.

"I'm going to get you back," he vowed to me in such a way that I believed him.

"How?" I breathed, placing my hands over his, savoring every second of this moment. His touch. His words. Being near him again. All of it felt so right. *So* real.

I chose to believe it was.

"I'm figuring that out," he answered, his voice as tender as his touch. "You just stay alive until I can get to you. Okay?"

I nodded, choking back a sob. "Okay."

He pressed his forehead to mine and whispered, "I love you, Sage. We will be together again. I promise you."

And then he was gone.

But his words remained—*You just stay alive until I can get to you.*

For the first time since I awoke in these unfamiliar lands, I felt that small, sacred spark within—the one we all had burning inside of us, the one that made life worth living. The one that made it all worth fighting for.

That voice within me said, *Get up.*

"Let the battle begin!" the blonde woman standing on the balcony announced, and the spectators cheered and clapped.

Get up, that inner voice said again, this time a bit more urgently.

The giant charged at me, and the ground trembled.

Get up! the voice roared, filling my veins with

adrenaline.

My heart leapt into my throat, and I spurred into action. I scrambled onto my feet, my muscles firing, trying to recall what they once were capable of. I flung my hand to my side, searching for my powers, but—

Nothing. They didn't respond.

The giant brought her ax down, and I narrowly missed being cleaved in two as I dove out of the way. I slid across the ground, the sand scrubbing at the top layer of my skin, causing ichor to brim in the small, rash-like wounds.

"Ugh," I growled as I came to a stop.

Roaring, the giant tugged on her ax stuck in the ground. Freeing it, she spun toward me, coming for me again.

I jerked upright, back onto my feet. I jumped as high as my weary muscles would allow, tucking my feet in. The ax sailed right underneath me, the current so powerful, it nearly sucked me to the side.

Collectively, the audience roared in astonishment, cheering at the blow that nearly chopped my legs off.

Adrenaline shot through my veins, filling me with strength. I darted to my left, fumbling for my powers. Still, they would not answer my call.

"Damn it," I hissed under my breath.

What was stopping them? I wore no iron, and there was nothing on my person to suppress my powers, so why wouldn't they answer? In the Spirit Realm, Von had wards placed around his castle preventing people from light walking in and out. My eyes darted to my left, then to my right, scanning the perimeter of the arena, high and low, as my legs carried me, my feet churning up sand.

There! I internally cried out in victory when I spotted them.

Where the lower and upper sections of the amphitheater were separated, four mounted statues sat on pedestals overlooking the arena below. They were spaced evenly apart, each one different—a bear, a wolf, a fish, and a cougar.

For a brief second, I was transported back to the Cursed Lands, to when the elders had met in Valenthia to decide what to do to fight Aurelius and his army of Demi Gods. Ezra had sat upon a table, a table she'd struck with her cane when the room erupted into chaos, a table with the *exact same* animal carvings on its legs as I was seeing now. The words she had spoken back then as she'd gestured to me repeated in my mind—*Behold. Your savior.*

I didn't know it back then, but Ezra hadn't just been speaking to the rest of the room—she had been speaking to me. *Future* me. The one who needed her powers more than ever.

And now I knew what was stopping them.

I eyed the statues, my mind churning out a quick plan.

"I'm listening, Ezra," I wheezed under my breath as I came to a swift halt, facing the giant. I was done running.

I charged straight for her.

Reaching the center of the arena, she swung her ax.

I dodged to the side of it, feeling the weapon sail past me, biting into the ground and spraying sand, some of which pelted my back. As she worked on tugging it free, I raced as fast as my legs could carry me, running beside the length of her handle.

With a mighty roar, I hurtled into the air, landing on the giant's wrist.

"Get off of me, you maggot," her booming voice roared as she tugged her ax free, swinging it upwards in an attempt to fling me off. She didn't have to try very hard because when I was above her head, I let go.

I sailed through the air like an awkwardly Sage-shaped arrow loosed from a bow. The faces of the people in the crowd, which had looked so small before, became a whole lot bigger as I flew straight for them. They scattered, like a stepped-on hill of ants, racing this way and that, right before—

Crash!

I smashed into the stands, snapping a wood bench in two, causing a plume of dust and an explosion of wood. I wheezed, the wind knocked out of my lungs. *Fuck me.* That might not have been one of my best ideas, but it worked. Rolling over, I did a quick mental check on my body. Apart from some bumps, bruises, and cuts, miraculously, nothing felt broken.

Perhaps my immortality was finally kicking in.

"About damn time," I panted under my breath.

As soon as the dust settled, someone yelled, "Get her!"

I didn't care to find out who it was.

Grimacing, I shoved myself back onto my feet and locked my gaze on the ward that was closest to me. Then, I moved, albeit rather sloppily. I felt like milk in a butter churn, because my whole world was swirling.

"Come here," a guard snarled as she jumped into my path, fists raised. She fired a punch, hoping to connect.

Somehow, my forearm caught hers, blocking her swing. I thrust the heel of my palm into her chest, knocking her back onto her ass.

I stumbled like a newborn fawn around her, pressing forward. I was so close to the ward, almost there, almost—

A spectator grabbed me, her arms wrapping around me like a python, squeezing me tight. As if my lungs weren't desperate for air enough—the last thing I needed was this.

"I've got her!" she screamed victoriously in my ear.

Fighting my disorientation, I rammed the back of my skull into her face, and her arms immediately released me.

"My nose!" she cried out, the sound garbled, telling me I'd probably broken it.

Stars peppered my vision, blinking in and out. I shook my head, and they cleared somewhat, then I moved.

I reached the ward, and I pressed my hands against the cold stone. My teeth cut steel as I shoved with all my might, forcing it ahead. The statue began to move.

Holy shit, I was doing it—

My scalp screamed in agony as a hand grabbed my hair, wrenching me backwards, pulling me against my attacker. I sent my elbow into their abdomen, an audible *oof* sounding from her, and she wobbled backwards. The hand let go and I shot toward the ward.

Roaring, I collided with it, shoving it over the edge. The fish statue fell from its pedestal, rotating in the air until it smashed into the ground, breaking into hundreds of pieces.

I grinned in victory.

The moment was short-lived.

Hands shoved me forward, back into the arena.

The wind tugged at my hair as I fell toward the ground, spiraling faster and faster. Frantically, I reached deep down, searching for my powers. A breath before I turned into a silver splatter upon the sands, my water beast came roaring to life. My hands shot out as a hurricane of water swirled from my palms, blasting against the ground beneath me, against the remnants of the shattered ward. The force of it was so strong I was released from gravity's pull.

I landed on my feet, on the drenched sands, water dissolving from my hands.

I was given less than a second to think, because the giant was already coming for me, her ax swinging back behind her head, ready to deliver that final blow—

But I *would not* let her have it.

An animalistic roar tore through me as I harnessed my power. Like a runaway horse, it came stampeding to the surface, and I unleashed it.

Fire erupted from my hands, blasting toward her.

She dropped her ax and crossed her arms, trying to shield herself from my flames, but it was of little use. Fire chewed into her exposed skin, and she let out a horrific scream that shook the entire amphitheater. Her metal armor began to glow orange, as hot as a pyre, searing into her skin. The scent of burning flesh, like meat cooked in a pan, permeated the air. She tore her chest plate from her torso, ripping off bits of cloth and skin with it, revealing a gruesome truth—

What my fire had done to her butchered, charcoaled chest.

My flames cut off, and I dropped my hands. I peered down at my palms, mortified at what I had done.

I realized at that moment, I had lost a piece of the person I used to be. There had been a time when the girl from Edenvale would stand amongst the crowd, watching as the Cursed were burnt at the pyre. It had made my stomach heavy, like an undigested meal.

Now, here I was, doing the exact same thing I had once despised—burning someone alive. Was this the price of—

No. She was going to kill us, the goddess within argued.

But the noble part of me, the hero part, was having a hard time listening.

People yelled and screamed, darting out of the way as the giant stumbled back into the stands. She fell into one of the sections, crushing the platforms, benches, and stairs underneath her. A second passed, maybe two, and they started to catch fire. The wood benches were so old that the moment the fire touched them, they lit like a torch soaked in oil.

I watched as my flames engulfed the amphitheater.

Piercing cries sounded from above, the noises unnatural and distorted, haunting and chilling. They were hard to explain, forged from high-pitched screams that seemed to echo around me. But they weren't just sounds, they were a warning—

I jerked my face skyward, eyes stretching wide.

A wraithlike creature, double my size, descended from the sky like a nightmare come to collect screams. Its talons, the color of pale milk, stretched out toward me, the curved nails as sharp as knives. Underneath a hood, cut from shadow, it possessed a bird-like skeletal face. A vulture, perhaps. Where its eyes should have been, there was nothing—only bottomless, empty holes.

And yet, they bore into me.

I forged an azure blade, pointing it at the creature. With a snarl on my lips, I warned, "Get back."

"I mean you no harm," the creature screeched, her voice about as pleasant as metal against tooth. It slid across my bones in the most eerie and unnatural of ways, causing a shiver to race down the length of my back.

Hundreds of others, just like it, began to emerge all around the blazing amphitheater. They seemed completely unbothered by the flames as their fearsome beaks picked at the dead giant, snapping her charcoaled skin from her bones and gobbling it down. Others attacked those who were trying to find their way through the flames, toward the exit—grabbing hold of them with their talons and carrying them off.

"What are you?" I asked, my voice breathless.

"I am a vuleerie. My kind is loyal to Nockrythiam and by extension, you," she answered, floating above me.

I did not lower my blade, keeping it firmly pointed at her. "Why are you here?"

"We received a message from an unknown source, written on a scroll with information about you, that you had returned and the empress was sending you to this arena to have your soul crushed. A white hair was wound around the scroll. My niece tasted it and confirmed that it did indeed belong to you. And so, we have come to rescue you," she replied.

Avriel. That's why she'd needed my hair. She must have been the one to send the scroll to them. And somehow, it had worked. The priestess seemed to believe that the vuleeries would help me. I took a breath, hoping she was right.

I dissolved my sword, and asked, "How do I get out of here?"

"I'll take you," she said, flying over top of me.

With surprising gentleness, her talons clutched onto my shoulders. My hands wrapped around her scaly legs as she lifted me. She flew us out of the blazing arena, high up into the azure sky.

Chapter 19

Sage

"Where are we going?" I asked the vuleerie, unsure if I had made the right decision as I peered down at the sprawling hills. We were very, *very* high, and if she dropped me, I'd be flatter than roadkill. *Scratch that.* I'd be microscopic Sage splatter. I squinted. How did that work with immortality, especially when I couldn't heal myself? Would I spend an eternity like that, misted upon the ground?

I swallowed uncomfortably. *No. Nope.* I didn't like that thought.

"To the Moriel Forest," she answered, voice as disturbing as ever. *Loved* that for me.

"What's there?" I inquired curiously.

"Not what, but *who*," she replied.

I decided to bite. "*Who* is there?"

"You'll see," the spectral creature said, then her beak snapped open and she let out an eerie sound. I realized with a degree of horror she was . . . *chuckling*.

Fuck me.

What had I gotten myself into?

I took a breath, forcing it inside my frozen-stiff lungs, and tried not to lose my shit. Which, all things considered, I think I had a right to lose.

I was in an unfamiliar land, ruled over by an evil empress who wanted me dead-dead for reasons I didn't fully understand—reasons, I surmised, attached to yet *another* past life I'd clearly had. Not to mention I'd lit an entire arena on fire, burned a giant alive, and now, I was being flown to an unknown location by a shadow-ghost-skull-faced-bird who laughed like a homicidal lunatic.

I repeated—*fuck me*.

It was all so much to process—*too much* to process.

Forcing an exhale, I focused on my breathing and tried not to think about *everything*. Instead, I lied to myself. I was just enjoying a leisurely flight to a cottage in the woods. Nothing more. Nothing less. I breathed again. Repeated the lie. Another breath.

Wash. Rinse. Repeat.

In truth, the only thing that kept me going was Von's promise—

I'm going to get you back, his words repeated inside my mind.

In the arena, when he had knelt before me, I had struggled to decide if he was real or not, but something within me told me that he was. So I leaned into his words, letting them be the spark that ignited the fire within me—to fight, to make it out alive.

Deep down, I believed we would be together again.

I believed we would find our way to one another.

I just had to stay alive long enough for that to happen, which meant I needed to keep my wits about me. I needed to stay alert. Track my surroundings. Form a mental map and learn the geography of this foreign world. It probably wouldn't hurt if I tried to recover some of the memories from my past life too.

Down below, the great expanse of rolling hills gave way to a lush, densely packed forest. Towering trees, unfathomably large, shot up hundreds of feet into the air. Their branches were full of so much foliage it was impossible to see through them. It was almost like a blanket of green clouds, covering that part of the world and keeping it closed off to outsiders.

When we reached the tallest one, the vuleerie left the current she had been riding, and we dropped like a lead weight, plunging toward the dense canopy below.

"Wait!" I shouted, my eyes widening as I braced for impact.

As if the tree had spotted us coming, dozens of branches moved like stiff, creaky arms. They swayed apart, allowing us a small section to pass through. In some ways, it felt maternal, like a mother welcoming a child into her embrace.

. . . A child.

Sadness brimmed, dragging me down into its dark depths.

But I had little time to sit in the feeling because thousands of eyeless sockets were fixed on us. Vuleeries upon vuleeries perched in the giant tree. I could not even begin to guess how many there were. If they all were to take to the sky, it would look like a sea of black. They watched us as we descended past them, their heads lowering as we made our way further down through the never-ending branches.

While the leaves of the tree were lush and green, the bark was smooth and completely black.

"This is Hollow Tree, and it is our home," the vuleerie told me.

"It's huge," I marveled. "How many of you live here?"

"There are about ten thousand of us," she replied.

I swallowed at that, digesting the information.

That was *a lot* of vuleeries.

It took us a while just to fly through the branches, and we weren't going at a slow speed. When we finally reached the last of them, we continued to descend beside the trunk, which was so large, there was no way I could see around it. It was a mountain in itself. I imagined it would take quite a while to walk around the entire thing.

I looked down at the mossy forest floor, my brows knitting together—

Below, two females stood, peering up at us.

The one had dark-brown hair falling in lush, sultry waves. Her features were strong, her eyes wise and kind. She was beautiful. Her nose was a bit prominent, curving downward ever so slightly at the end, but it suited her face.

She wore a white, gauzy chiton fastened with a gold brooch on her shoulder, the color complementing her light-brown skin tone.

Standing beside her was another female.

A female who looked a bit like . . .

Me.

Her eyes were as blue as a winter sky, crisp and bright. Her hair, the color of white moonlight, was styled in braids, falling well past her waist. On her skin, there were intricate blue markings that glowed with a constant, steady thrum. She stood proud, a warrior. Strong. Her clothing looked to be crafted from boiled leather, formed perfectly to her body, portraying the same message.

My feet contacted the ground.

"This is where I leave you," the vuleerie said, her talons lifting from my shoulders.

I was too stunned by the female standing across from me to say anything. Too stunned to thank the vuleerie for rescuing me as she began her ascent. Too stunned to speak a single word. All I could do was stare.

Slowly, the rusty cogs of my mind started to turn before they supplied a name. One I knew I had not spoken in my past lifetime, nor the one that came before it, which meant that it had been known to me a very long, long time ago.

"Artemesia?" I asked, my voice barely above a whisper.

"Hello, sister," she answered softly, tears forming on her lower lash line.

One second, we were standing there, and by the next,

we were both running toward each other. Crashing together, we embraced in a desperate hug, full of so much longing it made my heart ache. My fingers curled into her clothing as I held her tightly to me.

The voices from our past began to speak, circling around us like swirls of magic—the late-night laughter that made our bellies hurt and the sisterly fights where both of us were too stubborn to back down. Although I could not match them to a memory, I could hear the same message repeated strongly throughout—

Of *how much* we loved one another.

The *same* feeling I could feel right now.

"I knew this day would come, but I did not expect it to take so long," Artemesia choked out, her words ragged with emotion.

Mine was no different as I replied, "I have no memories of us, but I can hear the voices of our past, and I can feel how much love my heart holds for you. How long has it been?"

"Thousands of years," Artemesia sobbed.

Her words and the guttural sadness in her voice were like a dagger to my heart.

I held her tighter, an old instinct waking within me. It was covered in dust, but I knew it well—the need to be a protective big sister and reassure her. "It's alright. I'm here now."

She nodded, and we remained like that for a while, just holding on to one another.

"How did you know where to find me?" I asked softly.

"Two vuleeries showed up at my camp, telling me they

had received a scroll with a white hair wrapped around it. They said it belonged to you, then told me what the scroll said. I wanted to go with them to the arena to rescue you, even though it would have put my people at great risk, but the vuleeries assured me they would retrieve you and told me to wait here instead. That decision was not an easy one. However, now, here you are." Slowly, she pulled back from me, her eyes puffy and red. I imagined I looked much the same. Gently, she clasped my cheeks. "Creator below, it's so damn good to see your face."

"As it is yours." Then, we were hugging again, a mess of bubbly, happy laughs and heart-wrenching sobs.

When we finally got it together, Artemesia stepped back and gestured to the other female. "Sage, this is Vatara. Vatara, Sage."

"A pleasure," Vatara greeted me, the words rolling off her tongue with a mystical quality.

"It's good to meet you," I said, reaching out to shake her hand as she did mine.

The second our skin touched, an image flashed before my eyes. It was of an exceptionally large . . . egg. A memory, perhaps? It was gone faster than it appeared.

Weird.

"We should probably get out of here—we have a bit of a long flight to get back home," Artemesia pointed out.

"Where is home?" I asked.

"I'll show you," she said with a grin before she turned to Vatara. "Ready?"

"More than ever. You know I can't stand being in my

human form," she answered. A flash of light emitted around her. One second, a woman was standing before me, and in the next—

A mighty gryphon.

She had the head and wings of an eagle and the body of a lion. Her front legs were bird-like, her talons, sharp and deadly, digging into the ground beneath her. Her long, glossy brown feathers sparkled with bits of gold. They were her crowning glory. She was magnificent. Mythical. Like a creature from a fairy tale brought to life, right before my very eyes.

The vuleeries began to revolt, hissing and snarling, flapping their wings. Together, they crafted a haunting song, full of warning—*you are not welcome here*!

"Come on," Artemesia spoke to me, before she turned and mounted Vatara. "The vuleeries don't take kindly to other birds being near Hollow Tree so we best take our leave."

I nodded then followed after her, eager to escape their haunting melody.

Chapter 20

Von

The moment I saw her—collapsed and broken, the icy fire within her eyes gone—dark emotions laced through my insides, gutting me on the spot.

Urgency gnawed at me, the need to protect her, to get to her, overwhelming me. My mate was strong, yes, but something inside her was not as it should have been. Had her memories returned to her? Had she discovered the truth of our past—that she had died while pregnant? It was a question I didn't need to answer, because one look at her had told me the devastating truth—

She knew. She knew, and I couldn't be there for her.

A flurry of emotions blasted through me like a blade to my abdomen, cutting me open.

Rage for her mistreatment.

Frustration because I couldn't help her right now.

Urgency to get to her.

Relief because she was alive.

My mate was . . . *alive*.

The black fog lifted from my vision.

I'm coming, Sage, I promised through the bond, taking my hand from Soren's arm—who was still unconscious and unfortunately, *still* breathing. To my dismay.

"Your horns are gone," Folkoln said from behind me, voice groggy. "And your skin is back to normal."

I examined my hand—the black bolts had disappeared. My head felt lighter, too.

From her spot on the settee, Ezra was slumped forward, arthritic fingers covering her mouth as she cackled to herself, the sound full of disbelief, astonishment, and joy.

"Well?" Kaleb asked as he moved around me, eyes huge. Pleading.

"She draws breath in another realm," I said, leaning into the truth of those words, feeling the weight of them, like kindling to my starved fire.

My mate was alive.

Kaleb swayed, and then he crumpled onto his knees, one at a time. "Alive," he whispered, sitting down on the backs of his heels, his eyes filling with tears. He began to wipe at them with the back of his hand, unable to stop himself from smiling.

"She is!" Ezra exclaimed. "Our girl is not lost to us!"

Not lost.

Found.

And now I just needed to get to her.

Eyes darting to Ezra, I asked, "Do you know what

realm she is in?"

"No, but I will," Ezra said, holding up her hand, her thumb and forefinger nearly touching, but in between was the smallest piece of . . . sand. As if she were speaking to a baby, she asked it softly, "What is the name of your home, little one?"

Folkoln and I side-eyed one another.

Ezra moved her hand beside her ear, listening. "Aha. I don't know that one. Another. Oh, wait. Say that again. One more time. No, doesn't ring a bell. Try another. Uh-uh. Uh-uh. Wait! I've heard of that one!" She lowered her hand into her lap, and then said to us, "This sweet little dear spoke a great deal of names to me. The last one I recognize."

"What is the name?" I demanded, my patience long gone.

"The Ancient Lands," Ezra answered. "That is where Sage is."

"What do you know of them?" I asked, crossing my arms over my chest. I tilted my head to the side, waiting for her answer.

"Very little, only whispers here and there. It's hard to know which ones are true." The skin crinkled between Ezra's drawn brows as she contemplated something. Then, her lips twisted into a grin. "But I know *someone* who came from them, as do you."

"Who?" Kaleb asked, face red and soaked with tears.

Ezra pointed to the ground.

I glanced down, and realization dawned. She didn't mean anyone in this castle or even the other seven tiers beneath it.

She was talking way, *way* down—as far as you could go in the Spirit Realm.

I sighed. "Getting her to talk isn't going to be easy."

"We meet again, little god," the giant said as I approached her, in the lowest tier of the Spirit Realm. She lounged beside a sprawling lake of water, her hand dipped in as she swirled it around.

Ezra trailed behind me, cane tapping the ground.

"And you've brought another tiny friend with you. How quaint," the giant spoke sarcastically.

"Tiny friend," Ezra muttered grumpily under her breath. Of course, *now* she was insulted. But when the giant had been eating every immortal in sight, she had merely shrugged her shoulders and told me, *Good luck with that.*

"It's been a while," I said by way of greeting, my hands in my pockets as I continued my leisurely pace. I had no idea what to expect from this meeting, although I was more than ready to find out. If I needed to unlock the beast within to attain the information I sought, I would, although I was hoping to handle things a bit more diplomatically.

"A while doesn't even scratch the surface for how long it's been," she stated, flicking the water from her fingers a few times. She tipped her chin up and peered at us down the bridge of her nose. "Why have you come?"

"To have a nice little chat," I said, the left side of my

mouth curving upwards.

"You left me to rot for centuries. What makes you think I would be willing to talk to *you*?" She snarled the last word.

I stood about an arm's swipe away—a calculated position.

Tap. Tap. Tap.

Ezra walked up beside me. "In all fairness, you *were* eating people."

"I was sending *souls* back to the empress," she corrected. "It is what I was built to do—what we all were."

"By eating them?" Ezra asked, quirking a wiry, gray brow. "How does that work, exactly?"

Skeptically, the giant looked at us, and for a brief moment, I thought she might not reply, but then she said, "Ah, fuck it." She leaned back, using her outstretched arms for support. "I will answer your question, but do not mistake my willingness to participate in conversation—something I have not had in a very long time—for anything more."

"Fair enough," I replied.

She continued, "To your kind I am known as an Ancient One, but the proper name for my species is venum stoomic, and I was created for one purpose—to harvest souls from different realms, particularly male ones, and send them back to the empress."

"Poison stomach," I said, my tongue translating the foreign language all on its own. Where it came from, I did not know.

"Ah, you speak my language. Yet another sign you are not as you seem," she said with a soft laugh. "Perhaps we should cut you open again, hmm?"

The memory of her slicing my leg open and peering at my bones resurfaced.

"I'd rather not," I stated flatly.

"Aww, you're no fun," she teased with a coy grin. "Now, where was I? Ah, that's right. As the name suggests, the contents of my stomach are deathly corrosive. It breaks souls down into such small pieces, the soul can no longer exist here. Seeking to be remade, the soul returns to the Mother Realm, what you call the Ancient Lands. It is where all life originated from and where all life must eventually return to. But before any of that can happen, the venom within my stomach must gnaw through the body. It is so powerful that even the strongest of immortal hides and iron bones don't stand a chance." With her eyes on me, she licked her lips. "Yours would be no different. You would be a tasty treat."

"Eh." I shrugged one shoulder. "I don't think I would. I got a lot of muscle—probably be too chewy."

"Who said anything about chewing?" The giant chuckled. "I'd just swallow you whole."

Ezra turned to me. "You should probably take her up on that."

I sighed, knowing the old bird wasn't wrong. It was one way I could get to where Sage was, albeit I'd rather not be eaten by a giant today. I decided to try another avenue.

"How did you get here?" I asked the giant, trying to recall the events of that day. I had been in my office, signing different documents, when Zahra had come racing into the room, fear propping her eyes wide open, explaining that a giant immortal had just appeared and she was *eating* other immortals.

"With this," the giant answered as she lifted the blue gemstone hanging from her neck. It looked like a large sapphire.

"See?" I spoke through the side of my mouth to Ezra. "No eating involved."

"Take a closer look," Ezra stated smugly.

I studied the gemstone, noting that even when the light hit it, it refused to sparkle.

"This is an energy stone, in particular, a travel stone, and it is how my kind travel from realm to realm. Shortly after I arrived here, it quit working." She removed it from her neck and placed it in her palm, studying it. "For centuries, I have waited to see it glow once more, so that I can return home."

"Do you know why it quit?" I inquired curiously.

"It's a question I've wondered many times, but I don't have an answer," she replied. "All I know is that it hasn't worked for a very long time and I'm starting to think it never will." She reached forward, dangling it before me, the stone larger than my head. "Do you want it?"

I raised a brow. "What do you want in return?"

"A simple exchange. If you figure out a way to make it work, you let me use it to get home."

I nodded in agreement. "Alright."

"Good," she stated. "Hold out your hand."

I did. The necklace shrank, and she dropped it in my

palm.

I surveyed it for a moment before I handed it to Ezra. "What do you think? Could you get it to work?"

She raised it to her ear, listening for a moment, then said, "I can take it to my sisters, but it could be a while before we discover anything. *If* we discover anything. And even if we do, there is no guarantee we can fix it."

"How long is *a while*?" I asked, peering down at her.

"Days. Months. Years." She handed the stone back. "Time we don't have."

My shadows swam around it, dissolving it and placing it in their storage.

I crossed my arms over my chest, mulling things over. I could wait for Ezra to take the travel stone to her sisters, but, as Ezra pointed out, there was no guarantee they could get it to work.

I thought of Sage, and I knew what I had to do.

Not that I was going to like it.

I loosed a breath.

"It's a good choice," Ezra said before her face swiveled in the giant's direction. "Would you like him salted or unsalted?"

Of course, she grinned.

Chapter 21

Von

"Don't worry, Von. I'll look after it," Dameon reassured me as he, Zahra, Folkoln, and I left my council room—the voices of the conversing immortals inside cut off as the door closed behind us. After Ezra and I returned to the castle, I'd called a meeting, assigning my council members various tasks to take care of in the wake of my absence. Some weren't qualified for half the jobs I had handed over to them, but desperate times called for desperate measures or some bullshit like that.

I had no idea how long I would be gone for, no idea how I planned to get back, and for all I knew, time could move differently in the Mother Realm.

But the one thing I did know with every fiber of my stubborn, bastard self?

I was going to get Sage back.

"I appreciate it," I answered Dameon as the four of us

began to walk down the hallway. There was one last thing I needed to do.

From behind us, flapping wings sounded, followed by a flash of light. "Wait!" Kaleb called out, his voice echoing off the glass walls.

Ignoring him, I continued forward.

Kaleb jogged up beside me and opened his mouth to speak—

"No," I stated firmly, already knowing what he was going to ask.

"I didn't even say anything," he protested.

"You didn't need to. The answer is still no."

"She's *my* sister," he argued. "I'm coming with you."

"Let him come," Folkoln cajoled. "It'll make things more entertaining."

"I see no harm in letting him go with you. You never know—you might be able to use the help," Zahra added, like the little mother hen that she was, always trying to look after me.

Folkoln chuckled at that. "Ah, dear Zahra, if I can assure you of one thing, it is that help is not in my brother's vocabulary."

"I'm well aware, but just because the big idiot doesn't understand the meaning of the word doesn't mean he doesn't need it sometimes," she snipped back. Her patience for Folkoln had fizzled out centuries ago. For my sake, they tolerated one another.

"You two realize I am right here, yes?" I asked. When neither of them said anything, I sighed. "Fine, you can come."

"Yes!" Kaleb decreed as we turned a corner. "When do we leave?"

"Within the hour," Folkoln stated.

"Great. I'll go tell Fallon. She'll want to come too," Kaleb said as he slowed his pace and began to turn around.

My shadows lifted from my shoulders, swirling in annoyance. Some formed into hands, threatening to reach out and grab Kaleb, who thought my yes *to him* was an open invitation to invite everyone else. Okay, okay, yes, it was just one more, but still. Sighing to myself, I reined them in.

While Dameon and Zahra spoke with one another, Folkoln fell into step beside me. Privately, he spoke inside my mind, *Fallon could be of use. We do not know anything about this . . . Mother Realm. We don't know what the terrain is like, or what or whom we will be up against. If we have her scout ahead, it could give us an advantage.*

Kaleb can do that too, I answered, casting the words over the private bridge that existed between the two of us.

Folkoln shot me a curious look. *What's this really about?*

I let out a sigh. *Fallon and Sage are a shit combination. I don't need them scrapping with each other the entire time.*

Folkoln's laughter echoed in my mind. *I see nothing wrong with that.*

My attention flicked toward him. *Says the jackass who feeds on emotions.*

Folkoln cracked a shit-eating grin, one that swiftly slipped away. His eyes narrowed. *Fate and Destiny have arrived.*

What do you sense from them? I asked.

They are conflicted.

As to be expected. Will you go to them and make sure they don't lose their nerve?

I can do that, Folkoln said.

I gave him a look, one that needed no words, because it was one I had given him thousands of times before.

He chuckled. *Don't worry, brother. I'll be on good behavior.* And with that, tendrils of onyx smoke swirled around him, and in a blink, he was gone.

"Where'd he go?" Dameon asked.

"To greet the Spinners. Although," I sighed, "knowing Folkoln, he'll probably torment them instead."

"Perhaps Dameon or I should have gone?" Zahra suggested with a degree of concern.

"That probably would have been wise," I answered, nodding as we walked down a small corridor, the north and south walls checkered with doors. "Well, I suppose, if anything, he'll keep them entertained."

Dameon chuckled. "That he will."

I opened the door, and the three of us filtered inside the small room. Harper and Lyra were lying on the small bed, on top of the covers, their legs entangled. Harper had one arm thrown around Lyra's shoulder and the other rested over her abdomen, her fingers linked with Lyra's. On the other side of the bed, Ryker dozed in a chair—one long leg stretched out in front of him, the other tucked underneath it.

Slowly, he woke, his eyelids heavy. "Haaah," he

yawned, his mouth stretching wide.

"Afternoon, sleeping beauty," I greeted.

"What time is it?" Ryker groggily asked as he sat up in the chair. He scrubbed his hand over his face, fingers rasping against his stubble.

"About two o'clock," Zahra answered as she made her way to his side, her hand falling over his shoulder, giving it a tender rub. "Have you had anything to eat, hon? You've been sleeping a lot. The Spirit Realm can do that to the living. Let me go fix you something so you can get some energy back." She looked at Lyra. "You too, love. You should have something to eat as well."

Lyra nodded, but Ryker said, "I'm fine for now. Thank you though."

"Word of the wise, son—she won't take no for an answer," Dameon said, looping his arm around his mate's waist.

Zahra glanced from Ryker to Lyra to Harper. "I look after my family. Now, what can I get you two to eat?"

While they discussed food options, I said to Harper, "You look well."

She smiled. "I feel much better."

"Zahra told me the good news—you are getting released today."

"I am." Her eyes filled with emotion. "Thank you for bringing them here."

"I'm just relieved it worked," I answered honestly.

Her brows drew together. "How are things going with finding Sage?"

"That's what I came here to tell you. Sage is alive. She's in a place called the Mother Realm, and we are going to be leaving within the hour to get her back."

"I knew she couldn't be gone." Harper's eyes filled with happy tears.

"I knew it too," Ryker spoke softly as he brushed back a few of his own.

Lyra covered her face and silently wept into her hands. Harper wrapped her arms around her, placing her cheek against the top of her head. Dameon and Zahra dabbed their eyes.

In truth, there wasn't a dry eye in that room, not even my own.

Shortly after, Ryker asked, "Who's all going?"

"Myself, Folkoln, Kaleb, Soren, and possibly Fallon," I answered.

"I don't understand." Ryker shook his head. "Why would you take that traitor with you?"

"Believe me, I don't like it either, but he has a connection to Sage and might be able to help us find her quicker," I answered, folding my arms across my chest.

"Let me come with you," Ryker said. "Someone's going to need to keep an eye on him. Just face it, if your plan fails with Soren, you'll need a good tracker."

Harper jerked her head up. "If you're going, I'm coming too." Lyra tapped her arm and gave her a firm nod. "We're *both* coming," she corrected.

"Harper, dear, I don't think that's a good idea," Zahra countered softly, expression concerned.

"Sage is my friend," Harper argued with fiery passion.

"She is mine too. Rest assured, they'll get her back." Zahra's voice was gentle. "You just transitioned."

"*Because* Lyra and Ryker are here. I know they can't stay in the Spirit Realm much longer, but this will give me more time with them, which, as we now know"—Harper gestured to herself—"is good for me. So . . ." She looked at me and flashed a smile. "We're going with you."

Zahra opened her mouth to speak, but Dameon cut in, "My flame, she is as strong-willed as you, and this arguing will get you nowhere. If she wishes to go, then let her."

Zahra sighed before turning to me. "You will take care of my family, yes?"

I opened my mouth to say I had not agreed to any of this, but when I glanced from Harper to Ryker to Lyra and saw the plea burning behind their eyes—a plea to help get their friend back—I caved. "Yes, of course, I will," I grumbled then told the rest of them, "We leave in half an hour."

"Great," Harper said, giving Lyra a squeeze. "By the way, how are we getting to this . . . Mother Realm?"

"Is there a portal or something?" Ryker tacked on.

Turning to Zahra, I said, "I'll leave you to explain that one." I dragged my gaze over the rest of their faces. "And then we'll see if you all are so keen on tagging along."

My umbra swam around me, and I shadow walked out of the room.

Chapter 22

Von

"Are you sure this is the only way?" Soren whined as all eleven of us—Folkoln, Ryker, Harper, Lyra, Soren, Kaleb, Fallon, the Three Spinners, and I—approached the giant. She was lying on her stomach, her head propped on her hands, her huge feet swinging back and forth, a massive fucking smile on her face.

"It's the best we got, fingerless," Folkoln stated from behind him, his hands in his pockets. He looked at ease, while Soren—as well as some of the others—looked like they might shit themselves. I wouldn't be surprised if Soren already had.

The giant licked her lips as she purred with delight, "What. A. Feast."

"I'm out," Soren squeaked, and he turned back around.

Folkoln crossed his arms over his chest as he peered down at Soren, blocking him from going back. He raised one brow, and that was all the convincing Soren needed to continue walking forward with us.

"Who's first?" the giant asked as we fell into somewhat of a side-by-side line.

"Wait," Ezra said as she walked in front of us. She dipped her arthritic fingers into her bulging pockets and pulled out one small glass vial, half the size of my pinky. She raised it up for us to see. Inside it? A bubbling blue liquid. "Before you go, you must drink this. It will give you consciousness once you reach the other side and will remove the veil from your eyes."

"Are you sure this will work?" Ryker asked suspiciously, one eyebrow shooting upwards.

Ezra's curved shoulders performed a half-hearted shrug. "Not entirely."

Kaleb groaned.

"Reassuring, as always," Harper sighed, her hand reaching up to rub her temples, trying to ease the headache of Ezra.

"Have some faith, dear child," Ezra implored. "Catch." She tossed the vial in Harper's direction. It flew a bit short, so Harper leapt forward, her long arm reaching out to catch it before it smashed on the ground. She cradled the vial in her hands as both she and Lyra looked at it.

"It will work," the Goddess of Destiny said, moving to Ezra's side. Her gray-blue eyes, born from storm clouds and sea, swept over us all. Beyond those eyes, a powerful immortal lurked beneath, but externally, she looked nothing of the sort. Her shoulders were curved, her torso wilting like a dying flower. Her tunic was moth-eaten, her skirt a mosaic of mismatched patches. The hem dragged behind her as if it had been stepped on and torn. And then there was her face, weathered and hard, like leather left to cure in the sun.

Folkoln asked, "Did you see something?"

"I did," the Goddess of Fate answered as she stepped to Ezra's other side. Although the three sisters bore a great deal of resemblance to one another, Destiny and Fate could pass as identical twins. If Fate didn't stain her gray hair with streaks of red and purple, it would be hard to tell the two apart.

"The night before last, a vision came to me. Nine souls drifting among tumultuous waters under time-forged icicles." She reached above her head, looking up. "Icicles that glow like brilliant, twinkling stars. There, written in the sky, a message—six find their feet, two need time, one is broken."

"But there are eight of us going," Fallon said, her arms crossed over her chest, her hip cocked to the side.

"Not for long," Destiny countered with a grin, her eyes shifting behind us.

I turned to look over my shoulder. A muscle ticked in my jaw when I saw who was walking toward us—

"Saphira," I growled underneath my breath as my vision darkened, rage simmering in my bloodless veins.

There was a brief time in my long, long life where I'd tried to repair our sibling relationship, but the moment I learned Saphira had plotted to end my mate, that she was the one who'd given that fucking disgrace of a king the Crown of Thorns, any wish to fix the damage that she had done ended immediately. And then when I found out she'd forced Sage into making an impossible deal—trading the Blade of Moram for our child's feathers—I knew right then and there that I would end her miserable life. My hand flew to my side as I summoned my sword from my umbra—Death Weaver.

Folkoln stepped in front of me, his hand pressing against my chest. "Von, wait."

"I suggest you remove your fucking hand from me before I cut it off," I warned, my tone menacing.

Every set of eyes were stuck on us. The ground groaned, trembling beneath my feet as the giant moved into a sitting position.

Slowly, Folkoln retracted his hand. "Just hear what she has to say."

Realization punched into my gut. "You talked to her. You told her what we were doing today, didn't you?" I'd be a damned liar if I didn't admit I felt a sliver of betrayal.

"I did," Folkoln said, owning up to it. His voice switched to our private channel. *And you can hate my rotten guts for it. But here's the thing, when this fucking bitch*—his eyes flicked up to the giant before they shifted back to me—*killed Aryx, the Saphira we knew died too. I know Saphira has done brutal things to you, and I'm not condoning her actions—I never fucking would, brother—but this could be her chance to find Aryx again. If she does, she might become the sister we once knew, before this world broke her."*

I looked over his shoulder, watching as Saphira walked toward us, her cloak swaying behind her. For a moment, I could almost see the little girl who would ask me to go out and gaze up at the stars with her.

I turned my head to the side, looking down at my sword. I had a decision to make.

When Saphira got closer, Folkoln stepped to the side.

We stood face to face. I searched her emerald eyes. In them, I found nothing but . . . desperation.

"Please." Her voice was barely above a whisper. "I know that I have done unspeakable things to you and Sage, and you have every reason to hate me for it, but if there is a chance that Aryx is alive, please, *please*, let me have it." She got down on her knees. In her hands, a chest materialized, one I recognized immediately. She laid the box at my feet. "Freely, I give you your child's feathers back."

And then, the proudest goddess I had ever known bowed and pressed her head to the ground.

I stood there, silent, conflicting emotions warring within me. I didn't trust Saphira—her past actions were too loud to ignore, and when I thought of what her intentions might have been for my child's feathers, ice crept along my skin. However, as I watched my sister grovel before me, something she had never done before, I realized something—she would do anything to be reunited with her mate, just as I would Sage.

Fallon strode closer to us, and she said with a shrug, "Fate said nine."

Indeed, she had.

"Oh, for Creator's sake, this is taking too long," the giant sighed as she reached over and plucked Soren by the scruff of his tunic. He kicked and screamed as she tilted her head back, placing him above her parted lips.

"Wait!" Ezra yelled. "He hasn't drunk the—" Her words fell short as the giant dropped Soren into her monstrous, cave-like mouth. Ezra sighed. "Never mind."

True to her word, the giant didn't chew.

I could *see* Soren pass through her esophagus, like a snake swallowing a mouse.

We *all* winced.

"Hmm-hmm," she chuckled gleefully. Clearly pleased with herself. She licked her fingers and smacked her lips, then looked at us. "Who's next?"

I turned to face Ezra. "How many vials do you have?"

Milky-white orbs stared blankly as she replied, "Eight. I was unaware of my sister's vision."

My shadows swept around my sword, dissolving it. "Well, since Soren won't be needing his anymore." I held out my hand. "Give me two of them."

Without question, she collected two from her pocket and placed them in my hand.

My shadows swept around the chest of feathers, concealing them in their vast storage as I crouched and dangled a vial in front of Saphira's face. "I'm going to give you this, but so help me, Saphira, if you make me regret it, I'll destroy you once and for all. Understood?"

"Yes." She nodded swiftly, gratitude lighting her misty eyes.

I dropped the vial into her hands before I rose to my full height. I looked at Destiny, then Fate. "And you two will keep up your end of the deal, yes?"

"We will," Fate answered. She waved her hand, and two spinning wheels appeared. Nine spools landed beside them, neatly stacked. I spotted my own. "Although, we cannot promise it will work. We have never weaved past the Three Realms before."

Once we got to the Mother Realm, we would be in bad shape due to the giant's poisonous stomach. Fate and Destiny would snip that part from our spools and weave another truth—that the damage had never been done, reverting our bodies and our souls back to normal. The irony was not lost on me that when I had taken my dead mate to them, begging for this very thing to be done for her, they had been unable to, all because of Aurelius's fucking heart. It had been the conduit that gave her life here, but ultimately, it was not hers, and the damage done by the Blade of Moram was irreversible.

Tearing the cork from the vial with my teeth, I spat it to the side. I raised the glass to my mouth and shot the burning, salty liquid back before I tossed it over my shoulder. The small glass shattered when it struck the ground. With a grin, I said to Ezra, "For good luck."

Then, I walked toward the giant.

I had a feeling this was going to hurt like a son of a bitch.

Chapter 23

Avriel

"You incompetent fools," Empress Avena seethed, her voice trembling with repressed anger. She shoved her goblet into Aryx's chest, which he swiftly took before it fell. Her discerning gaze locked on the two trembling guards kneeling before her. She was seated in her rose-colored bathing pool, a harem of scantily dressed males lounging around her, in and out of the waters—Shadow included.

He'd been the first person I saw when I walked into the empress's bathing chamber with the two guards in tow, a few short moments ago. Like a statue, cold and unfeeling, Shadow towered behind her, his muscular arms crossed over his broad, soul crusher-derived chest. But when he saw me, there were the tiniest sparks of warmth in his onyx eyes, and it had filled my stomach with dancing butterflies.

For his sake, as well as my own, I did not dare to steal a second glance at him—something that was not easy to do, considering *all* six-foot-five-inches of him.

"You had one job," the empress enunciated, her nostrils flaring. "You were to ensure the traitor was executed."

One of the guards began to plead, her words bucketed from a well of desperation and dumped out before us. "Please, Your Majesty, we beg your forgiveness! There was nothing we could do! The vuleeries just showed up, and they took her—"

"Silence!" the empress roared as she jerked up out of the waters. Glistening droplets slid down her wet, naked torso, dripping back into the bathing pool. The only thing she wore was her favorite gold cuff around her wrist. Her hair was stuck to her skin, clinging on for dear life as she strode toward the stairwell. The railing groaned under her mighty grasp as she grabbed hold of it and stormed up onto the main level.

One masked male strode forward, offering her a towel, but she walked right past him, clipping a fearsome pace toward the guards. Water pooled beneath her feet as she cast the kneeling, armored females in her umbra, her expression filled with disgust. They dropped onto the polished opal floor, laying their hands out, groveling like worms before her.

Slowly, she crouched, one long fingernail reaching underneath the pleading guard's jaw. She tipped her face upwards, forcing her to meet the empress's scrutinizing gaze. "You will go to the Moriel Forest and demand to find out what they've done with my prisoner."

"But Your Majesty, the vuleeries will tear me to shreds

the moment I step foot in the forest," the guard sputtered. "You know this."

"That is none of my concern," she said with malice, stroking her finger upwards and slitting the female's chin open. The guard winced as ichor brimmed. The empress stood and turned to me, her voice resolute. "Arrange a council meeting."

"Yes, Your Majesty," I said, bowing.

"Oh, and Avriel dear, Victor has requested a private audience with us later tonight. Clear your schedule."

I nodded again, stealing one small glance at Shadow, it was no more than a whisper of a look, and although it was brief, I noted that his arms had fallen to his sides. Noted the clench of his fists, the way his skin had turned white over his knuckles, as if the bone beneath might burst through.

And I didn't know why, but that vision burned like an iron, searing itself into my thoughts. It stuck with me as I left the room, as I arranged the council meeting. It stuck with me until the sun dipped its weary head and bowed to dusk. It stuck with me until I found myself in the empress's private dining room.

A long candlelit table stretched on and on, all but three of the surrounding chairs empty. The empress took up her imposing throne-like chair at the very end. Directly across from me was the male who always sent my fingers into a tizzy, itching to grab hold of the rabbit's foot—

Victor.

While the empress remained lost in her private thoughts, her attention cauterized to the innards of her goblet, which she swirled around and around, Victor watched me. His smarmy eyes swam all over my body like a pair of unwanted hands, peeling back the layers of my clothing and exposing my naked flesh.

I hated every second of it, but just as the countless other women who had become the dreaded epitome of his obsession had done before me, I endured.

My mother had been one of those women.

I could still hear her stifled cries as she wept into her pillow when she'd come back to our room late at night, trying not to wake me. Those sounds had only become louder with time, haunting me. They had been like a calling, begging me to take action, begging for retribution. There'd been a time when I had plotted to end Victor's life in order to put my mother's spirit to rest, but I'd realized Victor was only a small part of a much bigger problem, a problem that was allowed to persist because of the empress, because of her biased, unjust laws—which she, herself, broke frequently.

So, like a snake donning the furs of a rabbit, I had set my sights on the real enemy. For years, I had bided my time, waiting for an opportune moment to strike. Then, Sage had appeared, and I couldn't explain it, but I knew she was it. So, earlier today, when I'd heard the guards update on her, that she had been taken from the arena, I realized I'd successfully made my first move against the empress.

Now, I just needed to get through this incredibly uncomfortable meal with two of the people I hated the most.

A plate of food rested before me—smoked salmon,

rice, carrots, and peas. On my fork, I lifted a bite of green and orange to my mouth. Had I been in my private chamber eating this meal, the roasted vegetables would have tasted quite good, but because I was *here*, with *them*, they turned to a ball of ash on my tongue. When I swallowed, it felt like my esophagus had shrunk, the mashed-up vegetables lodging like sludge in my throat. I grabbed my goblet and drank some of the water down.

My mother had always warned me never to drink the empress's *special* wine, which was being served tonight, saying that it had caused the downfall of the emperor, as well as many others, and if I were to let a mere droplet of it pass my lips, it would cause my downfall too.

So, I heeded her words.

"Is something not to your liking?" Victor asked, his voice about as pleasant as a black-snake whip splitting open flesh.

"Oh no, it's all very delicious," I lied sweetly as I set the goblet down and picked up my knife. How badly I itched to bury it into one of them, but I eyed the salmon on my plate and decided it would have to do. Lightly, I pressed down, severing a small piece of pink, flaky meat.

"You eat with such grace," Victor said, leaning back in his chair, his arm stretched across the table, his finger rubbing the neck of his goblet in long, slow strokes. Up and down. Up and down. At least it wasn't his repulsive tongue for a change.

"Thank you," I answered then tried the salmon. It tasted no different than the peas or carrots.

"You are most welcome," he replied.

I made the mistake of looking up at Victor, only to see that his lips had parted, and his tongue had begun to squirm in the corner of his mouth. A leech searching for blood.

Apparently, I had spoken too soon.

My stomach revolted.

"Do you think the general will be successful in finding Sage?" the empress asked, her attention lifting from her goblet and landing on Victor.

He pulled his disgusting tongue back into his mouth. "If there is *anything* left to find, I imagine she will be the one to do it."

"Anything left to find," the empress scoffed. "Might I remind you that the vuleeries were loyal to Nockrythiam in the past. Considering who she is to him, I sincerely doubt that they'd harm a white hair on her head."

"Loyalty has an expiration date. Who knows where their allegiances lie now. For all we know, they showed up early to the event simply because they were hungry," Victor said with a shrug.

The empress cocked her head to the side, eyes narrowing. "Does *your* loyalty have an expiration date?"

A chill swept through the air, as cold as winter's caress.

I went rigid.

Victor let out a raspy chuckle that quickly turned into a bout of coughing. He grabbed his handkerchief and hacked into it, spitting out a gob of luminescent green mucus. Dropping it on the table, he turned to the empress and spoke with vehemence, "Avena, my dear, I am the exception to the rule. I will remain by your side until one of us is six feet beneath the ground."

"Good," she said, her expression softening. "Now, might I ask why you requested this dinner?"

"You may, you may," he said, a stomach-heaving smile spreading across his grotesque lips. "As you know, I have served you for a great number of years. I have devoted my life to your goals and aspirations, and through my hands, I have helped them come to fruition. It has been my greatest honor to serve you, to continue to serve you. But as you see, my work has taken a toll on me, and my vessel is not as it used to be. However, my soul remains young."

"If you are asking for permission to create another vessel, then you have my blessing," the empress said with a wave of her hand. "In fact, I'm surprised you haven't already."

"That is the thing—I do not wish to create a vessel for myself," Victor said.

Unease crept like a spider walking over my skin.

"Then what are you requesting?" the empress asked, her tone growing bored.

His eyes slid to mine. "I would like to have one *made* for me. The old-fashioned way. I would like this beautiful priestess to stitch a new vessel together within her womb. I would provide the seed, of course. Once the child has grown into a man, I will extract the soul and install my own."

My fork clattered against my plate.

"But I have taken an oath," I sputtered, my tongue firing out words faster than I could think. "I cannot lie with another." My eyes jerked to the empress's, pleading with her to end this madness before it had a chance to begin.

But I was a fool, and I should have known that the empress was not my savior.

Her gaze abandoned mine as she looked to Victor. "Because of your years of service, I will allow it."

No! I screamed internally.

Somehow, despite the mass hysteria taking control over me, I was able to spin a bit of logic from my tongue. "But Your Majesty, if the people were to find out, there would be outrage in the streets. *Your* new law comes into effect next month—making it illegal for women to have children, a crime punishable by death. If the people found out that you allowed your priestess, a woman of the cloth and under oath, to be impregnated under your blessing, what would they say? They would question your reign. They would—"

"Enough," the empress snarled, her voice a cold blade, slicing off my words.

I held my tongue, but my thoughts were a tempest, swirling with rage.

"If I may?" Victor cut in.

"Of course," the empress said.

"I have a manor in Burgania, nested in a remote location. There's nothing but trees there. No people. Absolutely nothing other than a few of my most trusted servants. The priestess can live there, away from prying eyes and wagging tongues. After she has delivered the vessel, she can return to the palace, and my servants will raise the child."

"That will work," the empress said, nodding her head.

"Your Majesty." My words were barely audible. "Please, do not make me do this."

Her gaze slid to mine, cold as death, as she said, "It has already been decided."

Tears raced down my cheeks as I ran through the palace halls, unable to rein myself in. My carefully honed mask hadn't just slipped—it had shattered into thousands of pieces, and right now, decades of repressed emotions and my fear of the future were dragging me into its murky depths.

I was being treated as if I were a device. A factory. As if I had no say over my body. I fucking hated it. Hated that I had no say in the matter. Now I knew how males felt—their bodies used and abused and treated as if they were objects void of feeling.

There was one person in this creator-forsaken world I needed to see.

I tossed the door open and stumbled inside the room, scented with the smell of burning coals and melting iron. Shadow stood over his anvil, a long strand of black hair, damp with sweat, tumbling over his forehead. He looked at me and dropped his hammer. His voice was filled with concern as he asked, "Avriel? What's wrong?"

"She's sending me away to be impregnated by Victor and forced to carry his child. All so he can take the body over and use it for himself," I sobbed, my words using up the last of my strength. My legs gave out from under me, but just before I fell, Shadow was there. Strong arms wrapped around me, pulling me into his protective embrace.

His voice was as hard as the blades he forged as he vowed to me, "I won't let them."

Chapter 24

Sage

Over the past couple days, we'd flown with few breaks. Sometimes, I'd feel my body grow weary and I'd fall asleep, dreaming of Von, our child, and the family we should have had. In my waking hours, Artemesia would tell me about the lands we flew over, the history behind them—who lived there before and who lived there now. She'd tell me about the empress's laws and the ways of this realm, portraying it as a matriarchal society where men had no rights.

Talking with Artemesia was easy, simple, and even though we'd been split apart for thousands of years, our sisterhood had picked up right where it had left off.

We had a great deal of things to discuss, and I had dozens of questions I longed to ask her—about how she'd managed to survive all of these years, what she could tell me about my forgotten past . . . if she knew why the empress wanted me dead. And then there were the things that I wanted to tell her—about my life in the Three Realms, about Von . . . about the child we'd lost.

I wanted to tell her about it all.

But I was tired—both mentally and physically.

And I think she sensed that which was why she kept the majority of the conversation light. Something I was grateful for.

Apart from my exhaustion, I was hungry. Starving, to be exact.

The turkey leg and burnt bun Avriel had delivered to my cell was the last semi-decent meal I had. Come to think of it, it was the only meal I'd had since arriving in these lands.

When Artemesia received word from the vuleeries that I was alive, she had left in such a hurry that she had collected only a handful of supplies. Which meant we had very little to eat. Something our protesting tummies made well known.

We reached what Artemesia called the Forgotten Mountains, a place she explained didn't exist on any public map, because the mountains seemed to pick and choose who they showed themselves to—who they allowed to live within them. Artemesia said not even the empress knew of their existence, and that when outsiders came here, they would only see flat land. When I asked her how that was possible, Artemesia told me she didn't know, but it was like there was some exterior force protecting them, that perhaps the mountains were sentient beings, much like the Hollow Tree.

The setting sun illuminated the wintery snowscape, causing it to glitter as if it were crafted from millions of tiny diamonds. Although the temperature was not nearly as cold as it could get back in Meristone, it still was cold enough that my teeth began to chatter.

"There's a saddlebag behind you, on your right. You'll find a cloak and a spare pair of boots in it," Artemesia spoke over her shoulder as she steered Vatara forward. "They should fit you."

Shifting, I looked behind me, located the saddlebag, and began to search through it. Soft fur brushed against my fingers. Grabbing onto it, I pulled the cloak from the leather bag and put it on. My body shuddered in response, thankful for its warmth. Next, I located the boots. They were brown in color, crafted from animal hide and trimmed with rabbit fur. I tucked them under my arm and closed the flap. Trying my best not to go ass over teakettle and fall off Vatara, I took my time slipping the boots on.

Artemesia was right—they fit perfectly.

Not long after, Vatara landed smoothly, the snow crunching under her heavy weight.

Artemesia and I dismounted.

Gently, Vatara nudged Artemesia with her beak, making a small, pleading squawk. Reaching up, Artemesia stroked her forehead, her gaze fixed forward as she said, "We made it."

Nestled between the steep slopes of the mountains was a valley, bisected by a turbulent river partially covered in ice. On both banks was an encampment. The round, small tents were crafted from a white fabric, making them almost disappear in the snow. Despite the simple nature of the structures, there was something magical about what I was seeing. A whisper of the past breathed itself into me—

There was something familiar about the tents.

Had I stayed in something similar in my past life?

A voice within me answered, *Yes*.

"Come on, it's been a long flight, and I can tell we have much to discuss," Artemesia spoke softly as she began to walk ahead, Vatara at her side.

I followed after her.

When we reached the edge of the camp, a young girl who was rolling a ball of snow jerked her head up, looking at us. Her face lit with joy as she offered us a big toothy grin. Scrambling to her feet, she raced to the tent closest to her and yelled, "Chieftain Artemesia is back!"

A man and a woman came racing out, their expressions shifting from concern to relief when they saw my sister. The woman took the little girl's hand while the man went to another tent. Quickly, people began to spill out from it. Two boys who came from that tent dashed to another. More smiling faces emerged from the one they ran to. This process was repeated until nearly everyone stood in front of their tents.

A man with chestnut hair and a sturdy build walked up to us and embraced Artemesia. "I am so happy you are back, chieftain."

"I am too," she replied, returning the hug before she took a step back. "This is my sister, Sage. Sage, this is

Novack."

Novack bowed his head. "It is an honor. I have heard a great deal about you."

"All bad things, of course, like when you lost my favorite hunting bow," Artemesia jabbed. She let out a dramatic sigh. "I still think about that bow to this day."

A memory flashed before my eyes—of me and Artemesia in our shared chambers, in our family's summer home.

"I didn't take it," I said as I stoked the coals in the fireplace.

"I don't believe you," she stated.

"I'm telling you, I didn't take it," I sighed, putting the wrought-iron fireplace poker in the cradle that held the rest of its kin.

"Did it just sprout legs and walk out on its own?" Her voice was sarcastic.

"I mean, it could have. It was enchanted, after all." I shrugged.

She crouched beside me, the flames casting an orange glow across her face. "It went missing the same day you did. Just . . . tell me what happened. I don't even care about the bow."

"Sage?" Artemesia asked, her voice threaded with concern.

"Sorry, I think I'm getting some of my memories back," I replied, letting out a breath of air that made a small cloud.

"We have much to talk about," she said with a soft

smile. Turning to Novack, she asked, "Can you let Millie know we've returned and have her prepare some food for us?"

"Of course," he answered, leaning in to give her a kiss.

She didn't move to meet him. Instead, she pressed her finger against his nose, smooshing it, and effectively stopping him from advancing any further.

For a brief second, he went cross-eyed, peering down at her finger. Redness tinged his cheeks. Retreating, he rubbed the back of his neck sheepishly. "I'll go see about that food." He quickly scurried away.

When he was out of earshot, I whispered to my sister, "That was awkward."

In agreement, Vatara let out a screech.

"It was," Artemesia said, petting her. She lowered her voice. "I slept with him once and now he thinks we're an item. I'm going to have to have a talk with him."

Vatara and I nodded.

For the next half an hour or so, Artemesia introduced me to the clan. They all seemed so relieved to have her back home. I could tell they thought a great deal about her. Somewhere throughout the many introductions, Vatara got bored, unfurled her wings, and flew off into the trees. During our journey here, Artemesia had shared with me that Vatara hated being in human form—it felt suffocating to her—so ninety-nine percent of the time, her gryphon form was what she donned.

As night fell, Artemesia walked me over to a pair of tents and pointed at one. "That one is mine." Her finger moved to the other. "And this one is yours."

On the outside, the tent appeared to be no bigger than a carriage, but when we stepped inside, it was huge. A light tinge of magic hung in the air, which explained the tent's shift in size, as well as the radiating heat. A few cabinets sat beside a table surrounded by four wooden chairs, an armoire, and a couple sizable chests. A large bed covered in fur pelts, its frame made from stripped logs, sat off to the left, flanked by end tables.

"These should have some clothes in them," she said, walking over to the armoire. She pulled the doors open, showing me the garments inside—cotton tunics, a few pairs of trousers, a jacket, and a white cloak trimmed with reddish-brown fur. "Nothing too fancy."

"They are perfect," I stated, moving beside her. I ran my fingers over the various fabrics, thankful that there wasn't one stuffy dress to be found. Reaching the jacket, my hand stilled, recoiled, then reached out. A lump formed in my throat as I ran my fingers down the sleeve of the leather coat, dyed midnight black. It made me think of Von. A physical ache pierced my chest, stabbing me right in the heart.

Gently, Artemesia clasped my shoulder. "What is it?"

I gave her a sad smile. "It reminds me of someone I love."

She returned the look. "I understand." Her brow furrowed. "Do you want me to get a different jacket for you?"

"No, I like this one. I'll wear it . . . for him." The

thought lessened the pain in my chest.

"Alright." She patted my shoulder comfortingly.

"Excuse me, chieftain, but I have some warm food to fill your bellies," spoke a woman on the other side of the entrance.

"Coming!" Artemesia called out, walking over. She pushed the tent flaps open, holding them so the woman could enter.

"Thank you," the woman said as she stepped inside, a covered wood tray in her hands. She headed over to the table and set the tray down. "Can I get you anything else?" she asked, turning to face us.

"No, that will be all. Thank you, Merita," Artemesia responded, offering her a kind smile.

"A pleasure, as always," Merita replied as she bowed her head and then left, a waft of cool air rushing into the tent with her departure.

I moved to the small, round table, resting my hands on the chair as I watched Artemesia remove the lid. On the tray were two plates full of steaming food—a dark, sliced meat, mashed potatoes smothered in gravy, and various boiled vegetables diced and mixed together. My mouth watered, my stomach churning with hunger.

"Have a seat. I'll get us something to drink," Artemesia said as she turned toward the cabinets. Sitting on top of the one were three jugs and a few drinking horns. "Wine okay?"

"Wine is great," I answered, sitting down.

"Perfect." She reached for the middle jug and filled the two horns. When she was done, she brought the horns over to the table and handed one to me. "I'm famished. Let's eat."

Our conversation was light as we filled our tummies with delicious, warm food—grilled trout, boiled potatoes, and warm, golden buns—and refreshing red wine. When our plates were empty, we both reached forward and pressed a thumb against the plate, securing a crumb. Like that, our attention caught on one another's, and we both started to laugh.

"I see the empress never did make a lady out of you," she chuckled before she popped her thumb into her mouth.

My smile faltered at the mention of the empress.

"I'm sorry. I shouldn't have brought her up," Artemesia apologized.

I wiped my fingers on the cloth napkin. Now that I had food in my belly, I felt ready to talk about the harder topics. "Actually, I'm glad you did. I'd like to learn more about my past, including the parts about her."

She picked up her plate and placed it on the tray. As she did this, she said, "I can tell you what I do know. Maybe it will help fill in some of the gaps?"

"Yeah, that would be great." I nodded. "Talking about it might help some of my memories return."

"Let's give it a shot then." She pursed her lips in thought, then said, "You and I were born to Luna and Herulf." Warmth spread through my chest at the mention of their names. "Before the Great Divide."

I raised a brow. "The Great Divide?"

"Oof, you don't remember much, do you?" she asked.

"No," I answered.

"Do you recall anything about Emperor Alaric?"

I gave her a blank look.

She blinked. "It's going to be a long night." Sighing, she got up, collected the wine jug, and brought it back to the table. Deep red liquid refreshed our drinking horns, misting the air with the scent of fermented grapes. She peered inside the jug, swishing the contents from side to side as she muttered to herself, "We might need more of this."

"Perhaps we should start with what we have," I suggested, eager to hear more.

"Very well." She sat down, looked at me, and then she started, "In the beginning, all realms were connected together and ruled over by Emperor Alaric, also known as the Creator. On his great anvil, he forged life, from mortals to immortals to the plants and everything else in existence. It was he who discovered that when he took a star from the sky and broke it in half, it created two souls, eternally bonded."

My heart ached. I couldn't help but think of Von and how much I missed him.

"For a long time, he ruled these lands alone, but one day, his gaze slipped from his anvil, and he found a pretty goddess with lilac eyes, a witty mind, and a sharp tongue—Avena, the Goddess of Women and protector of femalekind. It wasn't long before he fell for her and made her his empress. At first, she had noble intentions; she saw the horrors happening to females—the lack of equality, the raping, the senseless murders. So, she took her concerns to the emperor. Together, they enacted new rules, protecting all females. The empress merely spoke her wishes, and the emperor would make it so. Eventually, nearly half of the realm began to praise Empress Avena's name, thankful for all that she had done for our gender. Some would even visit her temple and hand over their power, their magic, in her honor.

"For a while, the emperor and empress were happy, so much so that he plucked a thread of his being and gifted it to her, allowing her the ability to create as well. But as the centuries passed, the mass amount of power she was given began to twist her mind and corrode the goodness within her." Artemesia paused for a moment, picked up her horn, and drank. Then, "One day, a rift opened between the emperor and the empress. People speculated a great deal of things, but the rumor that became the most prevalent was that he had been unfaithful to her, although that was never confirmed. Something in her snapped, and unbeknownst to the rest of the realm, she began to plot and scheme. That's when she showed up on our manor's doorstep, looking for you."

I glanced down at my cup, peering at the dark red liquid inside. Something about the color, about all of this, shook a memory free.

Chapter 25

Sage

I stood with my ear pressed against the red oak door of my family's summer home, my fingers gently resting against it. Hushed footsteps sounded behind me, followed by a cupped hand placed softly to my cheek and the tickle of warm breath on my ear.

"What are they saying?" Artemesia whispered before she pulled back.

I gave her a stern look and pressed my finger over my mouth.

She stuck her tongue out at me and then tiptoed closer to the door, placing her ear against it, listening in.

My father's voice was diplomatic as he said, "I do not mean any disrespect, Your Majesty, but Sagentia is the future chieftain of my people. If anything were to happen to her . . ."

"Herulf and I would not be able to live with ourselves,"

my mother finished for him.

The conversation stalled, and the room filled with silence.

Then, Empress Avena asked, "What is your price? Surely, Mrs. Belmont, you must have one."

"I beg your pardon?" Mother spoke with disdain.

"Luna," Father cut in. I didn't need to be on the other side of the door to know that he had probably placed his hand over hers, trying to calm her.

"It is fine," Empress Avena said with a light chuckle. "To put matters plainly, change is upon us, but for it to happen, I will need your daughter by my side, and so, you see, I will not take no for an answer. So what is it you want? You mortals always hunger for something. Riches beyond compare? Health for everyone in your clan? Just say what you want and I—"

"Our daughter is not for sale," Mother growled.

"Luna," Father warned.

There came a pregnant pause, and then, Her Majesty said, "Do you ever get tired of the way he reprimands you?"

"What?" Mother asked, the word a hiss upon her breath.

"The way he covers your hand as if he can control you. The way he says your name in a bid to silence your tongue. I have devoted centuries to making the genders equal, and still, despite my best efforts, we are not there yet. Your husband is evidence of that." She huffed a mocking laugh. "The only way us females will ever be able to live in peace is if the male gender were to cease to exist."

Artemesia and I shot each other strange looks, both of us wondering what we had just heard. I could only imagine the look on Father's face; I doubted he'd be able to mask his expression.

"Prior, you spoke of the future of your clan. As chieftain, your people must be of great importance to you. That is something I can understand," Empress Avena started. "As I said before, change is coming, and it is coming in the shape of a great war. If you agree to send your daughter with me, in exchange, I will sign an agreement that will protect you and your people from the war. Your clan will be left untouched, unharmed by my forces."

"And if we do not agree?" Mother asked.

"It's quite simple, really. Your daughter is a vital part of my plan. If you don't agree, I will take her regardless and leave your clan to suffer the consequences. So you see, the choice is yours."

Unease filled my stomach.

This was my home, and becoming chieftain was my future. I had never aspired to leave these lands, but now, that all could change. Please tell her no, *I silently beseeched my parents.*

But instead, Mother said, "Will you ensure that same security will pass over to our daughter?"

"If she does what I ask of her, then she will be safe."

My breath stilled in my chest and my hand fell from the door, seeking the comfort of my sister's, which was already searching for mine. Our hands clasped tightly together.

"But our daughter is headstrong," Mother said, her

voice almost pleading. "She beats to her own drum and is not one to do as she is told. I cannot assure you that she will do as you ask of her."

"You have another daughter, yes?" Empress Avena asked.

"Yes . . ." Father begrudgingly said. It was impossible not to notice the turmoil in his tone, as if it was an answer he didn't want to give.

"Does Sagentia love her sister?" she questioned further.

"More than anything," Mother answered.

"Good." The direction of her voice changed as she projected it toward us. "Girls, you may come in."

My sister and I exchanged confused looks before we did as we were told. The rusty hinges squeaked in annoyance as I pressed the door open. Somewhat hesitantly, we stepped into the small receiving room. In the middle sat a table surrounded by chairs. On the far side was an unlit fireplace—a painting of our family, set in a golden frame, hung over top of it.

We bowed, keeping our heads like that until the empress said, "You may rise."

When we did, I took her in. I had seen her likeness before, painted on murals and stitched into tapestries, but in person, she was exquisite. The very definition of beauty and grace.

Her gaze swept over my sister from top to bottom before it shifted to me. "Your parents tell me you love your sister more than anything. Is that indeed true?"

I swallowed, then answered, my voice shaky, "It is."

"Aw, that is a beautiful thing. Sisterly love, how wonderful," she exclaimed with a sunny smile, one that slowly faded. A foreboding darkness began to taint the air. She let out a heavy exhale and shook her head, offering me a look of sympathy. "It is such a shame that she will not make it to her twentieth birthday."

"No!" my mother wailed, leaning forward in her chair as tears filled her blue eyes, twin to my own. Swiftly, my father went to her side, and he took her in his arms.

My blood turned to ice. "What do you mean?"

"There are two deadly events that stand in her way. If the first one doesn't kill her, the second will. One of those events just happens to be"—her eyes flashed with malice—"today."

My sister started to choke, as if she had a piece of meat lodged in her throat.

I turned to her, my voice panicked. "Artemesia, what is it?"

Father and Mother scrambled over to us, their expressions as terrified as my own.

"What are you doing to her?" Mother yelled at the empress, as she held my sister.

Artemesia clawed at her throat, her fingernails cutting into her skin. Father grabbed Artemesia's hands, holding them to stop her from hurting herself.

"Stop it." I turned to the empress, pleading. "Make it stop. I'll do anything you ask of me."

"I was hoping you'd say that," Empress Avena said,

light shifting across her eyes once more.

Wheezing, Artemesia fell to her knees, gulping down mouthfuls of air as my mother tried to comfort her. Father looked at the empress, his eyes full of fiery rage.

"I will give you a moment to pack your things, while your parents and I sign this contract," Empress Avena said as she waved her hand and produced a stack of papers on the table, accompanied by a quill and inkpot.

"Wait," I whispered under my breath. I met the empress's gaze. "Before we go, I have one more request."

"Pray tell, child, what is it?" she indulged me.

"You said my sister will die before her twentieth birthday." The words tasted bitter on my tongue. "Is that true?"

"It is," she conceded, and my mother began to sob again.

I clenched my fists. "Then you will make her an immortal so she can live."

She scoffed. "I am one of the most powerful goddesses, but I cannot just grant immortality."

"I'm sure you know a workaround or two," I stated.

She studied me for a moment, debating her answer. "You've got fire. I'll give you that." She rolled her wrist and bolts of electric light began to spark from her palm, forming a giant cerulean egg. She swished her hand, and the egg floated to my sister, who was kneeling on the floor, still trying to catch her breath.

"What is it?" I asked.

The empress answered, "It is an immortal creature

called a gryphon. When it hatches, your sister will be able to bind her lifespan to the creature's, thus granting her immortality. Only when the gryphon dies will your sister die, but considering some are even older than me, I imagine she will now live a very, very long life."

Chapter 26

Sage

"You remembered something, didn't you?" Artemesia asked, her hand reaching across the table, falling on top of my wrist. Her touch was warm, comforting. Instinctually, my hand fell over hers. How incredible it was that her existence had been exempt from my memories, but the moment she stepped back into my life, that same love I'd held for her in the past had returned immediately, untarnished and unwavering.

Slowly, I nodded. "I did. It was of when the empress came to our family home."

"That was a very dark day," she stated, her solemn expression emphasizing the weight behind her words.

"Please, don't take her!" Artemesia's young voice called out as she tried to keep up with the carriage, her hand reaching for mine.

"Artemesia!" I cried out, wedging myself through the window, my fingers reaching for hers. We were so close.

But the coachman cracked his whip, and the carriage picked up speed.

"Sage!" she cried, tears racing down her rosy cheeks as she tried to keep up.

"Artemesia!" I bellowed her name as my heart was cleaved apart.

Pulling back from the memory, I looked to my sister, and with a lump forming in my throat, I asked, "What happened after that?"

"You went with her," she said somberly, her gaze falling to the table, "and I never saw you again."

For a time, we sat there, silently grieving the past. The sadness that we felt for being pried from one another's lives. And although neither of us shed a single tear, because we had given enough, someone else cried for us—

The wind. Outside, it began to pick up, and now it howled *for* us.

For the loss of two close sisters who had been torn apart.

I gave her hand a gentle squeeze. "I am glad that we have found each other once more."

"As am I, dear sister," she said.

We remained like that for a while.

I think she knew that I needed the quiet, so I could come to terms with everything I had just learned. In my last lifetime, I had been forged from the womb of the moon and given a goddess's title, but in the lifetime I had just recalled, I had been a mortal. I'd had parents—a mother and a father. I looked across the table—a sister.

Merging from the depths of my thoughts, I asked, "What

happened to them? Our parents?"

"They lived, and eventually, they passed from old age, their deaths occurring three days apart," she answered. "I buried them at our family's summer home, although there wasn't much left of it. Mother always loved it there so much." She smiled warmly. "She always said she loved—"

"The long summer nights where the moon was close enough to touch," I said along with her, my mother's favorite words returning to me.

"Yeah." Artemesia smiled, and we both chuckled.

After, I asked, "Before, you mentioned something called the Great Divide. What was that?"

"Right, okay, I'll get to that. First, I need to finish what I was telling you before," she said, shifting back in her chair. "After you left, the realm fell quiet for a few years, to the point we wondered if the empress had called off whatever she had been planning. Then, one day, word reached us that the creators were at war. Father desperately wanted to travel to Avolonia to see if he could find you, but Mother didn't seem to think that was a good idea. I remember being so mad at her. We argued and fought, until she took me to the kitchen and told me that the safest place for you to be was with the emperor. I knew Mother was religious and she strongly believed in him, but I couldn't understand why she thought you would be with the emperor when it was the empress who had taken you. Mother refused to tell me any more and told me not to speak a word of what she had said to Father." Artemesia paused. She gave a gentle shake of her head and an apologetic smile. "Sorry, I got a little off track there. Anyway, the empress ended up beating the emperor in the final battle. With his dying breath, he drove his mighty sword into the land and fractured it apart, thus ending the old realm and creating hundreds of others. Then, with a mighty roar, he used the last remnants of his powers to cast the realms out into the universe thus creating the Great Divide."

My eyebrows furrowed. "Why did he do that?" I asked. "Why break the old realm apart and create hundreds of others?"

"He discovered what the empress had planned, that she was going to strip all rights from males and force them into a life of slavery. He didn't want that for his creations, and so, in a last attempt to protect what he had made, he broke the realm apart and sent them away so they could be free of her."

I sat with that for a bit, my gaze flicking back and forth on some random spot on the table. There was still so much I didn't understand, and in truth, knowing that the realms had been cast far into the universe made me feel . . . lonely.

Because it meant Von was way out *there*, and I was here.

I reminded myself of his promise, held tight to it.

Looking up at Artemesia, I asked, "Do you know if there is any way to travel between the realms?"

"The empress can send souls to different realms, but there is no way to travel between them."

"Ah," I said, dragging my hand over my face.

"You look tired," she noted.

"I am," I answered honestly.

"Perhaps we should pause this conversation for now. I'm sure this is a lot to process," she said, standing up from her chair.

Following her lead, I stood too, and stretched out my neck.

"Do you need anything else for the night?" she asked.

I glanced around the tent. It was a far cry from the cell I had been locked inside. "I think I'll be fine."

She wrapped her arms around me. "Alright. If you do need anything, you know where to find me."

"Thank you, Artemesia. For everything." I hugged her back.

She responded warmly, "What are sisters for?"

After she left, I peeled the clothes from my body and crawled under the soft sheets. I knew I was filthy and I should probably wash the grime from my skin, but I was too tired.

The doors to the armoire were still open. The black leather jacket very much *there*.

"I miss you," I whispered to the darkness, longing to hear his voice.

But all that replied was lonely silence. And it was deafening.

A tear slipped down my cheek, landing on the pillowcase. *Plip*. Then another. And another. Until I was shaking and sobbing. Until I cried myself to sleep. But, as I would soon find out, nothing but horror awaited me there.

Chapter 27

Sage

"Come along, girl, and be quick about it," the empress called out after me as she thundered down the long corridor—one of hundreds inside her and her husband's illustrious castle, forged from opal stone. My head whipped this way and that as I took it all in, my eyes bathed in splendor and riches, unlike anything I had ever seen before. The guards followed us as we began to walk down a set of winding stairs, leading into the bowels of the castle. When we reached the bottom, we walked a bit further, until we came up to a door, clad with strips of heavy iron. The guard opened it, and the empress gestured for me to go inside. *"Go on."*

Hesitantly, I stepped into the room.

The hairs on the back of my neck stood.

The windows were covered with a thick, dark cloth, blocking out any natural light. In its place, wrought-iron *candelabras burned with an eerie blue flame. The room smelled of copper and honey, and . . . a sinister, tainted magic. In the middle was a horizontal slab of stone, large enough I could lay on it.*

Lead filled my belly. I took a step back, colliding into something hard.

The empress's hands landed softly on my shoulders. "All is well, my child. You have nothing to fear."

Said the spider to the fly, *my inner voice commented.*

Swiftly, I stepped forward, eager to get away from her.

Along the far wall, there were dozens of cages, filled with various animals and creatures. The sound of a rodent running on a wheel caught my attention. I walked over to it, feeling the empress's eyes on me. Bending forward, I looked into the cage, finding no animal inside, and yet, the wheel moved. Suddenly, it stopped. A breath later, the food inside its bowl began to shift and move.

"What is it?" I asked, marveling at the small, invisible wonder.

"I haven't decided on a name for it yet," said a clear, languid voice.

I turned to face the doorway. In it, stood an attractive male, dressed in a black, heavy leather jacket fastened with thick straps and shining metal buckles. His short, brown hair was impeccably styled, neat and trim, as was the rest of him.

He smiled, showing off his perfectly straight teeth. "Perhaps you have a suggestion?"

I glanced back at the cage before my gaze returned to

his and I shook my head. "I do not."

"Well, if you think of something, you'll have to let me know," he replied before he turned to Empress Avena and bowed his head. "Your Majesty."

"Victor," she said by way of greeting. She waved her hand, and a heavy tome—wrapped in brown leather— appeared, floating in front of her. Glowing symbols were written in its flesh—a language I did not recognize. She swished her fingers, and it moved toward him.

Victor took it. Slowly, his fingers drifted over the cover as he whispered to himself, "This is the emperor's." He shook his head in disbelief. He opened it and began thumbing through the pages. "It's all the notes on how he built his anvil and his hammer. How did you get it?"

"The how *is not important. What is, is that you copy his notes swiftly so I can return it before he notices it's missing. He is away right now but will return in a few weeks' time. You have until then."*

"I can do that," Victor agreed. "I'm guessing you want me to create something based off of these as well?"

"Indeed, but make it something more . . . feminine. Something I can wear, like a necklace."

Victor hummed in thought. "A necklace wouldn't work; it needs to be closer to your hand, just as his hammer is to his. A ring or a bracelet, perhaps?"

"Whichever one you think. Just don't make it gaudy."

"Alright," Victor replied, the book disappearing before my very eyes.

Her piercing gaze shifted to me. "You will not speak a

word of this to anyone, am I understood?"

I nodded. "Yes, Your Majesty."

"Good. Now—" She flicked her hand at me. "Remove your clothes."

"I beg your pardon?" I implored, crossing my arms over my chest. Victor began to undo the buckles on his jacket. My eyes stretched wide as I realized where this was going. Panic saturated my veins. "Your Majesty, please, do not ask this of me. I have never lain with a man before."

"You think I'm such a monster? I would never ask such a thing of you, nor any female for that matter. That is what men do. They rape and they use, and they try to take control over our bodies, but there will come a day when the reverse is true, when it us taking control over theirs. Mark my words, us women will be the owners of this world, and men will have nothing. I've heard the prayers of my people, and I will answer them." Her expression softened. "I know none of this makes sense to you right now, but someday you will understand this all was necessary so we could create a better world for our gender."

Victor had fallen silent. If he had any qualms about the empress's plans to remove his rights, he didn't seem to care.

"I'm failing to see how removing my clothes has anything to do with creating a better world," I retorted, keeping an eye on Victor as he hung his jacket on a hook that was secured to the wall. He reached for the leather apron beside it and put it on. It reminded me of the ones the blacksmiths wore back home. Reaching behind his back, he pulled the straps and tied them.

The empress moved toward me, stopping an arm's reach away. "The reason I have asked you to come is because I need you to get closer to someone who is known as Nockrythiam. I need you to earn his trust and learn what his weakness is."

I had heard a great deal about the rumored Ender of Realms—Nockrythiam. I knew he was not someone I should ever try to cross. Yet, the empress was asking me to do exactly that.

There were only two reasons why someone wanted to know someone else's weaknesses—to use the information as blackmail, or use it to destroy them. Something in my stomach told me it was the latter. Still, I asked, "Why do you want to know what his weakness is?"

"Nockrythiam is loyal to my husband. When he learns of my plans for the future, he will stand against me and do everything he can to protect the emperor. I am extremely powerful, yes, but I am not naïve enough to think I would be guaranteed victory in a battle against Nockrythiam. And so, I need to ensure the odds are tipped in my favor."

She was going to kill him . . . with the information I fed to her. Despite the horrible stories I had heard about Nockrythiam, my stomach churned with unease. A grimy feeling settled over my skin.

"Why me? I'm a nobody, a mere mortal. Surely, there are thousands of better candidates for this task."

"Indeed, there are, however, you possess something no one else does," she said.

My eyebrows shifted together. "Which is?"

Victor started, "You are Nockrythiam's—"

The empress held up her hand, silencing him immediately. "That is of little importance. The fact of the matter is you are the only one who can do this. Now, about those clothes."

I was Nockrythiam's what? It was a question I had no answer to.

"Sage," the empress grated.

Still hesitant, I kept my arms crossed. "I want you to tell me what's going to happen first."

She pinned me with her glare. "Stubborn girl. Have you forgotten the deal you made with me? Your compliance ensures your sister's safety."

"And I will comply, but I want to know what I'm getting myself into," I stated, tilting my chin upwards. To her, I might look like some feeble mortal, but I was the daughter of a great chieftain.

"Very well," she answered, her heels clicking as she began to walk around me, circling like a vulture looking over a carcass, wondering which part it should snap off first. "Nockrythiam is among my husband's best work; he is a handsome immortal, and you are a plain mortal. If you are going to catch his stubborn eye, we're going to need to modify your vessel and make you appear immortal." She stopped in front of me, her lilac orbs meeting mine. "Satisfied?"

"I suppose," I said, my voice distant as I struggled to come to terms with what was about to happen to me.

"My patience is becoming very thin," the empress

warned, her voice snapping me from my private thoughts.

With trembling fingers, I began to remove my clothes. First, my tunic, which I slid over my head. I dropped it on the floor and then began to kick off my shoes and remove my trousers. Lastly, my underwear.

I felt the empress's gaze, as well as Victor's, rove across my skin, leaving a smear of invisible dirt in their wake—one that made me want to plunge into a bath and scrub it from my flesh.

"The body isn't half bad, although those scars will have to go," the empress said as she began to walk around me once more.

Victor stood in front of me, his hand scrubbing his chin as he debated something. "She's a bit short, is she not?"

"She is." The empress grew quiet, pondering something for a moment. "If you were to stretch out her bones, how long would it take?"

Stretch my bones? That sounded horrible, something I did not want any part of.

"It can be done, although it is no easy task. There are so many bones in the body. I imagine it would take me three to four weeks at least."

"We do not have enough time for that. The height will have to remain." She let out a frustrated breath. "One thing you must do is dispose of her red blood and replace it with ichor. If Nockrythiam sees, he'll know immediately she is mortal."

"Very well," he said, his gaze drifting to my chest. His eyes burned hot, searing into my flesh. "And what of the

breasts?"

I banded my arm over my chest, hating every second of this.

"I'm not worried about them," she replied. Gently, she clasped my chin, tilting my head from side to side. "The face is agreeable. Smile," she directed me. Unwillingly, I did. "The teeth are horribly crooked. Those will need to be straightened. Lengthen the canines so they look like the rest of ours."

"Thoughts on making them retractable?" Victor asked.

She raised a brow. "For what purpose?"

"For convenience and to appease my inventive mind. If the retractable fangs work well, we could try it out on the new god species."

"Will it take any longer?" the empress asked.

"It shouldn't."

"Then go ahead."

"Very well, Your Majesty. Is there anything else?"

"No," she replied before she turned to me. "I will return for you in two weeks' time."

When the empress left, Victor gestured to the stone slab. "Shall we begin?"

Chapter 28

Sage

Someone was screaming.

The sound was so chilling it was like winter had plunged her hands beneath my skin and frozen my muscles stiff. Yet somehow, I was slick with sweat. The strange combination of cold and hot made me feel sickly.

I jerked upright. My mouth snapped shut, and the terrible sound stopped.

My hand flew to my lips, covering them—

I was the source of that *horrible* sound.

That desperate scream for the pain to stop, for the cutting and the slicing to end, but my words were never heard. Through all of it, Victor had used his dark alchemy to keep me conscious. He said having someone to talk to helped pass the time, even though the only sounds that came out of me were desperate pleas and endless sobbing. In the beginning, at the end of the day, when he was done working on me, he would leave me on the cold slab, blow out the candles, and leave me in the dark with his imprisoned, howling animals. All of that changed the day I tried to stab him with one of his torturous tools. After that, he would shove me into the cages, locking me in for the night.

By the time he was finished, a part of me had died inside.

Despite his *drastic* change in appearance over the years, I had no doubt the Victor from my past was the *same* Victor who worked alongside the empress now. If there was one thing I knew it was that he was a ruthless monster. There was not an ounce of humanity to be found within him.

"Sage?" a frantic Artemesia asked as she rushed in through the tent's flaps, her expression full of concern. "I was down the river, but when word reached me that there were screams coming from your tent, I dropped what I was doing and raced back here. What has happened?"

"Just . . . the past catching up with me," I replied, weaving my fingers into my hair, pushing it back from my forehead.

"Do you want to talk about it?" She sat on the side of the bed.

"I'd rather not." I forced a deep exhale and slipped my hand through the rest of my hair. "I'm sorry to have frightened you."

"I'm just happy you are alright." She gave a soft smile.

Eager to leave the nightmare behind and think about something else, I changed the topic. "What were you doing down the river?"

"Fishing."

"Did you catch anything?"

She shook her head. "Nothing worth keeping. I swear, the fish get smaller every year."

A memory returned to me, of us as young girls, fishing with our father. She'd said that same thing back then, too. "You've been claiming that since we were little," I teased.

"To which Father would always say—" She propped her fists against her hips, broadening her shoulders, and tipped her chin up ever so slightly, trying to channel our father. "That's because you are getting bigger," she said, imitating his voice.

I chuckled. "That's right. I remember him saying that."

She grinned. "Are you hungry?" She thumbed over her shoulder. "We can go get something to eat—it's a bit past noon, but that won't matter. Millie always has something yummy cooking."

"I didn't realize it was so late in the day," I said, peeling the covers off my legs so I could change my clothes. "But yes, food sounds good to me."

My stomach rumbled in agreement.

Shortly after, Artemesia and I were standing inside of a tent that smelled absolutely divine. Baking bread, roasting meat, various herbs and spices—instantly, my mouth began to water. Placed in three neat rows were long stretches of wooden tables, flanked by benches made from split logs. To my right, in the corner, was a large hearth crafted from stone.

Flames licked at the bottom of a bubbling, steaming pot. To the side, a giant, mouthwatering slab of seasoned meat was being spit-roasted—a middle-aged man working the crank.

A woman with rosy cheeks and bright-blue eyes walked over to us. "Good day, chieftain." She looked at me, her smile growing even bigger. "And you must be Sage."

"I am," I returned with a smile. "You must be Millie?"

"Indeed, indeed," she spoke with a great amount of glee. "Come, have a seat." She gestured to one of the benches. "You must be hungry."

"Knowing my sister, I can almost guarantee that," Artemesia replied with a chuckle.

Following Millie's instructions, we sat down.

"I'll be back in a moment," she said warmly before she hurried back to the bubbling pot.

"She's so sweet," I whisper-spoke to Artemesia, who sat across the table from me.

"She really is," she agreed. "One of the kindest souls I've ever met."

We chatted for a short while, before Millie returned with two steaming bowls, which she set in front of us. "Some nice deer stew for you two. Fresh from the pot."

We gave our thanks and then we dug in, reminiscing as we ate. Somewhere between my sister's laughter and the good, hearty food, I could feel the icy grasp of the chilling memory I'd recovered beginning to melt away.

After we finished eating, the plates were cleared, and we had profusely thanked Millie, Artemesia slung her arm over the back of her chair and looked at me. "Sooo," she started, dragging out the word. "Do you want to tell me what you've been up to all of these centuries?"

"That's a loaded question," I answered honestly.

She smiled. "We have nothing but time."

"I suppose you're right."

Then, I told her all of it. Every little detail. Sometimes in order, sometimes not. I cried at some parts, laughed at others, but throughout it all, I longed for Von. He was stitched into every inch of my story. His name was carved upon my soul, in my bones. He was my other half, and I was incomplete without him.

When I got to the part about the child we lost, Artemesia reached across the table and squeezed my hand. With misty eyes, she said, "I do not know what it is like to lose a child, but I do know a little about loss. I know that when we love someone, we cut a piece of our heart out and give it to them. So, when they die, in some ways, we do too. But the thing is, we carry a piece of them with us, and so, in their honor, we must do the impossible without them—we must live."

Pressure built between my eyebrows, and my eyes blurred with tears. They brimmed on my lower lash line, then spilled over, trickling down my cheeks. My voice crackled with emotion as I choked out, "That is beautiful." Finding it hard to speak, I pressed my lips together, trying not to give in to the weight of sadness I felt welling within me. My gaze fell, and I shook my head. "I just wish I would have gotten the chance to know them."

Softly, she squeezed my hand. "Who knows what comes after this realm. Maybe someday, you will."

Chapter 29

Von

An icy grip clutched at my limbs, dragging me under, but it was the heat boiling beneath my skin that shoved me to consciousness. With the speed of an arrow released from a bow, my eyes flashed open. I was in dark waters, among hundreds of glowing souls, their unconscious spectral forms tossed around by the tumultuous currents. When the current dipped low, one was shoved into me, her body drifting through mine, passing to the other side.

As I had zero desire to stay down here, I called upon my shadows to shadow walk me out of here. My umbra answered, sweeping around me, and then—

Nothing.

Nothing happened. My body didn't move an inch. That was odd.

I supposed I'd have to do it the mortal way—I began to look for the surface.

There. The slightest bit of light gnawed at the shifting surface. Biceps firing, I started to swim toward it, heeding little mind to the phantoms as they passed through me. The waters fought against me, trying to pull me back down, but my will was unyielding.

When I reached the surface, I swam toward the jagged edge of the shoreline—viciously carved by the iron bite of the river. Placing my hands on the rocky ground, I heaved myself out of the waters. Kneeling there, naked as the day I had emerged from the soil, I took in my surroundings as the water dripped from my body. The innards of a mountain stretched over top of me, tunneling around the river. The light source that had guided me to the surface was from brilliant, glowing stalactites that lined the cave's ceiling.

As I gazed up at them, I couldn't help but think of Sage. Had she seen them too? Had she been *here*?

Now that I was in the same realm as she was, I wondered—

Sage, I spoke through our bond, my breath ceasing as I waited.

Silence was my only answer.

I tried again. *Little Goddess*.

Still, nothing.

Further down the river, Folkoln emerged from the agitated waters. He had one arm banded around an unconscious Kaleb's chest while he used the other to swim toward the shore. Swiftly, I moved.

"Here!" he yelled over the roar of the river, passing me Kaleb.

"I got him," I said as I pulled Kaleb up and out onto the rocky ground.

Folkoln emerged beside him, crawling on all fours. He flopped over onto his back, and with a wild smile, he panted, "Now *that* was a rush."

I chuckled. Only someone as screwed in the head as my brother would enjoy getting eaten by a giant and shit out into a river of the dead.

"If that's what you want to call it. Did you see anyone else?" I asked.

"No, just Kaleb. Figured I better grab him," Folkoln said as he got up, shaking his head like a dog, water droplets spraying out everywhere.

I scanned the surface of the river. "We'll have to find the others."

Folkoln nodded.

I checked Kaleb over. I couldn't see any visible damage, everything looked intact—ten fingers, ten toes, one pint-sized mortal cock. Check. Check. Check.

Fate's words replayed in my mind, *Six find their feet, two need time, one is broken.* Folkoln and I were two of the six who had found their feet, which meant Kaleb either needed more time to wake, or he was the broken one.

Only time would tell.

A frustrated scream echoed through the tunnel, bouncing off the walls like a boomerang. I looked further up the river.

Saphira was standing there, going in circles. A long, black appendage with a piece of fluff on the end swayed behind her, twirling as she rotated.

Folkoln started, "She's got a . . ."

"Tail," I finished as we stood there gawking at our infuriated sister who swirled around and around. A black, snarling cat chasing her own tail.

Finally, grabbing ahold of it, she tugged on it and let out a pained yelp.

Folkoln burst into laughter.

And because I was every bit of the asshole he was, I did as well.

"Why are you laughing?" Saphira snarled as she thundered toward us, her eyes glowing with anger. "Did you do this?" Accusingly, she shook her tail, caught in in her firm grip, at Folkoln.

"No." Folkoln shook his head, cackling as he said, "Although I wish I had."

Saphira looked at me, and the fire in her eyes wicked out. Still on her good behavior act, she dropped her tail and didn't dare ask if I had something to do with it.

"Ezra's concoctions have side effects sometimes. I'm presuming this is one," I speculated, crossing my arms over my chest.

She let out a frustrated sigh. "Do you think it will go away?"

"Hard to say," I answered with a small shrug.

"Help!" an unfamiliar voice called out over the rushing waters. The three of us jerked our heads toward the river, looking to see who it was—

Lyra!

Without a second thought, I raced for the river and dove back in.

Arms churning, muscles firing, I swam to her.

Lyra's wide eyes met mine as she struggled to keep herself upright. Underneath the water, in her arms, was Harper. Lyra gasped as she tried to keep the two of them from being dragged under. I grabbed them both, keeping the three of us above the water.

"Grab onto me," Folkoln said to Lyra as he reached us.

She nodded, her hands wrapping around his arm.

When we were out of the river, Lyra crawled to Harper's side. Her small fingers held Harper's face as she knelt over top of her, small, strained whimpers coming from the back of her throat. Her tears plipped, falling on Harper's unresponsive face.

I placed a reassuring hand on Lyra's shoulder. "She'll be alright."

She turned toward me, gave me a nod, then wiped her tears in the crook of her arm.

"You were so brave to call for help. I'm proud of you, Lyra," I spoke softly, and her eyes grew cloudy once more. "Hopefully, we'll get to hear more of that voice someday."

Her hand fell over mine, clutching it in thanks.

I was reminded of when I had found her, barely alive, on the floor of a tent in one of the mortal king's training barracks. Her body had been laden with bruises and wounds—both new and old. Looking at her, I had thought she was not long for the Living Realm. I still remembered the way her weak hand had reached for me—as if her soul understood I was Death, and that I could make her suffering end. I had seen thousands of mortals die before, but in that moment, something came over me—perhaps it was because of Sage and the way she cherished the living. Before I knew what I was doing, I had picked Lyra up and taken her to Ezra.

Removing my hand from Lyra's shoulder, shadows swarmed into my palm, conjuring two towels and a set of clothes. I handed them to Lyra. She placed them beside her, used one towel to cover Harper, and then proceeded to wrap herself in the second.

When you lived as long as we immortals did, nudity didn't bother us. It was our natural state, after all. But mortals were modest creatures.

Turning my attention to Kaleb, my shadows weaved a third towel, and they placed it over top of him.

As I sauntered over to Folkoln and Saphira, my umbra swirled around me—dressing me in a pair of leather pants, a simple black tunic, and a set of black boots. Black and silver rings wrapped around my fingers, Sage's white feather weaving into my hair.

"We're still missing a few," Folkoln said, black eyes scanning the river as I stepped beside him.

"We'll find them," I stated. "Can you sense anything?"

"No, but for all I know, the river could be interfering with things. All I can sense are the emotions rolling off of you three. Which, other than the small one's sadness and fear, are relatively bland." He rolled his neck, looking at Saphira and giving her a lopsided grin. "How's that tail treating you, sis?"

"Fuck off," she snarled, and crafted a long black dress that reached down to the stone ground, its neckline a plunging v cut. Beneath the silk fabric, her tail twitched from side to side.

Folkoln leaned back, eyeing it. "Nice try, but it's definitely still there. I wonder if it's going to be permanent?" He tapped his chin.

"Do you know what *will* be permanent?" Saphira snarled as she shot Folkoln a look so deadly that I could feel the daggers pierce him when it landed. "The imprint of my heel, stamped on your face."

Folkoln inhaled, and when he exhaled, smoke curled from his nose. He groaned in ecstasy, "Yeah, that's the stuff."

"You emotion-sucking leech," Saphira hissed in disgust.

"Would you two shut the fuck up?" I growled at my inferior siblings, pinning them both with my gaze. I looked back to the river. "I'm trying to decide what to do."

They grew silent.

Saphira stepped around Folkoln, toward me. "If I may . . ."

"You may not," I cut her off, my face shifting to hers. My anger was leashed, but my words had bite as I spoke between clenched teeth, "Your tongue speaks nothing but lies and treachery. I will not have it poison my thoughts."

"Understood," she said coldly before she spun on her heel and headed down the river, clipping a thunderous pace.

Good. That should get rid of her, at least for a little while.

I could only hope she kept going and didn't turn around—one less soul to concern myself with.

Folkoln opened his mouth to say something, but I shot him a look that made my intentions clear—I was not in the mood to discuss anything that had to do with Saphira.

Proving he had half a brain cell, he shifted directions. "So . . . what's the plan? How are we going to find the others?"

"Tunnel makes it pretty clear. We have two options. Go the way Saphira went or head upstream," I answered, mulling over what made the most sense. "Whichever direction we go, we should be doing sweeps of the water." I jerked my chin to the river. "They could still be down there."

Folkoln glanced in the indicated direction. He was quiet for a moment, thinking, then, "We could split into two groups. One group goes downstream, the other goes upstream. We'd cover more ground that way."

I shook my head. "Splitting up is counterproductive if our goal is to get the group together. Besides, we know nothing about these lands and what lurks in them. It's better if we stick together."

"Fair enough," Folkoln replied. "So what do you want to do?"

"I think we do a quick sweep of the water. If we find nothing, we head further downstream. If some of the others did surface further up the river, then hopefully they'll travel the same direction as us. We'll leave a message, written on the wall, with an arrow pointing downstream so they know where to find us."

"Alright. I'll go back in, see if I can locate anyone else before we move ahead."

"Don't get lost," I ordered, my tone serious.

"I'm insulted you think I would," he said with a cocky, arrogant grin before he dove into the waters with little care, as if he were going for a leisurely swim. I looked down, peering beneath the surface, watching the souls as they drifted by.

This river reminded me so much of the Da'Nu.

Turning away, I walked over to the wall of the cave, contemplating what message I should leave behind. I didn't know who or what might be lurking in this place so I wanted to make sure it was something only Fallon, Ryker, or Soren would understand.

Then, it came to me.

Slowly, I waved my hand from left to right, and my shadows went to work. Tiny bits of rock sputtered out from the wall, as if they were being removed by chisel and hammer.

When I was done, sitting over an arrow that pointed downstream, were the words—*Four found their feet, two need time.*

Chapter 30

Sage

The snow crunched beneath our boots as Artemesia and I ambled through the camp, chatting with one another about insignificant things like the weather. It was nice having a light conversation with her. It felt nostalgic. Simple. Easy. But best of all, it served as a distraction—one that kept my mind occupied, away from the heavy throes of sadness.

A man walked toward us, a deer slung over his shoulders. That was one thing I had noticed about this place—there always seemed to be a steady stream of game brought into the camp. To the extent I wondered what they did with it all; surely, they couldn't eat *that* much meat. Following behind the man were a boy and a girl who looked maybe a year apart.

"It doesn't matter, mine is bigger," the girl huffed as she held up the sizable rabbit she had caught.

"Yeah, but I caught two!" the boy snipped back. Sure enough, in his hand, strung by their hind legs, were two jackrabbits.

"That's enough, you two," the man scolded them softly. When he reached us, he dipped his head and said, a bit out of breath, "Good day, chieftain." He nodded to me, and I returned the gesture.

"Good day," Artemesia greeted him. "Nice looking buck you got there. Where did you find it?"

He nodded over his shoulder, toward the woods—the branches of the green spruce trees were dolloped with fluffy snow. "Near Cocoah Lake."

"It's been a good spot lately," Artemesia stated, then introduced the two of us. By the time she did that, the kids had started to argue again over who was the better hunter.

The man shot them stern looks, but the flicker of his grin made the look fall flat. Heaving the deer further up on his shoulders, he looked at us and said, "Well, I suppose I better get going before these two end up in a fistfight."

"Fair enough," Artemesia chuckled, blue eyes glancing at the children. "Go easy on your father, you two."

"Yes, chieftain," the boy and girl replied in unison, flashing big, toothy smiles before they raced ahead, following after their father.

I watched them for a moment, wondering what *that* must feel like—to have your little ones trailing after you. I wondered what it was like to teach them how to hunt, to watch them grow . . . to tuck them in at night and kiss their foreheads. I wondered what it was like to have a place for your love to go, rather than it all being stuck inside your chest, yearning to be spent, but no child to give it to.

Grief drifted to the forefront of my emotions, standing there with her solemn face. She took me in her arms, wrapping them around me. The weight of her hug was crushing.

"Sage?" Artemesia asked, her hand clasping my shoulder. "Are you okay?"

I took a breath. Then, another. "Sometimes yes, sometimes no," I answered. That was the strange thing about grief, it was constantly coming and going, ebbing and flowing, always changing. One second, I felt okay, but by the next, I was breaking all over again.

"I think that's a pretty normal way to be, all things considered." She offered me an understanding look. "We can go back to your tent if you would prefer."

"No." I shook my head. "The outside air is good for my soul."

As soon as the words left my tongue, the wind picked up ever so slightly. I felt the cool breeze run its fingers through my hair, felt its touch dance across my cheek, and it reminded me of Von—of the promise he'd made to me in the arena. That promise was what kept me going. It kept me from fracturing apart and reverting to the person I'd been before—the broken goddess of nothing, lying on the floor in the empress's dungeon, covered in her own urine. Yes, being outside was exactly what I needed.

"Alright," she said, giving my shoulder a gentle squeeze before we continued forward.

As we walked, I took in the world around us, marveling at the mountains. They stood like royalty—towering and majestic, wearing crowns of sparkling, craggy stone and cloaks made of rich, lush forests.

"It's strange," I started, thinking out loud. "The tents are familiar to me, but this place isn't. It's so beautiful, you'd think it would have ingrained itself in my memory."

"That's because you've probably never been here before," she answered. "The clan was originally from the Centeria region, but we had to relocate here."

"Why?" I asked curiously.

Artemesia took a breath before she replied. "The empress held up her end of the bargain. She left the clan untouched as her war raged around us. However, after it was finished, the realm became unsafe. The empress didn't harm our clan, but she didn't protect it either." She shrugged her shoulder. "Mobs beget mobs, and when they learned the men and boys of our clan lived freely, well, you can imagine how well that went over."

I could see the flames of history burning in my sister's eyes, telling me where this part of the story was headed next.

She continued, "Two other clans, who were previously allied with ours, joined together and attacked us in the middle of the day. They burned our homes, slaughtered the women, and tried to take the men and boys. Those of us who survived were forced to run into the forest." She paused for a moment, her eyebrows weaving together. "There, I saw a deer with a strange white marking on its neck, and it led us all the way here." She gestured to the mountains. "That was many centuries ago. For all I know, the empress probably thinks our clan was wiped out during that time. I've done all I can to keep a low profile, hoping she'd think I returned to the soil long ago."

"If that's the case, it's probably a good thing she doesn't know you are still alive," I answered, thankful they had been able to escape.

"Agreed." Her eyes flicked from side to side, scanning our surroundings before she whispered, "I need to show you something."

We stepped inside a tent where the air smelled of tobacco.

Chests lined the perimeter of the tent, piled on top of one another, some of which were open, showing off the rich pelts inside. In the middle sat a table with large maps strewn about, their curling ends held down with weights. Sitting on the thick papers were small, carved animals that looked to be strategically placed—rabbits, deer, elk, and so on. Standing around the table were a few women and a couple men. An elderly woman rested her weary bones in a chair, a pipe in one weathered hand and a carved deer in the other. Their gazes swung up to meet ours.

"Chieftain," the elderly woman said, and they all bowed their heads.

"I'm sorry to interrupt, but we need to pass through," Artemesia replied.

"Of course," said the woman standing near the end of the table, and they all began to move.

One of the men helped the elderly woman stand up. He handed her her cane, which she took as she sucked on her pipe.

Smoke curled from her mouth as she relied on her cane to carry her over to a chest. She plopped down on it, an audible sigh leaving her lips.

The men picked up the table and moved it, careful not to knock too many of the pieces over. Next, the women crouched by the edge of the rug and began to roll it up. Underneath was a wood floor. The one waved her hand over top of it, and then—

Part of it *opened* like a trap door.

I peered into the vast hole in the ground, but I couldn't see anything.

One of the women moved to stand in front of it, turning her palm face up, and a small ball of fire grew in it. She raised it to her mouth and blew. The fireball burst forth, shooting into the hole. It bounced from side to side, lighting sconce after sconce, until a path of never-ending stairs appeared.

"Come," Artemesia directed before she began to walk down them. I followed after her.

I did not know how long we descended into the belly of the mountain, but when we reached the bottom, Artemesia looked to me and said, "Welcome to Veshameer, the Hidden City."

Stretching before me was a vast network of streets, shops, and homes, all carved from stone. I eyed the shop sign closest to me, noting that it did not contain words, but rather a picture—a loaf of bread, a few swirls placed over top.

"There are many languages spoken here," Artemesia stated, her attention fixed on the sign, "so shops use pictures instead."

"That makes sense," I replied. "How many people live here?"

"Thousands."

"Is that why you need so much meat?" I inquired, although I was fairly confident I already knew the answer.

"It is. Unfortunately, animals do not fare well down here, and so the clan hunts all winter long to supply the city with meat. But we only supply a third of it. The rest is purchased with gemstones and diamonds mined from down here," she answered.

Underneath the bakery sign, the wood-slat door opened, and a man and a little girl walked out. The smells of rising sourdough and cinnamon wafted toward me. I breathed them in. With his little one in tow, the man rushed over to Artemesia. "I do not have much, but it would be a great honor if you would accept this bread, savior." He held up what I imagined was the bread wrapped in a creamy beige linen, offering it to my sister.

Artemesia placed her hand on the linen, gently pushing it back to him. "I am so honored that you would gift it to me, but you and your daughter need it more than I do. So please, keep it."

"But you do so much for us," the man replied, his voice wobbling with emotion. There was something about the way he looked at Artemesia that was familiar. It was the same way the people in the Cursed Lands had looked at me—with admiration so deep you could feel it in your bones.

"And yet, it doesn't feel like I'm doing enough," Artemesia responded honestly.

"But it is," the man said as he gently pulled his daughter up beside him. "This is my daughter—we named her after you. She wouldn't be here if not for you."

"It's wonderful to meet you both," Artemesia said kindly, smiling at the two of them.

After the man and his little girl said their goodbyes, Artemesia and I continued ahead. Every once in a while, someone would come over to us and offer Artemesia something, which she would always politely decline. With every interaction, it was evident how much they respected her, and how much she cared for them.

Some time later, as we walked down a residential street, I asked, "Did you rescue *all* these people?"

"Some of them directly, yes. Others are descendants of those I've rescued over the centuries," she answered, our paces perfectly matched. "When I saw what the empress was doing to males, I felt so . . . powerless. It took me a great number of years to realize I wasn't."

"You've done a good thing here." I looked at her. "Do you remember the first person you saved?"

"I do." A light chuckle passed her closed lips, her mouth curving ever so slightly as she reminisced. "My very first rescue was a young boy. After that, things just . . . well, they spiraled. Once I got a taste for saving lives; I couldn't stop. I still can't stop. Although, as I bring more and more people back, the weight on my shoulders increases. If the empress were ever to discover this place . . ." Her lips thinned. "It would be the end of all this."

Chapter 31

Shadow

Three days had passed since Avriel told me about the empress's plans for her.

Plans that filled my lungs with a fiery rage. The kind that could burn a person to ash, if I let it get out of control. Something I refused to do. I wouldn't let it, wouldn't let my anger and frustrations consume me, because now there was something much larger at play. The only female that I had ever cared for was going to suffer the same fate I had experienced every time the empress commanded me to go to her bedchamber.

I would do everything within my power to prevent *that* from happening to Avriel. I wouldn't allow that horrible excuse of a man to touch her. Which meant I needed to keep my fucking wits about me.

Avriel had learned Victor was planning to leave with her early next month, which didn't give us much time to figure out how we were going to escape together. Still, I didn't trust that grimy fucker around her, and I knew we were already working on borrowed time.

That was why it had absolutely gutted me to go to Virtus City for today's soul crusher games. Avriel had told me to go, telling me we needed to act normally. Otherwise, we would arouse suspicion. It had taken everything within me to listen to her, although I knew she was right.

And besides, it would give me the opportunity to speak with another soul crusher without the concern of prying eyes and eager ears.

I walked through the hypogeum, a subterranean network underneath the arena, past the men chained to the walls, their eyes fixed on me, pleading for mercy. With each glance, I repeated the same message to them—the only mercy I could give them was a quick end.

Back in the depths of one of the hallways, where there was little light, stood the soul crusher I had been looking for—

Commodus. He was a towering male, close to my height. The great expanse of his lifetime had easily clipped mine dozens of times. He was a good immortal to know, because he possessed a great deal of things, and if he didn't have what you were looking for, then he knew someone who would. He was an alumnus of the empress's harem, one of the very few she allowed to live beyond the palace walls, due to the millennia he'd spent serving her. Through cock and sword, he had gained his freedom.

"Shadow," he said, his voice unfathomably deep, as if

he'd reached inside himself and plucked the words from his brass balls.

"Commodus, you old goat," I replied, slapping him on the shoulder. "It is good to lay eyes on you."

He chuckled, his hands bracing my arm in friendly reply. "Ah, it is good to see you too, brother."

Even though there was not a droplet of blood shared between us, all of us who served within the empress's harem were brothers. We all understood one another's pain, of being used and abused at the empress's hands, a toy for her to play with.

"How is Aryx doing?" he asked, a hint of fondness in his voice. Commodus had been to Aryx what Aryx was to me—someone who had raised the other, taken them under their wing. I used to feel sorry for the poor bastard who tried to take refuge under mine, considering they wouldn't provide much protection, but now that my plans had quickly changed, I supposed that was something I wouldn't be around to do anyway.

"Aryx is doing good," I answered.

"Is he still mourning his sweet Saphira?" he asked, his mighty arm returning to his side.

"I don't think he'll ever stop missing her," I spoke honestly.

"No, I don't suppose he will. A love like that is one you never forget," Commodus said, a hint of sadness whispering into his eyes, swept away when he blinked.

Commodus had once been married before the War of the Creators. Although he didn't speak of those days often, once, when he was drunk, he'd opened up to us about them. About the goddess he had once loved before the empress had taken him from her. He had made a deal with the empress, that if he served her for one thousand years, she would retrieve his wife for him. But the empress had never specified whether she would be living or dead, and on the day that she was set to arrive, her vessel came in a casket. A hole through her chest.

"Say, what do you know of that arena that burned to the ground in Lorphiah?" he asked curiously, tipping his head back.

"Not as much as you, I would suspect."

He chuckled at that.

I answered him anyway. "I heard that a female who was condemned to have her soul crushed managed to find her way up into the stands. There, she pushed one of the wards off and it shattered upon the sands. She scorched the opponent to ash, causing the rest of the arena to light on fire. Then, the vuleeries took her. The empress was rather furious to learn of all this."

Commodus let out a low whistle. "That's *some* female."

"Indeed," I chuckled. "What have *you* heard?"

"I've heard that version and a thousand others from the old rumor mill," he said. Footsteps sounded above us. "People are starting to arrive. I should let you get ready for the games."

My voice dropped to a whisper. "Before I go, I need a favor."

"Name it," he said, voice quiet.

My gaze held his. "I need a map of the Mother Realm."

"Why would you need that, brother?" he asked, voice wary.

"It's better you don't know."

"Then I won't ask, but I will get it for you. Are you staying for tomorrow's games?"

"No." I shook my head, voice returning to normal. "Leaving tonight."

"Alright, I'll meet you back here after the event is over."

I nodded. "Thank you, brother."

"Good luck."

"I don't need luck," I told him.

"Something tells me that you are going to need all the luck you can get." He gave me a concerned look and then patted my arm. "I'll see you after the games."

A short while later, I made my way to the iron gate. My heart beat like a stallion's hooves, pounding adrenaline through my veins. The armor I donned was crafted from onyx-dyed boiled leather. It had taken me months to make the armor, after many, *many* prototypes. I doubted I'd ever get it perfect enough for my standards. I rolled my arm, peering down at the new, thicker strap I'd recently installed on my vambrace. I tugged at it, ensuring it was tight.

Nixus, another soul crusher, walked up to me, carrying

a soulius.

I looked at the gauntlet, made from dragon hide and claw. There was once a time when I had aspired to be able to fight in the arena, but over the years, the soulius had lost its luster. Now, when I looked at it, all I saw was death.

I put it on then set my sights on the arena.

The gate groaned as it lifted.

"Good luck, brother," Nixus offered before I walked out.

"Thanks," I replied, thinking that perhaps the old goat was right—perhaps I needed it after all.

Chapter 32

Von

"I feel like I snorted a line of salt," Folkoln grumbled as we ambled forward, matching Lyra's much slower pace. Folkoln carried Kaleb on his back while I had Harper on mine.

I grunted in reply.

He wasn't wrong. The briny, damp air was relentless. It saturated my nostrils, stuck to my skin, dampened my clothes. It was a menace. One I was eager to get away from. Also grating against my frayed nerves were the ceaseless sounds of the rushing river and the water that trickled from the cave's mouth. Just like this tunnel, it was never-ending.

Drip. Drip. Fucking drip.

We hadn't seen Saphira since she'd stormed off, which was probably for the better. Ryker, Fallon, Soren—not one of them had turned up either.

It was just us five, the endless river, and the salty

fucking air.

We had been walking for four days, only stopping when Lyra needed to rest. As there wasn't a speck of natural light to be found, I relied on her sleeping patterns to measure the time.

Mortals were like little clocks, their sleeping and waking hours revolving around night and day. Although time was relevant to us all, mortals were passionate about it, and as usual, they liked to claim it was one of them who had created the concept of it. Take the calendar, for example. For thousands of years, people had fought over who invented it. Some would say that it was this scholar or that great king, or oh no, it was Pharaoh Such and Such. And while they claimed this, they would completely ignore the fact that women's bodies ran on a thirty-day cycle—just like the calendar.

I rolled my eyes. *Morons.*

The ground started to shake beneath my feet, causing small stones to jump from their resting state. *Something* was on the move. Something big.

Folkoln and I exchanged brief glances.

A screeching roar sounded from up ahead, followed by another, and another. From one to the next, they were vastly different, which meant—

"There's more than one," Folkoln whispered. "What do you want to do?"

"We're not going back," I stated firmly, my mind fleshing out a plan.

Lyra's fingers slid under my arm as she stepped closer

to me, her attention locked on the direction of the monstrous sounds. Her complexion had paled, her heart pumping at a thunderous rate. I needed to find her somewhere she could hide, as well as the others, so that Folkoln and I could advance and figure out what we were up against.

Eyes searching, I looked over the wall of the mountain. *There.* A crevice.

The ground shuddered again. Worse than before.

"Quickly. Follow me," I commanded, hoisting Harper further up on my back before I took off toward the fracture. Folkoln and Lyra followed behind me.

Reaching it, I peered inside the sizable crack, my immortal eyes seeing through the darkness. About fifteen feet in, the fissure opened up to a small cavity—just enough space to lay Harper and Kaleb down. Shadows swam from my shoulders, gently taking Harper's body and sliding her through the fissure until it reached the small, open space, placing her there on the ground. Umbra returning, they took Kaleb from Folkoln and did the same.

I turned to Lyra. "You're next."

Eyes as wide and bright as two full moons, she nodded, and then began to slide inside.

As I went to turn away, I felt a small tug on my sleeve. I glanced over my shoulder. Lyra looked up at me with pleading eyes, her message clear.

"Don't worry, we'll be alright," I reassured her.

She gave a small nod before her hand slipped away, and she slid into the crack.

Folkoln and I advanced, sticking to the shadows. I

cloaked us in my umbra, but considering some species could see through that, we weren't about to take any chances, so we crouched low to the ground and ducked behind a massive boulder with a flattened top.

Muscles tense, I raised my head slowly until I could just see over the top of the rock, laying eyes on the gigantic, snarling beast—

A *hydra*.

It had at least a dozen heads. Its wet scales glistened like a layer of black, impenetrable armor. Dark, sinister eyes glowed with malevolence while razor-sharp teeth hissed and snapped as it slithered after its prey.

"Guess we found them," Folkoln stated.

Ryker raced in our direction with Fallon on his back. She was awake, although by the way her scrunched face was contorted in pain, something was definitely wrong.

Both she and Ryker were wearing clothing made of large, green, leather-like leaves, secured in place by a braided rope that looked like it was made from the root of something. Wherever they came from, there were plants. If I knew one thing, it was that plants with leaves like that needed sunlight to survive, which meant they'd made it outside, or at least found a space that was open to it.

Hope filled my chest, but it was quickly smothered out—the hydra was gaining on them.

One head struck, just narrowly missing Ryker as it plunged its teeth into the ground, causing a spray of stone. Fallon screamed in horror.

"Keep the others safe," I commanded Folkoln as I

stood. My shadows plummeted from my hand, producing my Vischordian blade—Death Weaver.

Then, I charged.

"Von!" Ryker exclaimed, relief spreading over his face.

"Keep moving," I growled as I passed him.

I'd never faced a hydra before, but I knew enough about them to know there weren't many ways to kill them. The best way to do it was to cut off each head. The problem with that? The heads were immortal and able to replicate, so if I sliced one off, two more would grow.

Luckily, I had an idea. Not a fucking clue if it would work, but it was worth a shot.

My quadriceps fired up as I leapt from the ground, wings bursting from my back, snapping outward in one swift movement. With a mighty flap, I shot forward like an arrow loosed from a bow. Two dozen monstrous eyes turned on me, tracking my movement as I flew straight for them.

"That's right, beasty, I'm what you want!" I shouted as the heads reared back, readying to strike.

The first one released, launching at me, its snapping teeth stretched wide. Twisting to my left, I dodged it with ease. I darted this way and that, moving through the heads, looking for an opportune moment to test my theory.

Finding it, I tucked my wings in as I launched toward two entangled necks, which resembled the number eight. Passing through the top hole, fire engulfed my blade. In a blur of onyx steel and flame, I swung it, slicing through scales, tissue, and bones. The scent of cooked meat, like a pig roasting over a spit, permeated the damp, briny air. The head fell onto the ground in one, loud *thunk*.

A cacophony of bloodcurdling roars erupted from the beast, their heads swiveling back toward me.

Wings flaring out, I flew higher, out of its reach.

Turning around, breath locked in my chest, I watched to see if another head grew from the swaying stub or if my flame had cauterized it fast enough.

When none did, I grinned. My idea had worked.

One down. Eleven to go.

Shooting back toward the hydra, I focused on my next target.

Death Weaver found purchase, and another head fell to the ground below.

And then another.

And another.

I chopped and hacked and cut, every chance I got, until I was bathed in the ichor of the hydra.

My powerful wings cut the air, blasting me forward as I flew toward a recoiled head, readying to strike. It shot toward me, but before my blade could find its mark, pain lacerated my outstretched left arm. A mouth full of razor-sharp teeth clamped down on it, piercing through muscle and sinew and—

Snap.

My humerus broke under the beast's mighty bite. It jerked its head to the side and tore my arm off. I roared in agony.

Crunch. Crunch. Crunch.

Chewing, the beast's mouth opened and closed,

revealing my arm—or rather, the mushed-up version of it. On the hydra's forked tongue, I spotted a bit of silver. My black phantom heart dropped instantly.

Damn it! I *really* liked that ring.

The other heads noticed and began to fight with the one that had taken my arm, completely forgetting about me in the process.

I landed on the ground, my lungs heaving as I looked at what was left of my shredded arm. Scraggly bits of flesh, cloth, and jagged bone were all that remained.

"Fuck," I groaned painfully.

"Need a hand?" Folkoln taunted as he walked up beside me, the flat of his blade resting against his shoulder.

My eyes sharpened on the jackass. "You're a prick."

He chuckled, lowering his sword to his side. Tendrils of smoke curled around it, and within seconds, it lit with a black flame. His wings flared out, and he surged from the rocky ground. Wind blasted against me.

Clank. I tossed my sword on the ground so I could support my aching nub, watching as my brother took on the hydra. Folkoln moved with speed, skill, and precision, smoke curling around him, tracking his movement in a blur of onyx.

It didn't take him long before he chopped off one head.

"Show off," I panted under my breath as I plopped down on my ass, watching as he went after the next one. He cleaved its head free, sending it spiraling, blood spraying out before it landed on the ground, rolling to a stop. Its lifeless eyes peered at me, its mouth stretched unnaturally wide from the way it had landed.

Something sparkled in the back of its mouth, caught beside its tooth.

I squinted—

Well, I'll be damned.

Instantly, my spirits lifted. Fingers curling around the handle of my sword, I grunted like an old man as I got up. I walked over to the head and used the tip of my blade to flick the shiny round object out of the beast's mouth.

Ting. My skull ring landed on the stone.

A tendril of shadow swirled forward, scooping up the ring and taking it back into its storage. It wasn't like I could wear it now anyway, all things considered.

I looked at the ongoing battle, noting there were only two heads left.

As if I was going to let the insufferable ass gloat for the rest of eternity about how *he* had defeated the hydra. Ignoring the pure agony of my left arm, my wings slammed downward, and I shot up from the ground.

"You crazy bastard!" Folkoln howled as I flew to his side.

"Can't let you have all the glory," I grunted through the pain.

"Have you ever?" he chuckled.

"Never." I grinned. "Which one do you want?"

"Left one."

"Alright." I set my sights on the right one and launched toward it. A mighty roar sounded from both of us as we clashed in a battle of teeth and sword.

With my good arm, I sent my iron fist, backed by the handle of my sword, into its jaw. Droplets of the beast's saliva sprayed into the air before the sap-like gobs answered the call of gravity and rained back down on me. Before the beast had a chance to retaliate, I delivered my final blow and severed the head clean off. It slid off the neck and tumbled to the ground below.

I landed and started back toward the group. A few seconds later, Folkoln let out a victorious roar, and the monstrous beast fell on the ground, the stone to trembling beneath my feet.

Folkoln emerged beside me, wings tucking in.

"Took you long enough," I said, glancing at him.

Fuck you, he mouthed at me, and we both burst into laughter. But the sound was quickly cut off as a surge of pain shot through my left arm. I grunted, dissolving my sword as I reached for my arm to help support it.

When we returned to the group, Lyra and Ryker were kneeling beside Fallon. Her face was scrunched in agony, her hand wrapped around her leg, which she had pulled close to her body. A sharp yellow fang was stuck in her thigh.

Heads swiveled toward us.

Lyra's mouth fell open, the color leeching from her face.

"Holy shit, Von," Ryker drawled as he got to his feet, his eyes fixed on my mangled arm. "That doesn't look good."

I looked down at it, eyeing the torn bits and pieces. A

chunk of flesh dangled, a small bit of sinew keeping it there. Gritting my teeth together, I gripped the meat and tore it free, tossing it on the ground. "Yeah, it's not great, but it'll grow back," I said, continuing to inspect it. Already, I could see small bits of muscle and tissue slowly beginning to repair. With time, it would heal.

Fallon moaned in pain.

"Fallon?" Kaleb's groggy voice called out from inside the crevice.

Lyra dashed over to it, disappearing inside. Not long after, she and Kaleb emerged.

"Easy now, tough guy," Folkoln said as he strolled over to them. "You've been out for a while.

"How long?" Kaleb spoke wearily, his arm slung over Lyra's shoulders.

"About four days," Folkoln replied.

"Did we all make it?" Kaleb asked.

"Soren is the only one unaccounted for," Folkoln answered.

Kaleb nodded, drowsy eyes shifting over to us, then—

"Fallon!" he yelled, voice desperate. Seeing her, as she was, must have been like a bolt of electricity, because he was racing over to us. Lyra scrambled after him.

At Fallon's side, he sank to his knees, their gazes locked. He slid his shaking fingers to her cheek, and she cupped his hand, her fingers stained with blood. "It's going to be okay," he said. His head jerked up to mine, face etched with worry. "What do we do?" His eyes locked on my arm, and they grew even larger. "Shit!"

"It'll grow back," I reassured him. "Worry about Fallon."

"Reassuring," Fallon grimaced, voice saturated with sarcasm.

"Should we take the fang out?" Ryker asked, looking at me. "Or is it better to leave it in?"

"It's not the fang I'm worried about," I said as I surveyed the wound. Surrounding it, a web of black had started to spider out. My attention shifted to my arm, looking to see if I, too, had been infected by the hydra's venom, but I spotted nothing. Either the toxin hadn't had a chance to spread yet, or the head that bit me wasn't venomous.

My gaze returned to Fallon.

Back home, Fallon couldn't die again because she was already, well, dead. But here, in these foreign lands, I didn't know what would happen to her soul.

I *could* suck the venom from her, but if I wasn't immune to it, like I was with snake venom, that could cause a host of problems—problems that could deter me from getting to Sage, and that was something I was not willing to risk.

"We need to find someone who knows about the hydra's venom," I told them. "A healer."

"Fuck the healer," Folkoln hissed as he crouched beside Fallon's wounded leg. His hand wrapped around the broken tooth, and he pulled it out before anyone could stop him.

"Folkoln," Ryker growled.

But Folkoln paid him no mind. Carelessly, he tossed the fang to the side, sending it skittering against the stone. He bent forward and, with his eyes on Fallon's, said, "Just remember, Little Bird, out of all these *so-called* men, who had the balls to save your life today."

"Folkoln, wait," I snarled, reaching for him with my good hand—my only hand.

But he flipped his middle finger at me as he placed his mouth against her wound and began to suck out the venom.

Chapter 33

Von

"This is it," Ryker said hours later as we approached a section of the tunnel partially caved in on one side.

The crumbled stone had fallen into the river, squeezing off the passage of water and forging it into turbulent, angry rapids. Rubble was strewn about, making the terrain treacherous and uneven, a good place for a mortal to break one of their many brittle bones. Through the jagged hole, daylight beamed, giving the reddish rocks a yellow glow.

"Finally!" Kaleb exclaimed as he jostled Fallon further up on his back. Lyra leapt up and down beside him, sharing in the small victory.

"There are plenty of plants and game on the other side. A freshwater stream as well," Ryker said, an unconscious Harper in his arms. "Fallon and I made a camp out there where we stayed during the nights. During the day, we'd come back inside the tunnel to try to find you guys. Little did we know we were going to find a fucking hydra."

"Did you ever travel further downstream?" I asked, my gaze set ahead, while the rest of them looked at the exit.

Fallon picked up her head from Kaleb's back. "No," she rasped, her voice weak but slowly improving since Folkoln had sucked the venom from her wound a few hours ago. "We had planned to go tomorrow if we didn't find anyone today."

"Soren could have floated further down the river," I stated, hating the idea of remaining in this fucking tunnel any longer, but it was something that might be necessary—Soren was essential because he was the only connection we had to Sage. Since we arrived, I had tried to speak to her through our bond, but that private bridge remained broken.

So, if I was going to find Sage, I needed to find Soren first.

A truth I despised.

I studied the weary faces, now turned toward me, waiting for me to decide. They did not possess the same immortal stamina as me or Folkoln, although I'd seen bits of it shine through Harper and Ryker, as they were descendants of Dameon and Zahra. But all in all, the group was tired.

"We'll spend a night at Fallon and Ryker's camp so everyone can rest up," I decided. I could see the relief spread from face to face. "We'll reassess in the morning."

Fallon and Ryker's camp was fairly simple. They had crafted a small shelter, just big enough to fit the two of them—something I know made Kaleb do a double take. Small, slender tree trunks stacked together formed the sides. The roof was made out of large, leather-like leaves. Those same leaves were what Fallon and Ryker had made their laughable clothing out of. The leaves were placed over top of one another and slanted to the side for runoff. In front of it was a small stone pit. Inside, the ground was untouched, not a speck of ash to be found—which meant Ryker had been using his own flame to create a fire within it.

Lyra watched with solemn eyes as Ryker gently placed Harper's unresponsive frame inside the shelter. When he backed out, the leaf he wore failed its job, causing Lyra to swiftly look away. For her sake, I would make him clothes—as well as Fallon. However, I would have to wait until later because the regeneration of my arm was chewing up a great deal of my power.

I rested on a fallen log, eyeing my stub, which had grown about halfway between my shoulder and elbow. My old tattoos began to stitch themselves back into my skin. The top of the tattoo of Sage's hand holding an apple was starting to form again. Seeing it there was like oxygen to my lungs, breathing life into me. Reassurance.

Folkoln sat beside me, his sights set ahead on Kaleb and Fallon.

Slowly, Kaleb lowered her onto the mossy ground. She winced as he slid his arms from underneath her. When Kaleb pulled back, she caught his hand, a silent conversation taking place between the two of them.

My gaze shifted to Folkoln, who was still watching them.

What am I looking at right now? I asked, shoving the words through the cracked door linking our minds.

Absolutely nothing, came his reply.

Absolutely nothing, my ass. Sucking the venom out of her leg could have put you at risk, and yet, you did it anyway. Why?

He shrugged. *I was doing my good deed for the decade.*

You, my brother, are many things, but selfless is not one of them. You haven't taken your eyes off her since you sat down beside me. So, I'll ask again, what am I looking at?

At first, he said nothing. Which was unlike him. Then, *Fallon and I never shared a personal connection; it was always just intimate. When Kaleb came into the picture, she called things off. Which I was completely fine with, but then we came here, and it's like something has shifted in me.*

I raised a brow. *How so?*

That's what I'm trying to figure out. I don't know if it's because I like the idea of being with her, or if it's broader than that. But I find myself wondering things that have never crossed my mind before. Like what it would be like—he nodded to Kaleb and Fallon—*to have someone.*

I thought of Sage, of how much she had enriched my eternal life. She brought me happiness I had never known was possible. Understanding, patience, kindness, love. And above all else, she had shown me the power of forgiveness. She wasn't just forged from the moon—she *was* the moon, and it was my world that revolved around her, not the other way around. I believed she could learn to live without me, something I would want for her if that were to happen, but I could never do the same.

What I was doing now was a testament to that.

The truth was, I needed Sage. Like an addict needed their next fix. Like the birds needed the sky. Like a beginning needed an end.

She was the light to my darkness.

She was my *everything*.

My attention drifted to my arm, locking on my vine tattoo, my brows lifting ever so slightly as I breathed out the words, "There is no better feeling."

"I never understood your and Saphira's infatuation with the stars, nor did I understand why either of you wanted to find your mate so badly. But now, I feel this strange . . . tugging." He rubbed his hand over his chest.

"I know that feeling. I feel it with Sage. Like a rope is tethered to my insides and I'm being pulled toward her."

"I was thinking more in terms of a boat seeking a lighthouse, but that's a good way to describe it." He glanced back at Fallon and his hand stilled.

I could see the mismatched wheels beginning to rotate in his chaotic mind. Before they could start to spin any faster, I said flatly, "She's not your mate. If she was, the bond would have forged the first time you slept with her."

"I'm not a dumbass. I know how the bond works," Folkoln said, his gaze still fixed ahead. I followed it—

Fallon and Kaleb seemed to be having some type of

dispute, but before I could listen in, Kaleb spun and started for Ryker, who had his back turned to him. Kaleb's fists were clenched so tight the skin over top of his knuckles had turned white.

Folkoln leaned over, saying, "This ought to be good."

I nodded.

"Hey! Ryker!" Kaleb shouted.

Ryker turned to look at him, but just as he did, Kaleb's fist smashed into the side of his face. Blood and saliva misted the air as Ryker swirled and fell onto the ground.

"You are a real asshole, you know that?" Kaleb spat out the words, his face glowing cherry red.

"I deserved that," Ryker said as he rubbed his jaw.

"You deserve that and so much more," Kaleb hissed, voice laden with anger, raw and deep, like a jagged shard of glass, ready to cut.

Ryker held up one hand in defense. "I know this is shit for you, but Fallon and I had something in the past and we're just trying to figure things out."

Kaleb bit back. "Fucking each other when she is with someone else is *not* figuring things out."

Lyra, who had popped her head out of the shelter, watched the scene unfolding before us all, her mouth wide open.

Fallon looked rather pitiful as she dragged her leg behind her, making her way over to the two of them. She stepped in front of Kaleb, her eyes pleading as she said, "Kaleb, I know you're mad at me, and you have every right to be, but please try to understand. What Ryker and I had in the past was real, and we never got to see what could have been. I won't deny I have feelings for him, but I love you too."

"You love me *too*?" Kaleb's eyes narrowed. "Does that mean you *love* him?" His slit pupils shifted to Ryker before they landed back on Fallon.

Fallon's mouth went slack, tripping over her words as she said, "I-I-uh, I'm trying to figure that out. Those feelings don't just go away."

Kaleb went to take a step back, and Fallon tried to grab his hand, but he pulled away. "Don't touch me." His voice was as cold as the dead of winter.

"Kaleb, just hear us out," Ryker interjected. "We never would have gone that far—"

"No," Fallon cut in. "We wouldn't have, but the berries we found that night messed with our thoughts. It loosened our inhibitions, and next thing I knew, it just happened."

"I feel like I'm going insane. You are blaming your infidelity on . . . fucking *berries*?" Kaleb shook his head in disbelief.

"Kaleb, it's true, please," Fallon pleaded.

"I'm done," Kaleb said, and then turned to walk away.

Fallon and Ryker called after him, but there was nothing they could say to keep him from walking off into the trees.

I sighed and said to Folkoln, "Look after the others. I'll be back shortly."

My right hand propped up my nub as I made my way through the forest, the mossy floor covered in small twigs that snapped underneath my boots. The earthy scent of decaying leaves and fresh pine hung heavily in the air, a welcome change from the briny tunnel.

When I caught up to Kaleb, I slowed to match his pace.

For a while, we walked like that, our silence occupied by the sounds of the forest—the natural rustling of leaves, the chirping, tweeting birds, and a babbling brook not far up ahead.

I knew of the inner turmoil Kaleb must be feeling right now, because there was a time, not so long ago, when I had felt it too. When Sage had decided to sleep with Aurelius, a choice she made without the sway of his ichor, it made me wild with anger. With possessiveness. So, I went to her, and I asserted my claim. Over her. Over her pleasure. She was *mine* in every sense of the word. She *belonged* to me.

As I to her.

Despite what she had done, I could not stay mad at Sage. To do so would be incredibly short-sighted.

Sage's *actions* had been because of *me*.

She had learned of our twisted past, where I had cursed her and taken away the one thing she longed to do—create. I had left her to suffer through the fever, which ravaged her for days on end, causing her unspeakable pain as her body and mind were torn to shreds.

I could still hear her tormented screams as she writhed on the cottage floor, begging for the agony to stop. And like a heartless asshole, I just sat there, watching her. Like that, in her weakened, desperate state, I had taken advantage of her, forcing her into another bargain—

I am willing to offer you a deal. I will give you an apple seed to plant. My own words echoed inside my head.

I scowled at the memory.

Back then, I had been so caught up in my need for revenge I had ignored all the signs—that she was my mate. I had wasted precious time I could have had with her, if only I hadn't been so painfully blind.

I hated what I had done to Sage, and yet, she had forgiven me for it. All of it.

So, if she could do that for me, I could do it for her.

In fact, I already had.

Kaleb sighed. "I miss Sage."

"I do too," I conceded, looking up at the swaying green canopy. Creator above, *how* I missed her.

"I wish she was here so I could talk to her about Fallon," Kaleb said, the anger in his voice gone. Now, all that was left was sadness. "She'd know what to do."

"I know I'm not nearly the listener that she is, but I can try to be, if you want to talk about it," I offered.

Kaleb gave me a skeptical look, but he let out a long sigh and then word-vomited all over me. "I don't know what to do. I don't. I had planned to ask Fallon to marry me, can you believe that?" He gave a sardonic chuckle. "But then Sage died, and I put everything on pause. I just . . . I couldn't imagine committing my life to another and not having my sister—my best friend—there. When we learned she was alive and where she was, I felt hope again, so I started to think about asking Fallon to be my wife." He shook his head in disbelief and scoffed. "I'm an idiot. I thought what we had was strong, but clearly, I was wrong. She tossed what we had to the side so easily." He began to wipe at his watering eyes with his bruised hand, the knuckles split and bloody.

I didn't know what to say.

Kaleb and I were vastly different. And despite there being some similarities with this situation—our females fucking someone else—the elements at play were vastly different. Ryker wasn't Fallon's *purely trash* ex-husband. Kaleb hadn't robbed Fallon of her powers and tormented her for decades. Kaleb also hadn't hunted Fallon down in the forest, shadow chained her, and tricked her into forging the mating bond with him through a hate fuck. Kaleb hadn't forced Fallon to live with him in his castle, knowing the bond would keep her from running away. Kaleb hadn't—

Fuck, I was a bastard.

It was a wonder Sage had been able to forgive me after all of that. And yet, she had. The goddess was a saint.

I let out a sigh and rolled my neck, looking to Kaleb. "Do you want my thoughts or what I think Sage would say?"

Kaleb stopped and turned toward me. "What Sage would say."

Facing him, I put my hand on his shoulder, as I felt like that was something Sage would do. "Do you need me to go kick her ass?"

Kaleb barked out a laugh.

I cracked a grin.

"Yeah, she would say that. She'd be all too happy to go another round with Fallon," Kaleb said.

I was about to reply, but I heard sounds—voices coming from the north, which was the opposite direction of our camp. I looked at Kaleb, whose mortal ears probably hadn't detected them yet, and placed my finger against my lips.

What's wrong? he mouthed, his eyebrows weaving together.

I pointed over to a large rock, indicating we should hide behind it.

He nodded, and we crouch walked our way over to it, my shadows wrapping around us.

The voices became louder—two females.

Through the trees, I got a glimpse of them. They were strange-looking beings—gray skin, white markings, tall, and obscenely slender. It was as if their bodies had been stretched out, arms, legs, and necks elongated.

"Since Imari returned, she has become a menace. Acting like she's better than everyone else. There is no way we can get the new system up and running in two months' time," said the female whose hair was pulled tightly back, secured with a leather tie. She was the tallest of the two.

The other one replied, "We do not have a choice. It is an order that has come from the empress herself, so we must do all that we can to make sure we get it done."

"Wow, look who sounds like Imari now," the taller female huffed, her speed picking up.

The other one quickened her pace so she could catch up

with her. When she did, she said, "I'm sorry, I didn't mean for it to come across that way."

"It's alright. I'm just frustrated. The empress casts her shining eye on Imari. Imari, of all people! When was the last time she extracted a soul and didn't break it?" asked the taller female.

"Yes, it has been a while. Oh, speaking of, how are you making out with the mortal soul, the one with the vessel that's missing fingers?

Kaleb and I looked at each other.

"It's kind of a cutie, you know, for a human," the shorter female continued, her voice growing more distant the further they walked from us.

I gestured for Kaleb to follow behind me. He nodded. Quietly, we moved through the trees, staying hidden while keeping up with them.

"Right? I think it's cute too," the taller one said. "The vessel has been repaired, and the soul is nearly finished as well. I imagine I'll be done tonight so we can ship it off with the others."

"That should work. Can I ask you something?"

The taller one nodded. "Of course."

"Do you ever wonder why the empress has us rebuild male souls and vessels if they are just going to be sent to the arena to be crushed anyway? Why not just have *us* do it?"

Ponytail lowered her voice. "I heard this from a friend of a friend who works at the Celestial Opal Palace, but the empress likes to look through them. Although it's rare, sometimes she'll keep some of the male souls. That's how she built her harem."

"Wow, can you imagine being hand-selected by the empress?" the other one exclaimed as they walked up to the foot of the mountain.

"It must be an incredible feeling," the taller one said as she raised her hand, and a glowing, oblong slit emerged in the stone, opening it to the tunnel and the rushing river of souls. They walked through it, and it sealed shut behind them.

"We need to get back to camp," I said. "Now."

Chapter 34

Shadow

Everyone had a defining moment in their life, one they thought back on and knew that it had changed the entire trajectory of their path. As I peered down at the map laying on the table before me, contemplating where Avriel and I could go, I could only hope that this was my defining moment, one that would lead to a better life for us both.

But I was no stranger to the ways of the world and the many obstacles we would face once we were on the outside. Specifically, my lack of rights. I was a possession, something to own. No more than an acre of poor land, one to be bought and raped. I found it ironic that in the arena, spectators cheered me on, treated me like a god, but outside of it, the ichor coursing through my veins and the skill of my blade were long forgotten.

A champion in the arena but a slave outside of it.

Aryx used to tell me stories about his past life, about a

place called the Three Realms. He said that there, immortals known as Old Gods were treated equally, regardless of sex. However, the mortals who resided in the Living Realm lived differently. He drew parallels between the way women were treated there and the way men were treated here. He said that kings and lords were the ones who possessed female concubines.

Female concubines. I had scoffed at the thought.

I still couldn't imagine such a thing.

Aryx had also said that women, especially those born into poverty, would go missing and then their souls would turn up in the Da'Nu, something which he explained functioned the same as the Miyakai River here. I had asked him what caused their deaths—did they have arenas they sent women to? I still remember the way Aryx shook his head, sadness washing into his eyes as he told me women didn't die in an arena, no; it was in the privacy of their own homes, something the Living Realm turned a blind eye to.

Sometimes, when the nights grew long, I'd sit in the quiet of my room and think about that, a glass of spirits in my hand. I knew what it was like to die behind closed doors; I experienced it every time the empress called me to her room. I hated that the women in the Living Realm had to experience that too. Hated that things were so . . . out of balance.

I drew a heavy breath.

Lungs reaching their fill, I returned to looking over the map.

The Mother Realm was comprised of three

continents—Fiarnia, Eaylandrea, and Airenyl. I always thought Fiarnia and Eaylandrea looked faintly like dragons, fighting over the meat in the middle—Airenyl.

Fiarnia was a brutal land, comprised of steep, treacherous mountains, barren wastelands, and scorching-hot deserts. Eaylandrea, where the majority of the population lived, was the opposite, with its fertile, rich soil, bountiful forests, and gentle snow-capped mountains. Both continents had a small hint of one another within them, like yin and yang. Airenyl was a mix of the two.

I eyed the floating island of Avolonia, the empress's imposing palace sitting on top. This had been the only so-called home I had ever known.

I held no love for it. No loyalty either. And if it weren't for my brothers, Avriel, and the other innocent people forced to live in this creator-forsaken place, I would have lit it aflame a long, long time ago. Just to watch it burn to ash.

"Do you know how you got your name?" the empress's voice echoed in my ear, her arms wrapping around my shoulders.

I didn't respond to her apparition, knowing that it was my mind conjuring her.

"Not much for words today, hmm?" she purred, voice soft. "That's alright, I'll tell you anyway . . . It's because when you were just a boy, you would always try to stick to my side. Just like a little shadow." Her translucent fingers slid up my neck, floating across my mask. "Do you want to hear another story?"

I continued to ignore her.

If there was one thing I knew, it was that if Avriel and I managed to escape, the empress would never stop looking for us. Which meant we needed to disappear entirely. Just like the white-haired female had—the one the empress was trying to find.

Better yet, the one the empress *hadn't* been able to find.

I looked at the Moriel Forest, a curious brow raising.

"Oh, come on now," the empress said, her imaginary fingers pulling on my face.

I jerked my head to the side, away from her.

The door was nearly soundless as it opened swiftly, soft footsteps ushered inside, and then the door closed shut. I looked up, and my heart quickened at the sight of her. Avriel. She offered me a small smile, and the empress's phantom instantly disappeared.

"Well, did you come up with a plan?" she asked, rushing to my side to look over the map. Her scent hit me, and I couldn't help but take a step closer to her, desperate to breathe her in.

"I have ideas, but none I'm extremely fond of," I replied. "I was thinking about the white-haired female—"

"Sage," she cut me off gently. "Her name is Sage."

"Alright, I was thinking about *Sage* and the vuleeries, particularly the Moriel Forest. Perhaps that is where we should go," I said, my attention drifting back to the map.

"The vuleeries would tear the meat from our bones if we tried to enter their forest," she countered. "Unlike Sage, we're not Nockrythiam's mate. They have no reason to help us."

"But you helped Sage," I said. "That has to be worth something."

She was quiet for a moment, thinking it over. "I don't think it's worth the risk. Plus, the empress already has guards watching the forest, looking for any sign of Sage." A brief pause. "What about the Northern Mountains? They are more secluded, and fewer people live there, so we wouldn't have to worry about someone recognizing us as much," she said, then giggled. "I'm sure we could find a cave to call home."

I smirked at that. I'd happily live in a cave with her, if that's what it took for us to be together.

She let out a breath. "I've never seen them before."

"The mountains?" I asked, unable to pull my gaze from her.

"Mhm. I've heard they are beautiful. That the snow sparkles like diamonds when the light hits them. I've never seen the sea either, but my mother used to talk about it with such fondness. She grew up by it. Right"—she tapped a spot on the map—"here. In a small village called Okanoe." A tendril of hair slipped beside her face.

Instinctively, I swept it back, tucking it behind her ear. "Then I will take you to both places," I promised her.

She looked up at me, eyes wide with those unspoken feelings, the ones she had kept buried for years. "You would do that for me?"

"I would do anything for you." My hand moved to her cheek, caressing it. Her skin was so soft. So warm. Everything I had dreamt it would be.

Her hand rested over mine as she whispered, "Will you take your mask off? So that I can see the real you?"

"You will not like what you see," I warned.

"I doubt that."

I paused in a brief moment of hesitation.

"Please," she whispered.

My fingers slid from hers as I reached behind my head and unfastened the clasp. I removed the mask and waited for her to gasp in shock, waited for her to step back.

But she did nothing of the sort. Instead, she raised her delicate fingers beside my face, and asked, "May I?"

I nodded.

When her fingers met my cheek, I sucked in a breath. I had imagined this moment thousands of times before, but I had no idea her touch would feel like . . . *this*. Tender. Loving. It was a feeling I would never get enough of.

"Did *she* do this?" Avriel asked, her fingers tracing one of the scars.

"Yes." I leaned into her touch, desperate for her never to stop.

"The night she sent you to be with that other woman," she said, tears filling her eyes.

When one spilled over her lash line and dribbled down her cheek, I swept it away with my thumb. "No. I do not want you to cry over something that happened centuries ago."

"Then what would you have me do?" she asked, her voice shaky.

I lowered my hand, cupping her cheek. "I would prefer

to see you smile."

She mustered a small one, just for me, and like the morning sun, it scattered the darkness of my life and made all the pain and suffering worth it.

Avriel was *the reason* I endured.

"Can I kiss you?" I brushed my thumb over her heart-shaped mouth.

She nodded, her eyes hooked on mine.

I lowered my face to hers and then I did the very thing I had been longing to do for centuries . . .

I kissed her.

I pulled her into me as her arms enveloped my neck, her fingers weaving into my hair. Her lips were soft and plush, everything I had dreamed they would be. Everything and more. The smile she wore transferred to my mouth, her breathy laughter mingling with mine. My hands roved up and down her sides, feeling the wealth of her body.

In that moment, I knew—

I was the richest immortal alive, all because I had her.

Chapter 35

Von

Rushing back to the group, we found an unexpected but welcome surprise—Harper was awake. She was sitting near the fire, Lyra and Ryker flanking her sides as she sipped from a wood bowl containing water. Relief unburdened my shoulders, and they fell ever so slightly. Fallon and Folkoln were over by themselves, out of earshot, privately conversing. Her attention swiftly swung to Kaleb, but he did not meet her gaze.

"You're awake," I said, walking up to Harper.

"I am," she replied, voice raspy. Tired. She nearly dropped the bowl when she saw my arm. "Oh, my gods! Are you okay?"

"I'm fine. It's growing back," I reassured her, unintentionally shifting it forward for her to see. The movement only made it throb worse.

"How are you feeling?" Kaleb asked as he knelt beside

her.

"Like a giant ate me," she said with a disbelieving chuckle.

Lyra nodded in understanding. I think we all did.

"We have something we need to discuss," I said, turning to Folkoln and Fallon. I jerked my head, motioning for them to come over.

Folkoln helped Fallon up and they joined us.

Fallon looked miserable. Her black lashes lifted as she searched Kaleb's face, her expression pleading, like she was trying to get him to look at her.

Kaleb gave her nothing.

"What's going on?" Folkoln asked us, the white flames reflecting off his dark eyes. He crossed his arms, threading them loosely, as he waited for an answer.

Taking the bull by the horns, Kaleb stood up and said, "We saw two strange, gray-skinned females. Unlike any species I've ever seen before. They had these white markings inked into their skin, eyes completely black."

I added, "They were talking about a human soul. Said the vessel is missing fingers. Sound familiar?"

"Soren," Ryker grated between clenched teeth. His posture became visibly rigid.

"Yeah." Kaleb nodded, putting his issues with Ryker to the side so we could focus on what mattered right now. I had to admit, it made me respect him even more.

"Did you follow them?" Folkoln asked, small bits of smoke breaking off from his skin, much like my shadows did with mine.

"We did," I confirmed. "But they opened a passage in the wall of the mountain. Through it, I could see the tunnel and the river of souls. It closed immediately after they walked through it so we couldn't follow them any further."

Folkoln looked in the direction we had just come from, then to the hole all of us had walked out of earlier today. "They must be further down the river then."

I nodded in agreement, my hand propping up my throbbing arm. "The one female said she would be finished working on the soul tonight, just in time to ship it off with the others. Which means we need to move swiftly."

"Alright, let's go," Folkoln said, taking a step forward.

I shook my head. "No, I need you to stay here with the others."

"We'll all go," Harper suggested.

I gave her a soft half-smile. "Although I appreciate the offer, Harper, you are just recovering. Fallon can barely walk. Time is of the essence right now. It will be better for you all to stay here."

Ryker stood up. "You and I can go. I know I'm not as skilled of a fighter as Folkoln, but I can hold my own, and you know it." His eyes darted to my nub. "Plus, if you get into any trouble, you might need some help."

I debated for a brief moment, then said, "Alright. Let's go."

"Wait," Folkoln said as he turned his palm skyward. Smoke drifted from his fingers, thinning into tiny threads. They began to weave together until a thin cloth was formed. He wrapped it around my arm and tied it into place behind my neck, taking some of the weight off my nub.

It was all so very . . . *brotherly* of him. I quirked a brow, wondering where this act of selflessness had come from.

Then, because Folkoln was Folkoln, he smacked the side of my half-eaten arm, like the bastard he was. Pain exploded, and I winced.

He smirked in that asshole way of his, like he had a secret he didn't plan to share, then jabbed, "Don't take long . . . you know I can't stand babysitting."

"Fuck you," Harper hissed. Lyra squinted at him.

I could hear Zahra chuckling all the way back in the Three Realms.

Ryker and I moved at a swift pace, keeping up with the rushing waters. The tunnel seemed to stretch on and on, but we kept going, knowing what would happen if we didn't reach Soren in time. The constant roar of the river washed out the sounds of our feet, well, more so Ryker's than mine, since mine were nearly silent—one of many skills I'd honed over my lifetime.

The iridescent light from the stalactites began to change, becoming much brighter—almost blinding, as if they had harnessed the power of the sun and were using it to shine.

Up ahead, the tunnel forked. To the left, the river kept, but to the right, it swerved, growing in size. At the end of it, there was a cavernous room.

"We need to get closer," I whispered to Ryker.

"Agreed." He gave a firm nod.

We kept to the shadows as we approached, looking for any signs of life. If the gray-skinned creatures had been here before, they weren't now.

Cautiously, we continued to advance.

Neatly hung around the walls were a variety of strange instruments—ones I had never seen the likes of before. Some were cylindrical glass devices attached to clear hoses or sharp, strangely hollowed needles. Others had multiple legs, like a metal spider, with clasps on the ends—used for plucking something, perhaps? There were so many of them. In the middle of the room, where the light was even brighter, there were rows of altars that looked to have been chiseled from the mountain itself. On some of them, there were bodies, lifeless and still.

I walked by one, peering down at it.

A female, her long, brown hair strewn about, her eyes closed. She looked peaceful, much like the dead back in the Spirit Realm when they floated along the Da'Nu. Hovering above her chest were hundreds of glass pieces, some so small they would not be visible to the mortal eye. My mind began to draw lines from one piece to another, mapping them out. This way and that. The image continued to play out, of what would happen if I combined all of the pieces. The shards would be made into an orb—

"A soul," I whispered to myself, somewhat mesmerized.

I had seen and collected hundreds of thousands of souls

before, but they had never been shattered apart like this one; they were always whole. Fascinating. Although part of me itched to move the pieces, to complete the puzzle, that was not why I was here.

Returning to the task at hand, I continued to pass by the tables, looking for Soren's ugly mug.

"He's not here," Ryker stated after we'd searched the bodies.

"No," I growled under my breath, clenching my jaw. A muscle ticked inside of it as if it were trying to squirm away. The beast within me roared in frustration, begging me to grab one of the altars and send it careening into the wall. Knowing that wasn't going to help, I kept my composure and began to walk around the room, looking for anything that might help us.

A faint whisper of clicking heels sounded, echoing in our direction.

There was no time to move anywhere else, so Ryker and I ducked behind the altars we stood beside.

One of the gray-skinned females that we had seen before, the taller one with the pulled back hair, appeared. She hummed softly as she walked through the rows. A glowing magic swirled behind her, grabbing hold of a stool and plucking it from the ground. As she continued forward, the stool followed. She stopped at the end of an altar—a man rested on top of it.

She placed her clawed fingers on his face, gently turning it from side to side. "Pretty good work, if I say so myself. Now, let's see about that soul of yours," she said.

Her magic dropped the stool at the foot of the altar, and she sat down on it. She waved her hand over the stone, and a rectangular black slate appeared. She began to study it, humming softly to herself.

As Ryker was closer, and he had two good arms, I flicked my head toward her.

He nodded. Without a moment's hesitation, he leapt from his spot and grabbed her, pinning her arms to her sides. He shoved her face forward, right between the man's two feet.

"How dare you touch me!" she snarled, blue magic shooting out behind her, reaching for the serrated knife a few altars down. Grabbing hold of it, she flung it toward Ryker.

Just before it plunged into his back, I caught it.

I placed the blade against her throat and said in warning, "I wouldn't try that again."

She ceased her struggle, turning bone stiff. That told me a great deal. Either she was afraid of pain, or she was afraid to die by the knife. If it was the latter, it meant she was not immortal, which could mean the rest of her kind wasn't either. I archived that information.

I lowered my face to hers. "There was a human here, missing three fingers. Where has he been sent to?"

Her empty black eyes shifted to a wall before they swiftly flicked back to mine, narrowing. "How should I know? We get plenty of vessels that are missing things—fingers, eyes, heads." Her gaze flicked to my sling. "Arms."

I glanced at the wall. "What lies beyond it?"

"I don't know what you're talking about," she hissed.

"Oh, I think you do." I pressed the blade further against her throat. "Now, I will only ask one more time. What lies beyond the wall?"

Her voice was barely more than a whisper. "It is where we store the bodies until they are taken."

"Show us," I demanded.

Reluctantly, she did. She used the same magic she had used before, parting the wall and enabling the three of us to step inside.

The room was lit with a dim glow, the air different. In here, there was a steady, lively hum—as if it flowed with life. There were carts, stockpiled with bodies. I peered at the one's face, and although it didn't move, I could *feel* it looking back at me.

All of these souls were conscious, but still they were unable to move. It was like there was a disconnect between soul and vessel.

"Which one is he in?" I asked her.

"That one." She nodded to the one at the end, her movement limited due to the blade I held at her throat. We walked over to it, my eyes darting from face to face, searching.

Finally, I spotted the little fucker, stacked on top of the others.

Ryker climbed up the cart and dragged Soren to the side. Lifting him over the wood wall, he brought him down then placed him on the ground.

I peered into his eyes. Inside, I could see a circular,

repetitive movement, like a mindless rodent running on a wheel. Over and over again. But there was no feeling there. Only numbness.

"Why is he like this?" I inquired.

"Because there is a veil over top of him, which does not allow him to connect with the world, and therefore he cannot connect with himself," she answered.

"Remove it."

"I need to bend down to do so," she grated at me.

"Don't get any ideas," I warned, pulling the blade from her throat.

She knelt beside Soren, her hand moving to the middle of his chest. With a plucking motion, she pinched at nothing, but when she pulled her hand away, a sheer bit of fabric emerged from his skin. She discarded it to the side, and it dissolved on the ground.

Soren came sputtering to life.

I grinned down at him. "Hello, Soren."

Chapter 36

Sage

The air was different that morning.

It wasn't cold and bitter and full of spite, as winter could so often be. It was warm and peaceful, with a hint of something in the light, breezy wind—something fresh and full of promise. Like the earth was stretching her arms after taking an exceptionally long nap. I *knew* that scent. It made no difference that I was in a different realm, it smelled the same as it did back home—

"Spring," I whispered, breathing it in, savoring it. Although the ground was blanketed in a good layer of snow, I could sense the life waiting to sprout below.

"Smells good, doesn't it?" Artemesia exclaimed as we walked alongside the frozen river. She had a fishing rod in one hand, and our lunch, packed in a basket, in the other. An ax was tucked underneath her leather belt, a sword on the other side.

I carried a fishing rod and a wooden tackle box—full of different types of fishing supplies. "It really does," I hummed in reply.

Artemesia eyed a spot by the river, a few large rocks—perfect for sitting on—resting there. "I caught rainbow trout like crazy over there last week." She nodded to the spot. "Should we give it a try?"

"Might as well," I answered, starting toward it.

A short while later, after we'd taken turns using her ax to carve out a sizable hole in the ice, we were perched on the rocks, and our hooks were in the water.

"It's a bit surreal," Artemesia started. "Sitting here with you, fishing. Just like we always used to do. It's nice."

I smiled. "It *is* nice. The only thing missing is Father."

"He would have loved to be here with us."

I nodded. "He would have."

Eyes shifting to the sky, I watched as the cottony-white clouds drifted lazily by. They moved slowly, as if they had all the time in the world to get where they were going—wherever that was. It made me wonder . . .

I finished the question out loud, "In the Three Realms, when mortals die, they end up in Von's Spirit Realm. When mortals die here, what becomes of them?"

"It depends on who you ask. Some believe that mortal souls go to Elysium, a place full of golden, swaying crops and azure skies as far as the eye can see. Others believe that when a mortal soul dies, that is simply the end, nothing comes beyond it. I suppose that belief would align with what we believe happens to immortal souls—that when their souls are crushed, it is truly the end." She paused for a moment, jigging her rod. "When immortal souls die in other realms, they return here, just as you did. I suppose for immortals, the Mother Realm is their Elysium. Or at least, that's how it should have been."

I glanced down, the space between my brows crinkling—

When immortal souls die in other realms, they return here, just as you did.

I gasped, nearly dropping my rod. My face swung toward hers. "Wait, our child would have been immortal. Does that mean their soul would have returned here as well?"

Artemesia shook her head slowly. Sadly. "You were too early in your pregnancy for them to receive their soul."

"But I *felt* them." My fingers splayed over my stomach.

"What do you mean?"

"On our wedding day, when I found out I was pregnant, I had intended to keep it a secret from Von until I could tell him later that night, but he showed up without warning. The babe knew of my wishes, so they helped me by using their magic to hide the sprouted Neptuah seeds before Von had a chance to see them."

Artemesia looked stunned. She opened her mouth to say something, but no sound came out. She closed it. Opening it for a second time, she tried again, "Then, yes, your child could very well be . . ."

"*Here*," I finished for her. *For me*.

I could hardly believe it. There was a chance our child's soul *could* be in this realm.

A chance!

The shackles of grief fell from my limbs. One by one, the invisible anchors struck the ground. For so long I'd felt heavy, drowning in the ocean of loss. But now, I felt featherlight, as if I could drift up to the sky. Because now there was possibility. There was *hope*. And it was a powerful thing.

Tears misted my eyes. Overwhelmed with joy, I let out a laugh. And then another, and another, until I was a mess of happy laughter and guttural sobs.

"Oh, honey," Artemesia said gently. Emotion twisted her face, spilling over her lower lash line. She leaned over, embracing me in a hug. I wrapped one arm around her. Dropping my fishing rod, I added another.

"They could be here," I whispered, my chin tucked on her shoulder. Hers on mine.

If only Von was here, if only I could tell—

Sage! a familiar voice yelled inside my head.

I jerked back from Artemesia.

I *knew* that voice. Just as well as I knew the sound of four tiny feet scampering across my mind. It was a sound I'd never expected to be thankful to hear, but at that moment, I was.

"What is it?" Artemesia asked, her platinum eyebrows weaving in concern.

But I didn't get a chance to answer, because a shadow mouse appeared at the forefront of my mind. It twisted and turned, growing and growing until . . .

Soren? I asked, somewhat in disbelief, as his darkened

silhouette emerged in my thoughts.

Sadness and regret swam within his eyes as he said, *I know I'm probably the last face you want to see, but still, it's good to see yours.*

How is this possible? I asked, grappling to believe. Real or not real?

We're all here, in the Mother Realm, he answered.

Von? I inquired softly, voice wobbling. My chest throbbed.

Yes. Kaleb, Harper, Ryker, Lyra, Folkoln, and Fallon too. Where are you? Soren asked. *We'll come to you.*

They were all *here*? My mate? My brother? My friends? *I'm . . .*

I trailed off.

What if this was a trap? What if it wasn't really Soren? The empress had seen my thoughts . . . what if she was using this as a way to find me?

Swiftly, the clouds in my eyes cleared.

Soren took a step toward me as he said, *It's really us.*

Artemesia's voice pulled me back into the present. "Sage? You're scaring me." Her hands were on my shoulders, her eyes rounded at the corners. "What's going on?"

"Von and my friends . . . they *might* be here," I told her, hope brimming inside, hope that I didn't want to let grow, because I would be devastated if it were all a lie.

We are, Soren's voice was soft. *By the way, Von is getting really impatient.*

"Did you have a vision or something? How do you

know?" Artemesia questioned.

My lips vibrated as I blew out a breath of air. I wasn't exactly sure how to explain this one, but hey, my sister rode a half eagle, half lion, so I was sure she wouldn't blink twice at a shadow mouse living inside my brain.

"Back home, there was someone by the name of Soren. We were friends . . . once, until he forced himself into my mind, without my consent, and then used it against me in order to save himself." Even though I spoke the words to Artemesia, I watched Soren, noting how his head dipped as I voiced his transgressions against me. "Right now, he stands on the forefront of my mind, telling me that he and my other friends are here in the Mother Realm."

"That is terrible for a friend to do that. Such a person is not to be trusted," Artemesia spoke with disdain. She raised a brow. "Does this mean he is privy to your thoughts? Memories? Things you've seen?"

"Yes. He has access to everything," I said, the growl in my voice lost when I realized—

I won't tell anyone about Veshameer, Soren vowed as he took a step toward me. *I promise.*

Just hearing him speak the Hidden City's name made me clench my fists. His promise was meaningless. His actions had proven that he was not one to be trusted. And so, I would not give that to him now. Not until he showed me otherwise.

I will, Sage. I'll earn back your trust. I'll—

Ignoring him, I looked at Artemesia. "I know this could be a trap, but if there is a chance Von and my friends are here,

I need to go."

"You are my sister. I'm not letting you go alone." Her voice was firm. "Ask this *Soren*," she hissed his name, "where they are, and *we* will go to them."

"Alright." Turning inward, I looked at Soren.

His reply came swiftly. *We are moving further into the forest, east of the Verita Mountains. The others had a camp set up, but Von and Folkoln don't want to stay there because they think the gray-skinned creatures will come after us. Considering Von left one of them tied up, when they find her, I imagine they will.*

"The Verita Mountains," I said to Artemesia. "Do you know where that is?"

She nodded. "I do, yes. The Miyakai River runs through them. I'll get Vatara, and we can leave within the hour."

A small seed of hope sprung inside.

Von . . . Is it really you? I asked across the broken bridge that linked us, and although I could not hear his reply, I *felt* it—

A small gust of wind brushed over my cheek, caressing it with a loving touch.

"Before we leave, I want you to tie this over my eyes," I said to Artemesia, holding up a bit of cloth, the edges frayed and torn. I'd ripped it from the fabric of my pillowcase a short fifteen minutes ago as I'd quickly packed a bag for myself.

"Why?" Artemesia asked as she stroked Vatara's head, the two waiting for me outside of Artemesia's tent.

"I don't trust Soren. I won't risk showing him how to get here," I said, handing it to her. "Which means I can't know the way either."

Her fingers curled around the cloth as she answered, "Alright."

She whistled, and Vatara lowered so we could mount.

I sat in front of Artemesia, feeling the immense warmth radiating from Vatara. I patted her neck while Artemesia tied the sash in place. My vision went dark.

"Can you see anything?" she asked, a bit of air moving in front of my face. I imagined she was waving her hand back and forth.

"No," I replied. "Nothing."

"Alright, we're off then," she said, clicking her tongue.

Vatara whistled a melodic note, and then she leapt from the ground, taking us to the sky.

I had experienced seasickness before when riding on boats, but it was nothing compared to the way my stomach revolted now. Apparently, flying through the air at high speeds with a sash covering my eyes was not the best idea I'd ever had. We'd had to stop six times so that my rumbling stomach could find relief. The one time, we hadn't been fast enough, and poor Vatara's side had borne the worst of it.

"How are you doing?" Artemesia asked, one hand rubbing my back, the other on the reins.

"Feeling like we're never going to make it at this rate," I spoke groggily.

"You can take the sash off," Artemesia said. "There are *other* ways we can ensure this *Soren* does not speak of Veshameer."

"It's alright," I said, forcing a deep breath of air into my lungs. Even though my world was a pit of black, I closed my eyes. I recalled that strange feeling, of how it had felt to be disconnected from my body, unable to feel my arms or legs, unable to move. There was no sensation. Only nothingness. I focused on it, told myself it was what I was feeling now.

Keep going, spoke the ethereal female voices inside my head, effervescent and sparkling, like a cup of bubbling wine. I had heard those voices before, when I was rejected by the Endless Mist.

You once asked me who I was, I said to them. *When I said I was Sage, you did not accept that answer. Why?*

Because your answer was incorrect, they said.

And if I reply that I am the Goddess of Life, is that correct? I asked.

You are getting closer, but there is still so much you don't know. Turn inward, and you will find the answer.

A hallway of doors appeared inside my mind, stretching on and on. I reached for the one closest to me, opened it up, and stepped through it.

Chapter 37

Sage

If I were to ask the people of this realm one place that they would like to see with their own eyes, I would have been given one common answer—the Crest of Salvation, the emperor's legendary arena. No mortal had ever been allowed inside before. The grounds were considered sacred, a place where only immortal ichor could be shed.

And yet, here I was, a mortal, seeing it now.

I stood on the private balcony, my hands settled on the stone railing as I took in the incredible arena. The Crest of Salvation was positioned between the peaks of two mountains, the sides carved to look like an eagle's wings piercing the sky. In them, were thousands of rows of seats, filled with gods and goddesses—all dressed in the finest of robes.

The empress sat behind me, in her throne forged of opal stone. Beside it was another, the seat empty.

"You should sit down, child. Your eagerness makes you look like you do not belong here," she said softly, the words delivered like a suggestion, but underneath the allure of them, I heard the command.

I turned to face her, opening my mouth to reply that I didn't belong here, but then an immortal stepped through the open doorway. Streaks of gray ran through his brown hair, tucked back by a laurel crown. The leaves and branches were forged from a polished silver metal. That same silver color wrapped around his body, making him glow. And even though there was no breeze today, the hem of his chiton flowed.

When he saw me, his eyes flared wide, his lips parting in surprise. Swiftly, he swept the look away.

Thinking little of it, I dropped to one knee and bowed my head, for I was in the presence of greatness—the emperor, the creator of all.

"Why is a mortal here?" Emperor Alaric inquired, but his voice was not cold.

"Because I wish for her to be," the empress answered, not a hint of warmth to be found.

Sandals appeared in my line of sight, along with a flowing hem. I could feel the immense power radiating before me, like standing in front of an open fire. "Rise, Sagentia, daughter of Luna," said the emperor.

I did as I was told. "How do you know my name?"

"I remember every soul's name," he answered, a flicker of an unknown emotion flashing across his face. Gone faster than it appeared.

My eyebrows raised at that, for I could not imagine how

vast his knowledge must be.

I felt a sharp prick against my forehead, like the tip of a dagger was being pressed against it. My gaze shifted to the empress, finding her fierce, glowing eyes glaring at me. Her fingernails dug into the arms of her throne. Teeth clenched like a bear trap, she grated, "The games are about to start."

"I suppose we best sit down then," the emperor said, giving me a wink.

I didn't know if it was because I was standing in the presence of greatness or if it was something else, but I felt my heart warm at the gesture.

"A grand idea," the empress replied sarcastically as we sat down—the emperor in his throne, and me on the other side of the empress.

A short while later, the games began. The first one was to test speed. The immortals moved so fast that they looked like blurs, racing around the tracks until a horn blared. When the victor raised her hands, the crowd's roar was so loud it shook the heavens. Our attention shifted to the left of the racetrack, where the archers prepared for the next game.

"Would you like to make a wager, my love?" the emperor asked, his hand reaching across the space between their thrones.

"No," she said as she pulled her hand from the arm of the throne and placed it in her lap, something I caught just out of the corner of my eye.

Her actions confused me.

I, a mere mortal, had barely spoken to the emperor and she had hurtled daggers in my direction. I was no stranger to the stories surrounding the empress's jealous nature. Most of which were filled with terrible accounts of what she had done to anyone who dared to look at the emperor too long. However, he had just tried to be tender with her, and she had pulled back. That begged the question—why?

Five bullseye targets sat beside one another, each one at the end of a lane. The first archer stepped up, nocking their bow with not one, but five arrows. Releasing the string, the arrows shot forward like bolts of lightning bursting from the clouds. They whistled, slicing through the sound barrier.

Thunk. Thunk. Thunk. Thunk. Thunk.

All five hit the bullseye mark.

Again, the spectators cheered. I found myself doing the same.

Clapping, I spared a quick glance at the emperor and the empress, seeing if they shared the same excitement as the rest of us. The empress looked bored, but the emperor's eyes were on . . . me. Upon our gazes connecting, he quickly looked back to the arena.

I did too—not wanting to risk the empress's wrath.

After the archers finished, there was a series of other games that tested strength, agility, and endurance. When they were over, our attention turned to the middle of the arena, to an oval space covered in sand. Four giants stood on the one side of the arena. On the opposite end was a square hole in the ground.

The sound of stone sliding against stone became audible. It grew louder and louder until a carving of an eagle head emerged from the hole. It was huge, larger than four

Clydesdale horses stacked in pairs. I had never seen such a grand display before, and I did a quick mental check to ensure my jaw wasn't slung open.

Silence spread from tongue to tongue, and the spectators grew quiet. All eyes were locked on the larger-than-life carving. The beak opened and shadows began to pour out from it, cloaking the ground in a blanket of black. so thick not even the powerful sun could penetrate it.

Horns blared and drums rumbled, swelling and building—the message loud and clear—

Something big was going to happen. No, not something—

Someone.

A dark god. Cut from the fabric of night itself and painstakingly stitched together.

The crowd erupted—their cheering so loud that the ground beneath my feet shook with the power of an earthquake. The energy was so potent, the hairs on the backs of my arms stood.

There was something about the way the immortal moved, confident and purposeful, a lethal predator on the prowl. A black cape swayed behind him, breaking off into bits of umbra. His helmet covered his face, his armor crafted from the blackest of blacks. On his one shoulder, a skull, dipped in silver, and on the other, vicious spikes. Every inch of him screamed one message—built to kill.

I was no different from anyone else—we all had heard the stories of the emperor's champion. Second to the emperor, there was no name spoken with more reverence than that of—

"Nockrythiam," I said under my breath.

"Is he to your liking?" the empress inquired, her eyes studying mine, searching for answers deeper than the question she had just asked. A truth I could feel deeply.

"It is hard to say when I cannot see his face," I answered. "Besides, would it matter if I was unattracted to him? It is not like I have a say in any of this."

"No, I suppose you don't. However, I can promise that when you do get to see his face, you will be pleasantly surprised, for my husband has never worked on perfecting a vessel as long as he did for his. He spent weeks collecting this item and that, even longer when it came to forging him on his mighty anvil." She paused for a moment. "Do you know what they call him?"

"Yes, I've heard the title they attach to his name. The Ender of Realms. To be honest, it makes no sense to me."

"It makes no sense to anyone." She glanced at the emperor. "Isn't that right, dear husband?" There was nothing endearing about the way she said the word, twisting it grotesquely on her tongue.

"You are correct," the emperor said, eyes fixed ahead.

I followed his gaze, looking at Nockrythiam. How could he be the Ender of Realms when there was only one realm? I spared a quick glance at the emperor, wondering if he knew.

Another horn blew, and the battle began.

I watched in awe as Nockrythiam moved. Despite being pitted against four other men, he made it all look so simple to cut them down. No sooner than the fight started, it was over, and Nockrythiam stood victorious.

After Nockrythiam left the battlegrounds, the fallen warriors were cleared and another fight began.

"Wine, Your Majesties?" asked a female voice from behind me.

I turned toward her. She was beautiful, just as all the immortals were. She held a wine jug in one hand, a circular tray with four goblets balanced on the other.

"Why not," the empress said, plucking two goblets from the tray. She handed one to the emperor. "Here, love." The endearing word sounded dead on her tongue. How the emperor didn't notice was a curiosity to me.

"Thank you," he said, taking it.

The empress grabbed a third and handed it to me. "You might as well have one too. The games are far from over."

I nodded and took the goblet. The sweet, smooth liquid bloomed on my tongue, and I realized I was tasting the nectar of the gods. It was divine, and before I knew it, I had downed one glass and accepted another.

Boots struck the floor behind us, and I turned to see who it was.

There was no mistaking that sleek, black armor or the mighty, dark god behind it—Nockrythiam.

"Your Majesties," he said, but he did not bow. He didn't need to.

He removed his helmet, and dark, endlessly black eyes met mine. His hair was cut short on the sides but left longer on the top. The tousled raven strands were tossed carelessly back, one piece falling over his forehead. His face was angelic, although his sinfully shaped mouth suggested he was nothing of the sort. He was the epitome of devastation. The kind of immortal who sunk his fangs into you, spread his venom into your system, and then left you for dead.

I knew because that's exactly what he had done to me.

"You!" I exclaimed, jumping up from my seat, charging at him.

Before I knew what I was doing, I tossed my wine at him. Red splashed across his tanned skin. It dribbled down his face, dripping off his strong, sharp nose and steel-cutting jawline, down onto his armor.

I stood there, my lungs heaving, my world feeling as if it were caving in on itself. I could feel the emperor and the empress's eyes very much on us while Nockrythiam's remained locked on me.

"I deserve that," Nockrythiam rumbled in his deep timbre. His tongue brushed over his bottom lip. He pulled it in, sucking off the wine. "Despite the wine to the face, it is good to see you again, Little Mortal."

My mouth fell open, and I grabbed the fourth goblet from the tray, tossing that in his face for good measure. "Don't you dare call me that, you bastard!" I snarled as I stormed through the doorway and out into the hallway, my fists clenched. My teeth felt as if they might combust under the iron clench of my jaw.

Unbelievable. This was unbelievable.

Had the empress known? Was that why she'd set this up? For him?

I hissed at the thought.

"Sage, wait," Nockrythiam called out from behind me.

He grabbed hold of my arm and spun me to face him. "Please."

"You told me your name was Von!" I hissed.

"Technically, it is. Nockrythiam is the name the emperor gave to me upon my creation. Von is the name I have chosen for myself."

"You told me you would come back for me."

His voice was like granite. "I had planned to."

I scoffed. "But you didn't." I tore my arm from his grasp. "Do you have any idea how long I waited for you? How broken I was when I realized that you were not coming?" My voice shook, my words chopped apart from my emotions, as violent as the ocean tide in a storm.

"I'm sorry, for all of it," he said, his hand reaching for my face.

"No." I shoved his arm away and pulled back. "You lost the privilege to touch me."

And then I turned and walked away from the male I had been a fool to entrust with my heart. Tears brimming, I wiped at them as I turned the corner, walking right into the empress.

"Explain everything," she snarled at me. "Now."

Chapter 38

Von

Through the swaying canopy of leaves, I would catch glimpses of the crescent-shaped moon. It didn't matter what realm I was in, all moons reminded me of Sage and the day I'd first felt her presence call out to me. And like a ghostly vessel lost at sea, finding land for the first time in centuries, I'd gone to her. That day stood at the summit of my memories, above all the rest, because it was the day I first saw her. She had stood behind Aurelius, peering over his shoulder with eyes full of fear. I couldn't blame her for her reaction to me—it was as strong as my reaction was to her.

But in place of fear, all I felt was need.

Need to carve myself into her bones, to ink my markings into her skin, to hear my name on her lips. I needed to consume her just as she had consumed me.

And most importantly, I needed to lay a claim—*mine*.

At the time, I had no idea why that feeling had been so

strong, but as the years passed by, the cosmos revealed the truth—

She was my bonded. My mate.

We were two halves of the same star. Destined for each other, long before the Creator plucked us from the sky and broke us apart. Ever since then, we had been clawing at the fabric of fate, desperately trying to be together but always brutally torn apart.

There was *nothing* I wouldn't do to be reunited with her.

I sat on the forest floor, leaning against a tree. One of my knees was bent, my healed arm draped over top of it. Tattoos reborn. Silver rings in place. Good as new. I closed my eyes and tilted my head back, resting it against the trunk.

My thoughts were adrift, lost in the ocean of her.

Soren had contacted Sage three days ago. Three. Long. Fucking. Days. Ago.

She said she would come to us, giving us a location to travel to. And so, for the past three days, we had worked our way here, to the lake full of purple shimmering waters. How she knew of its whereabouts, I didn't know, but I suspected she had someone helping her.

I didn't know if it would take Sage days or weeks to get to us. I didn't know how she was traveling or who she was traveling with. I didn't know *anything*.

Sage had refused to hand out any information regarding her whereabouts. And although not knowing where she was aggravated me, considering Soren's involvement, I understood why. She didn't trust him.

A smile twisted my lips. *Clever, infuriating goddess.*

Wings flapped, followed by the scrape of claws against the ground.

"No sign of her yet," Kaleb said as he landed beside me.

I opened my eyes, peering down at his raven form. "Thanks for checking."

He nodded. "I'll go do another round."

"Alright," I answered.

His wings flared out beside him, and he flew through the trees, out over the top of the lake, and then shot up toward the sky, his caw piercing the night. Fallon, who was seated with the others around a fire Ryker controlled, looked over her shoulder, peering in the direction Kaleb had gone. She sat like that for a while, her proud shoulders caving in. When she turned back around, she drew her legs to her chest, wrapped her arms around them, and lowered her chin to her knees. The reflection of Ryker's fire danced in her weary, sad eyes.

Ryker, who was seated directly across from her, noticed her reaction. And for a brief second, he looked as if he were going to get up and go to her, but Harper gently placed her hand on his arm and shook her head. Fallon had asked Ryker to give her space to sort things out, and so he was trying to be respectful of that, but I could tell how hard it was on him.

How hard all of this was on all of them.

Especially Kaleb.

Folkoln stood and started toward me, a spit with a fire-roasted fish in one hand and a half-eaten fish in the other.

Apart from the fact that I was a miserable, grumpy fucker, *what* they were eating was part of the reason why I was sitting by myself—it didn't matter if fish were cooked or uncooked, I couldn't stand it.

So naturally, my shit brother waved the spit in front of my face.

I curled my upper lip and let out a low growl.

"Oh, come on now, princess, try a bite," he said, trying to torment me further.

"This—" I grabbed the stick. "Is low, even for you, you emotion-sucking leech." I shoved it away.

Folkoln chuckled, but the sound was cut off. His expression turned stern as his eyes darted past me. Searching.

Swiftly, I was on my feet. "What is it?" I asked.

He breathed in, his chest rising. "Excitement. Urgency. Fear . . . Pain."

A piercing caw sounded from above. *Kaleb*.

My wings sprung from my back, and I shot from the ground up through the trees.

Kaleb flew to me, shouting, "Trouble! Over there!"

To the south, under the gaze of the moon, warriors riding winged horses tracked toward us. Over half of them were archers. Their arrows were nocked, ready to shoot at the creature flying ahead of them. It had the head of an eagle, but the body of a lion. A gryphon. Something was wrong with its left wing, making it struggle to stay in the air. On its back, were two riders. One of them—

"Sage!" I roared, the might of my voice striking the

mountains, causing the world to tremble as I tore through the air, trying to get to her.

"Von!" she screamed, her voice wild with fear—lighting every protective, predatory cell within my body on fire. She had one arm reaching behind her, steadying the other rider, her free hand gripping the reins.

"Fire!" shouted the warrior at the front of the pack, the metal of her blade catching on the light as she dropped her arm.

"No!" The word shredded through my throat as they released *their arrows* on *my mate*. Power, ancient and brutal and unforgiving, charged through my veins before it erupted from my hand in the form of a howling, vicious wind. When it passed by Sage, it softly caressed her skin, but when it met the arrows, it stopped them dead.

For a brief second, they hovered in the air, subdued by my power.

I rotated my hand, causing the arrows to turn, and then I fired them back at the warriors who dared to harm my female. When the arrows found their marks, the sky exploded with splotches of ichor and blood—like mini fireworks painting the night.

The labored gryphon let out a pained roar as it tried desperately to stay upright. It gave one last flap of its wings—

It's going down!

Panic lashed at me, spurring me into action. I moved as fast as my wings could carry me, pushing them harder than I ever had before.

I reached for Sage as she reached for me, her other arm still tucked around the rider.

Our fingers were *so* close—

But a horse barreled into me, knocking me backwards.

"Von!" Sage let out a piercing cry.

My wings flared out, biting into the air, anchoring me in place.

The gryphon gave up its fight and it began to fall, taking them with it.

In my peripheral—a glint of steel.

I swung toward it, Death Weaver emerging in my hand just in time to answer the call of the warrior's sword, slicing straight through it. Before the top half of the blade could slide off, I shoved my palm forward, using my powerful winds to blast her right out of her saddle. She and her mount went careening backwards, flying through the air.

I peered down, searching for Sage. *There!* Spiraling toward the ground.

Wings tucking in, my sword dissolved, and I dove for her.

She tried desperately to hold onto the other rider, but a current of air fractured them apart.

Folkoln! I yelled through our private channel.

I got her, came his reply as he flew about thirty feet below. He caught the other rider while I flew for Sage. This time, when we reached for one another, we connected.

Swiftly, I pulled her into the safety of my arms. Relief flooded me.

"The gryphon can't die!" she yelled at me, her blue

eyes filled with worry. "My sister. Their lives are connected. Von, you have to—"

I kissed her.

I couldn't help myself.

It didn't matter if the next group of riders were coming for us. It didn't matter if she had just revealed to me that she had some long-lost sister. All that mattered was her.

When she tried to pull back, I bit her bottom lip, forcing her to stay connected to me. A low, possessive growl emitted from deep within my chest, the sound more animal than man.

No, I spoke firmly through the bond, even though I knew she couldn't hear me—something I would rectify the first chance I got. I kissed her again and again, her lips so soft, so plush against mine. She was heaven and earth and everything in between. And I couldn't get enough.

As I kissed her, my left hand faced down, and a shadow chain shot from it, faster than a bolt of lightning. When it wrapped around the gryphon's leg, there was a slight tug, briefly jerking us down, but my wings held firm, keeping us suspended in the air.

This time when she broke the kiss, I let her. She looked down, eyes searching.

"Folkoln's got her, and I've got the gryphon," I reassured her. "But most importantly, *I've got you.*"

Beautiful blue eyes returned to mine. Creator above, how I had missed those eyes. How I had missed *her*.

"You bastard," Sage whispered, her brows pressed firmly together. Then, her expression softened. "What took you so long?"

I looked at her in disbelief, an amused grin tugging at the corners of my mouth. "Out of *everything*, that's what you have to say to me?" I teased, unable to help myself.

Her eyes filled with emotion, one I knew well—regret. "Von, I'm so sorry about—"

"No," I interjected. "That can come later. Right now, all that matters is that you are in my arms. Breathing and alive. We'll figure out the rest."

A low-pitched roar emitted from above us. It was the sound of a stallion letting out a final warning before battle. Our faces jerked upward. A winged horse flared its nostrils as its rider charged straight for us. Five more riders behind it.

Six azure daggers, made from densely packed water molecules, formed around us. They shot forth, five of them finding their mark. The rider who managed to dodge the one corrected her altered course and started for us. Sage conjured another dagger, sending it straight for her. The horse swerved to the side at the command of its rider, but it wasn't fast enough, and Sage's dagger chewed into the rider's thigh.

She let out a scream, falling off her mount, and plummeting to the earth below. The horse chased after her, wings flapping, neck straining.

"Impressive," I said to my mate, unable to keep myself from placing another kiss on her lips.

Softly, her fingers traced the length of my cheekbone. "How many nights I dreamed of touching this face." They drifted over my mouth. "These lips."

I leaned into her touch. Savoring every second of it. Of her.

"Hey, lovebirds, we've got company," Fallon, now in her raven form, hissed from beside us.

I sighed, looking at the next wave of warriors coming for us, swords raised. *Fools*. The lot of them. Wings powering up, I flew us closer to the ground, allowing for the gryphon to be placed against it first. My shadows disappeared and I descended the rest of the way.

After we landed, I stole one more moment with Sage.

I brushed my thumb over her bottom lip. "I'll be back for these shortly."

I let her go and took to the sky, conjuring Death Weaver.

Chapter 39

Sage

A gust of air crafted from the powerful downthrust of Von's incredible wings sent my hair twirling as he shot from the ground. In his wake, amber and sandalwood clung to me, wrapping me in his rich, masculine scent. I had missed the smell of him so much.

Missed *him* so much.

Vatara let out a small noise, and I rushed to her side. I ran my hand over her beak, petting her. "Lift your wing for me and let me see."

Slowly, she did as I asked. I brushed my hands along her neck, stroking her softly as I moved down to her lifted wing.

Walking under it, I ran my hand through her silky feathers, feeling for the arrow. Finally, I found it. In comparison to the massive wing, four times the size of me, the arrow didn't look much bigger than a sliver, but it was where it had landed that impacted the gryphon's ability to fly. It was right at the elbow joint.

Gently, I wrapped my hand around it. Her watchful eyes connected with mine, and I said, "I'm going to remove it now. This might hurt."

She nodded in understanding.

Swiftly, I pulled it out, and she let out a pained screech. I tossed the arrow on the ground.

"Shhhh, sweet girl. It's done now. It's over," I reassured her, rubbing and patting her side as I inspected the wound. Ichor wept from the injury, but to an immortal gryphon, I doubted it would be fatal.

I moved back by her head, my fingers stroking the soft, silky feathers on her forehead. Holding her gaze, I said, "Thank you for getting us here. I am indebted to you."

She let out a melodic whistle, the sound of it magical.

Twigs snapped to my left and I twirled, a ball of flame emerging from my hand.

As soon as I saw who it was, I put it out.

"Folkoln," I breathed in relief.

He walked toward me, my sister in his arms. Her face twisted in pain as she applied pressure to the wound in the crook of her elbow, blood oozing from it. The wound had appeared at the exact same moment Vatara had been hit by the arrow. However, on my sister's arm, much smaller than Vatara's wing, it looked much worse.

I rushed over to them. "Thank you for catching her."

"Of course," Folkoln replied. "It's good to see you, Sage."

I smiled. "I can't believe I'm saying this, but it's good to see you too."

"Fucking hell," Artemesia moaned. "Why do arrows have to hurt like such a bitch?"

"You've got a mouth on you," Folkoln purred. A smirk twisted his lips, making his snake bite piercings look even more wicked.

The way he looked at her . . . he was *smoldering* at *my* sister.

I sharpened my gaze. Pinned him with it. "Don't even think about it."

"A bit late for that," he said, his shoulders performing an unapologetic shrug. The action caused bits of smoke to break off from his tall, muscular body.

"Put her down," I snarled.

"Alright," he said, looking down at her as she writhed in pain.

I waited. Nothing.

Folkoln made a strange face. But he didn't budge an inch.

"Folkoln," I grated. "I need to inspect her injury."

"How strange," he spoke quietly, more to himself than us. His dark eyebrows shifted together. He shook his head as if he couldn't believe it himself. Then, they lifted. Onyx eyes met mine. "I can't feel her emotions."

"Considering that's what you feed off of, it's probably a good thing. Now—" I gestured to the ground. "If you would be so kind."

Still, nothing.

"What's your problem?" I asked.

"I can't," he said, pulling her closer into him.

"For fuck sakes, Folkoln, quit playing around. She's in pain," I hissed at him. My power shifted, just beneath my palm. I'd shove a blade into his abdomen if he didn't hurry up and comply. This was ridiculous.

"I am," Artemesia moaned.

"Folkoln," I said, taking a step closer to them.

His top lip curled back, and he bared his teeth at me, a deep, low growl emitting from his throat.

Swiftly, he cut it off, shaking his head as if he were trying to free himself of whatever demon had possessed him. Lids sprung open, his black eyes flaring wide. Then his arms fell down to his sides, like they'd lost all of their strength, and he dropped Artemesia as if she were a scalding-hot potato.

She landed with a heavy *thud*.

I rushed to her, kneeling beside her. I glared at Folkoln, my mouth about to form a word, but she beat me to it—

"Asshole!" she moaned as she rolled over onto her side, curling into herself.

"What the fuck?" Folkoln snarled in shock as he looked at his hands. His face shifted to my scowling one then to Artemesia's pained one. As if *he* were *afraid of her*, he took a step back. Then another. "I'm going to help Von." His wings flared out behind him, and in a blur of smoke, he was gone.

My sister groaned. "What is *wrong* with him?"

"Many things," I said honestly. On a good day,

Folkoln's actions were strange, but like Von, there was always an angle to what he did. Typically, it was so he could feed off emotions. That's what I had suspected he was doing. But then when he snapped his teeth at me like a predator guarding its meal . . .

I knew *that* look.

It was the exact same one Von had given me hundreds of times before. Particularly when I tried to squirm away from his *relentless* tongue, my mind gone squirrely from too many orgasms. Like he hadn't drank his fill. Like he hadn't had enough of me.

It was possessive, protective. *Primal.*

It was . . . the bond.

"Shit," I muttered under my breath.

"What?" Artemesia panted, blue eyes shifting to mine.

"I'll tell you later," I sighed, turning my attention to her arm. I held out my hand. "Let me see."

Artemesia complied, and I inspected the wound. It was a clean, deep puncture, the surrounding tissue swollen and covered in blood. "How do things like this work with you and Vatara?"

"When she heals, my arm will too," Artemesia answered.

"How long will that take?" I asked, releasing her arm.

"As long as the arrows were not dipped in dragon's blood powder, it shouldn't be very long. Vatara heals rather swiftly."

The space between my eyebrows crinkled. "Dragon's blood powder?"

She gave a small nod. "Dragons were wiped out during the War of the Creators. The empress had their carcasses taken to Avolonia, in hopes of recreating the species, but to this day, she has been unsuccessful, a failure some have taken notice of. Anyway, she had her stygian forgemasters harvest what they could from the mythical creatures— scales, bones, teeth, claws, organs. Everything. While experimenting, they discovered when dragon blood was left to dry, not only did the consistency change, but its abilities were altered too. The blood that kept the immortal creatures alive, when dried and ground into powder, became lethal."

"How so?" I questioned softly, watching as Vatara came over to us. She laid down and placed her head on the ground beside Artemesia, setting her worried eyes on her.

Artemesia took a breath, wincing. "It cuts off immortality and prevents healing. Ultimately, making the vessel die." Artemesia held up her arm, eyeing her injury. It looked smaller than before. It was healing, which meant—

"No dragon's blood powder," Artemesia sighed in relief, dropping her head back on the ground. With her good arm, she reached up to rub Vatara's head.

"If the empress had the carcasses of the dragons taken to Avolonia, what became of their souls?" I wondered.

"In truth, nobody seems to know, although nearly everyone has a theory. Some think the emperor cast them into the other realms, sending them away with everyone else, while others believe the empress collected them and has them all hidden somewhere." Her eyes shifted skyward as she continued to pet Vatara. "I think they returned up there, becoming one with the stars once more, from which they were taken."

Head shifting, I followed her gaze.

Like the river searching for the ocean, I looked for Von.

My breath faltered.

Four warriors surrounded him, reminding me of the recent memory I had recovered of him in the arena. He still moved with that same precise skill, every swing intentionally placed, never missing his mark.

You can have an army of ten thousand, but it is the brave acts of one that will bring them home, spoke a strong, male voice from a time long forgotten. *That, my dear daughter, is the warrior.*

My brow furrowed. Was that something my father had once told me?

If so, why didn't his voice sound like . . . his?

In the distance, across the lake, flame arrows shot into the sky toward the winged horse riders. I looked down, tracking where they had come from. Through the trees I could see them—

Harper. Ryker. Lyra. My heart performed a mighty kick, emotion choking me up.

It was *really* them.

"Sage," sniffled a voice from behind me.

I *knew* that voice.

It had been there ever since we were children. Strong and steady.

Unable to stop the tears from bubbling up, I turned around. Kaleb walked toward us. He looked exhausted, like he'd been dragged through a forest for weeks on end. And yet, he was here, before my very eyes.

"Kaleb," I choked out his name.

We raced toward one another, embracing and sobbing.

"I'm so happy to see you," Kaleb spoke through his tears.

"Me too," I said, sounding equally as pitiful as him.

Pulling back, I wiped at my wet cheeks as we smiled at each other like idiots.

"I have someone I need you to meet," I told him, taking his hand. I pulled him over to Artemesia. "Kaleb, this is my sister, Artemesia. Artemesia, my brother, Kaleb."

For a moment, there was silence. Then, Artemesia gritted her teeth as she got up, wincing as she put too much pressure on her injured arm. I rushed to her side, helping her. Kaleb came over.

When she was standing, she killed the distance between her and Kaleb and tossed her good arm around him, giving him a tight hug as she whispered, "Thank you, Kaleb."

"For what?" he asked, hugging her back.

"For taking good care of our sister."

There was something full circle about this moment, about seeing Artemesia paying Kaleb respect. It made my heart proud. Warm.

My lips wobbled. I sucked them in, trying to get ahold of my sappy self.

Gently, Kaleb pulled back, his eyes puffy and swollen from our sob fest. He placed a hand on Artemesia's shoulder. "Thank you for taking care of her first."

Tears pricked my eyes.

And then *all three* of us were sobbing.

I knew from that moment on, regardless of blood or birth, of parents or origin, the three of us would forever be connected.

Family.

Chapter 40

Sage

Large branches snapped like brittle twigs as a blur of white fell no more than twenty feet from us, colliding with the ground. Feathers exploded into the air like a wagon full of pillows struck by cannon fire. A winged horse laid there, unmoving, no rider in sight.

"Is it dead?" Kaleb inquired, daring one step forward.

I eyed its side, illuminated by moonlight, looking for any sort of movement. Just barely, I could see its ribs rising and falling. "No, it's alive," I answered.

The horse burst upright, and it charged at us. Nostrils flared, white mane flying straight back, its wings spread out.

Vatara was quick to move, using her tail to protectively sweep Artemesia into her. Kaleb and I leapt in the opposite direction from one another as the horse stampeded past us.

I swirled around to face the horse, reaching for my powers, bracing for it to come at us again. But it didn't turn back—it just kept going, racing off into the distance, which eagerly swallowed it whole.

Loud, rumbling sounds, like stone smashing against stone, came from the direction the winged creature had gone in, as if a rockslide was happening on one of the mountains in the distance.

A thunderous, unnatural roar blasted from there—like a violent wind being forced through too small of a space, amplifying it. The hairs on the back of my neck rose in standing ovation for the haunting bellow—one I did not care to hear an encore for.

"Winged horses can't make that sound, can they?" Kaleb asked, wide eyes fixed straight ahead.

"Nope." Artemesia popped the p.

Trees cried out as their branches and trunks snapped in two. The ground groaned, as if a heavy, unbearable weight were being placed upon it. The forest floor trembled beneath my feet, shooting shockwaves up into my legs, growing in force with each passing second.

"And they probably can't do that either, can they?" Kaleb chuckled nervously.

"Definitely not," Artemesia confirmed. She turned to Vatara, who lowered immediately, the two working in perfect tandem. Artemesia reached up, her arm now fully healed, and she slung herself over the side of the gryphon. Urgently, she directed us, "Come on. We need to get out of here."

Kaleb stood with his mouth agape as he stared in the direction of whatever was coming toward us.

"Come on, Kaleb," I urged, snatching his hand and dragging him over to Vatara.

When the three of us had mounted, Vatara flared out her wings and shot from the ground. It wasn't until we were above the tree line that I looked back and saw *it*.

A giant, forged from the mountain behind it. Clumps of trees stood on the cliffs of its vessel, creeks stretching across it like a network of veins. I had thought the giant I faced in the arena was huge, but in comparison she wasn't even half this beast's size.

"What is it?" I asked Artemesia, my arms wrapped around her waist, Kaleb's around mine.

"Something we won't stand a chance against," Artemesia hissed as she steered us away from the giant. "It was most likely conjured by a priestess who can bend the will of earth, which means we need to find her first."

I scanned the indigo sky. Von and Folkoln had led the empress's warriors away from us, across the lake, bringing the battle closer to the ground, using Harper and Ryker's flame arrows to aid them.

I didn't recall seeing so many fighters before, which meant reinforcements must have come. Dozens of them. Still, Von and the others were holding them at bay.

I zeroed in on a female, positioned behind the others. She hovered in the air, her purple robes floating around her. Her hands were raised, her eyes fixed on the giant.

"There!" Kaleb and I exclaimed at the same time.

"I see her," Artemesia replied as she pulled her sword from its sheath and handed it to Kaleb. "Take this."

He unwrapped his arms from my waist and took it. "Thanks?" Kaleb replied with a degree of question as he eyed the sword.

"Vatara, we need to get closer," Artemesia told her.

Vatara let out a piercing screech in reply.

"Hold on," Artemesia warned us as Vatara angled upwards, shooting us high into the sky, above the battle below.

The well within me swelled with power, nudging at the surface as if it wanted to show me something. Trusting in it, I allowed it to overflow into my palm. I curled my fingers, and a round handle formed within them, the color of gold tinted with rose. It shot out from one side to the other until it was eight feet long. At one end, twin prongs formed, chiseled into the shape of slender, curved wings. The points were lethal and sharp. *Deadly*.

Vatara tipped her beak to the ground, tucked her wings in, and dove straight for the earth bender.

"Guard the priestess!" shouted one of the riders as they charged for us.

Heeding their command, more and more warriors started to fly toward us, looking to cut us off.

It was now or never.

Using every ounce of my immortal might I could conjure, I fired the bident at the earth bender. It tore through the air, whistling as it headed straight for her. At the last possible second, her head swiveled up, and she formed a round shield out of thin air.

The bident chewed into it, the brunt of it shoving her

downward.

With a snarl on her lips, she tossed her shield, along with my bident, into gravity's clutches then set her furious sights on us. "Get *her*!" she yelled, her eyes narrowing on me.

Artemesia pulled up right before we collided with a handful of riders who had formed a protective barrier between us and the priestess. They chased after us as we flew upwards. I glanced back down, looking past them. Instinctually, my hand reached out, searching—

The bident answered my call, returning to me from the ground below. A hum sounded as it flew toward me, still stuck in the shield. The lip of the round shield collided with a rider, knocking her off her horse. The force was so great it freed my bident.

"Nice," Kaleb exclaimed.

"That was dumb luck," I chuckled as the bident returned to my hand.

I surveyed the weapon. I had never created anything like it before, but it felt good. Familiar. Powerful. A title came to me, whispered into my thoughts . . . *Guardian of Creation.*

Was that the name of the bident?

Something in me whispered *yes*.

A rider, standing on top of her horse's back, daggers in hands, emerged beside us. She leapt across the distance, her weapons ready to bite. I took aim with my bident, released it, and held my breath. It impaled her chest, knocking her back with such force her hands and legs curved in front of her torso. She screamed as she fell toward the ground, her horse scrambling after her.

I flexed my hand over the air, and like a faithful old mare, the bident returned, the twin points saturated in ichor.

Another rider leapt from up above and I thrust my bident upwards. It impaled the rider, my immortal strength kicking in as I held the fully grown immortal over the top of us, speared like a fish on a stick. She kicked and squirmed, horrible gurgling sounds coming from her mouth. Grunting and muscles contracting, I heaved her over the side.

Gravity tugged at her, pulling her off the sharp points of my weapon.

The metal tang of swords sounded behind me as Kaleb fought with another.

Their mount collided into Vatara's side, and I swayed at the force of it.

Kaleb won against the other rider, earning us a few seconds to breathe.

Eyes searching, I looked for Von.

He was back to back with Folkoln, the two of them surrounded by riders, so many that I could just barely make them out.

"Von!" I yelled my mate's name, my heart stampeding in my chest, frantically shooting blood through my veins. Urgency clawed at me as I watched the riders close in on them. We had to help them. We had to—

A tidal wave of immense power blasted through the air, and the soldiers who surrounded Von and Folkoln were sent careening backwards, their armor crumpling like tin cans. I could *hear* the sound of bones breaking, followed by desperate, pleading wails, something I had heard once before, back in Edenvale. Immediately, I knew who the lethal force had come from. Only my mate was capable of such raw, incomprehensible power. Only Death could crush bones as if they were made from brittle leaves.

Down below, Harper and Ryker continued to shoot their flame arrows. Lyra, Soren, and Fallon were with them—the three of them fighting the riders who had taken to the ground.

The giant was drawing closer to them. Closer to us all.

"Shit," Artemesia swore. "I've lost visual of the priestess."

I scanned the sky, searching for the earth bender.

"She's over by the giant!" Kaleb shouted.

I glanced back, toward the mountainous beast.

Sure enough, Kaleb was right.

The priestess hovered by the giant's shoulder. She lowered her hand, and the giant reached down. Like two monstrous shovels, his stone hands dug into the ground, pulling a huge chunk of it free—trees and all. Bits of soil crumbled beneath the slab as he raised it over his head.

"Oh fuck," Kaleb muttered under his breath, voicing what we all were thinking.

The giant roared as he threw the mass of land at us.

"Hold on!" Artemesia yelled as she pushed Vatara to her limits. She flapped her wings faster and faster. I peered behind us, my eyes stretching wide—

We weren't going to make it.

Get up, commanded a voice as strong as steel. A voice from my memories—Ezra. *Now fight for him, child, with everything you have.* Those were the same words she had said to me when Kaleb got lost in the blizzard. I looked at Kaleb. I knew what I had to do.

I leapt to my feet, core contracting, muscles firing as I kept my balance.

Time almost seemed to pause.

Just as I could feel the water molecules in the air, I could feel something else—the life force of the trees, the warmth of the ground. My fingers tingled, a new power forming—no, not forming, *awakening*. It came from some deep, forgotten crevice within, something that had been there all along, just hidden.

I leaned into it, and like a powerful wave, it swept over me, dragging me down in its immense power.

Light illuminated from me, encasing my body in a bright, white glow. A mighty roar passed my lips as I thrust my arms into the air, raising my bident above my head, my hair floating around me.

The ground groaned. Then, it heeded my command.

Trees, stones, clay, and earth shot into the sky, forming *mountains*, made by my own will. Like a mighty fist, they smashed into the soil-crafted asteroid and sent it careening off course, obliterating the riders caught in its destructive path.

"Holy shit," Kaleb spoke in a stunned voice as the mass sailed over us, blotting out the light of the moon.

My legs trembled, my hair fell, and the light emitted

from me wicked out.

I collapsed back down, panting as my lungs cried out for air as if I had been holding my breath, even though I hadn't. My body felt weak, zapped for energy. Like a well, drained of water, albeit I could feel the droplets slowly starting to trickle back in.

"Sage, you just *made* mountains," Artemesia whispered in wonder.

"Fucking mountains!" Kaleb exclaimed.

In the land mass's wake, the current it created was so strong that it sucked Vatara in, sending us into a spiral. I let go of my bident and held onto Vatara for dear life. Kaleb and I screamed, while Artemesia desperately tried to correct us.

The world went around and around and—*oh gods*. Like a butter churn, my stomach rolled, the contents working their way up my esophagus.

Finally, we quit spinning, but the damage had already been done.

"I'm going to be sick." I covered my mouth.

"Don't you dare puke on her again," Artemesia hissed with disdain, having all but forgotten the miracle I'd performed a few seconds ago, thus saving our lives.

"Or me," Kaleb interjected.

Apparently, he had too. *Ungrateful siblings.*

"You two suck," I groaned, fighting another wave of nausea. When I felt the acidic contents of my stomach start to glob up on the back of my tongue, I leaned over to the side.

"No!" Kaleb cried out.

But it was too late—I hurled my guts like a cat evicting hairballs. Yes, with an *s*. One after another. Some of it landed on Vatara's side, the chunks sticking to her fur. Some of it landed, well, I don't know where it landed.

She let out an insulted screech. I couldn't blame her. I would feel the same way if things were reversed.

"Sorry, Vatara," I wheezed, my eyes stinging. Creator above, that stunk.

"Sage," Kaleb said, voice flatter than roadkill.

"Yeah?" I asked as I wiped my mouth with the back of my sleeve.

"I have . . . puke spray on me." He gagged.

"Don't you dare, Kaleb," Artemesia warned.

"I'm okay, I'm okay," he replied, although he sounded nothing of the sort.

My stomach eased, a sense of relief washing over me. "I feel better now," I stated, smacking my lips. My energy seemed to be swiftly returning too.

"I'm so glad," Artemesia replied sarcastically. "Now, if you are done chundering, can we get back to focusing on the priestess?"

"Um, girls?" Kaleb said.

"What?" we asked.

"You might want to look to your left."

Artemesia and I did as he said.

My breath stilled in my chest. "Von," I whispered.

"No," Artemesia spoke softly. "That's Nockrythiam, the Ender of Realms."

Standing taller than the mountain giant, was a lethal

figure painted in shadows. Forged from darkness itself. His presence was commanding, terrifying. Powerful.

Onyx horns shot out from his head, sleekly twisting back, tipping up at the points. Sharp and menacing. The black of his pupils claimed the whites of his eyes, making him look . . . *other*. A species entirely of his own. And then there were the veins beneath his tanned, tattooed skin. They had doubled in size, feeding his muscles with immense strength.

"Retreat!" one of the riders screamed.

"No!" the priestess yelled, but no one seemed to care as the warriors began to flee. "Cowards!"

Von raised his sword, pointing it at the giant. Moonlight reflected off the wickedly sharp edge, highlighting its lethalness.

Then, he charged, and the world trembled.

Bits of shadow broke off behind him, unable to keep up.

Taking a defensive stance, the priestess dropped into a crouch and raised her fists beside her face. The giant did the same. They threw a punch at Von's sword, but the giant's slowness caused it to miss, and Von's blade sailed through the air, narrowly missing the priestess and finding purchase in the giant's neck, sweeping all the way to the other side and cleaving the giant's head straight off.

The priestess floated up higher, eager not to make the same mistake again of being too close to the battle.

Von leapt back, lowering his sword to his side, watching as the giant's head slid off its neck. When the head struck the ground, the earth shook, and the sound cracked like thunder. So loud that we covered our ears.

Snarling, the priestess thrust her hands forward, and the headless giant began to move toward Von, its fist still raised. Von held firm, waiting for it to come to him.

The giant threw another slow punch at Von, which Von caught.

His grip turned crushing, and the giant's hand disintegrated, as if it were made of sand, not stone. Von shoved the giant back, his movement agile and swift as he raised his leg. In one mighty move, he kicked the giant square in the chest, sending it careening backwards. When it fell to the ground, it crushed the trees behind it, causing a plume of dirt and debris to erupt into the air.

Again, we covered our ears.

The priestess raised her hands, and slowly, the giant started to get back up again.

"Can you get me another shot?" I asked Artemesia, eyes on the priestess.

"You bet I can," she said. With a click of her tongue, we veered to the left, giving a wide berth around the ensuing battle.

As we closed in on the priestess, her back turned to us, I readied my bident.

And this time, when I fired it, I did not miss.

After the battle was over, Vatara landed in front of Von.

Horns receding, he returned to normal size, which by mortal standards meant he was still a goliath. A muscular, tall, tattooed, dripping with unbridled masculinity, positively sinful, *definitely* going to ruin me later goliath.

Above all that?

He was *mine*.

I leapt down from Vatara, my legs picking up speed as I rushed toward him and he to me. Blood evacuated my veins, replaced by urgency—urgency to get to him. It lit every fiber within my body on fire.

Conquering the distance between us, I leapt from the ground and threw myself into him. My arms wrapped around his neck, my legs around his waist. His grip turned crushing, his arms like shackles as they banded around me, holding me tightly to him.

We were two desperate souls, finally returned to one another.

Together.

The place where we both belonged.

"Never again," he pledged, his heated breath drifting across my skin.

"Never again," I promised, nuzzling into his neck and inhaling his scent. There was once a time when the smell of burning birch reminded me of home, but now, that had changed. Now, home smelled of amber, sandalwood, and leather.

Unfurling my arms, I took his face in my hands and kissed him with such intensity I realized I was starving for him. It was a hunger like no other. It wasn't just sexual—no, it ran much deeper than that. It was a need, like how the rain needed to fall, how a seed needed to sprout, like the stars needed to glow.

It was a need to live. Like blood in my veins. Air to my lungs. I needed him as if my body had been poisoned and he was the antidote, the only thing that could save me.

I *needed* him.

So, I kissed him. Until the world fell silent, until it was just us.

Until I swore I heard the moon whisper to the wind—
They've found each other at last.

Chapter 41

Von

Sage and Harper had their arms looped around one another, conversing and giggling as we all made our way through the forest, traveling on foot. Lyra's hand was in Harper's, an excited bounce in her step. She, too, was happy to see Sage.

We all were.

I hadn't been able to take my eyes off her since the battle had ended a couple hours ago. In truth, a very large part of me wanted to grab her and fly her away somewhere private so I could hoard her to myself. But when I saw how happy she was to be reunited with the others, I refrained just so I could see that smile of hers a little bit longer.

Sage and I had much to talk about, and some things were not going to be easy. Right now, all that mattered was that she was alive. Safe. Happy. We'd get to the rest after.

Artemesia led the group, her gryphon walking with her, Kaleb beside them. After them came Fallon and Ryker, separated by Soren, who had spent the last two hours reliving his heroic efforts in the battle—most of which we all took turns calling bullshit on.

Apart from a few bumps, cuts, and bruises, we'd all fared rather well.

Well, everyone but Folkoln, who had been as quiet as a temple mouse ever since the fight ended. Quiet and Folkoln—it was an oxymoron.

My brows raised slightly as I glanced his way. "What's going on with you?" I asked, voice low.

No reply came at first.

Then, "She's my mate," he whispered, eyes fixed ahead.

I traced his gaze, landing on Artemesia. "How do you know?"

"Because I want to snap Kaleb's neck for talking to her."

I chuckled at that. "That doesn't mean she's your mate."

"She is." His tone was serious, yet another strange thing for the God of Chaos to be.

"Explain."

"It's like I said before—ever since we arrived here, I've felt this constant tugging. When she was falling, I didn't just go to her because you asked. I physically felt compelled to do so. And when Sage asked me to set her down, it was like . . ." He glanced down at his hands. "My body had a will of its own and wouldn't listen."

"Like you couldn't physically part with her," I said, recalling the time when Sage had fallen unconscious and I had taken her to Ezra. Ezra had asked me to lay her on the bed, but as hard as I tried, my body would not comply. It felt as if she were safer in my arms.

"Yeah." Folkoln sighed. "And I *might* have growled at Sage when she tried to get close to us."

That was something I, too, had done multiple times. Although, it had nothing to do with Sage getting closer to me; it was always because she was trying to squirm her fine little ass away from me when I wanted another taste of her.

"It does sound like the bond," I admitted, rolling my neck and tipping my face toward him. "So what are you going to do about it?"

"I don't know yet," he said as we passed through the last of the trees and stepped out into a clearing.

A rolling landscape stretched before us, the grassy hills bathed in the golden light of dawn. The group fell quiet, cut off from their private conversations, as the uncertainty of what to do next weighed on all of us.

"So . . . now what?" Soren asked, pressing his hands against his hips as he stretched out his back.

Artemesia rubbed the gryphon's neck as she said, "Vatara needs to rest before she'll be able to fly us anywhere. I also don't think she'd mind if I washed her side, since Sage vomited on her. Again."

"*That's* what that smell is!" Fallon exclaimed, batting her hand in front of her face.

"I wouldn't mind washing myself too," Kaleb tacked on, his gaze sliding accusingly to Sage, telling the rest of us all we needed to know.

"That's so gross," Soren said, unable to help himself from chuckling.

Sage crossed her arms over her chest.

"I could use a bite to eat," Ryker tossed in, taking some of the heat off Sage. She shot him an appreciative look, and he gave her a wink.

"Okay, Weyfern is a small city, about a forty-minute walk"—Artemesia pointed to the west—"that way. There's an inn I've stayed at before. Beds aren't anything special, but the food is good, and the innkeeper doesn't ask questions."

"Will it be safe for us?" Harper asked, slinging an arm over Lyra's shoulders.

"Define *safe*," Artemesia responded.

"Will the winged horse riders be there?" Harper clarified.

"Although I can't guarantee they won't be, I honestly doubt that they will. I imagine they'll be rushing back to Avolonia, scrambling over one another, hoping to be the first to tell the empress what they witnessed today," Artemesia answered, turning away from Vatara to face me. "That Nockrythiam has returned."

Silence fell. Eyes shifted toward me.

Nockrythiam. The name wasn't foreign to me, but the past it was connected to was.

"Von, were you from *here*?" Ryker asked, his tone full of wonder as he tried to fit the pieces together.

But it was Sage who stepped forward and said, "We both were."

Ryker paused, examining this new bit of information. "Wait a minute." His eyes shifted from Sage to Artemesia. "Are you two sisters?"

"We are," Artemesia answered.

"I thought you were just helping Sage," Ryker said with a gentle shake of his head, as if he couldn't believe he hadn't figured it out before. "Although now that I look at you both, I can't unsee it. You two share resemblances. Namely the white hair."

"They do," Harper agreed, her tone less amazed than Ryker's.

He turned to his twin. "You already knew?"

"I didn't," Soren stated, not that anyone cared.

"I've been walking with Sage for the past two hours. What do you think we were talking about?" Harper chuckled. "Although the one thing we didn't discuss . . ." Curiosity lifted her eyebrows. She looked at Sage. "Why were the riders after you?"

"Because the ruler of these lands, Empress Avena, condemned me to have my soul crushed, from which there is no coming back," Sage answered, voice soft as she revealed this truth, turning my bloodless veins colder than the glaciers themselves. "Wraithlike creatures known as vuleeries rescued me from the arena. The riders were sent by the empress, tasked to collect me." She shrugged. "There's a bounty on my head."

An image of her appeared in my mind, of how broken she had looked when I saw her collapsed in the sands of the arena. My muscles tensed, realization stringing them taut.

"The day Soren linked us to you. That was the day you were going to have your soul crushed, wasn't it?" I asked, my voice sharp.

She didn't look at me as she answered, "Yes."

Anger flared red-hot, branding the truth into my skin.

"You were just going to *give up*."

"I was dealing with *a lot*," she fired back at me, pain lacerating her words.

I took a step forward, shadows breaking off from me. "What if I hadn't shown up that day? What would you have done?"

She didn't respond. She didn't need to.

She had been ready to give up.

Confliction slit me open like a knife, gutting me where I stood.

I wanted to grab her by the chin and roar at her that she wasn't the only one dealing with a lot. That we both had lost *so* much.

But how could I?

I'd had centuries to process the loss of our child, but she had only just found out. Naturally, the weight of it crushed her, just as it had me.

"I hate to break up this lovers' quarrel, but we should probably decide what we're doing next," Artemesia cut in.

While the group discussed traveling to the city, Sage and I held one another's gaze, so many unspoken words floating between us. For a brief moment, we faded from the discussion.

I'm sorry, I said, sending the words down the private river that once linked our thoughts.

And although I knew the words hadn't reached her, I could tell by reading her eyes that she was saying the same thing back.

"Alright, it's settled then. We'll spend the night at Weyfern," Artemesia said. She gave a low whistle, and Vatara, who had been sitting beside her, lowered down to the ground. Artemesia unbuckled one of the saddlebags, flipped the flap open, and began to rifle through it. She started taking out ropes, dropping them on the ground. "Since you all are new here, let me give you a rundown of how things work in the Mother Realm. By law, males have no rights. Most are sent to the arena, where they have their souls crushed for sport. Some are allowed to live as slaves—it's less expensive to keep ones who are not . . . intact. The extremely pretty ones who know how to handle a sword, both cock and weapon, become part of the empress's harem. So—" She tossed the last rope to Kaleb. "While in public, you will have to act accordingly, otherwise you'll risk getting all of us into trouble." She began to search through another saddlebag. She pulled out a handful of scarves, consisting of various patterns and colors. "Males are not allowed to show all of their faces either, so you will have to wear these."

"So, what exactly are we supposed to do?" Folkoln asked, arms crossed, a tattooed hand playing with a lip piercing.

She walked over to him, shoved a pink scarf against his chest, and said, "Be a good male, look pretty, and shut up." She winked at him. "Us females will take care of the rest."

I cracked a smirk. Folkoln was going to have his hands full with *that* one.

Chapter 42

Sage

"How many are slaves and how many are castrated?" the innkeeper asked as she folded bed linens that smelled like they'd been dragged through a field of lavender. Each time she dropped the folded linen on top of the pile, a waft of the floral scent filled the air.

Poor Kaleb, who was allergic to lavender, hadn't stopped sniffling and sneezing since we set foot inside the inn.

Artemesia, who was leaning against the counter, briefly glanced over her shoulder at the guys to do a quick head count. Looking back at the innkeeper, she said, "Five. Also, I have a female mount that will need a sizable stable. And no, they are all intact."

"Alright, will they be sleeping in the stables, as well?" the innkeeper asked, reaching for the last linen.

"No, they'll stay with us," Artemesia answered.

"Are you sure? I can have one of my eunuchs chaperone them," she said. "It wouldn't cost much more."

"Thank you for the offer, but they'll stay with us."

"Very well. That will be four cords then."

"Your prices have gone up," Artemesia noted.

"Blame the empress for raising the slave tax again," the innkeeper sighed as she smoothed her hands over the linen, giving them a final pat, another waft of lavender bursting into the air.

"Achoo!" Kaleb sneezed.

The innkeeper side-eyed him. "It's getting more and more expensive to keep them. I have one who is intact, but I fear I might have to have him castrated soon. Such a shame." She shrugged, shoved the linens to the side, and then held out her hand.

From her coin purse, Artemesia retrieved four strings of coin, ten on each, and handed them to the innkeeper. They plunked in her palm.

Jostling them a few times, the innkeeper tested their weight. "That oughtta do it. Your rooms are on the second floor. I'll have some food brought up."

"Thank you," Artemesia said, tapping the counter twice before we all headed upstairs.

Later on, I rested my hands against the windowsill, feeling the fresh breeze dance over my skin. Across the street, a woman swept the sidewalk in front of a shop with windows full of plants. Above her, the wood sign swung gently from side to side, the well-oiled chains that held it in place making nary a whistle. Etched into the wood, in a language I did not know the name of but surprisingly could read, it said, *Root Tonics*.

The woman, the shop, the name—it all reminded me of Ezra.

I couldn't help but miss her.

Soon enough, we would find each other again.

As per the rule of the lands, intact males were not allowed to be left unchaperoned. The chaperone had to be either a female or a eunuch. Because of this rule, it meant one female had to stay with one male. Earlier on, deciding who was going to stay in what room was a process, about as organized as a monkey shit-fight. Which, when it came to Folkoln, who put up the biggest stink about staying with Artemesia, wasn't a stretch from the truth. Surprisingly and begrudgingly, she'd agreed to stay with him, but not before she threatened to chop his cock *and* balls off if he tried anything on her.

Go, sis. Talk about ambitious.

Then, there was the whole situation between Kaleb and Fallon. He had refused to stay with her, which I found even more odd, something I made a mental note to ask him about later. So, he ended up with Harper, while Fallon roomed with Soren. Lyra and Ryker stayed together. Which left me with—

Tattooed, muscular arms wrapped around my torso, pulling me against his strong, unyielding frame.

Von.

I brushed my fingers over his prominent, thick veins, feeling the potent power thrumming through them as they filled with blood for me. The warmth of his skin was like fire against my cool fingertips. My wandering hand stopped, finding a new path to trace—the vine tattoo inked into his arm. It was just as I remembered it, the thorns sharp and menacing, twisting this way and that. The masculine twin to the one he had given me when I made the deal with him, promising him everything. My gaze shifted to my forearm, to where the ink used to be.

So much had happened between us. I had betrayed him. Betrayed *us*.

"Von, I—"

"Shh," he purred the word, the sound deep and low. Throaty.

It made my knees weak.

He made my knees weak.

For him and him alone, I would kneel, just to get a taste of him.

"I know we have much to discuss, but I want you to memorize how this feels," he continued, his deep cadence like a wicked, dark spell cast over me, tethering my every thought to him. His fingers drifted along my jawline, gently angling my face up to his. "Because after we're done talking, and after we're done fucking"—he gave a roguish smirk—"I want you to fall back into my arms, just like this, right where you belong. Where you will *always* belong."

Warmth spread throughout my heart. I understood the

message behind his words. No matter what, his love for me was unwavering.

While I had been fickle and confused, Von had remained strong and steady.

The one person I could always rely on.

We stayed like that for a long, long while, just watching the people on the streets below.

And for a time, life was so beautifully simple.

Until it wasn't.

"Von." I took a breath, knowing I was going to need it. "I have to tell you something."

"Alright," he said as I turned to face him.

My hands rested against his broad chest, feeling the stone-like muscle beneath the soft cloth of his tunic—steel and cotton. Dark, smoldering eyes met mine, rimmed with natural strokes of kohl, making him look otherworldly. A light stubble etched out his strong jawline, emphasizing his high cheekbones. His black hair was untethered, my small, white feather tied to the end of a slender braid.

"I don't know if you need to sit down or . . ." I trailed off.

"You know I'm not much of a sitter. Stop stalling and tell me." His gaze was unwavering, his words a soft command.

"Alright." My fingers slid down his chest, drifting along his arms. I gathered his hands in mine. It was amazing how hands as rough as his could still feel like velvet against my skin. It defied logic. Everything about this male defied logic. Slowly, I started, "On the day of our wedding, there was something I was going to tell you . . ." Sadness crept into my voice. I had no idea how I was going to tell him this.

"I know," he said, the words so quiet I barely heard them.

My lips parted in surprise. "You do?"

"Yes, and I will never forgive myself for not being there for you that day." His gaze lowered to my stomach then returned to mine. "For you both."

I took his face in my hands and said with every fiber of my being, "What happened was not *your* fault."

"No, but . . ." His thick brows drew together. "I could have prevented it had I been more careful. I should have placed more wards, had more guards. I should have been there to protect you two. And things would have been very different."

My hands slid back to his chest. "We can't change the past, but we can look to the future. All immortal souls return to this realm upon their death. What if our child's soul is here? What if this is our second chance?"

He gave me a soft, sad smile, his voice gentle as he said, "Sage, my love, that's impossible. The fetus would not have had a soul yet. Immortal or not, the vessel would not have been strong enough to house the divine. You know that."

"That's what I thought too, but I'm telling you, *somehow,* ours did. I had intended to keep my pregnancy a secret until after the wedding, but then you showed up unexpectedly, and the Neptuah seeds were sitting out. You would have seen them, but our babe must have heard my wishes because they hid them." I pressed my hand over my stomach. "I *felt* them, Von."

Black lashes lowered as his gaze drifted to where my hand rested. He was silent for a moment, the beautiful, dark god processing my words. His expression was unreadable, that mask he wore held so carefully in place. Always so controlled, my mate.

Until he wasn't.

He took a breath, and I think it was the first shaky one I had ever heard come from him.

"Then there is a chance they could be here." He spoke the words slowly, as if he needed time to adjust to their meaning.

"Yes," I said, hope lifting my tone.

"But if they were male gendered, you know what that might mean." His voice was soft, so heartbreakingly soft.

I swallowed that solemn, bitter truth. I felt it go down like a ball of ash, lodging in my throat. "I do," I choked out.

The Mother Realm was not kind to male souls. Considering most of them were sent to the arena to have their souls crushed, there was a high chance that would have been our child's end as well.

The thought was heartbreaking. Devastating.

Still . . . I finished out loud, "If they met their end here, I want to know."

Von breathed in, a muscle feathering in his jaw. Finally, he said, "Alright. We will find out what happened to our child."

I nodded in reply then asked with a downturned smile,

"Is it bad that I wish for them to be a girl now?"

"No, not in this context," he answered, his arms wrapping around me and pulling me into his warm, steely frame. "To be honest, it is something I wish too."

My fingers bunched in the fabric of his black tunic. "What do you think she would be like?" I asked, lowering my cheek to his chest.

Rhythmically, he stroked my hair. "If she's anything like you, then definitely stubborn."

I jerked my head up, squinting at him.

He gave a playful grin. "I'm not finished."

Still, I squinted.

He chuckled then continued, "She'd probably have that same irritating hero mentality as you, always wanting to save everyone."

"Von," I hissed.

His rich laughter was light, and I couldn't help but soften further into his arms. I cursed my weak backbone, no better than a limp, overcooked noodle when it came to him.

"Alright, alright," he said, his voice deep, pulled from the lowest part of his chest. "She'd be smart, so smart. Courageous and brave and kind. She'd stand for what's right. Stand up for those who couldn't. And she'd do it unapologetically. Just like you."

I reached up, my fingers sounding against his stubble. "And what would she get from you?"

"I think that should be obvious," he spoke seriously, despite the curve teasing the corner of his mouth. "My handsome good looks, of course."

I rolled my eyes, chuckling as I said, "You are something else."

"Indeed, Kitten, I am," he purred confidently, his attention drifting to my lips. The way he looked at them, accompanied by the sensual cadence of his voice, had my thoughts spinning.

My lips parted, opening in invitation for him.

Knock. Knock.

Von growled at the door, "Go away."

I shoved my hands over his mouth, whispering and giggling, "You are going to get us kicked out of here." I threw my voice. "Who is it?"

Playfully, Von nipped at my fingers. I gave him a warning look.

"It's me," Kaleb's muffled voice spoke from the other side.

I pulled away from Von, opened the door, and swiftly ushered Kaleb inside. I peeked out into the hallway, ensuring Kaleb wasn't seen walking on his own, before I swiftly closed it.

Kaleb pulled the scarf from his face. "Can I talk to you?"

"Yes, of course," I replied, concern drawing my eyebrows together. "What's going on?"

Von sat on the windowsill, the breeze pulling his long, black hair to the side. Loosely, he threaded his heavily inked arms over his chest.

Kaleb plopped down on the bed, lying back on it. "Fallon and Ryker had sex," he groaned as he stared up at the ceiling.

I nearly fell over.

They what?

Swiftly, I hurried to the bed and sat beside him. I looked down at him, his arm tossed over his face. Gently, I clasped his arm and lifted it. "I'm sorry. Come again?"

Knock. Knock. Knock. Knock. Knock.

Knuckled rasped against the other side of the door, the sounds fast and hard. Whoever was on the other side sounded incredibly impatient.

"Hold that thought," I said, blowing air through my lips as I returned to the door and cracked it open.

"You would not believe what the asshole said to me," Artemesia growled, her eyes filled with fire. "Can I come in?"

"Yeah," I answered, taking a step back so she could enter.

"Von, your brother is a real piece of work," Artemesia snarled, her mouth snapping shut as she saw Kaleb. "Oh . . . hey, Kaleb."

He raised a hand, waving at her as he remained laid out on the bed.

"Am I interrupting something?" Artemesia asked.

Kaleb sat up. "No, it's fine. Everyone else knows, so you might as well know too. Fallon and I were together. Actually, I had planned to propose to her, but she cheated on me with Ryker."

"Oh shit," Artemesia said, sitting beside him. "Do you need me to go kick her ass?"

Von cracked a grin. Kaleb did too. Their gazes connected—an unspoken message shared between the two.

"What's *that* about?" I asked, my finger flicking between them.

Kaleb chuckled. "That's what Von said you would say when I told you about Fallon and Ryker, so it's funny that's what Artemesia said. You two are definitely sisters."

"I mean . . . I will," Artemesia said with a shrug. "I haven't known you for a long time, but I can tell you are a good person. That *Fallon* girl has no idea what she's missing out on."

"Thank you," Kaleb sighed.

"Of course," she replied.

"When did this happen?" I asked, sitting on the other side of him.

"Shortly after we arrived here. When we emerged from the river, we were split up from them. They said they ate some berries, and the next thing they knew, it just happened—as if the *berries* had convinced them to do it. Can you believe that? *Blaming it on berries*?" Kaleb scoffed as he shook his head.

"Actually . . ." Artemesia gave him an apologetic look. "I hate to tell you this, but if they were surrenderberries, which are known to grow at the foot of mountains, then I can believe it."

"Surrenderberries?" Kaleb asked, curiously tilting his head to the side.

Artemesia nodded. "As the name implies, they weaken inhibitions and make one surrender to their desires. They are so powerful that one alone can do the job. However, the more one eats, the more powerful they become. Castalia, the ancient Goddess of Trickery and one of Empress Avena's sisters, was said to be the creator of them. As the story goes, Avena went to her sister and asked for her aid in helping her advance her relations with the emperor. And so, Castalia made them and instructed her sister to have the emperor eat them. It wasn't too long after that their nuptials were announced and she became empress. They say up until the day the emperor died, she always had some put in his wine, unbeknownst to him."

I thought back to the memory I had recently recovered, of when I'd sat with the emperor and the empress in the great amphitheater, known as the Crest of Salvation. We had drunk wine—wine I had found all too easy to toss into Von's face. Had he deserved it at the time? Perhaps. Although I didn't fully understand the context of my actions, I could remember how freely they came to me. How easy it had been to surrender to my wants. It made me wonder . . . had the empress drugged both the emperor and I with her surrenderberry wine?

Granite filled my stomach—she wasn't the only one who had done that to me.

Aurelius had done the same, but instead of wine, he'd used his ichor.

This is how things will be for you now, Moonbeam, his ghost whispered in my ear. I could taste his ichor on my tongue, feel it pouring down my throat into my belly. The bed dipped under his weight as he crawled over the top of

352

me.

No!

My body tensed, knowing what was going to happen next.

He's not here, I reminded myself, chanting the words like a mantra until I broke free from the memory.

I glanced down at my shaking hands. Swiftly, I tucked them beneath my legs. I didn't dare look at Von, but I could *feel* his eyes boring into me.

"I haven't spoken to Fallon since it happened," Kaleb said with a sigh.

"Perhaps that might be a good place to start," Artemesia replied, giving him a sympathetic smile.

Kaleb blew out a breath of air, tipping his head from side to side as he weighed her suggestion. Finally, he said, "Yeah, I suppose maybe I should."

Artemesia gave him a pat on the back.

"Now, since we've hashed my problem out. What happened with you and Folkoln?" he asked.

A small smile touched my lips. I was happy to see the two getting along so well and offering one another support. It was sweet. Heartwarming.

"You aren't going to believe this one. He said we are bonded. *Bonded*!" Artemesia rolled her eyes. "No offense, Von, but your brother is absolutely ruthless. I'm well aware he wants to get into my pants, but to use something as sacred as the bond as a ploy is atrocious."

"Artemesia . . ." I took a breath, knowing I was going to need it.

"Yes?" she asked, eyes meeting mine.

Now, it was my turn to offer her an apologetic look as I delivered the news she clearly was not ready to hear. "I actually think he might be telling the truth."

"Fuck off," she said, staring at me in disbelief.

When I didn't budge, her gaze shot toward Von.

"I believe you two might be mates as well," Von said.

Artemesia's mouth fell open. She snapped it shut, then opened it again, like a fish out of water trying to survive the uprooting of its entire world.

Finally, she said, "I need a drink. A *really* stiff one."

"Me too," Kaleb agreed as the two of them looked to the small liquor cabinet across the room.

Chapter 43

Sage

"Boop," Kaleb said as he pressed the meaty pad of his finger against my nose, smooshing it in. I finished tying the scarf over the bottom half of his face and then gently took his hand and lowered it to his side. Reaching up with his free hand, he squished my nose again. "Boooop!" he repeated, his voice higher pitched this time. His breath, which smelled like the bottom of a barrel, washed over my face. Scowling, I batted his hand away.

Artemesia snickered. "Do it again."

Sighing, I took a step back, out of Kaleb's reach. I eyed my highly inebriated siblings. The two looked like willow branches swaying in the wind. One soft push and they'd surely fall over.

"Don't worry, I'll get him back to his room," Artemesia said, slinging her arm over Kaleb's shoulders.

"Mhm," I replied with a degree of skepticism, shooting

Von, who was tidying up after my siblings, an unimpressed glance. He looked as if he were tempted to laugh.

"She will," Kaleb said with a hiccup. He tipped his head and looked at her, his eyes no more than slits. He smiled drunkenly. "It's so nice having another sister." He lowered his voice. "One who isn't so bossy." He rolled his shoulder inward, trying to hide his thumb as he pointed it at me and whispered loudly, "*Some* sisters—not saying any names—are *really* bossy."

"Alright," I interjected, maneuvering around them so I could open the door. "Let's get you two back to your rooms, shall we?" I glanced over my shoulder, meeting Von's gaze. "I'll be back shortly."

A wicked grin. "I'll hold you to that."

"I'd expect nothing less," I retorted playfully then gently steered them out. We walked to the room across the hall, and I knocked.

Not waiting to be called in, Kaleb opened the door and slurred, "Harps, I'm baaaack."

Lyra, Harper, and Ryker were all inside. The three of them were sitting on the bed, chatting. Ryker's muscles stiffened.

As soon as Kaleb saw Ryker, he said, "No thank you," and turned around to go back out the door.

I caught him by his shirt. "Kaleb, come on. You can't drunkenly wander around this place. You'll get us all in trouble."

"See?" Kaleb said to Artemesia. "Absolute stick-in-the-mud."

She nodded in agreement.

I squinted at them both. Drunkenly, they smiled back.

I sighed.

After some arguing, Kaleb finally agreed to stay in his room, but *only* if Ryker left, which Ryker was fine with doing.

Ryker was a loyal, good friend, and the discord between him and Kaleb was uncomfortable for us all, although I understood it. Ryker had crossed a very big line with Fallon; still, I wanted to hear his side of the story. I also thought he should know about the effects of surrenderberries.

Lyra got up to accompany him back.

"It's alright. I'll walk him to his room," I said, and she nodded. I looked to Ryker. "I was hoping we could have a word?"

"Alright," he answered, voice like gravel.

We stepped out into the hallway, silence lingering between us. A few doors down, we entered Ryker and Lyra's room. It was much like the one Von and I were staying in. I noted there was a bed made on the floor beside the actual one. Without a doubt, I knew Ryker was the one who had offered to sleep there so that Lyra could have the bed for herself.

I leaned against the wall beside a painting of rolling hills, my arms threading loosely over my chest. Oxygen rushed into my lungs as I stole a deep breath. "So . . . you and Fallon."

Broad back facing me, Ryker plucked a jug of water

from a wood cabinet and poured some into a cup. "The whole thing is a mess, Sage. I like Kaleb; he's a good guy. I never intended to hurt him or get between him and Fallon, but things . . . they just happened that night. I know it might sound unbelievable, but in some ways, I didn't even feel like I was in control of myself. I don't know what happened, and by the time I did, it was too late to take it back."

"I know the feeling," I spoke softly, watching as Aurelius's ghost entered the room, gold ichor seeping from his wrist. He held it out in offering.

He's not real, I reminded myself, looking back at Ryker.

The apparition disappeared.

I cleared my throat. "And no, it doesn't sound unbelievable at all. Ryker, there's something you should know. The berries you and Fallon ate that night might be partially to blame for what happened."

Ryker turned to face me. He leaned against the counter, cup in hand. "What do you mean?" he asked curiously.

"Artemesia told us that there are berries called surrenderberries. They grow at the base of mountains, and they tend to loosen one's inhibitions. If you and Fallon consumed them . . . it would have made it increasingly easy to give in to your wants."

Ryker sat with that for a moment then said, "That would explain a lot of things. Still, it does not excuse our actions."

"Although it does help explain them," I countered.

"I suppose," he answered. Lowering his cup, he peered

down at its contents.

Silence lingered.

I broke it. "So what do you plan to do about Fallon?"

"I don't know." He shrugged a large, bulky shoulder. "She wants space right now as she tries to figure things out with Kaleb, so I'm doing my best to give her that, but gods, *it's hard*." He rolled his neck back, exposing his prominent Adam's apple, and looked up at the ceiling, his eyes searching for answers among the exposed wooden beams.

"Give things time," I suggested softly, kindly. "If you and Fallon are meant to be, then you will. And if she is meant to be with Kaleb, that means someone else is out there waiting for you. I know it might be hard to see right now, but things will work out as they are supposed to, Ryker. Have faith."

"Thank you, Sage. I'll try to remember that." He gave me a small smile, his rich brown eyes lacking their usual vibrancy.

Ryker and I chatted for a bit after that until I remembered that Folkoln and Von were both alone and technically unchaperoned. If a maid or someone became aware of this, it wouldn't bode well for the rest of us.

"I'll see you in the morning," I said to Ryker, before I left the room and returned to Harper's.

I knocked lightly, then stepped inside. Kaleb was sprawled across the bed. A string of drool rivered down his cheek as he snored loudly—so loud it was a wonder the floor above hadn't lifted off.

Artemesia was still awake but barely. She was telling a

story to Harper and Lyra about the biggest fish she'd ever caught. Half of what she said was unintelligible. The three of them were seated on the floor.

I made my way over to them.

"Thanks for looking after her," I said to Harper as I lifted Artemesia's arm and hoisted her up on her feet. She wobbled at my side.

"No problem. How's Ryker doing?" Harper asked.

"He'll be okay." I looked at Kaleb. "They all will."

Harper nodded in reply, her attention drifting to Lyra, watching as she stood up. Uncrossing her legs, Harper stood as well. "I'll see you in the morning," she said to Lyra, and the two shared a sweet, tender kiss.

The love between them was as strong as ever.

After I said good night to Harper and Lyra, I helped my bumbling, stumbling mess of a sister down the hallway, toward her and Folkoln's room. When we reached the door, I tapped it with my foot.

From inside, boots swiftly crossed the floor, and the door swung open.

Folkoln looked . . . stressed. Tendrils of smoke floated around him, twisting and turning as if they were in agony. His hair was tousled back, as if he'd swept his fingers through the midnight-black strands multiple times.

"Hello, *mate*," Artemesia slurred sarcastically.

"You're drunk," Folkoln stated, pupils narrowing into slits.

"No," she said, feigning seriousness. "I'm not."

"Uh-huh," Folkoln said, his gaze shifting to mine. "Did

she tell you?"

"She did, but I sort of figured it out when you growled at me," I answered with a slight shrug.

"Sorry about that," Folkoln apologized.

Artemesia hiccuped. "Oh look, there are two handsome bastards now. However will I choose between the two? I know . . ." She reached across, her hand latching on to Folkoln's pec. She gave it a squeeze then whisper-yelled to me, "Gods, this one is *hard*."

Her hand lowered, but Folkoln caught her wrist. "Careful, love," he warned.

"*You* be careful," Artemesia slurred, her body swaying unpredictably—back and forth, back and forth. I tried to stabilize her, but then she swayed ahead and nearly face-planted.

Folkoln caught her, his arm tucking behind her legs as he swept her off her feet. She lowered her head to his chest, eyes closing.

I followed as Folkoln carried her over to the bed, gently laying her down with such tender care, I wondered if he thought she was made of glass. I had never seen the God of Chaos act so . . . careful.

"What do you plan to do about the bond?" I asked, standing beside him, watching as Artemesia curled in on herself. She let out a small yawn then nestled further into her pillow, her long braids spilling across it.

"I'm trying to figure that out," Folkoln said as he pulled up a blanket from the end of the bed and placed it over top of her.

"You two are from very different worlds. She has a life here, one I can't see her leaving," I said, thinking of all the people who relied on her. I couldn't imagine the weight of what that must feel like, but I knew the loyalty and love she felt for her people. I had seen it firsthand. No, Artemesia wouldn't leave them. Of that, I was sure.

Folkoln turned to face me. "It's too early to think about that. I think she and I need to learn more about one another first." His starless eyes shifted back down to her. "Then we'll figure out the rest."

Chapter 44

Sage

When I returned to our room, I closed the door behind me and backed against it, taking a moment to admire the God of Death. He cut a striking figure as he stood, barefoot by the window, his tall, masculine frame bathed in silver moonlight. The sleeves of his tunic were rolled up, displaying his muscular, tattooed forearms full of prominent veins. He had a drink in one hand, the other placed casually in his pocket. Face fixed forward, he teased, "Did you get the *children* settled in?"

"I did," I answered, making my way over to him.

I leaned against the window frame, my gaze drifting outside.

Above the steep rooftops, a canvas of black framed a bright, glowing moon. Down below, the flickering glow of lanterns lit the brick-paved streets—streets that were void of the hustle and bustle of everyday life that had existed earlier.

The world was quiet, and it was *finally* just . . . us.

There was so much we needed to talk about, but most importantly—

"I'm sorry, Von," I started, my voice soft, sincere. I faced him. "For everything that happened with Aurelius. I was confused, and I didn't know who to trust, or what to believe. I let my anger and my hurt guide my choices and I acted on impulse. In the end, I betrayed you. I betrayed *us*."

"Your apology is unnecessary," he replied, attention shifting to his drink. "You didn't just make those choices on your own. Your entire world had been turned upside down. You were recovering memories from our twisted past, discovering . . . *how horrible* I truly was to you back then. Add on that you were being drugged by Aurelius's ichor and persuaded by his narcissistic charm. His heart beating within your chest certainly did not help things either."

"Yes, all of those factors played a part, but I refuse to let them be a crutch. I want to own up to what I did." My eyebrows drew together, cinching the space between them. "I'm sorry for betraying you, Von. Will you forgive me?"

He looked up at the starry night sky and let out a rough sigh, painted with raw, deep emotion. "The moment I held your lifeless body in my arms for the second time in my life, it brought me clarity. I knew then that everything else was inconsequential." He glanced at me, and my heart nearly stopped. "I have already forgiven you, Little Goddess."

I stood there in awe, unsure what I did to deserve him or his boundless love.

I looked down at the floor, smiling despite myself. I

hadn't realized how much I needed to hear those words from him. I hadn't realized how much guilt I had been carrying around with me. But now, I did.

Did his forgiveness erase what I had done? No.

But it meant we could start anew, that we could move on.

"There's something I've been wanting to ask you about." He placed his cup on the windowsill, then turned toward me. "Why were your hands shaking earlier?"

My stomach sank. This was one conversation I really didn't want to have tonight.

In truth, I didn't have the slightest idea how to tell Von. After *it* happened, I had made a solemn vow to myself that no matter what, I wouldn't tell a soul about that day. Because if I told someone, that would make it *real*. And although some part of me knew that it was, another part was quite fine with pretending it had never happened—I didn't want it to be what defined me.

"Sage . . ." he pushed gently, closing the small distance between us.

I opened my mouth to speak, but the words withered on my tongue.

Adept, long fingers slid under my jaw, gently tipping my face up to his. His endlessly black eyes captured mine. "I might not be able to feel your emotions anymore, but I know when something is deeply affecting you. Whatever it is, you can tell me."

I swallowed, my throat suddenly parched. "What if it breaks me to tell you?" I whispered, my insecurities dampening the strength of my voice.

His hand shifted, caressing my cheek. I couldn't help but lean into his touch. "I do not think keeping it in is good for you either," he said. "I know your hands as well as my own, and I know it takes a great deal to make them tremble as they were."

I took a breath. Then, another. "What if you look at me differently?"

"How could I *ever* look at you differently? Have my actions not shown as much?"

"What if you think I'm weak? What if—"

"What *if*," he cut in, "you told me and gave me that chance to prove all your what ifs away? What if I love you regardless?"

My eyes shifted between his.

I realized that a small part of me *wanted* to tell him.

I just . . . I didn't want tonight to be about Aurelius. I wanted it to be about us. If I knew anything about my mate, he was strong and steady, yes, but he was going to need time to process when I told him what Aurelius did to me. As was I. And that was a path I did not want us to walk down tonight.

I took a breath and vowed to him, "I promise to tell you. Just . . . not tonight. I want tonight to belong to us and only us. Please give me that."

His eyes studied mine, a soft interrogation. Finally, he said, "Alright, Little Goddess, have it your way. I will not press any further tonight."

"Thank you." My words held weight, driven forth by

the rapid strumming of my heart—Creator above, how much I loved him. His willingness to bend, to honor my wants, and take care of my needs were attributes I never knew I needed in a partner. But now that Von had shown me what that was like, I realized how Aurelius had starved me of it.

Von, in so many ways, was an answer I didn't know I needed.

Through him, I'd learned *I was worthy of love*.

That I *was* enough, just as I was.

All because he was . . . good to me. *Kind to me*.

Loving and understanding.

Safe.

Everything a partner *should be*. Everything Aurelius *wasn't*.

I looked up at the handsome male standing before me—completely mesmerized by him and all he stood for. If I were to tell the outside world what the God of Death was truly like, when it was just me and him, I doubted anyone would believe me.

On the outside, he was a fearsome, dark immortal who commanded reapers and was the keeper of the dead. Von was the type of male who, when he stepped into a room, others cowered from because they didn't want any trouble.

Ah, but underneath . . . underneath, he was a teddy bear.

Von's thumb brushed over my curved lips, tracing them. "And to what do I owe the honor of this sweet gift?"

"My smile?"

"Mhm," he purred, eyes fixed on my mouth.

"I was just thinking how thankful I am for you." I slid my hands up his torso, feeling the hardness of his muscles beneath his tunic. Resting them against his chest, I leaned into him. As if the walls were listening to us, I spoke in a hushed voice. "And that you don't have to worry. Your secret is safe with me."

"What secret is that, love?" Moonlight caressed the side of his face while the other remained darkened by shadow. In that moment, I could see the two sides of him— good and bad, and both were breathtakingly beautiful.

"That . . . Death might look like a big, scary Doberman, but underneath his towering, muscular, tattooed exterior, he's a golden retriever."

Like a spark bursting into flame, something wicked lit his dark eyes. "The only thing I have in common with that breed is that I retrieve what is *mine*." Slowly, his fingers drifted down my neck, sweeping possessively across my sensitive skin. "You belong to me. Your wants. Your needs. Everything about you. From your silky white hair to your decadent lips, to your soft, supple breasts, to your sweet, *sweet* sex, and all the way down to those darling little toes of yours. You are mine, love, and I am yours."

His words left me breathless and filled with fever.

He grinned, knowing the control he had over me.

Pulling his hand from my neck, he returned it to his glass, lifting it from the windowsill and bringing it to his smirking mouth. His commanding gaze remained locked on me as he drank. Lowering it, he said, "Now, there's something else we need to discuss, which I must admit isn't very . . . golden retriever of me, but I am a god of my word."

"What?" I asked, my curiosity piqued—my body aching for more of his touch.

"I made *two* promises to you. Do you remember what they were?"

"Two promises?" I asked, my brow furrowing as I raked through my thoughts.

Then . . .

I'm going to ink these by hand, his phantom growled softly in my ear. I could feel the heat of his large hand on my breast. My nipples budded in desperation as I recalled what he had said next as he had pinched the one. *And as for these? I'll pierce them with my silver.*

My lips parted, a small gasp escaping me. Heat crept up my neck, flushing across my cheeks. "I remember."

"Ah. I'm glad you do," he said, infinite black eyes meeting mine. His voice lowered, striking a deep, primal chord. "I *fully* intend to keep those promises to you, although I am willing to alter *some* parts if you wish."

A shiver strolled through me, arcing up my spine then back down into my core.

"Do you like the thought of wearing my ink? My silver?" he asked, his words a sensual purr.

I snatched the glass from his hand and took a deep pull from it. With a bit of liquid courage in my system, I admitted, "I find the idea intriguing. Arousing, even."

He smirked, running his wicked teeth over his bottom lip, tugging it back slowly. One black brow raised in question, his eyes smoldering. "Do you want to know what kind of tattoo I plan to give you?"

"Yes," I answered, my throat suddenly parched. I took another sip.

Thick, black lashes lowered as his gaze slowly drifted down, taking every inch of me in. "Take off your tunic, and I'll show you."

"In front of the window?" I asked, eyes flicking toward it.

"Does it excite you?"

"Yes." I had no idea what had gotten into me.

His fingers played with the fabric at the bottom of my tunic. "Then take it off."

"Who are you, and what have you done with the territorial male I know?" I set the glass down on the windowsill.

He gave a dusky laugh, the sound of it a dark, sensual melody—one I longed to hear over and over again. "Letting other people see as I touch you *is* a way of me staking *my claim*."

Fire licked at my skin, burrowing beneath it, into my veins.

Creator above, *this* male.

He watched as I removed my tunic, pulling it over my head. My hair fell against my skin, pooling down my back, over my breasts. I dropped the cloth onto the floor, beside my feet. I decided to take it one step further, unbuttoning my pants.

Von quirked a curious-but-not-sad-about-it brow.

Grinning up at him, I said, "So you can get a full view

of your canvas."

"Ah, so very thoughtful," he answered, giving me an approving nod.

I took off my shoes and wiggled my way out of my pants then removed my underwear and dropped them on top of my tunic. Moonlight shone against the swell of my breasts, resting against the flat of my stomach, highlighting the curvature of my hips.

I could *feel* Von's heated gaze as it swept over my naked flesh, eliciting a shivering response out of me.

"Exquisite," he praised, coming closer to me. Notes of sandalwood and amber washed over me, making me feel weak in the knees as he leaned in, gathered my hair, and swept it behind my shoulders. He took a step back and crossed his arms over his chest, rubbing his jaw in thought. A sinfully handsome artist debating what part of me to start painting first.

While he studied me, I took him in—*all* nearly seven feet of him. Inch by *incredible* inch. Von was a masterpiece, forged from the rawest, purest form of masculinity. He was a safe harbor, a place where my femininity could dock, unload, and thrive.

Reaching over to the windowsill with his long arm, he dipped two fingers into the cup, wetting them. I sucked in my breath when his fingertips touched my skin, the middle of my sternum, beneath my breasts.

"I'd start right here with a rose." He began to draw it out, his fingers shifting as he drew the petals. When they became dry, he dipped his fingers into the glass again and returned them to my skin. "And here"—he followed the curvature of my breasts—"I would take my time, drawing slender, intricate vines." He mimicked the same motion underneath my other breast. "From them, small chains would dangle." He wet his fingers again then worked up from the rose. "Leaves would curl between your breasts, reaching up toward a crescent-shaped moon. I might even hide a little skull in there somewhere, just so I can stamp my symbol on you." He smirked at the thought, and it was a wicked, devastating thing.

I had once hated the idea of belonging to him, but now I wanted nothing more. I wanted him. All of him. I wanted the bond and the connection that came with it. I wanted to wear his inky markings, his colors, his silver. I wanted to be his wife. His queen. And the mother of his children.

More than anything, I wanted *us*.

Gaze lifting to mine, he asked, "What do you think?"

"It sounds beautiful." I bit my bottom lip then released it. "Can you do it now?"

A dark, handsome grin appeared on his lips. "Only if you are willing to make a deal with me."

"What do you have in mind?"

His black lashes lowered, shadowing his gaze as it swept over me, taking *all* of me in before they rose back up to mine. "That tonight, you become *my* wife."

Chapter 45

Sage

"I know you wanted a traditional mortal wedding with the dress, the people, the celebration, but I have waited centuries to call you my wife, and I do not wish to go another day without being able to do so," Von said, stepping toward me. His knuckles drifted down the length of my arm, taking my hand in his. Something cold touched my skin, and my fingers curled around it. "So, Little Goddess, will you do me the honor of becoming *my wife* tonight?"

I lifted my hand, looking at the beautiful, dark, ethereal ring. An emerald stone sat in the middle, surrounded by intricately woven vines and tiny, dainty leaves. The emerald reminded me of the color of Von's eyes, and I couldn't help but marvel at it. Nestled beneath the glimmering stone were white and black diamonds—a nod to us both. The metal was a silvery-black color, as if the night and the moon had been harnessed to craft it.

Tears misted my eyes. So much detail had gone into this ring. So much *love*.

"Did *you* make it?" I asked, my voice crackling with emotion.

"I did. I had planned to give it to you on our wedding day," he admitted, his words holding a great deal of weight.

My brows wove together, my chin trembling as I peered down at the stunning ring, which suddenly felt so much heavier. "All this time . . . you've been holding on to it."

Gently, he tipped my face up toward his. "I've carried your wedding ring with me every day, every year, every decade, every century. I held on to it until I could finally give it to you. Until today."

My heart missed its beat.

I thought back to the limited time we had spent together after I reincarnated—from the moment he took me from the village square to the time I spent working in the bathhouse, all the way to when he had traded his life for mine, making that deal with Arkyn.

All that time, I had been so suspicious of him, mistrusting. Little did I know he was carrying my wedding ring with him, that he had for centuries—

I would not make him wait any longer.

"Yes, I want to become your wife. Tonight," I exclaimed, smiling up at him.

"Good," he replied, and then he closed the distance between us as his lips found mine. His kiss was ravenous, his desire scorching. I enveloped my arms around his neck, careful not to drop the ring. My body pressed against his, while his hand clasped my jaw, keeping me there as he kissed me senseless.

I pulled back and asked, "Do we need to find a priestess or something? If that's even possible, all things considered."

He raised a questioning brow as he spoke in a low, amused tone, "Are you asking *me*, the maker of deals, if I need *someone else* to marry us?"

A laugh blossomed from my lips. He had a point. "Are *you* going to marry us then?"

He smirked, pride flickering in his eyes—the look akin to a cat with a mouse in its mouth. "I am, although it will not be done in the traditional sense."

"What do you mean?" I couldn't stop smiling.

"We're going to make a deal."

"Are we now?"

He gave a confident nod. "We are."

"And the terms of this deal?"

"Give me the ring, love."

Unweaving my arms from his neck, I handed it to him.

His fingers brushed against mine as he took it. Holding it before me, he said, "Tonight, you become my wife, and I, your husband. Tonight, you agree to give what is owed to me. You agree to give me your soul."

"Will you give me yours in return?" I asked, voice light. Playful.

"I cannot," he answered, his dark eyes glinting with amusement.

My smile faltered. "Why not?"

"Because it's always been yours. *I've* always been yours."

"Oh," I whispered, my heart ready to stampede straight out of my chest. *This* male.

"However . . ." Von took my hand as he got down on one knee. "What I can give you in return is my vows."

My eyes pulled wide. "Wait, are you doing it right now?"

"I am." No arrogance was spared in those two words.

My mouth popped open. I gestured to myself. "But I'm not wearing *any* clothes."

A wicked grin played on his lips. "I see no point in conjuring you a dress, considering it will not last very long."

He had a point.

Still, that didn't explain . . . "Why are you kneeling?" I finished the thought out loud.

"Because this is how it should be when a husband commits himself to his wife. Bending the knee is how you show honor, respect, humility. This is how I want to enter our marriage, by surrendering all that I am, all I possess, and everything I will be to you."

Air escaped me as I looked at the strong, proud god. A king among kings. Ripe with dark, unimaginable power. And he was bending the knee to me.

My beautiful, dark villain who had become the hero I desperately needed.

With his eyes holding mine, he spoke in his velvety-rich, deep tone, "I surrender to you, Little Goddess. From this day forth, I vow to be your protector—your sword and your shield. I vow to be steadfast—my loyalty unwavering and true. I vow that my body will be a sanctuary to yours— my arms a safe fortress, my chest your place to rest. I vow to *always* hold space for your dreams, to honor you, our bond. I vow to be a *good* husband. I vow to be *yours*."

My soul danced to the song of his words as tears spilled from my eyes.

Lowering to the floor, I knelt in front of him, taking his free hand in mine. I brought it to my lips, kissing his tanned skin, before I met his gaze. Utilizing every cell of my being, I pledged to him, "I vow to love you through the bad and the good. I vow to give you my life, my love, and all of myself, every piece of my heart. Completely and irrevocably. I vow to be a good wife to you. I vow to be yours, Von, beyond the end of time."

I had never seen him look so happy.

He asked in a voice that was barely audible, but so very him, "So we have a deal, Little Goddess?"

"We do," I said, my cheeks starting to hurt because I couldn't stop smiling.

And as it would seem, neither could he.

Creator above, he was beautiful. Heartbreakingly so.

Smoothly, he slid the ring onto my finger, where it would forever remain. The ring was a perfect fit. Of course it was. Because he had made it for me.

I marveled at it. At *him*.

Shadows pooled down his arm, encircling his ring finger, conjuring another ring—the masculine version to my own, marked with white and black diamonds. Our colors.

"You made us matching wedding bands," I whispered, unable to pull my gaze away from the wedding band on his finger. I brushed my fingers over it, getting to know it.

"Of course I did," he said, his fingers intertwining with mine. He slid his free hand to my jaw, gently tipping my face upwards. Then he kissed me with claiming need. He lengthened it, deepened it, until I felt like I was dancing amongst the clouds with him. Until I was certain that the remainder of the world had disappeared and all that remained was us.

That kiss was one I would remember for the rest of my life.

Because in it, there was only one language to be found—love.

Sweet, beautiful *love*.

Smiling like a fool, his lips released mine, and we both glanced down.

The moon shone brightly across our hands, illuminating our rings. Illuminating our vows to one another. Under its silver, watchful glow, we were wed.

Husband and wife.

At last.

I watched in awe as the tattoo he spoke of earlier began to form. It was even more beautiful than I could have imagined. I lifted my hand, tracing the delicate design, stopping on the crescent-shaped moon above my breasts.

"What do you think?" he asked, standing, and taking me with him. He wiped away my happy tears.

"I love it," I answered wholeheartedly. I missed the

other tattoos he had given to me, because through them, it had always felt like I had a piece of him with me.

In truth, I was honored to wear his ink once more, to see it marking my skin.

Relieved even.

I looked at his chest, hidden beneath his tunic. "Do you wear the matching one to mine?"

"Sort of, but mine is a bit simpler."

"Can I see?" I asked.

He raised a brow, his handsome face almost too much for me to handle looking at right now. "Eager to get me naked, *wife*?" he teased, his voice a shot of bourbon.

Pride overwhelmed me, just hearing that word on his lips.

"Say it again," I murmured, mesmerized by the power of it.

"Wife," he purred then kissed me. Like a thief in the night, he stole the very air from my lungs. No matter how many times he did it, I never seemed to see it coming.

"Again," I beckoned breathlessly in between kisses.

I could feel his lips shift into a smile. "Wife."

I let out a deeply satisfied sigh.

"Is that a turn on?" he asked, pulling back.

I grinned. "You tell me, *husband*."

"Mmm." A masculine, throaty moan passed his sexy full lips, stoking my coals with oxygen. "I understand now."

"Right?" I chuckled.

Glancing down, I traced my fingers over his arm, following the lines of his ink. "Are some of these ones you've done by hand rather than using magic?"

"Some are, yes," he acknowledged, rolling his arm over so I could continue to explore his muscular arm, his skin hot beneath my touch.

"I hadn't realized that before. I had thought all of your tattoos were from deals you had made." I looked back up at him.

"Most of them are, but some I've gone over. The ones I couldn't reach I had Folkoln redo. Like the ones on my back."

"Why?"

Eyes meeting mine, he answered slowly, each word ripe with deep meaning. "Sometimes, you need to feel the pain of something to feel like you've earned a right to have it."

My breath hitched in my throat. He wasn't just talking about tattoos. I sat with that truth for a moment before I asked, "Which ones?"

His eyes burned like liquid fire. "The ones that matter the most. The ones I made with you or on your behalf."

"Von." I spoke his name softly, my heart beating wildly in my chest. I had no idea what I'd done to deserve him, but I couldn't help but feel gratitude toward the Creator for making him. A memory from a lifetime ago conjured in my mind, of a dark forest and an even darker male, of mud and rain, of a newly formed bond, of my lips tattooed on his—

My gaze shifted to the prominent bulge in his pants, which was pressed against my bare abdomen. The seam of his leathers stretched taut, emphasizing what waited for me beneath the onyx-dyed fabric.

Although I had been well acquainted with his length in the past, I realized that I had only seen it once in my current lifetime, and that was when he was in his phantom form.

My brow furrowed. "When you came to me as a phantom, the tattoo of my lips . . . I don't recall seeing it."

"It took every bit of remaining power I had left to send my apparition to you that day. Because of that, I had to pick and choose, which meant I was missing a *few* things," he answered. "It's a good thing you didn't look down, because I didn't have any feet either."

"Stop," I said, cracking a smile—one echoed across his lips.

"It's true. My feet are big and my cock is big. I had a decision to make. When I saw you on your knees, mouth open in invitation, it was an easy one."

My cheeks ran hot at the memory—his hands in my hair as he'd *filled* my mouth. Heat pooled in my lower belly. I wanted to do that again.

"So then, are my lips still there?"

He gave me mischievous grin. "They are."

No better than a dog narrowing in on one exceptionally large bone, I hooked my finger into the waistband of his pants, feeling the hardness of his body on one side and the smooth leather on the other. "I want to see. All of you."

Heat scorched the air between us, his dark eyes fixed on mine. "Then see *all* of me."

Chapter 46

Sage

I slid my finger upwards, unhooking it from Von's waistband, his skin smooth and taut. And oh, so masculine. I was a lucky, *lucky* girl. My hands drifted to the hem of his tunic, curling into the black fabric. I lifted it up, pulling his shirt over his head, and discarded it on the floor.

At the sight of him, my breath quickened, while his remained slow and steady. Controlled. It was the very nature of his being. And I'd grown to love every bit of it. Of him.

Heavy, sculpted muscle rested beneath a layer of ink-marked skin, illuminated by the caress of moonlight. His body was a lethal weapon, honed to perfection, built to command and forged to slaughter.

And right now, that was sort of what it felt like he was doing to me—

"Don't hyperventilate, love," he teased, a coy twist to his sexy mouth, showing off his deadly incisors.

"I'm not," I lied poorly, trying to calm my frantic, giddy heart.

I ran my fingers over his abs, tracing the steely ridges, his flesh warm against mine, inviting.

Gaze lifting, I paused my advance when I saw the new addition across the breadth of his chest—a crescent moon. Twin to my own, but much, much bigger, and it was completely white. It rested upon a canvas of black ink, making it stand out.

My hand slid upward, and I traced the new tattoo, taking my time with it.

"I thought the moon was fitting. It reminds me of you, particularly the day of your creation, when I stole you for the first time," Von said, his voice low. Seductive. And outright illegal, filling my thoughts with bad, bad things. Things we most definitely were going to do—tonight.

"It's perfect." I buried my teeth into my bottom lip, unable to stop myself from smiling. Releasing it, I admitted, "I quite like seeing my brand on you."

His large hand wrapped around my side, and he pulled me closer in one, swift move. His thumb brushed underneath my breast, across the delicate design. "As I enjoy seeing mine on you." Our gaze connected, and his eyes turned molten. His voice dropped on octave. "I'm trying to be patient, love, to let you have your time to get to know my body again, but my pants are becoming *increasingly* uncomfortable."

We both looked down—

Sure enough, his hard and ready cock waited below,

pressed firmly against his pants, straining against the seam, ready to be released.

Desire trickled through my body, pooling at my sex.

My fingers drifted down his abdomen, anticipation swelling as I began to unlace the strings from his pants. The fabric fell to the side, leaving one final layer between me and him. I shifted the cloth down along with his pants, allowing his proud length to spring free. It bobbed, reaching past his belly button. Powerful veins thrummed beneath his taut skin, drawing my attention to the tattoo of my lips. Still there, just as he had said.

"It's larger than I remember," I acknowledged rather honestly, looking up at him and stealing another glance at his incredible naked body as his shadows swam around his pants, dissolving them completely.

The God of Death in all his glory.

Like the big bad wolf come to life, he leaned forward, his heated breath gliding across my skin as he growled softly, "All the better to fuck you with."

My core clenched, aching for him to do just that.

But first?

First, I needed a taste.

Like a good queen, I got down on my knees for him, my dark, dominating king. Now, it was my turn to show him my respect, my servitude. My devotion.

I slid my fingers around his length, feeling the unfathomably hard ridges and thick, prominent veins pulsating with power. My hand looked so small in comparison, my ivory skin against his darkly tanned flesh.

"Sage," he groaned as I started to stroke him, feeling the softness of his skin and the hardness of the granite beneath it.

I swept my tongue along the smooth tip, tasting the briny flavor of him. My eyes rolled back. *Incredible.* My hand continued to pump him in smooth, rhythmic motions as I tongued the slit in his tip, stirring a throaty, carnal moan from him. I craved to hear that sound again and again.

Licking my lips, I took his length in my mouth.

He gathered my hair, clenching it in one tight fist. "Such a good wife," he purred.

His praise had me wanting to please him more.

So, I took him deeper. The masculine sounds coming from him sent me into a frenzy as I sucked and licked and tried everything within my power to make the controlling male come undone. I wanted him roaring at my touch.

Just when I was certain he was about to orgasm, he stopped me by giving my hair a gentle tug. Black, smoldering eyes met mine. "Stand up, Little Goddess. It's my turn now."

Half-dazed on pleasuring him, I did as he asked. I released his length from my mouth and stood. His hand wrapped around my jaw, and he tugged my mouth up to his. His lips moved against mine, coaxing mine open, filling my mouth with his hot tongue. His hand slid down the length of my body, his touch speaking on behalf of his nefarious intentions. Stopping at my hip, his fingers locked in place, he maneuvered me so my back faced the window, steering me toward it.

Our mouths were ravenous, desperate and demanding. It was a game of cat and mouse, constant teasing and toying. My hands slid over his body, desperate for every inch of him, for all his hardness pressed up against my softness.

Reaching the window, he pushed the cup off the windowsill, sending it flying. It smashed onto the street below. Von lifted me, setting me on the sill, the wood frame just barely wide enough to hold me.

I clutched on to him as his mouth began to work its way down from mine, sucking and licking, tasting and teasing. He dragged his long canines along my neck, scraping the skin, stirring it awake.

I extended my neck to him, offering him my blood.

He pressed a soft kiss against my sensitive skin, his heated breath fanning over it. "Tonight, I'm not going to feed from your neck, Little Goddess."

"But isn't blood necessary for us to restore the bond?" I asked, looking at him.

"It is, but I'm going to drink from you elsewhere."

"Where?" I breathed, voice barely audible.

A sly grin appeared on his lips. "You'll find out." He ran his long, ringed fingers between my breasts. "You're sticky from the spirits."

"I am." I arched into his touch.

"I have just *the thing* to clean you." Lowering his face to my breasts, he ran his tongue between them in one, long sweep. He did it again. His eyes stayed fixed on me, driving me wild as he cleaned my freshly inked skin with his long, wicked tongue.

He began to move his way down my torso, biting and nipping, licking and sucking. His fingers dipped between my legs, rubbing circles on my clit, stroking pleasure into me with each tantalizing swirl.

I moaned, my hips rolling as I rode his hand. I could feel my wetness dripping from my center, slickening in eager anticipation. My hands gripped his shoulders, my core pulsing with desire, looking for something to clench around.

"Von," I begged, voice saturated with desperation.

My fingernails bit into his skin as he inserted two fingers into my sex, answering my plea. He curled them inside me, hitting that sacred spot that made my eyes cross. He lowered onto his knees, his commanding tongue pleasuring that sensitive bundle of nerves.

"Ahhh," I cried out, tipping my head back. The cool breeze brushed across my heated flesh, swirling across my skin, touching me everywhere.

I knew it was because of him.

He pulled his fingers out, and my walls stuttered at the loss of him.

He held them up for both of us to see.

Tattooed fingers were covered in my arousal, dripping down his wedding ring, painting the black-silver metal in the evidence of my need for him. His eyes locked with mine as he raised his fingers to his sexy mouth. Opening his lips, he slid his fingers inside, tasting me.

"Mmm," a deep, carnal growl sounded from him as he sucked on his fingers.

Seeing Von taste me *like that*, it made me feral.

He slid his fingers from his mouth, and purred, "Just like apples."

Then, he lowered his face back to my sex. His fingers parted my lips, and he plunged his tongue into my center. His hands slid to my thighs, gripping them with bruising strength, keeping me there as he *devoured* me. A dark symphony of throaty, masculine sounds came from him as he fucked me with his long, dominating tongue.

I gasped and moaned as he worked me toward my climax. Like a dam breaking open, a flood of arousal released from me as I came undone. Von lapped up every drop, and his eyes began to glow a brilliant, vibrant green.

Seeing the beautiful color return made pride swell within me.

"I need *you*," I groaned softly, voice etched with animalistic hunger.

He raised his head, licking his lips—a dark predator who had just feasted on his prey.

His hand released my leg, and his fingers found my swollen clit, sparks of lightning erupting at his touch.

"You need to show me you can take three of my fingers, love, before I'm going to give you my cock. I'm not going to break you." His fingers slid down my slick center, entering me. "At least not tonight."

I gasped at the delicious feel of him, my body aching for more.

"Von," I panted as he slid them in and out before he aligned his third. He pressed it in, filling me ever so deliciously. There was a bit of pressure, my walls being forced to stretch around him, to accommodate what the dark god was offering.

"That's my good girl," he praised as he worked me like that for a short time, preparing me for what was next.

Removing his fingers from my sex, he stood, his body towering over mine.

Stars above, he was *big*.

He slid his fingers over his length, smearing my wetness on it. He tilted his hips, angling his sex to mine. Tattooed cock in tattooed hand, he ran his crown along my slit.

We both moaned.

His hand clutched my hip, eyes holding mine as his crown slid past my entrance, stretching me wide. There was a sting of pain, but the promise of pleasure had me starving for more.

"Need *all* of you," I panted.

"So very bossy," he mused. Then, he began to conquer every inch of me, giving my body no choice but to accept his.

Adrenaline coursed through my veins.

I had never felt more *alive* as Death filled me with his cock.

"Look at yourself," he spoke seductively. "How tightly your cunt clutches around me, taking me *so well*."

I glanced down, amazed at how he had fit all of *that* inside me. It made me feel dizzy. It made me feel carnal. Still, it wasn't enough. A third of him was still unsheathed, and that simply would not do.

I spread my legs wider, needing to have all of him.

Obliging, he slid himself deeper. He was almost all the way in when—

I gasped at the strange sensation.

There was an intense pressure, making me feel so incredibly full. It was uncomfortable and delicious all at once, and I craved to feel it again. He pulled his hips back, granting me a second of relief, then pressed back in, hitting the deepest part of me, evicting the air from my lungs, the soul from my body.

"Does it feel good to have me so deep?" he murmured as he pulled back and did it again. "Claiming *my* cunt." And again.

"Yes, gods, yes," I cried out for him, at the unreal sensations starting at my sex, shooting throughout my body.

"Gods?" Von mocked, his fingers drifting into my hair. He gave it a gentle tug. "You pray to one, *wife*, and he is a territorial bastard."

He kissed me like a tempest beast, sweeping me away into his powerful storm, the flavor of me still in his mouth, saturating his wicked tongue.

Lips pulling back a breath from mine, he admitted darkly, "I promised you would wear my silver, and although I like seeing my ring around your finger and my tattoos on your chest, it isn't enough. I need you covered in my scent, my ink on your skin, my markings, my jewelry. I need to see my touch all over you. I need to own *every* part of you." His hand cupped my breast, the pad of his thumb toying with my nipple.

"Whatever you want. I am yours." I moaned as he delivered one long, sensual stroke.

He breathed it in, his fingers releasing my hair. "You are. You are mine, every piece of you."

A sharp pain shot through my nipple, the feel of it so vicious, I was yanked back from my budding climax.

Head jerking down, my mouth fell open—there was a shadow needle *in* the tender pink bud. The sight of it made me dizzy, my mind blaring that something so sharp did not belong in something so soft. And yet, there was no denying it—it was very much *there*, placed horizontally, *all* the way through.

Warm ichor dribbled from the pierced point.

My world spun, my vision tunneling.

"Stay with me, Little Goddess," Von directed, rolling his hips, drawing my attention to where we were connected, keeping me right there, with him.

The wicked things he was doing to me . . .

I would be lucky to have a sprig of sanity leftover when he was done.

His hand settled at the base of my breast, lifting it as he dipped his head forward. He ran his hot tongue over my flesh, licking up my shimmering ichor.

A husky, needy sound fell from my lips—the area was so incredibly sensitive, and yet it felt so damn good to have his tongue there.

I craved more.

My fingers wove into his hair as he took my nipple, shadow needle and all, into his mouth. His tongue brushed against it, and the stretching sensation I felt—suddenly, it was gone.

Like that, Von drank from the piercing.

It was a dizzying, sexy sight.

The pain dissolved, leaving nothing but pleasure in its wake. His mouth was scalding, but I felt something cool slide into my nipple—it felt no different than inserting an earring.

Von pulled back, and I looked down.

The wound was completely healed, in it a delicate, silver barbell.

Gently, Von moved his hips. His thrusts were slow, sensual, but they were *deep*. With each one, I saw stars. His fingers swirled my nipple, and I moaned at the stimulation, at his carnal thrusts. It all felt incredible.

He felt incredible.

"Do the other one," I rasped, unable to believe the words coming from my mouth. I hated needles, and here I was, asking for him to pierce me again. Surface level, I probably looked like a masochist, but deep down, this was so much *more* than that.

This was a reckoning, my payment to the God of Death for my sins against him. It was a pledge, of my devotedness to him forevermore. And lastly, it was symbolic of my *willingness* to surrender to him—my mate, my king, my husband.

"Lean back," he commanded, eyes burning like emerald fire.

Obliging him, I did, my torso hanging dangerously out

the window, my legs hooked around his hips as he continued to thrust inside.

"Tip your head to the sky." His hand swept down my neck, down my chest, lower yet.

I looked up, toward the bright, vivid moon—the only witness to the pledges we had made tonight.

His knuckles grazed over the unpierced flesh. Lightly, he pinched the soft bud. I felt something sharp press against it.

I buried my teeth in my bottom lip, anticipation swelling.

Von retreated, unsheathing himself almost fully.

At the same time his shadows pierced my flesh, he drove back in.

"Von!" I screamed, as pain and pleasure exploded, my world flashing with blinding white light. I didn't orgasm, no, but what I felt was on an entirely different level of bliss. And I had no words to explain it, but all I knew was that it was such an incredible high, an adrenaline rush unlike anything I had ever felt before. Like jumping off a cliff. It was *exhilarating*.

"I'm right here, love, I'm right here," he reassured me, his mouth finding mine, kissing me sweetly. "You did so well," he praised between kisses.

My arms enveloped his neck, his thrusts slow and sensual, purposeful, keeping my thoughts on where we were connected.

"That was unreal," I whispered, still half-dazed.

"We're not done yet, sweetheart," he promised. His

fingers played with the piercing. "What do you think of them?"

Them?

Blinking, I looked down, amazed to find he'd installed the other barbell as well. When he did it, I didn't know.

The one thing I did know?

Von was right—sometimes, you needed to feel the pain of something to feel like you had a right to have it.

"I love them." I looked up to him. "I love you."

Von lowered his forehead against mine, his arms wrapping around me. "I love you, Sage. More than anything." His long, deep thrusts were different now. They were purposeful, amplifying the truth behind his spoken words.

With each stroke, he drove that message into me—*how* much he loved me.

With each one, he carved his claim into me—*mine*.

There was just one thing missing . . .

"The bond," I moaned in a breathy tone, lungs searching for air.

"You remember what comes next, yes?" he asked.

"I do," I said. I tipped my head to the side, offering him my neck.

"No, I've already had your ichor tonight," he mused, his thumb stroking my nipple, a gentle reminder. "You need to take mine."

"But how?"

"Use your teeth, Kitten."

"I don't know how."

"You do. Your body does. Think of the *taste* of me. I promise, they'll come."

I leaned into the image, picturing my teeth piercing his skin, thinking of the way his powerful ichor had once tasted on my tongue, how intoxicating it was and how—

This is how things will be for you now, Moonbeam, Aurelius's voice whispered in my mind.

I went board stiff, my eyes stretching wide.

"Sage?" Von stopped abruptly, his hands flying to my face, caressing my cheeks.

I blinked.

"What's going on?" he asked, voice worried.

I clutched on to his forearms, peering into his eyes.

His beautiful green eyes, like home to me.

If I didn't drink Von's blood, the bond would never be restored. Aurelius *would* win. He would still have control over me. No, I refused to let him have *any* part of me. I refused to let him win.

"Sage?"

"I'm fine," I said, rolling my hips. "I need more of this."

"You're sure?"

I nodded. "I am."

He brought his mouth to mine, kissing me as he began to move his hips. My legs tightened around him, as he stroked my body higher and higher. I wrapped my arms around his shoulders, our bodies tangled up in each other.

He scooped me up from the windowsill and walked us over to the wall, pressing me firmly against it, locking me between two impossibly hard things as he drove himself into me with powerful thrusts. I kissed Von's jaw, going down toward his neck. I could feel the blood swelling beneath his skin, feel it calling out to me. I could do this, I could—

This is how things will be for you now, Moonbeam, Aurelius's voice repeated inside my head, his phantom still there.

No, I internally snarled back at his ghost. *Because Von isn't you, and he will never use me like you did.* Power filled my veins as my canines erupted from my mouth, and I plunged them into Von's neck.

"That's my girl," my mate purred as I *willfully* drank from him.

Raw, ancient power exploded across my tongue, filling me with incredible strength. It was intoxicating. It was divine. It was Von. And he was all mine.

Pulling back, I licked his honey-sweet blood from my lips and said, "I claim you."

"As I claim you," he answered, branding his vow against my lips with the seal of his kiss.

I cried out as our bodies moved, speaking a dialect entirely their own.

Ancient magic thrummed around us, swirling and twirling, building into a grand crescendo. It delved beneath our skin, and we began to glow, our joined bodies encased in silver light as our souls were welded back together.

Like winter caving to spring, what once was dormant began to bloom—

The bond was reborn.

His emotions, so full of pleasure and love, thundered through me, intertwining with my own. The power of it was so strong, it sent us spiraling over the edge. My inner muscles clenched around his length, tightening and releasing as I rode out my orgasm, his name on my breathless, trembling lips.

A predator's roar came from him as he spilled his seed inside of me, the sticky, hot substance filling me. Some of it leaked out, dripping down his beautiful length, smearing between my thighs—making a mess of us both.

Panting, he lowered his forehead to mine. "From the Three Realms until the next."

"And whatever comes beyond that," I rasped out the pledge, my body completely spent.

Chapter 47

Sage

I couldn't remember the last time I felt this . . . happy.

Von and I laid in bed together, his large body curled protectively behind mine, his length still in me, the two of us unwilling to disconnect from one another. His strong arms were wrapped around me, an impenetrable fortress, one I never wanted to leave again.

It was a problem I'd have to figure out in the morning, but the morning hadn't come yet. Thankfully. And right now, I was safe and warm, and tucked up beside the one I loved most.

"Von?" I asked, my fingers painting invisible symbols against his steely forearm.

"Yes, Little Goddess?" he said, his head tucked above mine.

"Do you think bond drunk is a thing?" My voice was soft, sedated.

He chuckled. "I'd say it is."

"I think so too," I said, a small yawn escaping me. "Von?"

"Yes, my love?" he purred then pressed a kiss against the top of my head.

"I know you don't need to rest, but will you fall asleep with me tonight?" I didn't know why, but it meant something to me—that he would let his guard down and join me in the land of dreams.

He was silent for a moment before he said, "If that is what you wish, I will."

"Good." Another yawn passed my lips. "I'll see you in the morning," I mumbled as my mind closed up shop and I handed myself over to the night.

I kept low to the ground, my sister's trusted bow in one hand, an arrow in the other. I had been tracking this buck for the better half of the morning, but every time I got within range, his ears would flip back, and he'd startle into a run.

I took a deep breath, reminding myself I had nothing but time. And if there was one thing that I wasn't doing, it was going back to camp empty-handed.

Through the trees, I spotted him—

A nice-sized mule deer with four beautiful points. It had a strange white mark along the side of its neck—it almost looked like a stroke of lightning.

Without a whisper of sound, I nocked my arrow and

prepared to take the shot.

I held my breath, steadied my hand, and released.

Thwishhhhh. It whistled through the air.

Just as the deer started to run, the arrow found purchase, but not where I had wanted it to hit. Because the deer had moved, the arrow bit into its hindquarter. It wasn't enough to kill it, but it did injure it, which to me, was worse. Guilt swept over me as I cursed myself for not being quick enough. I hated when an animal needlessly suffered.

I chased after it, knowing that if the animal went down, there was a good chance I wouldn't find it in the bush—I needed to keep up with it.

Lungs heaving, legs aching, I chased it for what had to be three miles—perhaps even more. My body strained from the exertion of running through the uneven, wicked terrain. My ankles cried out the most.

The deer stopped, and I was granted another shot.

I reached back, plucking an arrow from my quiver. When I went to take it, my footing gave way, and the ground caved underneath me.

I screamed as I slid through a tunnel-like structure. It was like a massive badger had burrowed his way into the ground, digging dozens and dozens of feet below, and now, I was falling through it—

A never-ending hole.

The ends of my fingernails snapped off as I clawed at the dirt, clay, and rocks, trying to fight against gravity's greedy pull.

I was spewed out of the tunnel, and for a brief moment,

I was airborne, like a bird in the sky. The only problem? I didn't have wings.

My body crashed into the harsh ground, and I came to a rolling stop, lying on my back.

It knocked the wind out of me.

Slowly, I moved onto my side, lungs wheezing for air, bones aching. I laid like that for a minute, maybe two, before I started to get my wits about me—recalling I had just fallen down a very long tunnel, to Creator only knew where.

I propped a hand against the ground and slowly lifted myself up, spitting dirt and saliva out. When I was done, I wiped my mouth with the back of my wrist.

Neck lengthening, I looked up, and up, and up.

I must have fallen at least a mile. It was a wonder I was still alive. The tunnel must have been at just the right angle, preventing me from falling too fast—although, at the time, it had felt like I was flying.

It was a long way back to the top, and the steepness of the canyon-like walls was not something I'd be able to climb. Gigantic trees, hundreds of feet tall, spread out before me. It was as if they were trying to grow their way out of this monstrous sinkhole.

Trickling water rivered down the steeply sloped sides that surrounded me. One stream led to a lake, not far from me. Out of it leapt a sparkling silver fish. It plunked back into the water below.

What is this place? *I wondered to myself.*

A low growl rumbled from the trees, the hairs on the back of my neck standing.

I patted the ground, searching for my bow.

Dammit. *I must have dropped it when I fell.*

I reached for my dagger, always strapped to my thigh, but it wasn't there either. The weight of my quiver was gone as well.

Shit! *I had no weapons, nothing to defend myself with. The tunnel had stripped me of—*

The tunnel!

Whatever was hiding in the trees let out another warning growl, spurring me into action.

Shooting to my feet, I swirled around, spotting the hole I had been tossed out of. I started for it, eyes searching the ground for my weapons along the way.

Please. Please. Please, *I repeated the mantra.*

I looked around, frantically searching but finding . . . nothing.

My heart sank.

Trees smashed behind me, and I spun around, ready to meet my fate.

A beast, cut from darkness itself, emerged. It had sleek, black scales that looked like impenetrable armor and vicious, snarling teeth.

Larger than life. It was—

A dragon!

"Stay back!" I cried out as it approached, knocking over the trees as if they were brittle twigs. My hand trembled, my lungs heaved, my knees wobbled. The stories my father used to tell began to sift into my mind—about the dangerous dragons that lurked in the shadows of this world,

only appearing when little children didn't do as their parents asked. Those children would be taken away and never seen again. Father would snap his teeth at us, his fingers tickling our bellies as he said dragons loved to eat little kids. As I grew older and I listened to the horrific stories passed among our clan, I came to realize—dragons didn't differentiate between children and adults . . . They'd eat anything that walked.

My foot collided with something in the dirt, knocking it loose.

*My eyes widened—*my dagger!

With lightning speed, I grabbed it and thrust it up into the air, holding it out in warning as I snarled, "I mean it. Stay back!"

The dragon tipped its head curiously to the side, eyeing my dagger—about the right size for it to pick its teeth with after it was done eating me.

Its endlessly black eyes, larger than my head, shifted back to mine. Although it was a beast, its eyes were full of intelligence. It was like looking through a glass window into the inner workings of a lethally sharp mind. I could see those sleek cogs moving, turning in thought and churning out a plan.

Probably to eat me.

I swallowed, waiting for the snap of those vicious teeth to end me in one swift bite.

But then, the dragon sat down.

Its tail curled around its monstrous body. It looked like a massive black house cat, but I wasn't foolish enough to try to pet it. The tip of its tail swished from side to side in anticipation as it waited to devour me.

It was as if the dragon was enjoying this . . .

My brow furrowed, my eyes shifting as I looked for an escape. I wasn't going to allow it to torment me like this. Perhaps if I could get the rest of the way to the tunnel, I might be able to climb my way out of it. But would I be able to get there in time before the dragon's iron jaw clamped around me?

I had to try.

Turning on my heel, I sprinted toward the hole. My blood thrummed in my veins, shooting adrenaline through me. My heart pounded in my ears, my body waiting for that deadly swipe of the dragon's claws. Reaching the hole, I didn't dare look back. I leapt up, trying to grab hold of the opening, trying to pierce the wall with my dagger. I tried again and again, but I had no luck. The wall was too hard to pierce. I chucked the dagger onto the ground and resorted to my fingernails, desperation making an animal out of me, unable to think logically. Deep down, I knew the opening was too high for me to reach. Still, I jumped, my fingernails biting into the dirt, but I never got close enough.

I didn't want to die down here. I didn't want to die!

Father Creator, please help me. *I prayed, begging for his aid. I made the plea over and over again, but my prayer was never answered.*

By the time the sun started to dip its head, I was exhausted. I turned around, rested my back against the dirt wall, and slid toward the ground, crumpling in a heap of exhaustion and frustration.

I looked up at the dragon, who was still sitting there, onyx eyes thoroughly fixed on me.

That damn tail twitching from side to side.

It infuriated me.

How dare the creature take pleasure in my suffering.

My fingers, raw and bloodied, patted the ground beside me. Landing on a stone about the size of my palm, my fingers curled around it. "Well! If you are going to eat me, just fucking eat me already!" I growled as I hurtled the rock at the damned beast.

It ricocheted off the dragon's head, landing on the ground beside it. The creature didn't even move. It was like watching a mosquito strike a crocodile.

"That wasn't very nice," purred the dragon, its voice rich and deep.

I bristled. "You can talk."

"Indeed, I can," he said, offering no more, those sinister eyes watching me, always watching.

"Are you going to eat me?" I asked, regretting the question the moment it slipped past my lips. Did I really want to know if that was what he had planned? Anxiety burrowed into my chest.

The dragon chuckled, the sound sensual, enticing. "I have no intentions of eating you right now."

The right now *part didn't sit particularly well with me.*

Maybe he preferred his food dead before he ate it?

My muscles tensed at the thought. "Are you going to kill me?"

"Do I look like a killer?" The dragon smirked, showing off its horrifically sharp teeth.

"Yes," I answered honestly, stuck on the fact that the dragon had just downright smirked at me.

"You're not wrong. I have taken thousands of lives, especially mortal ones such as yours."

"Why?" I asked. "Why kill innocents?"

"Who said anything about killing innocents?" he challenged. "The souls I end are corrupt."

My brows lifted. "So then, what are you? Some type of vigilante dragon?"

"No. I am the iron hand of the Creator. His will is done through me."

I sat with that for a moment. "If that is true, what are you doing down here?"

"I was in search of a princess, however . . ." His gaze drifted over me. "A pauper has found me instead."

"A pauper!" I seethed at the insult, looking for another rock to throw.

A second chuckle rolled out of him, just as intoxicating as the first.

I set my sights on him and asked, "Well, if you don't plan to eat me, and you are in search of a princess, perhaps we should continue on our ways. Would you be so kind as to give me a lift out of here?" I looked up at the darkening sky. Before long, we would be out of daylight.

The dragon tipped his mighty face upwards. "Unfortunately, I cannot do that."

"Cannot or will not?"

"Watch the bird," he directed.

"What bird?" I asked, looking up, eyes searching.

The dragon sighed. "I often forget how poor mortal eyesight is. I do not know why the Creator made your kind so blind."

"I'm far from blind," I assured him.

"Says the mortal who cannot see the bird," he huffed.

"You are extremely irritating," I snipped, eyes still searching. Finally, I could just barely make it out. Way up above, a bird floated over the opening, its wings flapping as it moved at a leisurely pace. Considering the distance between us and the bird, and the fact that I could see it from way down here, it must have been an eagle or something of similar size.

"I could say the same for you. Now, keep your weak mortal eyes on the bird," he growled softly.

"Pfft," I blew out a breath of air but did as he said.

The bird, spotting something, decided to dip lower, until it passed through the bowl. When it did, something shifted, making the sky above look as if it were rippling, as if we were standing under water. When the bird went to return higher, it bounced against the invisible barrier, unable to pass through. It tried over and over again, before it gave up and flew down to the ground, taking refuge in a tree.

"I've been stuck down here for three months," the dragon said. "What comes in cannot leave."

My heart sank as I realized—

I was stuck down here.

With a dragon.

"Three months is a long time," I stated, my teeth warring with my bottom lip.

"I suppose for a mortal, whose life is brief, it is," he noted. *"Although, immortal or not, I have grown tired of being trapped down here."*

"So . . . what happens when you get hungry?"

He offered me a mischievous smirk, showing off his wicked incisors. "Then I'll probably eat you, Little Mortal."

"Sage," the dragon called out to me.

"Get back, you damned beast," I snarled, sending my curled fist into his steel-derived jaw.

Whack! His teeth clattered together.

My fist groaned as the skin split over my knuckles, causing ichor to brim. I couldn't see it, but I could sure *feel* it.

I groaned in pain.

"Fuck me," Von snarled. A waft of magic tinged the air, and the candle on the dresser lit, scattering the darkness from my vision. Green eyes met mine, twin to the emerald stone I wore on my ring finger. "It's me, Sage. It's me."

"Von," I spoke softly, relief washing over me.

I gasped when I saw his chin—the skin was cracked open, blood dribbling from the laceration. Had I done that? I had, hadn't I?

I shook my head. "I'm so sorry."

"It's alright," he said, glancing down at my hand. He took it in his and raised it to his mouth, kissing the injury. Instantly, the wound healed. His gaze lifted to mine. "Do you want to tell me what that was all about?"

"I thought you were the dragon," I sputtered, trying to make sense of what I'd just seen.

"What dragon?" Von asked, his hand gently stroking my forearm.

"I don't know, but I think I might have been trapped with him in the past." I inhaled a breath of air, forcing it into my lungs. My brows wove together as I recalled the way the dragon had acted, how his voice had sounded just like . . .

"Von?"

"Hmm?" he asked.

"I think the dragon might have been . . . *you*."

Chapter 48

Von

My mate telling me she thought *I* was the dragon from her dreams was not something I expected to hear tonight, out of all things. Then again, I didn't expect her to crack me in the jaw, either, but—I dabbed at the blood with the back of my hand—here we were.

"Show me," I said, conjuring a small cloth.

"How?" she asked, snatching it from me. The fabric began to grow dark, water seeping from her palm. With gentle strokes, she began to clean the blood from my chin, the cut and bruising already starting to heal.

"Our bond enables us to do more than just privately speak to one another. It allows us to walk into each other's minds, as long as the other partner allows it. Think of the dragon, return to your dreams, but take me with you this time," I instructed her.

She handed the cloth back to me, and my shadows

swallowed it.

She shrugged a shoulder. "I'll give it a try."

"Alright."

We laid back down, and I pulled the blankets over us. I tugged her naked frame against mine, tucking her in close to me, right where she belonged. I slid my fingers across her cheek, tipping her head to the side so I could kiss her lips. Her arm wrapped around my neck, and she kissed me back.

I love you, she said through our bond.

I love you too, I answered back, kissing the tip of her nose. *Now go to sleep, Kitten, and show me this dragon of yours.*

I'll see you in my dreams, she spoke softly.

You will, I assured her, kissing her shoulder. I glanced at the candle and cut the oxygen going to it, effectively killing the flame and painting the room in darkness.

Lowering my head back onto the pillow, I gently ran my fingers along her side, stroking her until she finally fell asleep. When her breathing became slow and rhythmic, I closed my eyes and walked into my mate's mind, the door left wide open for me.

If the birds didn't stop their incessant chirping, I would roast them all to ash. All day long, that's all they did. Chirp, chirp, fucking chirp. It was becoming rather irritating. Although, it was not nearly as irritating as the mortal female

I was stuck in this giant hole with.

She was always up to something, always making noise. If she wasn't working on her shelter, she was fishing in the lake, and if she wasn't fishing in the lake, she was trying to dig her way out of here through the partially collapsed hole she had arrived in nearly two weeks ago.

I let out a sigh, stretched out my neck, and placed my head on the ground. My tail swirled in the cool lake water, the only thing keeping my temper at bay. When the Creator sent me on my last mission, I never expected to get trapped here.

Yet, here I was.

Over by the hole, there came a heavy thump, followed by an, "Oomph!"

I jerked my head up, squinting at the female as she rubbed her bottom.

"You are rather noisy," I growled at her.

"I'm trying to get out of here," she snipped at me. "Which is more than you can say."

"It will take you years to dig your way out, and even if you do manage to get back to the surface, how do you know the barrier does not extend to it? Your efforts will be in vain."

"Well . . ." She got back up on her feet and crossed her arms. She was a mess. Dirt was smeared all over her face, painting the white strands of her hair brown. "I'll deal with that when I get to it." She turned away from me and started climbing back up the ladder she had built out of fallen branches, returning to her hole like a little mouse.

I rolled my eyes and went back to my resting position.

It wasn't much longer, and her grunts became even louder.

My eyes narrowed. She was doing that on purpose.

That was it. I was going to eat her today.

I was feeling hungry anyway, and I couldn't stand the stomach-curling fish she kept trying to feed me, something I suspected she was doing to stave off my hunger.

Standing on my fours, I went over to the hole. "Come out, Little Mortal. I wish to show you some—

I sputtered as a pile of dirt landed in my mouth.

I spat it out then hissed, "I should breathe my fire into this tunnel and roast you alive for that."

"Oh, sorry. I didn't know you were there," she called, her voice echoing down the tunnel.

"You are a terrible liar," I growled.

"And you are a terrible companion," she tossed back.

A companion? I had never been referred to as such. The word struck me odd. Perhaps I was even a bit dumbfounded.

"Actually, you know what?" she snarled at me as she slowly crawled back down to the opening, careful not to lose her grip this time. She poked her dirty little head out at me. The gall of this woman. I didn't know if she was stupid or obscenely brave. She pointed her makeshift shovel at me. "You are the worst dragon I've ever seen."

"I'm the only dragon you've ever seen," I stated flatly.

"Yeah, well, that doesn't matter. Aren't you supposed to be powerful beings? But all you do is lay around all day like

some lazy house cat!"

I chuckled at that.

"You find me funny, do you?" she seethed.

"I do," I said. "Which is lucky for you, because I had fully planned on eating you a few moments ago, but now, perhaps I shall let you live for another day, for entertainment purposes."

I didn't bother to wait for her reply as I turned around. I was about to start back toward my spot when something smacked the back of my head. I barely felt it, yet it still annoyed me, because the act lacked respect. My claws dug into the ground, cracking the earth beneath me.

"I would advise you not to do that again," I warned.

"And if I do?" she challenged.

"Then I will drag you out from that hole, bend you over my knee, and give you the spanking you deserve for acting like a brat," I hissed.

She gave me a funny look, equal parts insulted and confused. "You can't do that. You're a dragon."

"On the contrary, I can, and I'm not just a dragon." My iron bones hissed and cracked as they started to shrink and rearrange themselves. The black faded from my scales as the gaps between them filled, and they became smooth as velvet. Tanned skin stretched over my forearms, inked with black markings. Clothes, forged from shadow, wrapped around my vessel. I stood as a god before her and raised my hand, eyeing it. "Well, would you look at that."

"You're a god!" she stuttered.

"Indeed, I am," I said, smirking.

414

Surprise lit her features as she went to press her hand against the dirt, but she wasn't looking, and she reached too far and went ass over teakettle. I caught her before she hit the ground. Her scent washed over me, her blue eyes locking with mine.

I had never realized how beautiful they were before. My gaze lowered to her plump lips. I wondered if they were as soft as they looked.

She cleared her throat. "You can set me down now."

"I could. I definitely could," I said, still mesmerized by her mouth.

"So then . . . why don't you?"

"Why are you so eager to get out of my arms?"

"You're being weird. I think I prefer the side of you that would rather eat me."

"I just caught you. A mere thank you would suffice," I hissed as I set her down.

She rolled her eyes. "Thank you. There, happy?"

I couldn't believe how rude she was. Had her mortal parents taught her nothing? Was she raised in a barn? Under a bridge?

Deciding I was done wasting my time with her, I stalked off, growling under my breath. "Infuriating mortal."

Infuriating mortal, indeed. I smiled as I studied the slumbering face of my wife—the enchantress who had come into my life and fully and irrevocably bewitched me. She had forged herself as my heart and taken permanent residency inside my rib cage. There, she would forever remain—ruling over me and all that I was. My body was hers. Her will, my hands. Her happiness, my purpose.

A small breath fell from her slightly parted lips, her eyes still closed. Her body was nestled against mine, my arms cocooned around her. An impenetrable fortress.

Slowly, she woke, her nose crinkling as she let out a yawn—much like a tiny lioness. *Adorable*. Her lashes flickered and her eyelids drifted open. Celestial blue eyes met mine and the corners of her mouth shifted into a dazed smile.

"You are a nice sight to wake up to," she spoke in her morning voice. Her hand slid from underneath the blankets, reaching for my cheek. Soft fingers stroked my stubble, sounding against the stubborn bristles.

I leaned into her touch. "As are you, love." Truer words had never been spoken, and yet, they seemed lackluster. Having her here in my arms, tucked away in my protection, made me so damn happy it was a shame there were no words available to explain such a divine feeling.

"We should make a note to do this more often then," she teased.

"I agree. Thoughts on now until the end of time?"

She thought it over for a moment. "I think I could get used to that."

I loosened one arm from her and stroked her hair, my touch tender. "Wonderful. I'll make the arrangements."

She chuckled softly then asked, "What are your

thoughts on the dream I had?"

"I have no doubt that was us in our past lives." A wolfish grin unfurled on my lips as I propped myself up on my elbow. "Probably a good thing I didn't eat you back then."

"Von," she scolded me, but her playful grin and the twinkle in her eyes betrayed her reprimand.

"Maybe just one little bite." I captured her fingers and brought them to my lips so I could nip at them.

"Von!" She giggled, trying to pull her fingers from me, but I would not relent.

"Just a taste," I teased in between light chomps. "I don't think you need this finger, do you?" I popped the one in my mouth and bit down, softly.

She let out a surprised mousy squeak, one that took us both by surprise.

I released her imprisoned finger from my mouth and said with a smirk, "That was adorable, wife."

She squinted at me, her message clearer than a mountain spring—*shut up*.

I chuckled at that. I cupped her chin and brought my mouth close to hers. "Hmm, I wonder what other noises I can get you to make."

Her lips parted, her tongue sharpened with a clever remark. Before she could speak, my lips laid claim to hers. I kissed her slowly, wickedly, deeply. Ensuring she knew who her owner was. Her keeper. Her protector. Her provider.

Hers.

When I pulled back, I cocked my head to the side.

"Were you going to say something, darling?"

"That was a dirty trick," she quipped, although she didn't look the least bit sad about it.

"Lucky for you, I have an arsenal of them."

"Please . . . feel free to use them anytime."

I brushed my thumb across her bottom lip. "I intend to." Fingers sliding from her jaw, I found her hand and raised her palm to my mouth, placing a gentle kiss against the soft flesh.

As I did that, she asked, "Did the dream bring back any memories for you?"

"No, it didn't."

"And what are your thoughts on the whole . . . shifting into a dragon thing?"

"I don't really know what to make of it, but apparently, at one point, I could."

"Perhaps you will be able to again."

"Perhaps," I said, wondering if it were possible. I had only recently been able to tap into my giant form. Would my dragon form soon follow? Perhaps one was a step to another? Time would tell. My gaze met hers. "Have you recovered any other memories of your life here or mine?"

"I have. Can I show you through the bond?"

I nodded. "You can."

Making herself comfortable, she nestled against my chest and then granted me access to all of it—

Together, we walked through the past.

Sage showed me the memories of her and Artemesia as they grew up together. She showed me the day when she was taken from her family's summer home, traded to the empress in exchange for the protection of her people. She showed me how the empress had planned to use her to find out what my weakness was.

One memory I found particularly endearing, of when I had fought in the arena and she threw a glass of wine at my face then stormed off. My feisty female.

Then, her memories shifted to more recent ones, spanning from the moment she was pulled from the Miyakai river, which, to her, had felt as if it were waterless, something I found rather interesting. It did indeed have water flowing through it. I wondered if it was because her soul had been disconnected from her vessel, and so she had been unable to feel it.

Memories moving forward, she showed me what happened between then and the moment she saw me, flying for her, with the empress's winged horse riders gaining behind her.

When we returned to the present, I held her in my arms for a long, long while.

After some time passed, she poked her head up and said, "There's something that has been bothering me."

"What is it?" I asked softly, tucking a strand of hair behind her ear.

"In the past, the empress wanted me to find your weakness so she could use it against you and win the War of the Creators. But then, she sent me to the Three Realms, to retrieve your soul. Why would she want to get rid of you and then go to such extraordinary lengths to get you back?"

I thought it over for a moment, combing through the memories she had just shown me. Until I stopped on one—of when Sage's soul and her body were still disconnected.

"The empress said I was . . . the key," I said, showing her the memory through the bond.

"The key to what, though?" Confusion drew her brows together. Then, they lifted. She jerked upright, eyes stretching wide. "What if it's because you were able to shift into a dragon?"

"What do you mean?" I asked, sitting up. I tossed an arm over my bent knee, my gaze fixed on her.

"Artemesia told me that dragons were wiped out during the empress's war. She had their bodies taken to Avolonia because she wanted to recreate the species, but she never succeeded. What if she thinks you are the key to making them again?"

My eyes flicked back and forth. What Sage was saying made sense, but . . . I finished the thought out loud. "Why would the empress care so much about making more dragons?"

"Artemesia said something about . . . Oh, how did she phrase it . . ." Sage chewed her bottom lip. A sliver of jealousy wedged its way into me—I should be the one doing the biting right now. Releasing it, she continued, drawing my attention back to the conversation. "She said something to the extent of *because the empress was unable to create dragons, it was a failure that some were starting to take note of.* Perhaps she thinks that if she can create more dragons, it will secure her reign for longer?"

I mulled it over. "It's plausible."

A light knock came at our door, followed by Harper's muffled voice. "Are you two up? Artemesia called a meeting in her room."

"We'll be right there," Sage responded over her shoulder, throwing her voice. She turned to me. "We'll discuss this later." Then, she had *the audacity* to start to get up.

I snaked an arm around her torso and pulled her back against me. "Yeah, no. You are not leaving the bed yet."

"Von," she laughed as I flipped her onto her back.

I propped myself over her, my arms falling on either side of her body, caging her in. "I'm starving."

She ran her fingers up my forearm. "I'm sure there's some food downstairs—"

"I don't want mortal food." I raked my gaze over her. "I hunger for *you*, wife."

"Oh . . . oh," she whispered, heat licking at her cheeks. Her eyes shifted down to my chest, the soft pads of her fingers gliding over the crescent moon tattoo. Drawing a breath, her lashes lifted, and her gaze returned to mine. "So you intend to eat me after all?"

"Mind. Body. Soul. *Every* inch of you," I promised her. I moved to the bottom of the bed, my gaze never losing hers. I stood, my hands locked around her ankles, and I dragged her down until her bottom reached the end of the bed.

She didn't fight me, no—willingly, she gave herself to me.

My knees met the floor, and I draped her legs over my

shoulders, one at a time.

Her sex was slick with arousal. My mouth watered.

"Do you enjoy getting on your knees for me, Death?" she asked, propping herself up on her elbows, a toying smile gracing her lips.

"Do you enjoy having your cunt licked, Life?"

She swallowed, then admitted, "I do."

"Then you have your answer." I lowered my mouth to her clit, my tongue swirling around it, and she let out a small whimper. I laved her sensitive bud, playing and licking until I couldn't take it anymore. Lowering my mouth to her center, I ran my tongue along her slit, a deep, primal, satisfactory growl emitting from my chest.

Just like a fucking apple.

Dark desire overtaking me, I slid my tongue into her core. The taste of her exploded across my taste buds, and my grip turned crushing against her legs. My veins swelled, filling with immense power as I feasted. I could feel the wood floor beneath me giving way, the walls around us disappearing, until my focus was solely on her, and hers on me.

I ate her until she was screaming and coming undone on my tongue, flooding my mouth with her decadent release.

"Mmm," a husky moan, born from somewhere deep, emitted from me.

Perhaps there was a bit of dragon in me after all.

Chapter 49

Sage

Fallon stood across the room from me, arms tightly crossed, back against the wall. She'd looked seething mad all morning. Her jaw was clamped so tightly it was a wonder her molars hadn't combusted, but then again, maybe they had. Even when Von and I had announced to everyone we had wedded last night, she offered only a brittle congratulations before going back to her brooding.

Apparently, she and Kaleb had spoken earlier that morning, but the conversation became heated, and Kaleb had decided to end things between them. Artemesia had whispered it to me before Von and I walked inside her and Folkoln's room a couple hours ago.

I was seated on the bed along with Lyra, Harper, and Kaleb. Lyra's fingers were threaded with mine, her head resting against my shoulder, her other hand linked with Harper's. Every once in a while, I'd sneak a glance at the ring on my finger, checking to make sure it was still there, that I hadn't just dreamt up last night, that Von and I really were husband and wife. Earlier, I'd shown everyone the ring, and the girls—plus Kaleb—had all squealed and fawned over it while the guys slapped Von on the shoulder in congratulations. Soren, who was more so cowering in the corner of the room, had spoken through our minds, offering me a small congratulations before he scurried back to his hole. Ryker sat in the chair next to us, his big body dwarfing it. Von and Folkoln lingered by the window while Artemesia stood in the middle of the room, leading the discussion surrounding what our plans were and how we were to get home. Von and I had yet to tell them about our plans to find out what happened to our child, but we'd get to that when the time was right.

During the meeting, the others shared how they had arrived here—which sounded horrible, by the way. Von showed Artemesia and me the travel stone he'd received from the giant. She conceded she didn't know a great deal about them or how they worked—however, she had plenty of ideas about who might know more.

"This . . . Goddess of Knowledge that you spoke of earlier," Folkoln started, his chin tipped ever so slightly, small bits of smoke breaking off from his imposing form. "Where would we find her?"

Artemesia turned to face him. "She resides in the south, in the Naftiah Desert. However, the palace she lives in is protected by a vicious sandstorm, something she herself was rumored to create in order to keep unwanted intruders out. It is said those who dare to tempt the storm are rarely ever seen again."

"I'm not opposed to it, but it does sound really risky," Ryker said, his fingers scrubbing at his beard—a new addition. It looked quite good on him.

"It is," Artemesia agreed, arms threading loosely over her chest.

Kaleb's voice came from beside me. "Perhaps we should try the miner town you suggested earlier, where some of the energy stones were once harvested from. Maybe someone there will know why they quit working."

I glanced at him. His hair was disheveled, eyes tired, and it wasn't just from the hangover.

Fallon scoffed.

My eyes turned into slits as I slid them over to her, my gaze cutting like a lethal blade. I unthreaded my hand from Lyra's, just in case.

"What?" Kaleb asked, his voice like death. Cold, harsh. Unwelcoming.

"Nothing," she said with disdain, shaking her head.

"Clearly, it's something, so why don't you just say it?" he grated.

The room fell silent, so silent I could hear the rapid drumming of Kaleb's heart. Perhaps it was mine—the whole situation had the rest of us on edge, wishing we were anywhere else.

"Alright, fine," Fallon stated, her chin raising in superiority as she looked down her nose at *my* brother. "It's just so *you* to pick the easier option, because that's what you do, isn't it, Kaleb? When things get tough, instead of fixing them, you fuck off."

The skin over my knuckles groaned as I clenched my fists.

Sage, Von warned, sending the words down the private river that connected our minds.

I didn't answer.

Still, Fallon went on. "Leave it up to you to take the easy way out. You are such a damn coward, and everyone in this room knows it."

That's it.

I flew off the bed, leaving a spray of sheets in my wake as I leapt at her, my fist sailing through the air. She charged for me too, but right before we collided, Von's arm wrapped around my torso and pulled me back while Folkoln grabbed her.

"You *do not* get to speak of my brother that way," I roared, pushing against Von's hands. *Let me go*! I snarled through our bond.

"What sort of man needs his sister to stand up for him?" she snipped back as she tried to free herself from Folkoln. "And besides, who are *you* to *judge me*? You had sex with someone else too, you fucking hypocrite."

Red bled into my vision.

I was going to kill her.

But Artemesia beat me to it.

Faster than a bolt of lightning, she swung, cracking her fist against the side of Fallon's face, sending her head careening to the side in a spray of blood, misting the wall.

The blow was so hard it made the whole room wince.

Folkoln released Fallon.

"Don't you ever speak to my sister like that again," Artemesia warned, her voice deceptively calm, the kind of calm that took place right before a devastating storm.

Kaleb and Harper shot up from the bed, Lyra following after them.

Then, Ryker was there, placing himself in front of Artemesia and Fallon. "Enough," he said, his voice firm. "Fallon is hurting right now, and the last thing she needs is everyone to pile up on her."

Folkoln maneuvered protectively behind Artemesia, his dark eyes fixed on Ryker, like a snake in the grass, ready to strike if given reason.

Fallon winced as she wiped at her bloodied cheek.

I glared at Ryker. "Just because she is hurting doesn't give her the right to treat Kaleb like shit or speak to me like that."

"No, it doesn't," he agreed, his voice soft, understanding. He took a breath.

I did the same. I think we all did.

"I merely spoke the truth," Fallon muttered under her breath.

I bristled at her words.

Von's iron arms loosened from my torso, the one swirling from my front to my back as he moved to my side. He towered over everyone else in the room, his head nearly reaching the ceiling above. "Move aside, Ryker," he commanded, his voice dripping with authority—a king speaking to a soldier. It was absolute, drenched with raw, unfathomable power.

The whole room fell silent.

Ryker studied him for a moment before he complied.

Fallon looked up, her wide eyes locked on Von, watching closely.

"Sage is *my* mate, *my* wife, and *your* queen. You will treat her as such. This is not negotiable, nor is it something I will ask again." Von's voice was a steel blade, his words cutting so precisely, it was like watching her skin being flayed open, leaving her vulnerable and bloodied. "You will show her respect, or you will find yourself on the wrong side of my sword. Am I understood?"

Fallon dropped onto bended knee, her head bowed in subservience as she stammered, "Yes, yes, my king."

I had never seen her so humbled before, so obedient.

I'd be a liar if I claimed it did not please the immortal side of me to see her like that.

"Good. Now—" He looked at me. "There is something else we need to discuss with the rest of you."

I breathed in, knowing this topic wasn't going to be an easy one.

After everyone returned to their places, we told them. About how I died. About how our child died.

It wasn't easy.

Some parts were like taking a knife and pressing it to my scars, slicing them open again and showing them all how my body wept for my loss—*our* loss.

Throughout it all, Von stood by my side, his hand

locked in mine.

When we finished, Harper stood. "We'll help you find them. Then, we'll all go home together."

I shook my head. "We can't ask that of you all."

"We aren't leaving anyone behind, and if your child is here, that includes them too. Besides, having more eyes and ears will be helpful," Ryker interjected.

"Or we might be slowing them down," Soren piped up from his spot in the corner. I'd all but forgotten he was here. "Perhaps we should concentrate on finding a way home and then take it."

Ignoring Soren, Harper looked to Artemesia. "The Goddess of Knowledge would probably be able to help us find out what happened to the child's soul, or at least point us in the direction of where to look, right?"

"She'd give us more of a lead than the mining town would," Kaleb added.

The group nodded—well, everyone except for Fallon and Soren.

"So, we're going to the desert then," Ryker stated.

"There is a third option," Artemesia suggested.

"Which is?" I asked.

"We split up and do both," she answered. "Vatara knows these lands better than I do. She can fly some of the group to Viscourt so they can speak with the miners. I'll take the other group to the desert."

"I'm not fond of the idea of splitting up again," Von stated, a muscle feathering in his jaw. Green eyes roved over mine. "But I also know the sooner we can leave these lands, the better."

Artemesia glanced at the rest of us. "What do you all think?"

"I think it sounds like a plan," Kaleb said.

"Agreed," the twins concurred.

"Alright then. Von, Sage, Folkoln, and Kaleb—you four will come with me to the Naftiah Desert while Vatara, Harper, Ryker, Lyra, Soren, and Fallon go to Viscourt," Artemesia said, and the rest of us nodded.

Chapter 50

Avriel

Warm blood trickled down my fingers as I raised the heart, freshly carved from a male goat's chest, above my head, for all to see. The throne room was filled to the brim with attendees, everyone wearing their finest clothes for today.

On the first day of every month, we offered a sacrifice to the empress on behalf of the people. It was a tradition that began shortly after she defeated the emperor. Originally, a heart was offered from an immortal male's chest, but as time passed and those became less easy to come by, priestesses had resorted to animals instead.

I looked at the heart in my hands and then at the poor creature lying by my feet. His pale tongue had fallen out of his mouth, eyes bleak and lifeless. The knife I had used lay beside his slit abdomen, entrails leaking out of him. It was a bloody mess.

All of this was a bloody mess.

In truth, I didn't see why this sacrifice was necessary anymore, but people had a hard time breaking with millennia-old traditions. And because of it—I spared one more glance at the horned goat—the innocent suffered.

The irony of it all was that half of the time the empress didn't even show up for the sacrificial ceremony, and some poor animal had to needlessly die because of it.

I relaxed my clenched jaw, remembering I had hundreds of eyes on me and then began to chant in an ancient tongue. The bottom of my pristine white robes swept along the ground as I walked up to the foot of the dais that housed the empress's mighty, empty throne.

Knees bending, I lowered onto them, the fabric of my ceremonial garb bunching stiffly under my knees, digging into my skin where the fabric had folded over.

I paid it little mind—the goat had suffered far worse.

Continuing to chant, I lowered the organ muscle into the bronze bowl sitting on the ground before me. The heart made the softest of plunks as it fell inside. I waved my hand over it as if I were stirring a pot. The bowl began to twirl, guided by the breath of my wind.

The monstrous doors groaned as they opened behind me. That was odd. No one was allowed in once the ceremony started.

My tongue stilled, and I glanced over my shoulder, my gaze falling right on the empress as she stampeded toward me.

My mind flared with panic.

Shit.

Did she know Shadow and I were planning to leave tomorrow?

No, how *could* she know?

We had told *no one*.

We'd been careful.

. . . Hadn't we?

I got to my feet, my bloody fingers itching to reach for the rabbit's foot, my legs ready to run, muscles on blaring alert. I'd toss myself out of the window if I had to—there was no way I was going to become Victor's vessel-growing factory. I'd rather die.

As she approached, I steeled my spine, readying for the worst.

"Get out of my way," she snarled with mirth, her manicured hand grabbing hold of my shoulder and shoving me to the side. I stumbled, but I didn't fall.

Swiftly, I turned to face her, watching as she grew to her giant size, strode up the stairs, and seated herself in her massive, imposing throne.

Realizing my paranoia had gotten the better of me, I quickly dropped into a bow, just like everyone else in the room. I'd made a fool out of myself, and I'd let the invisible mask slip. I was damned lucky that the empress had something else on her mind and hadn't seemed to notice.

"Everyone rise," she commanded. As we all did, she said to the guards standing near the door, "Tell them to come in."

The guards nodded and stepped out.

Seconds later, they returned with three soldiers from

the empress's imperial army. They looked weary and battle-worn. I recognized the one—a general by the name of Areon. She had been present during the meeting that took place a few days ago, when news first came to us that the Goddess of Life might have been spotted, flying with another female on the back of a gryphon. Upon hearing the news, the empress had dispatched some of her forces, tasking them to retrieve her.

My heart fell into my stomach—had they been successful?

And if so, where were they keeping her?

"Speak, General. Tell them *all* what you and your soldiers have witnessed," the empress commanded, her voice absolute.

Witnessed? Confusion tempted my brow, but I did not lower it. I would not let my invisible mask slip for a second time today.

General Areon stepped forward, her helmet tucked underneath her arm. "In all my years, I have never seen such power," she started, turning toward the crowd. "A short few days ago, we were tasked to retrieve the white-haired traitor, the female who escaped her fate in the arena."

Hushed whispers scattered across the room.

The general continued, "We did manage to find her; however, she was not alone."

Tension drifted around every one of us, hanging like fog in the air—dense and hard to see through.

The general took a shaky breath and then said, "Nockrythiam was there."

The throne room erupted into chaos, faces filling with shock, eyes stretching wide with horror. While they all panicked, I remained calm—

Hopeful.

If Nockrythiam was truly back . . . that could change *everything*.

"Calm yourselves." The empress's voice erupted like thunder, bouncing off the gemstone walls as she rose from her throne. "*I* stood against Nockrythiam in the past, and it was *I* who won that battle." She spoke with great conviction, taking her time to deliver the message because she wanted it to sink in. "I will do the same again. I will protect you all from the heathen and his ilk. I will ensure what we have built remains intact. No male will destroy the laws of our realm."

As the people around me nodded, I realized a sad truth—

They were all under her spell, blinded by her lies and the familiarity of what they knew.

"Do not fear, my loves," Empress Avena cooed performatively, placing a dazzling smile on her face. The charade came to her just as easily as if she were changing jewelry. "I will do all within my power to crush Nockrythiam and protect you."

People began to cheer and clap, endorsing her words.

I felt sick to my stomach.

She told them not to fear, but that's exactly the emotion she was trying to seed into them. That was how she had controlled them for so many centuries—by selling them her snake oil, convincing them there was a problem they needed her help taking care of, telling them a monster was prowling outside their doors, when the truth of the matter was, she was already inside.

Later that night, I was in my room, my stomach flipping and flopping. Tonight's dinner was one of my favorite plates—roasted, lemon-stuffed chicken and warm, creamy mashed potatoes, but I had barely touched it.

My nerves were bad, my palms sweaty, and I was shedding hair like a stressed-out cat.

There was *so much* riding on tomorrow.

After Shadow had retrieved the map, we'd debated for a few days, but we'd finally come up with a plan to escape. The only downside was that it put us dreadfully close to when Victor planned to take me away. However, it was the best plan we had, and it would allow us to travel a great distance before anyone realized we were missing. One of Shadow's soul crusher events was scheduled for tomorrow, in an arena with an underground river that ran directly beneath it. The river was going to be our horse, carrying us away faster than our legs ever could. Hopefully, it would give us enough of a head start.

Hopefully.

I finished going through the satchel we planned to take with us—for the third time that night—and closed it up, walking over to my armoire. As I stuffed it inside a skirt and hid it in the very back, a knock sounded on my door.

My heart leapt into my throat and my fingers went straight for my rabbit's foot . . . I thought I had been nervous *before*.

Knock! Knock! There it was again, and whoever it was did not sound patient.

I froze. I didn't know what to do. It was *very* late.

Too late for visitors.

"Avriel, are you in there?" Mercia urgently spoke from the other side of the door. "Her Majesty is losing her mind, and she needs all council members and priestesses to help her look."

I shoved a breath into my stiff lungs, forced myself to blink, and moved toward the door. By the time I got there, my sky-high blood pressure came down a few notches. I opened it and said with a fake yawn, "Sorry, about that. I fell asleep at my desk. You gave me quite the startle."

"I can tell. You look paler than milk," she said, offering me an apologetic smile. Tonight, her shoulders were coated with monarch butterflies. The orange and black beauties were lined up in a perfect row. The color and pattern in their wings matched the sleek, body-hugging dress she wore. "Sorry about that, but it's urgent."

"What's going on?" I asked, leaning against the door. Firstly, because I'd nearly almost had a heart attack a few short seconds ago and needed the support, and secondly, because I wanted to keep up the charade of being tired.

"The empress is looking for two souls she had stored in the Archive of Souls Tower, but she can't find them. She is having everyone go through every box. If they aren't found, High Priestess Calandra could lose her life."

High Priestess Calandra oversaw the highly secretive tower, which very few were granted access to. I had only seen her a handful of times, but from what I knew of her, she was quite kind. It made me sad to hear her life might be in jeopardy. Part of me wanted to help, but the other part of me knew I should stay as far away from the empress as possible—I was already on edge. I didn't need her growing suspicious of me at the last minute.

"But the tower is forbidden to lower priestesses like me," I said, hoping I could wiggle my way out of this.

"Not tonight it isn't," Mercia replied. "Besides, haven't you always wanted to see what the tower is like? I've lived here for two thousand years and I've never seen it. It could be the experience of a lifetime."

Or the end of one if the empress smells a runaway in her midst, I thought to myself.

"Are you sure the empress wants all priestesses there?"

"Yes, she demands it." Mercia's brows pressed together. "I'm surprised by you, Avriel. Everyone is flocking to the tower to help her, and yet you aren't even interested." She raised a brow. "Do you have something better to do tonight?" Her eyes flicked past the door. "You wouldn't be hiding a dirty secret in your room, would you? Perhaps," she whispered with a playful smile, "one of the empress's courtesans?"

"Don't ever say that again," I scolded her, my voice firm. "I would never do that to the empress. And I've taken an oath of celibacy, as all priestesses must do."

"Sheesh, you bunch are so uptight. I'm only joking," she said, a hand landing on her hip, which she popped to the side.

"Yes, well, it's not funny. Jokes like that could get my soul crushed," I hissed at her.

"I'm sorry, Avriel," Mercia apologized. It felt genuine.

"It's alright." I sighed softly, realizing I didn't really have a choice. If word got out that Mercia had asked me to come and I had decided not to go, even though the empress had requested it, that could arouse suspicions.

So, begrudgingly, I agreed to go.

Chapter 51

Avriel

Mercia and I walked down a heavily guarded hallway, tucked in a part of the palace closed off to everyone but the empress and a handful of her most-trusted high priestesses. Oh, and Victor. Of course.

Doors groaned as they opened, and we stepped inside the tower. It possessed the same layout as the Creator's Tower and was similarly sized, but in place of whirring tools and nightmarish screams, the space was as quiet as a library. There were shelves upon shelves full of small wood boxes—*millions* of them.

"Thank you for coming," Priestess Anna spoke in a hushed tone as she walked up to us, handing Mercia and me a piece of paper. On it was a painting of two souls. "This is what we are looking for."

One of the orbs was purely gold with unique markings on it. I peered closer. It was a sun with a crown floating above it. The soul beside it was also gold, but it was full of maniacal claw marks, no rhyme or reason to them. In the claw marks were hints of red, reminding me of blood pooling into a wound.

Priestess Anna continued, her voice barely audible, "Both souls were placed in a golden box. The gold one with the sun on it was a recent addition to the Archive of Souls, added only two weeks ago. The other one has been here for a few hundred years. High Priestess Calandra took the box out so she could add the new soul to it, as the two are kin. She said she put it back in its designated spot, but the box is no longer there."

"Who do the souls belong to?" Mercia quietly asked, tipping her head in curiosity.

"The empress hasn't told us; however, she says it is imperative they are found. Every box must be gone through," Priestess Anna replied.

"Has anyone found the gold box they were originally in?" I whispered, glancing up at the sky-scraping tower. Despite how many people were here, it would take us weeks to go through all the boxes, and I didn't have weeks—I had until tomorrow, which meant the missing souls needed to be found tonight.

"No, the box hasn't been found either," Priestess Anna answered.

"So then why go through *every* box? Why not focus on looking for the missing gold one?"

"That's a good question. Maybe *you* should go and ask the empress," Priestess Anna stated somewhat sarcastically, a pointed look to her expression.

Internally, I sighed, her message loud and clear.

"I'll leave you to it," she whispered, bowing her head before she walked off to another group who had just arrived, handing them each a paper.

"I'm going to go start looking," Mercia spoke softly before she, too, headed off.

So I did as well.

I picked a random row marked *unsearched* and got to work.

Hours later, my back was stiff from bending over and my fingers felt like they had collected a permanent layer of dust—enough to make a second layer of skin, honestly. All the souls inside the boxes were beginning to look the same.

At this rate, we were going to be here for weeks doing this pointless task.

This palace was full of goddesses and priestesses, and this was what we were down to? Manually opening and closing boxes? Surely, there had to be a quicker way to go through them, but the empress had decided this was the best option—not that I could fathom why. She was sadistic—maybe this was her way of making us suffer.

For what, I didn't know.

I shook my head and moved on to the next section. Bending over, I reached for a box lower down.

"Priestess," a voice spoke from behind me—one that

made my blood turn to ice.

I jerked upright and spun around. "Victor," I said.

He offered me a smarmy smile. "It's good to see you."

"You as well," I lied.

"Are you looking forward to our little getaway together?" he asked in a way that made my skin crawl. "I think it will be quite enjoyable for you to get out of the palace and see another side of life, wouldn't you agree?"

"Yes, I'm looking forward to it." Lie. Lie. Lie.

"Wonderful. Say, why are so many people here and at such a late hour?"

"Two souls have gone missing, so the empress is having us look for them," I answered, picking up the drawing of the souls from the shelf I had rested it on. My body screamed *no!* as I forced myself to step closer to him, handing over the paper.

Victor took it, studying it for a second. A strange look flickered over his face. It almost looked . . . calculated, but it was gone swiftly. "I know where they are."

"You do?" I asked, surprised at this development.

"Indeed." He handed the paper back to me. "I took them a week ago and have been working on bodies for them."

"And you didn't think to tell me?" the empress roared, her voice murderous as she stomped up beside us. Startled, I jerked my face toward her. Her hair whipped violently around her, caught on the current of her anger.

"I didn't think I needed to," Victor retorted, completely unfazed by her fearsome state. "Do *I* need to, Avena?"

She was silent. The storm passed in her eyes, and her hair floated back down. "No, you don't," she answered, forcing a breath of air into her lungs. "You said you are working on vessels for them?"

"I am, I am, and I'm glad to report they are close to being done. I had planned to surprise you with them before Priestess Avriel and I left. I figured they might be helpful to you in your search for Sagentia."

"I had the same idea, which is why I was looking for them, but it would seem you are steps ahead of me," the empress said, her tone much more friendly. "However, I have one more request."

"What might that be?" he inquired curiously.

Her lips twisted into a cruel smile. "I want you to make another set of vessels for them. If they succeed at their task, we'll give them their original vessel as a reward." Her eyes swung to mine, just noticing that I, too, stood there. "Go tell everyone else the souls have been found and they are to leave the tower immediately."

"Yes, Your Majesty," I said, bowing before I swiftly scampered away. I was more than happy to put some distance between me and them.

Come tomorrow, hopefully, it would be even more.

Chapter 52

Von

Three days had passed since we'd separated from the others. By now, they should have reached Viscourt. We, however, were only halfway to the Naftiah Desert, which Artemesia said would take us about six days to reach by flight. So, under the concealment of my shadows, Folkoln and I carried the girls as we flew toward our destination while Kaleb kept up in his raven form.

Every once in a while, we would stop so the girls could eat and Kaleb could rest his wings, which was exactly what we were doing now, although the girls had already finished eating and Artemesia was leading us to Creator knew where.

My boots struck the brick-paved streets as we strolled through the city of Westridge. From what I could see, the city was small enough that everyone probably knew their neighbors, but big enough that it had *plenty* of amenities. The center of the city was full of various shops, packed from wall to wall. Females, of many different races and species, flocked down the streets, moving like pack animals as they chattered.

Artemesia and Sage walked ahead of Folkoln and me, while Kaleb perched on Sage's shoulder. My hands were bound by Artemesia's sad, frayed rope, the bottom half of my face covered with a purple scarf embroidered with delicate flowers and finished with a frilly, white lace.

Did I look ridiculous? Definitely.

Did I care? Not really.

I was too invested in watching the sexy sway of Sage's hips as she strolled ahead of me. The little flick of her hips each time she took another step was doing wicked things to my thoughts, filling me with sinister intentions. I sank my teeth into my bottom lip, wishing it was her plump peach I was biting instead.

Enjoying the view, love? Sage purred through our bond, using my own words against me.

Cheeky female.

The corner of my mouth lifted into a grin. I left her waiting for a moment before I said in a husky tone, *Out of all the lands I've traveled to and the incredible sights I've witnessed, I've never seen a greater one.*

Her breathy laughter warmed my cold heart. *Such a charmer,* she teased.

I only speak the truth, I said, as we passed by a group of women. Some glanced our way, their curious eyes drifting over me and Folkoln. Their whispered murmurs were easy to make out—they discussed how rich our owners must be to have such *fine* stock.

My eyes met Folkoln's briefly, our egos thoroughly fed.

An astringent flavor burst across my tongue. It tasted bitter, like a rotten, sour lemon. I knew what it was—

Jealous, Little Goddess? I asked through our connection.

Territorial, she corrected. *I have half a mind to rip that cloth from your face and kiss you in front of them, just so they know you are mine.*

I chuckled. *My, my, how things have changed.*

She glanced over her shoulder, shooting me an innocent smile, then looked back ahead. If there was one absolute truth I knew, it was this—I would do *anything* for Sage. All she had to do was speak the words, and I would follow her to the ends of the universe.

We walked by another group of women. Following behind them, dressed in rags, with a collar around his neck and a mask on his face, was a man. His eyes were downcast, his shoulders curved from a lifetime of servitude. There was no pride in his step, no vigor in his wilting torso. He was but a shell, a vessel—the light from his soul long burnt out.

How far the male gender had fallen in this realm.

In truth, when I looked at the cruel and violent acts mankind committed back home, I could understand why they ended up as they had. I thought of Lyra and what those soldiers had done to her, leaving her so bruised and broken like that. She had been lucky to escape with her life. And even though her bones and scars had healed, the trauma they had inflicted still haunted her. She had chosen not to speak—because of *what* they had done to her.

Those soldiers had stolen her voice.

How many other men had done that?

How many had raped and murdered women?

And it wasn't like the New Gods were any better.

Aurelius had treated Sage as if she were his slave, forcing her to stand beside his throne while he sat on his lazy, pompous ass. He'd always wanted her to be less than him, never equal. When I thought of his intentions for her, to use her as if she were breeding stock, a factory to produce his repulsive little heirs, my bloodless veins began to boil. Sure, Sage would have been fine with that at first, but what happened when she grew tired of child rearing?

I knew the answer to that.

Aurelius was too self-serving to care what her wishes were. He would have done as he pleased, believing that he had a right to her body, to force his children inside her.

The thought fanned my fury.

You are serving up quite the tasty meal, brother, Folkoln's voice entered my thoughts. *What's gotten you so fired up?*

Men, I replied flatly.

Folkoln chuckled. *You and every other female.*

I didn't respond, didn't care to.

Folkoln said, *I spoke with Saphira today. Sounds like she might have—*

I swung my gaze at him, my eyes a well-sharpened ax cutting off his words. *I couldn't care less what Saphira is doing. If you want to talk to the traitor, go for it, but I don't need any updates.*

Aren't you a little bit interested in finding out what our sister has been—

No updates, I reiterated firmly, looking ahead.

Artemesia stopped. So did Sage.

The rope slackened as I walked up behind my wife.

"This is it," Artemesia said, gesturing toward the shop to our right. Unlike the other buildings, it didn't have large windows, but small oval ones, the dark stained glass making it impossible to see beyond them. Artemesia opened the door, a bell to chiming, and we all stepped inside.

Robed figures peppered the innards of the musty-smelling building. They stood with books in their hands, their faces covered by white porcelain masks. The wood floors were cluttered with stacks of books, leaving small paths to walk.

Sage leaned in to her sister and whispered, "I'm guessing they don't serve food here."

"No, they don't. Come on," Artemesia said as she started down one of the paths.

We followed behind her, winding our way toward the back of the building.

Sitting at a desk in front of a stairwell was a female whose face and body were covered in scales. Her slit pupils scanned each one of us as we approached. Her reptilian eyes landed on Artemesia. A thin, forked tongue flicked past her lips. "It'sss been a while," she said, hissing every *s*.

"It has," Artemesia acknowledged. "We've come for our meeting with the seer."

"Whossse name isss the booking under?" the female asked.

"Mine," Artemesia answered.

She looked down at the paper on her desk, running her finger from top to bottom. "I do not sssee your name on the lissst."

"Check again." Artemesia tossed a small cloth sack on the papers, the coins inside clattering in response.

"Ahh, here you are," the female said as she tapped the page. She slid the cloth pouch off the table and then gestured to the stairwell. "She'sss waiting for you."

A few minutes later, we were in the lower level, Folkoln and I standing at the back of the room. Sage and Artemesia knelt before an older woman, who sat crossed-legged on top of a small, elevated platform. Beads hung around her. Her eyelids were closed, a smear of black paint swept over her mouth. Her lips looked almost too big for her face, as if a lifetime of talking had made them that way. She looked incredibly pale, to the point one might think she hadn't seen a day in the sun.

"What an interesting group we have here," the seer said. She held out her hand toward Sage. "Come, child. The future summons you."

"Drop the bullshit, Helga," Artemesia cut in.

The seer's eyelids flipped open, and she let out a cackle. "Ah, Artemesia, I should have realized it was you." She looked at Sage, then me, then Folkoln. Her eyes started to twinkle, her lips curving. "Wherever did you find them?

"None of your concern," Artemesia replied, not willing

to part with any more information.

"Oh, come on now. Don't be so secretive all the time. I won't tell anyone." She paused. One long, bony finger tapped her paint-smeared lips. "Say, I know you aren't in the business of selling slaves, but what if you loaned one out for a little . . . ride? I like the one with the piercings. He looks positively wild!"

"They aren't for sale," Artemesia stated flatly, her expression like a slab of stone, cold and hard and unforgiving.

"That is a real pity," Helga said. Reaching over to a small silver tray that sat beside her, she plucked a matching silver pot. She began to pour a cup of what I imagined to be tea for herself. "Every time I see you, you have different slaves. Whatever do you do with them all?"

"I take them to the arena," Artemesia replied, shrugging a shoulder as if it meant nothing to her. "I find it rather amusing watching them scrap like dogs, fighting to the death."

"As do we all," Helga said as she blew on her cup, the steam swirling forward.

Folkoln eyed Artemesia, one pierced brow lifting ever so slightly.

I realized he didn't know what Artemesia was up to. However, because Sage had shared her memories with me, I did. Artemesia wasn't taking the men she rescued to the arena to be put down like animals—she was taking them to Veshameer, the Hidden City, where they could live freely.

It was all very . . . Sage of her.

It's a charade, I spoke into Folkoln's mind.

How so? he asked.

It's not my place to say. You'll have to talk to Artemesia about it.

Alright. He didn't press; he knew me well enough to know I wouldn't talk—a fish's watertight asshole had fuck all on me.

Helga took a small sip before she jerked the cup back from her face, causing some to slosh over the brim of her cup and spill on her hand. "Ooh, ooh, that's hot!" Swiftly, she put the cup down and dried her hand on her robes.

As she did this, Artemesia asked, "What do you know about the sandstorm the Goddess of Knowledge uses to protect her palace?"

"I've heard a few whispers here and there—however, it's going to cost you." Helga chuckled.

Artemesia reached for her coin purse. "How much?"

Helga flicked her hand, indicating she wasn't interested in money. "Five minutes with him." She nodded to Folkoln.

"No," Artemesia answered firmly, the smallest hint of a growl on the back of her tongue.

Interesting.

"Then, in that case, I know nothing," Helga said, reaching for her cup again.

"Perhaps," I cut in as I took a step forward, "we can make a different deal. I can trade you information that will be of use to you."

Her blue eyes flicked to mine, a hint of surprise in them. "Oh?" she asked. "And what might that be?"

Asserting my authority, I tipped my head ever so slightly, eyes narrowing on her with lethal aim. "How you will die."

She scoffed. "Impossible. Only Death itself knows when that day will come."

"Exactly," I said, my flesh and skin dissolving from one half of my face until there was nothing but iron bone left. I placed a casual hand in my pocket. "Your time is coming faster than you think, but if I tell you, you might be able to escape your fate."

It was a lie—no one could escape Death.

But she didn't need to know that.

"What *are* you?" she hissed, scrunching back. Her heartbeat quickened its pace, pounding her fear into my ears.

"You know the answer to that," I said as I let my shadows free. They crept up the wall behind me, twisting my likeness, making it more monstrous, with horns and jagged teeth. Some formed arms, reaching around my torso. And then, there were the ones that started to crawl toward her, their heads twisting unnaturally to the side.

Her eyes stretched wide with horror.

Something spicy and sweet bloomed on my tongue, making my mouth water. An invisible chain tugged, and I spared a brief glance at Sage, noting the sultry look on her face. She sunk her teeth into her bottom lip.

You are beyond sexy right now, her seductive voice came through the bond.

I tried not to smirk.

"What will it be, Helga?" Artemesia asked, going along with it. "Do you want the deal or not?"

"Yes, I'll take it," she said desperately, still cowering. "Just call *those things* off."

"Wonderful," I patronized, my face returning to normal as I reined my umbra in. A new tattoo formed on my forearm—a knife swirled in a ribbon of sand. "You go first."

"Alright," she replied swiftly. "There is a riddle I've heard. If you can find a way to solve it, you might just be able to pass through the sandstorm."

"What is it?" Sage asked.

Helga thought for a moment before she said, "I'm there at the beginning of life and I'm there at the end. You can see me in the water, but I never get wet. I have no voice, but I'm faster than sound. I am a symbol of hope, especially in darkness. What am I?"

Silence lingered.

"You can take your time to think about it," she said, her gaze shifting to mine. "Now, about your end of the deal?" She posed it as a question, even though it was something we had already agreed on.

"In exactly three weeks' time, someone close to you will slit your throat with a poisoned blade," I replied, eyeing the scars I could see forming on her flesh. Invisible to the others, but not to me.

"Who does it?" she asked, her hands wrangling in her lap.

"Just like the riddle you gave us, that's up to you to figure out," I answered.

"Light," Sage said, grabbing everyone's attention. "Light is there in the beginning of life and at the end. You can see it in water, but it doesn't get wet. It has no voice, but it's faster than sound. Light is a symbol of hope, especially in the darkness."

"That's it!" Artemesia exclaimed.

I grinned. *My clever, clever wife.*

Chapter 53

Shadow

I'd been pierced by adrenaline's arrow—I could feel it flowing through my veins, increasing my strength, sharpening my fight-or-flight responses. It had nothing to do with the bloodstained ground I stood upon right now. No, it had everything to do with the future, which was coming fast.

In a few hours' time, Avriel and I would hopefully be very far from here, and that was what had my system on high alert. Today was the day we'd leave it all behind and find a new chance at life.

Together.

For the briefest of seconds, I glanced toward the balcony, looking right past the empress, toward the female standing behind her—Avriel.

Her worried eyes met mine.

I knew she felt it too. The anxiety. The worry. The fear.

. . . The hope.

That was the key to this whole thing.

Pulling my gaze from hers, I set my sights on my opponent, handing myself over to the duty I was here to perform—crushing souls. With each life I stole, the crowd only seemed to become even more wild. They chanted my title, over and over again—

Soul Slayer.

It was a title I had grown to hate.

A title I couldn't wait to leave behind.

When the event was over and the crowd had had their fill of blood and guts, I returned with the other soul crushers to the underbelly of the arena to a washing chamber. Sweat, ichor, and death permeated the air, hanging over us all. The sounds of shifting stools, trickling water, and light conversation flowed throughout the room. I sat on a bench beside a few other immortals, directly across from Aryx.

His large body looked much too big for the stool he sat on.

"You seem distracted today," he said, wringing out a cloth over a bowl of steaming water. He handed it to me.

"I've got a lot on my mind," I answered him honestly, hoping he'd leave it at that. Steam curled around my hand as I took the ragged cloth. I pressed it to my skin, wiping the sand and blood from my arm. The heat felt good against my overworked muscles.

Aryx dropped a bulky forearm against his leg, resting it there as he peered up at me, his eyes like a hawk's talons trying to pierce through me.

A small part of me wanted to tell him the truth—I was

leaving with Avriel. But if I did, I knew the danger it would put him in, so I kept my expression as hard as the steel of my blade and turned my attention to washing my skin.

When I felt his reluctant eyes pull away from me, I felt the smallest bit of relief.

"Oy! Water boy, I'm out," Jacob, an immortal who I was certain was the descendant of a god who had fucked an ostrich, said, as he tossed his bucket at the newest member of our group, seated a few spots down from me.

The reason why I had developed my theory about Jacob was simple—ostrich brains were smaller than their eyeballs, which meant their eyes took up more space in their empty skulls than their brain did. The same could be said about Jacob, whose intellectual shortcomings were vast. If it weren't for the eighth Wonder of the World swinging between his legs, I was certain the empress would have had his soul crushed centuries ago.

"I'll get it," I said, dropping my cloth on the bench before I stood up.

Aryx eyed me, suspicion growing. Water duties were reserved for those who were new here. It was rare for someone such as me to go get more water for another soul crusher, but it wasn't completely unheard of.

I shrugged. "It smells like stale farts in here."

That got a laugh from a few of the others. Aryx only continued to eye me with a great deal of skepticism.

I grabbed the bucket from the floor and left the room, weaving my way through the hallways. A petite, hooded figure waited further down, a satchel on her back. Her body was tucked against the wall as if she were trying to become one with the shadows. Spotting me, she quickened her pace toward me. "Ready?" Avriel asked as she looked up at me underneath her hood.

"As ready as I'm ever going to be. Stay behind me, alright?" I said, the words a soft command.

She nodded, her hand finding mine.

Gently, I tugged her behind me, leading her into the room where water was gathered from a well fed by a subterranean river. It was then brought up and boiled in massive pots before it was delivered to the washing room.

"Boilerman," I said to the stocky fellow, his back turned to us. "We're out of water."

"Hold your horses. Next pot's a comin'," he replied, not bothering to look my way, his magic controlling the flames beneath the steaming pot.

That was a mistake.

Bang!

I sent the bucket sailing into the back of his head, sending him ass over teakettle. He fell onto the ground like a bag of coal.

"Is he . . ." Avriel looked at him and then up at me, eyes large.

"No. He'll have a sore head when he wakes, but he'll be fine," I said, dropping the bucket beside him. "Come on. We don't have much time." I gave her a pull, and we rushed over to the well.

I looked over the gray stone, down into the darkness waiting below.

The sound of rushing water could be heard, roaring and growling.

"I'll take the satchel." I held my hand out.

She nodded, pulled the strap from her shoulder, then handed it to me. It had a surprising bit of weight to it. I crossed it over my body, my eyes catching with hers.

This time, it was my turn to ask, "Ready?"

"I guess so," she replied, starting to lift herself onto the edge.

"No." I shook my head, my eyes flicking to her clothes. "Your dress will make it too hard to swim."

"Right," she said, jumping back down.

I looked the other way, giving her privacy as she undressed herself.

"What should I do with my dress?" she asked.

I glanced at the unconscious boilerman. Although he hadn't seen us, the other soul crushers knew I had intended to come to this room. Sure, they would tell the empress, but why should I leave any extra clues behind if I didn't have to? Things might point to where we'd gone, but I didn't need to spell it out for them.

"Toss it in the well," I replied.

"Alright," she answered before she hoisted the fabric onto the edge and then shoved it over. I glanced down the well, watching as the darkness swallowed it. We both did. Our gazes met, and my breath snagged in the back of my throat—I had never seen *so much* of her before.

A silk chemise clung to her sensual feminine curves.

She looked stunning. The swell of her breasts—

Focus, jackass, I scolded myself.

"You go first," I told her. "I'll be right behind you."

"Okay," she said, taking a deep breath as she got up on the side of the well. I didn't miss the tremble in her hand or the fear in her expression as she peered down the hole, looking our unknown fate straight in the eye. Her face tipped up to mine, her voice small. "Shadow?"

"Yes?"

"If this doesn't work—"

"No," I cut her off. "It's going to work. We're going to get out of here."

"It's going to work," she repeated with a firm nod. She kissed the rabbit's foot she clutched in her hand and then jumped inside the well, her scream echoing through the stone walls. It was abruptly cut off as she fell into the river—

Splash!

I hoisted myself up onto the edge and followed after her.

Chapter 54

Von

Night had fallen, painting the sparse, hilly terrain a deep shade of indigo. We'd been flying all day, no stops, and my mate had fallen asleep in my arms. Her chest rose and fell in a natural, steady rhythm. The further south we'd traveled, the hotter the sun became. Still, I held her tightly to me, unable to get enough of the heat radiating from her body.

Because it meant *she was alive*.

I knew what the opposite felt like—when the heat faded from her skin and her muscles turned stiff. I'd experienced that twice—losing her, holding her lifeless body in my arms. Both times, it had felt like someone had taken a sledge and smashed my rib cage open before they carved my phantom heart out.

For that was what Sage was—she was my heart.

My purpose.

My everything.

Her cheek was crunched up against my chest, causing small crinkles by her nose. She let out a soft, happy sigh, and the corners of her mouth tugged up into a smile.

It was a contagious thing, spreading to my own.

Are you dreaming, Little Goddess? I thought to myself.

Lately, whenever Sage slept, she recovered more and more memories of us, of when we'd been trapped together in the strange hole in the ground, when I was called Nockrythiam and she was the mortal daughter of Luna and Herulf. With each memory retrieved, a story had begun to unfold, of two souls, trapped together, who started off despising one another but slowly started to like one another, and by the looks of her smile right now, perhaps even *more*.

Unwillingly, I pulled my attention from Sage and glanced up, eyes scanning the horizon. Nothing but night sky stretched on before us. Folkoln flew beside me, Artemesia in his arms, Kaleb perched on his shoulder. His little beak kept tipping down as he tried not to nod off. Every once in a while, he would jerk his head up, shake it, then try to focus on the story Artemesia told.

Artemesia. That one was quite the chatterbox, not that Folkoln seemed to mind. He hung on to every word of hers more than he hung on to a bottle of bourbon. I never thought I'd see the day, nor did I ever think there would be a female out there who could run my brother, the God of Chaos, ragged, but one look at Artemesia, and I knew that's exactly what she would do to him.

Fucker deserved it too. He'd spent the majority of his lifetime tormenting others. Let him be the tormented one for once.

"Mmm," Sage softly moaned as she nuzzled further into me.

One of my brows lifted—now I was curious. Was she having a wet dream about me? Or was she remembering a time when I had ravished her?

Sage had opened her mind to me, a door she left unlatched so I could join her dreams and memories while she was asleep. Letting my wings take over and my shadows steer us, I focused on the bridge connecting our minds and walked my way into hers.

"Creator above, this is sooo good," the Little Mortal moaned like a female who was having her sex properly devoured, even though it was she who was doing the devouring. She sat across the fire from me, a fish in her grubby hands and a beaming smile on her face.

"It stinks horribly," I groaned, repulsed by her. She'd eaten so many fish, it was a wonder she hadn't turned into one. I could only imagine how horrible her arousal must taste—something I'd found myself thinking of more and more lately.

Not that I wanted to lick her. It would just be for . . . educational purposes.

"It does not. It smells delicious. Besides, what kind of dragon doesn't like fish?" she asked, shaking her head in disbelief.

"One with very good taste," I answered, crossing my arms over my chest as I leaned back against the tree.

"Or one who is just extremely picky," she quipped, before her blunt mortal teeth tugged off another bite of flaky, pink meat.

"It is not a bad thing to have refined tastes, Little Mortal—"

"Sage," she corrected, just as she had done hundreds of times before.

I smirked. Oh no, if she was going to sit across from me and eat fish every night—something I detested—she could have a taste of her own medicine. "I think I'll stick with Little Mortal."

She rolled her eyes, took another bite, chewed, swallowed, then said, "Speaking of names, we've been stuck down here for months, and I still don't know yours."

"Ah, you mean you've finally come to the conclusion it's not Bastard?"

She gave me a smug look. "I didn't say that."

Coy little creature.

I opened my mouth to give her my name, but something in me paused—perhaps it was the way people seemed to cower from me once I told them who I was. The stories attached to my name, although not always true, were horrible.

So naturally, people feared me.

I didn't know why, but I didn't want her to fear me too.

So, I didn't tell her my name was Nockrythiam. Instead, I said, "Von."

"Von," she said, tasting the name on her tongue. "Is that short for something?"

"Draevon."

"And of the two, which do you prefer?" she asked, her sky-blue eyes meeting my black ones.

"No preference."

"Then I'll call you Von."

The corners of my mouth lifted. "Von it is."

She giggled. "You are smiling like an idiot."

My expression snapped back into its normal scowling state. "I am not."

"You were," she teased, smiling back at me like the little brat she was. So proud of herself. She dropped her voice an octave, feigning seriousness. "Don't worry. I won't tell the other scary dragons you are a big softie."

I rolled my eyes.

She giggled some more then tossed a piece of fish at me. It landed beside my boot.

I eyed it, then her, quirking one brow. "Are you throwing food at me?"

"I would never," she lied.

"You just did." I flicked my eyes to the chunk of fish.

She tried not to smile. "How odd. How did that get there?"

"You're impossible." I cursed my destiny for leading me here into this hole, where I was stuck with a woman who had the mind of a child. A woman I was starting to care for. No. Nope. I was not catching feelings for her. Mortal lifetimes were brief, and I had no desire to fall for a woman

who'd only get to spend a few short years with me.

I needed to put some distance between us—both figuratively and literally.

Boots shifting, muscles contracting, I got up.

"Where are you going?" she asked, standing as well.

"Where it doesn't stink like fish." I turned to walk away.

Her bare feet padded against the ground as she rushed to catch up with me. "I'll come with you. I'm done eating anyway."

"I have to take a piss," I lied, hoping my words would deter her. "You want to come hold it for me?"

"Oh, sorry." She chuckled sheepishly, rubbing the back of her neck. "You go ahead."

I glanced down at her bare feet, toes wiggling in the dirt. Annoyance needled its way into my flesh, stitching itself in my words. "Why aren't you wearing your shoes?"

"Because I'm my mother's daughter," she answered. Cryptic as ever.

"Meaning?" I grated, voice rough.

"My mother taught me it's important to feel the earth beneath my feet every once in a while." She wiggled her toes some more. "It's good for the soul."

"You have delicate mortal skin, which has about the same strength as paper, and you are susceptible to infection. I don't know anything about treating mortal wounds or how to take care of you if you fall ill, so please, do us both a favor and put your damn shoes on."

She was silent for a moment, eyes flicking back and

forth as if she were reading a book, accessing its information. When they lifted to mine, her gaze was so intense, it could have leveled a mountain. "Why do you care?"

"I don't," I lied.

Then, without another word, I stalked off into the woods.

Returning from the memory, I glanced down at Sage, finding her looking up at me, her beautiful blue eyes awake. A few of her silken strands swirled around her face, dancing on the melody of the gently whistling wind.

"That day, I knew you were lying," she said, her hand reaching up to cradle my cheek, her touch soft. "I saw the truth behind your words, that you were starting to fall for me."

"I was an idiot for not admitting it to you back then, on that very day," I answered her. Air swept into my lungs, filling them on a long inhale as I took a breath. "In truth, I can hardly connect with the immortal I was back then. He seems so different from who I am now. Quite the pompous asshole."

Sage laughed at that. It was a sound I wanted to hear over and over again. "Your soul was young back then, and so was mine. That girl saw life in color. Even when she was stuck in a hole with a broody dragon, the world was vibrant."

"So then, what is it now?" I asked, the words rumbling from my chest.

She glanced around, looking at the sky. "They are different now, always changing, sometimes disappearing altogether. When I woke up in Clearwell Castle . . . when I thought you had died, all the colors faded into one—gray. It was everywhere. From the floors to the walls to the bed I cried myself to sleep on." Her gaze met mine. "But then I found out you were alive, and the blues and greens and yellows and reds, all of the colors returned. However, they were different, forever changed. As was I." She paused for a moment. "I suppose I'm a bit like your eyes, my love— without you, there are no colors."

"Then I will ensure I'm always by your side," I promised her, pressing a kiss into her palm.

"You better," she teased, her fingers stroking my stubble.

With a smile on my lips, I looked up.

The terrain ahead was beginning to change, the grass becoming even more sparse, the ground shifting into sand, glinting with gold mica, which meant—

We'd reached the Naftiah Desert.

Chapter 55

Avriel

If there was one thing I knew, it was that there weren't enough hours in the day. Not enough minutes. Not enough seconds. Although Shadow and I used every precious kernel to try to put distance between us and the empress, it never felt like it was enough time. I couldn't shake the feeling that we were running out of it, despite Shadow's constant encouragement.

Through the wind, I could hear the nickering of her winged horses, chomping at the bit to sink their teeth into us. Each time a branch scraped across my face, I could feel her wicked nails dragging along my skin, threatening to break it.

Still, we moved.

At first, it was through the river—through the tumultuous waters that pushed us further downstream, until we found a well, close enough to the water that we could crawl out of. *That* had not been easy, and if not for Shadow going up first and throwing the rope and bucket down to me, I would still be stuck down there. When Shadow pulled me out of the well, I realized we had emerged in a herdsmen's yard, beside a pasture full of sheep. One looked at me as if to say, *What are you doing here?* before it returned to its grazing.

That was the last thing I remembered of that place before Shadow grabbed my hand and pulled me through the pasture into the forest.

I couldn't say how many days had passed since then— they all seemed to blur together. Perhaps it was the constant state of shock. The fear I grappled with, the questions that replayed over and over inside my head . . .

What if she found us?

What would she do to Shadow for helping me?

My stomach churned at the thought.

"We should stop for a small break," Shadow said, slowing our pace, those worried eyes on mine. He'd lost his mask in the river, something I wasn't sad about. It was nice to see his handsome face, scars and all.

Lungs wheezing, I nodded at the male who was in much better shape. I stopped and leaned forward, tossing my forearms against my thighs as I gulped down breaths of air.

The forest floor was full of broken twigs, decomposing leaves, and various plant life. It was all part of a cycle of life and death—from soil to plant to animal to mortal and back to the ground again. Without the breakdown of the dead, the living could not flourish. One needed the other, and we all were connected to it, whether we liked it or not.

"Here," Shadow said, extending his arm, offering me the waterskin he'd pulled from the satchel.

"Thanks." I panted as I straightened, taking it from him. For a brief moment, our fingers brushed, and my lungs turned to stone in my chest, frozen by that one little touch.

Shadow looked down at his fingers and I wondered if he felt it too—

"Do you think . . ." I trailed off, the last part of my sentence dying on my tongue, slaughtered by fear. Fear that if I spoke the words, if I put the thought out there only to find out he didn't feel it too—

"I've suspected it for some time now," he said, his words an ax to my doubt, severing me from it.

I took a slow, shaky breath. So I wasn't the only one. I knew the odds, that the bond had become extremely rare after the emperor died, as he had been its primary driving force. But every so often, a star would fall from the sky on its own accord and shatter into two when striking the ground, thus creating a new pair of bonded mates. The connection between Shadow and I was so strong, it was hard not to wonder if we were.

I took a drink from the waterskin, wiped my mouth, then asked, "When did you first start to wonder?"

"When I was a teenage boy," came his answer. His firm jaw pulsed. "It was the day your mother officially introduced you to court."

Pressure built on my brow, lowering it as I tried to think back to that day, but the time that had passed between then and now had rendered the memory full of cobwebs, the picture faded and cracked. And it seemed so strange because that had been a monumental day in my life, and yet, I remembered so very little of it.

"That was centuries ago," I stated, grappling with what he was telling me.

"It was, but I still remember it as if it were yesterday, because that was the first time I really felt seen." He stepped closer to me, the twigs crunching under his sandals. "I was standing by the empress's throne, watching from above as you bowed before her. When you raised your head, your eyes met mine. And in that brief moment, it was as if you had removed the mask from my face, peered past the scars and damage, and saw the person inside. It was like your soul was speaking to mine." He gave a soft shake of his head. "Ever since that day, I've wondered if we are . . ."

"Bonded," I finished, taking a step forward and closing the distance between us.

There was a brief pause when neither of us moved.

The small moment before the spark erupted.

A breath. A glance. A striking of a heart.

A wish. A need. A hunger like no other.

We caved—and we collided. I dropped the waterskin and encircled my arms around his neck as he kissed me with fervency, his tongue lashing against mine. Years of pent-up desire ignited the flames of passion between us.

"We shouldn't," he said between kisses.

"We should," I countered, tipping my head back, offering him my neck. My fingers wove into the raven strands poking out at his nape. I was tired of longing for him, and now that we were free, I wanted to know what the weight of his body felt like on top of mine.

His hands slid down my torso, roving over every inch of me, exploring and learning. The silk of my chemise, which was lighter than a feather, became very, very heavy, scratchy too, as if it were made of wool. I needed to get it off.

I reached for the hem, but his fingers stopped mine.

He pulled back. "Have you ever lain with another before?"

"No," I answered him honestly.

A muscle kicked in his jaw. "You deserve better than this."

"Better than what?"

He didn't meet my gaze. "To be rutted like some animal in the woods."

I could sense he was battling with something much deeper.

I slid my hands to his face, forcing him to look at me. "Shadow, I don't care. If it's here in the woods or a bed in the clouds. All that matters is that it's with you. There is no one else I want to give my maidenhood to. No one else but you."

"You're sure?" His voice was but a whisper.

"I am."

A pause. "You truly want this?"

In that moment, I understood.

He wanted *my consent*—he wanted to be certain this

was something I wanted because the empress had never given him the option. She had only taken from him, regardless of what *he* wanted.

Looking deeply into his eyes, I vowed to him, "If the sun fails to rise tomorrow, and all of creation were to meet its end, I could die happily, knowing I got the chance to experience this with you. To be connected to you. So yes, Shadow, I want this more than anything. I want you."

His eyes searched mine, inspecting them for any hint of mistruth. When he found none, his fingers slid to the bottom of my hem. "I want you, too, Avriel, more than anything else in this world. I've dreamt of this moment between us for so long."

"Then take me," I whispered, my lips finding his. He started to lift my chemise—

"Disgusting!" a hateful, familiar voice roared from up above.

A blast of light, traveling faster than an arrow, shot between us, blowing us apart.

My body sailed backwards until I collided with a tree trunk, bringing me to an abrupt, excruciating halt. Something inside me snapped and I felt a burst of pain.

I moaned in agony, my hand shooting to my side, but the second I tried to touch it, I let out a yelp. Although I didn't feel anything broken on the outside, it sure felt like something was on the inside. A rib, perhaps?

Gritting my teeth together, I looked around, trying to find Shadow. He was lying a good thirty paces from me, unconscious, surrounded by the empress's soldiers.

"Shadow!" I screamed for him, tears pricking my eyes as I tried to crawl for him, my movement slow and weak, my body crying out in pain.

No. No. No! This wasn't how it was supposed to be.

The empress landed before me, her massive wings tucking in. Her eyes were like daggers, threatening to carve mine out. She shook her head at me, lip curled in disgust. "I'm not surprised you turned out to be no different than your mother. She wanted to take from me, too, and we all know how that ended for her, don't we?"

The adrenaline coursing through my veins made me ignorant of my pain.

I thrust my hand up, calling on my winds, sending them hurtling for her.

She glanced to her left and stopped my power dead before it reached her, not even a strand of hair knocked out of place. "Don't make me laugh," she mused. Then, I felt the weight of her power, like a knee to my back, knocking me over, forcing me to bow to her.

Again, an explosion of pain slashed at my side—something was definitely broken. Still, I ground my teeth, trying with every fiber of my being to break her hold. With a face full of dirt and leaves, I just barely managed to look up.

She placed a hand on her hip and glanced over her shoulder, commanding her soldiers, "Bring him over."

"Yes, Your Majesty," one of them replied as she leaned down to grab his arm.

"What are you going to do?" I wheezed, watching as

the soldiers dragged Shadow toward us. My heart ached with the need to go to him. And yet, I could do nothing.

"You're going to find out," the empress replied, grabbing hold of her skirts and flicking them to the side as she turned. "Put him against that rock," she commanded. "Over there."

The soldiers did as she asked, dragging him over to a flat-topped boulder, large enough to lie on.

"Secure him," the empress directed.

A soldier flicked her hand, and vines began to shoot from the ground. They wove around his wrists, circling round and round. They wrenched his arms downwards, pulling him taut.

"Please, don't hurt him," I cried out, trying to fight against her power as I remained pinned to the ground.

But the empress didn't pay me a sliver of mind.

In horror, I watched one of her soldiers use a knife to cut off Shadow's shirt. In horror, I watched as the empress conjured a whip made of slender rawhide strips, interwoven with wire barbs, making it sharp and hooked. In horror, I watched as she handed it to one soldier and told them to begin.

"No!" I screamed at the top of my lungs as the soldier threw back her arm and issued the first strike. The hooks dug into his flesh, splitting it open and taking out chunks as the soldier ripped the whip back. Ichor sprayed in gory display, trailing after the whip. It brimmed like a dam bursting open, filling the deep gashes with silver.

Shadow came to, roaring in excruciating agony.

There were two sounds in this world I never wanted to hear again, and the sound he made right then was one of them.

My vision turned cloudy. His name slipped from my trembling lips. "Shadow."

Chest heaving, he lifted his head, his eyes finding mine.

"Again," the empress demanded, the words a snarl.

Whooosh. Crack!

"Ahh!" Shadow cried out.

"Please," I sobbed desperately, the pain of my broken rib long forgotten as Shadow's anguish took the helm. "Please. Please. Please. Stop it."

The empress tipped her head, her eyes narrowing into slits. "Keep going."

Whoosh. Crack!

Whoosh. Crack!

Whoosh. Crack!

I begged and pleaded for the punishment to stop, words pouring out of my mouth, full of promises and pledges. Promises I would never disobey the empress again. Pledges I would go with Victor and do as she asked of me. I tried anything and everything to get her to stop.

Whoosh. Crack!

Whoosh. Crack!

The whipping was ceaseless. It went on and on and on.

There were moments when Shadow would black out from the pain, only to come roaring back to life at the crack of the whip striking him again. Throughout it all, my eyes never strayed from him. Because when he awoke, I wanted

478

him to see me, to know I was there for him, that I was deeply sorry. This was all my fault. I should never have told him about Victor's plans for me. I should have run away on my own. If I had, he wouldn't be here right now.

When I'd lost count of how many lashes he'd been dealt, his back a bloody massacre, the empress finally raised her hand and said, "Enough."

The soldier lowered the whip, and the vice that constricted my lungs eased its grip. Air seeped inside my chest for the first time in what seemed like hours.

The empress walked over to Shadow, standing in front of him. She grabbed his chin and angled it upwards, but he was too out of it to register what was happening. "You are lucky you are my favorite—otherwise, I would end you right now," she growled softly. Her thumb stroked his cheek, and then she let go. His head flopped downwards. She turned to face me. "Now, the question stands. What shall I do with you?"

"I'll go with Victor," I pleaded. "If that's what you want me to do. I'll do whatever."

"Victor has already found someone to replace you, so it seems you are no longer needed," she said. "And I can't have you in my palace anymore, considering you can't be trusted not to steal my things." Her gaze shifted pointedly to Shadow.

"I won't ever do something like this again," I decreed.

"Unfortunately for you, I've already seen second chances don't work." She rolled her wrist, and light wrapped around her hand, forging a soulius made from white dragon scales.

"Please, Your Majesty," I begged as she started for me.

Shadow's eyes, which had been closed mere seconds ago, opened to half-mast, as if he were fighting with himself to keep them open. "Avena!" he rasped weakly. "Don't you fucking touch her!"

She curled her upper lip. "I see you have not learned your lesson. We'll have to work on that," she snarled.

Her magic lifted me from the forest floor, pulling my arms out to the sides as I dangled in the air. She placed the metal-like nails over my chest, pushing them past my chemise and into my skin.

"Goodbye, priestess," were her final words before she tore my soul from my chest.

Shadow's desperate roar was the last thing I heard before she squeezed her fist, and my life came to an end.

Chapter 56

Sage

We had reached the desert two days ago, although, in truth, it felt more like five. If the intense desert heat bothered my mate, he didn't let on. I had my arm wrapped around his neck as his powerful wings flew us over the barren lands. It was like a golden sea, forged from sand, stretching on and on.

No civilization or vegetation in sight.

Only scalding-hot sand and a relentless, boiling sun.

My tongue swept over my lips, dry and cracked.

"Do you need water?" Von asked.

"I'm alright," I assured him. "I wish I could fly so I would be less of a burden to you."

"You, Kitten, will never be a burden. When I get a chance, I'll start working on a new prosthetic wing for you," he responded in a deep, soothing tone.

"Thank you," I said, my heart brimming at the promise

of being able to fly again.

Like a knife, Von's gaze cut ahead. His pupils narrowed—his tell.

I looked to my left, over my shoulder, toward what he was looking at.

There. A swell of sand shot up toward the sky like a backwards waterfall. It was a wall of pale orange, cutting off the rest of the horizon.

"That must be it," I whispered under my breath, and Von nodded.

The closer we got, the more powerful the winds became. Bits of sand flew at us, pelting us with tiny rocks. Von held me close to him, his one wing arching down to protect me. Still, like that, he managed to fly, his hair whipping around violently.

"This is terrible," Kaleb groaned, his wings flapping swiftly as he tried to keep up. Every once in a while, a gust of wind would send him careening to the side.

"Von, can you do something about the wind?" Folkoln shouted as he flew closer beside us, Artemesia in his arms. She held her hand over her face, trying to protect her eyes.

A muscle kicked in Von's clenched jaw. "I can't. They will not listen to me."

Folkoln said something, but the howling wind made it hard to hear. It was growing worse by the second. Folkoln must have repeated himself through his private channel with Von, because Von nodded at him, and we began to descend to the ground. When we reached it, we landed about fifty feet from the beastly storm. Von set me down, his wing still curled protectively around me. Kaleb landed beside the four of us, shifting into his human form.

We walked the remainder of the way on foot, fighting against the wind.

Reaching the monstrous wall of swirling sand, Von held out a hand in front of his torso, flipping his palm skyward. Tendrils of shadow poured out from it, plunging toward the sand. They sectioned off, moving in front of each one of us, producing five lanterns before they retreated to Von's palm. The lanterns had a metal frame surrounding five clear glass panels. Artemesia had purchased them in the last city we stopped in, and Von had so graciously agreed to store them for us. Von rolled his wrist, and a flame emitted inside each one.

While the others reached down to pick theirs up, Von's shadows lifted ours to us.

Thank you, I said through the bridge that linked our minds as I took the lantern. The handle was slender, the metal surprisingly cool against my skin. I didn't understand the mechanics of how Von's shadows worked or how they just magically stored things, but judging by the cool metal, it seemed a bit like a cellar.

"Hopefully, Helga was telling the truth," Artemesia yelled over the roar of the wind.

We all looked ahead to the wall of swirling sand, impossible to see through.

"Should one of us test things first?" Kaleb asked, voice raised.

Folkoln stepped forward, placing his hand, which had

the lantern in it, inside the storm. He pulled it back. "Flame is still there. Hand is still there. Is that a good enough test for you?"

"I guess," Kaleb stated, his expression telling an entirely different story—he was not convinced.

"Come on," Folkoln said then stepped inside, disappearing before us. Artemesia joined him.

Kaleb sighed then followed them.

Von gave me a look, one that seemed to ask, *Ready?*

I nodded.

His fingers intertwined with mine, and we walked into the sandstorm.

The moment I stepped inside the raging storm, Von's hand disappeared from mine. He was swallowed up by the beastly winds, vanishing, just like the others.

"Von!" I screamed, thrusting the lantern ahead of me, the flame still lit inside. I sheltered my eyes, trying to protect them from the blasts of sand while I looked for the others. Thousands of tiny, violent stones pelted against me. Any skin that was unprotected, they chewed into, as if the storm were determined to eat me alive. I spun around, swinging the lantern from side to side as I called out for my mate.

When no answer came, I tried through our bond. *Von?*

I waited.

Nothing.

Shit. I was lost in the sands. *I was lost!*

My chest grew painfully taut, like a monstrous hand had wrapped around it, squeezing the oxygen from my lungs. Warning alarms started to blare inside my head as panic grappled for the helm—

No! Breathe, Sage, breathe, I told myself, again and again, until the message stuck, until I was able to focus again and search for the others.

"Kaleb?" I yelled, my hair whipping wildly around me, lashing at my face.

Still, no answer.

"Artemesia? Fol—"

The winds grew in ferocity, sending a barrage of sand to assault my mouth—cutting me off. It stuck to the inside of my cheeks, coating my tongue and the back of my throat. I choked on it, gagged on it. My mouth turned exceedingly dry. It was a terrible feeling, like drowning in sand. I gathered what little saliva I could and spat, and spat, and spat.

It helped some, but not completely. I could feel the sand everywhere—in my mouth, my nose, my hair, my ears, under my clothes. It was relentless, constantly assaulting me.

Still, I trekked ahead—or at least I *thought* I was. For all I knew, I could very well be walking in a circle. Sometimes, the storm became so powerful, I couldn't see anything, and I was forced to close my eyes, waiting until the moment passed. When I could, I called out for the others. I did not know how long I continued like that.

Had I been wrong about the riddle?

I'm there at the beginning of life and I'm there at the end. You can see me in the water, but I never get wet. I have no voice, but I'm faster than sound. I am a symbol of hope, especially in darkness. What am I?

Light. It was the only thing I could think of.

The light from the fire *should* work. So then why wasn't it?

I churned the riddle over and over again, looking to see if I had missed something.

What else could it be?

Time?

Time was there at the beginning of life and at the end. But could you see it in water? In a poetic sense, maybe—when clouds passed over top—but still, that didn't feel right.

What else could you see in water?

Your reflection? Fish?

Neither of those worked for the rest of the riddle. It had to be light, that was all I could—

Von's flame burnt out as the storm *unleashed* itself. With the force of a spooked horse, it railed into me, sending me flying. I landed on my side, an involuntary *oomph!* escaping my mouth. The lantern came to a rolling stop—glass shattering.

No!

Shooting onto my fours, I scramble-crawled toward the lantern as fast as my limbs would allow. A second before I reached it, the handle tugged upwards, and the lantern rose into the air, as if plucked up by an invisible hand. For a second, it floated there, and then it was tossed into the storm, disappearing instantly.

I smashed my fist against the ground, growling, "Damn it!"

The sandstorm was sentient, looking for ways to keep me stuck there, and so far, it was succeeding.

I allowed myself to sit in my frustration for a brief moment before I shoved off from the ground. I stood then blew out a breath of air, unclenched my jaw, and tried to focus on what my next steps were. Getting out of here and finding the others was my top priority. But how? My voice was no match for the winds. I couldn't see more than ten feet ahead of me, sometimes less. I didn't even know *what* direction I was going in.

I looked down at the shards of glass broken in the sand—all that remained from the lantern. They jumped at the wind's call, but for some reason, it left them there. Apparently, broken glass wasn't a threat, but it had sure taken the lantern awfully fast.

My eyes narrowed.

That was it!

The second Von's flame had gone out, the storm intensified, which meant light *was* the right answer. It just wasn't *enough* to assuage the tempest beast.

I reached down deep, stroking my powers with a loving hand, rousing them from their slumber. They stretched and stirred, a loyal pet, rubbing against my hand, eager to do my bidding. Like the crescent of a building wave about to broach shore, I felt it swell, and then I unleashed it with a mighty roar.

Silver light coiled around my skin until I was glowing as bright as the moon. I thrust my hands up into the air, and light poured from my palms, so bright, I nearly had to close my eyes. It scattered the sand and governed the winds, clearing a path before me, leading straight up to . . .

A monumental palace ripe with ancient architecture. The behemoth had to be over thousands of square meters wide. Spanning its great walls were various symbols, images, and dialects. Stone-carved figures—comprised of animal heads attached to human-like bodies—stood vertically, side by side, weapons in hand. They stood in front of the entrance, guarding it from newcomers.

Forcing a breath of air into my benumbed lungs, I started toward it.

Chapter 57

Sage

Soft music, accompanied by the buzz of light conversation, greeted me as I walked through the massive, doorless entrance into a grand foyer. The palace was made from limestone and granite, the vast walls etched in ancient symbols and words—archiving the languages of this realm and possibly, even more. Various species—*both* male and female—stood around the foyer, studying the markings on the walls, not one mask or face covering to be found. Judging by the books in their hands and the robes they wore, they were scholars.

A great span of stairs sat in the middle of the room, leading up to a mezzanine.

At the very top, a towering female stood, wrapped in an aura that emanated grace, patience, and deep understanding—as if she knew the secrets of the universe and its inner workings. Curly, brown hair floated past her shoulders, marked by a coil of silver that sprouted from her left temple. She was dressed in a chiton spun from fine ivory silk that draped elegantly down her lithe frame. An open book hovered in front of her.

"Welcome," she said, her tone soft and mystical, "Sage, Goddess of Life."

"You know my name?" I asked, my voice hoarse from calling out for the others.

"Indeed. I know a great deal about you," she said as she began to descend the stairs, the book floating along with her.

She looked . . . familiar, although I didn't know why that was.

I decided to start with what I did know. "You must be the Goddess of Knowledge."

"I am, but you can call me Naia." She offered a kind smile. The book shut, and then it disappeared. "Welcome to my palace." She gestured grandly.

"Thank you," I said, glancing around, taking it all in—particularly the fact that men walked around freely within these walls, conversing and smiling, their faces free of cloth. They seemed . . . happy. It was a far cry from the men I had seen in the outside world. "The empress's laws do not apply here," I stated, more to myself than anything.

"No, they don't," she confirmed. "I believe that intelligence is something that must be protected at all costs, and, unlike the empress, I do not discriminate based on someone's gender. So, those who are able to figure out my ever-changing riddles and find their way past the sandstorm are granted sanctuary within these walls."

"Ever-changing?" I asked.

"Indeed. I feed them out into the world, and they find the ones they were meant for. The light one was specifically for you."

"So you knew that I was coming?"

"I did." Her voice was as calm as a glass lake.

I didn't know if that was good or bad, but I was here now, so I decided not to fester in it.

Curiously, I asked, "I'm guessing that the empress doesn't know that her laws are not followed here?" It certainly explained the sandstorm. It was a nasty guardian, keeping unwanted trespassers out.

"The fact that it still stands is evidence that she doesn't know," she replied. Her smile grew. "You look so much like him."

"Who?"

Her violet eyes began to glimmer, rich with insight. "Your father."

"You knew him?"

"I did. In fact, if my sister hadn't come along and stolen him, I imagine the two of us would have wedded instead." She didn't bother to hide the longing in her voice. "Things would have been very different then." She waved her hand. "Oh well, I suppose there's no point dwelling on the past."

"Sorry, I don't understand." I was doing my best to keep up with what she had just said, but it didn't make any sense. "My mother was mortal, but you are immortal, so how is it possible you two were sisters?"

Her brows wove together, pinching the space between

them. "Mortals on a Sunday, you don't know, do you?"

"Know what?"

"It is a bit of a long story. Come, we will sit in the gardens, have some refreshments, and I will tell you the truth of your origins," she said, starting to turn back toward the stairs.

"Wait!" I shouted unintentionally, my voice echoing, startling a few of the scholars, who turned and looked at us.

She returned to face me. "Yes?"

"Four others were traveling with me. Have any of them shown up?" My voice returned to its regular volume, perhaps even a shade lower, as I was quite conscious of the attention I'd garnered.

She opened her mouth to speak, but instead, her lips closed and her eyes flicked past me, toward the entrance and out.

I followed her gaze, turning around.

Outside, Von and the others emerged from the sandstorm, walking toward the palace, not a single lantern in sight.

They looked like a mirage—the blistering rays of the sun so intense, it almost made it seem like their silhouettes were distorted. For a moment, I wondered if I was just imagining them or if—

Were you worried about me, Little Goddess? Von teased through our bond, voice full of that signature swaggering charm.

Relief washed over me.

I rushed out of the temple, racing toward them.

Von moved swiftly, the two of us colliding as I threw my arms around him, and he took me in his. Leather, amber, and sandalwood wrapped around me. I breathed him in. How someone could walk through a sandstorm for Creator only knew how long and still smell as good as he did was beyond me. I wondered if that went right along with his little make-your-clothes-disappear magic trick.

Unwrapping my arms from him, I pulled back.

His lips thinned when he saw the state of my face, littered with tiny cuts and abrasions from the angry sandstorm. He glanced down at my hands, noting they were in a similar state. Scooping them up, he took my hands in his. One at a time, he lifted them to his mouth, kissing each one. Instantly, my skin healed.

"Thank you," I told him, heart brimming with love.

"You do not need to thank me, Little Goddess," he spoke in his deep timbre. His eyes shifted to my sister as she walked up to us.

We hugged one another. "I'm glad you're safe," I said.

"We're glad *you're* safe," Kaleb stated as he draped his arms around us, joining in. "We were so worried when we couldn't find you."

"*So* worried!" Artemesia exclaimed. "It was awful out there."

"How did you all find each other?" I asked as our arms unraveled from one another.

"A beacon of silver light came to each one of us, leading us to one another," Folkoln answered as he stepped closer to us, bits of smoke breaking off from him.

"We figured it was you," Von added, his arm wrapping around my lower back.

"Perhaps it was," I said, thinking back on the light that had emerged from me, scattering the storm. I hadn't realized I had sent it out to them, but somehow, I must have.

"Nockrythiam," Naia greeted my mate as she walked toward us, her expression friendly. "How many millennia has it been since we last saw one another?"

Von's gaze lifted from mine, traveling to the Goddess of Knowledge. He didn't respond right away, which told me all I needed to know. Although she recognized him, he didn't recognize her. By the tick in his jaw, I could tell he was analyzing, trying to figure out his hand before he played his cards.

My fingers threaded into his as I spoke through our private connection, *We've come here to seek knowledge. If we are honest with her about our lacking memories, perhaps she can fill in the gaps of our past.*

I hope you are right, Von's words entered my mind, before he said to Naia, "I apologize, but I do not recognize you."

Naia looked surprised at that admission. "Although I did not think you were the type, surely, you jest. We spent a great deal of time working together, serving the emperor."

Again, I felt his hesitancy.

Tell her, I urged him through our bond.

"I do not have memories of my life in this realm, so I'm a bit foggy on who I did and didn't know," Von said, following up on our private channel with, *There, happy?*

Very much so, I replied back, smiling up at him.

"Well then, we will have much to catch up on," Naia said, pausing for a moment, her gaze shifting over us. "You all look like you could use some rest and food. Please, if you would, follow me."

Chapter 58

Sage

A short while later, we were in the courtyard gardens, not a speck of sand in sight.

The vast grounds were as vibrant and lush as a spring meadow, the air fragrant with floral scents. We sat in the shade under a pergola, the stone structure wrapped in winding, green vines adorned with bright-pink roses. Two servants joined us, standing beside the pillars.

Von and I leaned back in a wicker sofa, his one arm tossed over my shoulders, my hand in his. Von's thumb brushed over the glimmering emerald of my ring, and a flurry of emotions bloomed on my tongue—pride, satisfaction, immense happiness. Although the feelings belonged to him, they mirrored my own.

Artemesia and Folkoln sat across from us while Naia took the chair at the end. In the middle, there was a rectangular table full of jugs of wine and stone platters laden with fruits, cheeses, and thinly cut meats.

In front of the pergola was a pond full of goldfish. The water glistened under the bright gaze of the sun. Kaleb stood by the pond, watching them swim.

"How do they survive the heat?" he asked, looking to Naia.

For a brief moment, I could see the person I'd grown up with, who had yet to be tainted by everything that had taken place after he was conscripted. Kaleb was a tinkerer, infatuated with how things worked. Even more so, he liked to try to come up with solutions to make life easier. He was an inventor at his core, and it was good to see those curious cogs turning within his eyes once more.

"Place your hand in the water and see," she instructed him.

Kaleb knelt, dipping his hand inside. Pulling it back out, he exclaimed, "It's cool."

Naia grinned. "Indeed. Now touch the plant floating directly in front of you. The one with the blue-tipped leaves."

Kaleb reached for it. "Ah!" he gasped, swiftly jerking his hand back, a small, surprised laugh escaping him. "It feels colder than ice."

"That plant is called winter's caress, and yes, it is frightfully cold. That is how we keep the pond cool," Naia explained.

"Fascinating!" Kaleb replied enthusiastically as he walked back over to us. He sat beside Folkoln. "I can't believe how cold it is. Folkoln, feel my fingers," he said, shoving his hand toward him.

Folkoln narrowed his eyes with the lethality of a blade poised to cut—the look was enough to make Kaleb retract his hand.

"Never mind," Kaleb muttered under his breath, turning his attention to the food on the table. He plucked a grape and popped it into his mouth.

Naia turned to Von. "Earlier, you said you do not have any memories from your life here."

"That's correct," Von confirmed, a muscle feathering in his jaw.

"Is that why you have traveled all this way? To see if I can help you find them?" she inquired gently, tipping her head back.

"Not quite, although if you know anything about our pasts—" Von glanced at me. "We'd both like to hear it."

Naia's intelligent eyes shifted to mine. "Ah, so is that the same for you? No memories?"

"Some have started to come back, although the gaps are vast," I answered honestly.

"Well, perhaps we should start with what you do remember," she said. "Then, we'll go from there."

"Alright." I set my glass on the table. "I know I was the daughter of Herulf and Luna, that Artemesia is my sister and the—"

"If I may?" Naia interjected.

"Of course," I answered.

"Although Luna was your mother, your father was not Herulf."

Artemesia and I looked at one another, both equally confused.

I leaned forward, trying to process what I was being told.

"That can't be," Artemesia denied. "Her mannerisms are just like our father's. From her posture to the way she talks—so much about her reminds me of him."

"Naturally, she would act similarly to him; he spent a great deal of time grooming her to become the future chieftain of your clan," Naia pointed out. "But Sage is not of Herulf's blood, and although he was a kind man, his pride for his lineage meant more than anything to him. He would not have raised Sage to become the future chieftain had he known the truth."

"Which is?" Von asked.

There came a pregnant pause before Naia answered, "Sage is the daughter of Alaric, the primordial God of Creation."

A faint ringing sounded in my ears, as if I had been struck upside the head.

"The Creator?" Folkoln asked at the same time Artemesia said, "The emperor?"

"*That's* why you have silver ichor coursing through your veins, as well as mortal blood," Von stated. I could tell by his expression that some great puzzle piece had just clicked into place, not that I could say I felt the same.

My head swirled with so many thoughts. Alaric was the Creator, the first of everything.

And I was his . . . daughter?

But how could that be?

Naia's voice was an ax, severing me from my chaotic mind. "I was there on the day Alaric plucked your star"—her eyes shifted between me and Von—"from the heavens. When he cracked it apart, the half that belonged to Sage—her soul—lifted from the anvil all on its own, something that had never happened before." She looked at me. "Your soul was radiant—a brilliant, shining crystal, forged from silver light, so beautiful it brought tears to our eyes." Slowly, she shook her head, as if she were still in disbelief. "There was only one other soul that glowed with such vibrancy, and that belonged to Alaric. In that moment, he knew you were destined to be his daughter. And although he was filled with great joy, he also knew because of your relation to him, it would put your safety at risk. People would seek to use you, take advantage of you, and those with jealous eyes might seek your power for themselves. Swiftly, he covered you with a cloth and made me swear an oath not to tell anyone what I had witnessed that day, unless it was *you* who came to me, seeking the truth." She raised her arm, showing the underside of it. Inked into her skin was a crystal, bursting with light, cradled in a pair of hands. Lowering it, she continued, "He crafted a silver locket and placed your soul inside, so he could wear you on his neck, where you would be safe. But he knew he would not always be able to protect you, and so he turned to the other half of the star and went to work. He did not leave his workspace for months as he made you, Nockrythiam. Painstakingly, he forged you, crafting you into the greatest warrior he had ever made.

Protective and cunning. Powerful and fast. Lethal and loyal. You were one of the two achievements he was most proud of. Sage was the other."

I took a breath. I needed it.

Reassuringly, Von rubbed my hand. I leaned further into him.

"So then . . . how did Sage come to be?" Artemesia asked, curiosity raising her brows.

We all looked at Naia, waiting for her to answer.

"Alaric met your mother," she said with a smile. Her eyes slid to mine. "Who is not my sister, by the way. Empress Avena is my sister."

I nodded, now understanding what she had meant when she said if her sister hadn't wedded Alaric, she might have instead.

Naia reached toward the table, plucking her goblet by the stem as she reclined in her chair. She took a drink from it, then continued, "Alaric and my sister had been married for quite a while at that point, and although he loved her dearly, the façade of the blushing bride had worn off, revealing the power-hungry goddess beneath. Alaric worried what Avena would be like as a mother—fearing she would only use a child to become more powerful. Searching for answers, he disguised himself as a mortal and went to live amongst the woods so he could be alone while he thought things over. One night, he heard a woman singing, her voice so lovely, he felt compelled to follow it. Looking through the leaves of a bush, he spotted a young woman dancing under the night sky, her song praising the moon.

The locket lifted from his chest toward her. Following its pull, he decided to introduce himself. Which didn't go well, considering it was the middle of the night. I believe Luna screamed, threw her lantern at him, and ran."

Von chuckled. *Like mother, like daughter*, he spoke through our bond, his voice a gentle caress.

I couldn't help but smile.

"Yeah, that sounds like Mum," Artemesia acknowledged. "She once threw a cast-iron pan at Father's head when he didn't take his shoes off and got mud all over her freshly washed floors. It was a good thing he had quick reflexes."

The memory emerged from the cobwebs of my mind, and my smile grew wider. Artemesia and I had been sitting on the floor, playing with our wooden toys at the time. The pan had been full of vegetables, and it made an awful dent in the wall. There were peas and carrots everywhere.

"I remember that," I acknowledged warmly, but then my smile faded as I realized . . . I looked at Naia. "Wait. Does that mean our mother was unfaithful to him—to Herulf?"

She shook her head. "She didn't even know Herulf existed. Perhaps that's why it was so easy for her to give her heart to Alaric over the short span of their time together. One night, under the gaze of the moon, with Luna's blessing, you were conceived, Sage. By the next morning, when Luna returned home, knowing she was pregnant with you, she learned her hand had been given to the future chieftain of an allying clan. When she conceded to her mother she was carrying you, her mother sped the wedding up and it took place within the week. Alaric was sick over it all, but he knew it was for the best. He also feared what Avena would do if she were to discover the truth. And so, he faded from Luna's life so you could live yours."

"How does that work exactly?" Kaleb interjected, prayer hands held in front of his face. He tipped them forward. "Like if Sage's soul was in a pendant, how does the conceiving happen?"

All of us looked at Kaleb.

"What?" he asked, throwing his hands up. "I'm just asking."

"It is a very mortal question." Naia laughed softly. "But I will indulge your curious mind. Souls predate time itself, although some are connected in one way or another. They are not made by the joining of a father and a mother, but the vessel is. And so, that is what would have been conceived that night. Once the body is strong enough to house the soul, the soul will go to it, and two will become one. Does that make sense?"

"It does." Kaleb nodded, his eyebrows raised in fascination.

All this talk of souls and vessels and conception had my thoughts wandering down a dark, lonely path. My thumb lifted to my stomach, brushing over it in one, small movement, so small, no one would notice.

Ask her, Von spoke inside my mind, proving me wrong—he *had* noticed.

Of course he had.

My gaze shifted up to Von's.

It is one of the reasons we are here, to find out what happened to our child, he said.

What if it's an answer I do not like? I replied.

Then I will tear the truth apart and craft a new one to your liking, he vowed to me. His large, tattooed hand slid over mine, giving it a reassuring squeeze.

I inhaled a deep breath, taking my time to let it out, before I looked to Naia and asked, "What happens to an unborn immortal child if the mother dies?"

Naia set her glass down on the table. She looked at Von, then back at me, studying us both. Her eyebrows furrowed ever so slightly, her voice soft, gentle, as she said, "I have seen that look many times before." A small pause. "How far along were you?"

"Not very far." I cleared my throat, my vocal cords strung tight. "Maybe five weeks."

"I am so sorry," she said, and by the solemn look in her eyes, I believed she was. She took another breath, then started slowly, "There is no easy way to say this, but five weeks is too young for a soul to enter a vessel, immortal or not, so upon your death, the child would have ceased to exist."

I knew what I was being told wasn't true, because I had felt our child's power, seen it with my own eyes; however, hearing *that* still took me back. It made the words I wanted to say dissolve on my tongue, stifling my voice as if something had taken up residence in my throat, blocking it off.

So, my mate spoke for me, his body solid against mine. "No, their soul was there. Sage had planned to keep her pregnancy a secret from me, and our babe helped her."

Naia's eyebrows lifted at that. "If that is true, then yes, the soul would have been there. The vessel must have been exceptionally strong . . . although considering you two are the parents, I suppose that shouldn't come as a surprise." She thought things over then her eyes flicked to mine. "Tell me more about your death."

I nodded stiffly. "It was an immortal one, but I did not return to this realm. I reincarnated in the one we were living in instead."

"That complicates things greatly," Naia spoke on a heavy exhale.

"How so?" I asked, eager to hear more.

"When immortal souls are retrieved from the Miyakai River, all that information is logged by the Ashamori. If you could gain access to their system, you might be able to track down what became of your child. However, because you can reincarnate, your child could possess the ability as well. Which means they could have reincarnated anywhere, with any family—which, as you know, there is no log for." She stopped for a moment, considering something. "There is a third possibility as well—your child might have chosen to reincarnate within you, and they are waiting for a new vessel to be formed. In some cases, if the vessel is split in the early stages, it will result in twins."

Silence lingered as I reflected on what I had been told. Essentially, if our child was alive, they could be anywhere, including within me. I suppose that gave me a place to start, which was better than nothing. "If their soul has decided to reincarnate within me, how would I know?"

Naia's face grew weary. "There are two ways. The first is far from foolproof, and the second, although it will give you a definitive answer, is something I do not recommend."

"What are they?" I asked, moving forward in my seat.

"Well, the first would be to become pregnant again. After the baby is born, you could take them to a soul worker and see if the child's soul is the same as before, although, I will warn you to be careful, as there are a lot of fake soul workers out there, looking to capitalize on the desperate."

"That would take months, and if it isn't our first child or the soul worker is wrong, it would mean they could still be somewhere out there," I said, shaking my head. No, that wouldn't do. "What is the second option?"

She hesitated for a moment, then answered, "A visual inspection of the womb."

Von bristled beside me.

"That doesn't sound pleasant," Kaleb stated, reminding me that he was still here. That they all were. I had been so fixated on what Naia had been telling me, I had tunnel vision and forgot about everyone else.

"It's not," Naia warned, the caution in her voice still present. "As Sage is an immortal, she would have to take an elixir to prevent her immortality from healing her. A chirurgeon healer would then cut into her abdomen, into the womb, and visually inspect it through a special glass that allows one to see souls, no matter how minuscule."

"I don't have the ability to heal so that wouldn't be an issue," I said. "Where can I find a chirurgeon healer?"

"There is one who resides within the palace," she answered.

My heart leapt in my chest. "That's great. When can they—"

"Sage," Von cut me off, voice razor-sharp. "Can I talk to you for a moment?"

"Of course," I answered, turning to him. A sharp, spicy taste emerged on my tongue, like I'd taken a bite out of a pepper. I eyed him. What was that? Anger? Passion? Why did they taste similar?

He looked at Naia. "Is there somewhere we could speak in private?"

"Of course. It's getting late anyway. Perhaps we should pause this conversation until tomorrow morning?" Naia asked.

"That would be good," Von replied with a single nod, his eyes shifting to mine.

"Wonderful," she stated, shooting a glance over to one of the servants. "Please show them to their rooms."

The servant dipped her head and then gestured to the doorway leading back inside. "Please, if you would all follow me."

Chapter 59

Von

I loved my mate.

I loved her more than anything.

But *sometimes* her carelessness was like a spark to my veins, dry as tinder—causing an inferno of frustration reducing patience to ash. Sometimes, her total lack of self-preservation made me want to lock her in a tower, or a cage, or anywhere else she couldn't put herself in danger. She was just like every other hero out there—filled with that incessant need to put others before herself.

Well, damn her. Damn her and her selflessness.

Yes, I wanted to find out what had happened to our child, but not at her expense, not if it compromised her safety. There had to be a line, and that was where I drew it. I would allow *nothing* to harm *my* wife, not even herself.

I stalked into our designated chamber, Sage trailing leisurely behind me.

My shadows connected to every crevice within the large, dimly lit room, ensuring no dangers awaited us. I scanned beneath the king-sized bed, behind the window curtains, throughout the bathroom—searching for anything that would have me grabbing Sage and flying her the fuck out of here. Naia might be going against the empress's laws, but she was still her sister, and who knew how deep her loyalties ran. I did not trust the Goddess of Knowledge. Then again, the list of people I trusted was rather small— and right now, Sage's spot on it was becoming questionable.

She closed the door behind her.

I ran a hand through my hair in a bid to cool my temper—something which lasted all of one second before I said *fuck it*, turned, and strode toward her. I grabbed her by the chin and guided her backwards—

Thump. She landed against the door.

"Von . . ." she breathed, her sky-blue eyes flirting with mine. Her breasts arched up toward me, begging for my undue attention. Whatever emotion she sensed down the bond from me was off, although it wasn't necessarily wrong. There was a part of me that wondered if I could fuck a little common sense into her, although if we looked at our track record, senseless seemed more accurate.

"Do you have any idea how infuriating you are?" I asked, my anger like acid, eating through my restraint.

Her eyes narrowed, her offered chest deflating. "What are you talking about?" she snipped back.

I let out a low, rough, irritated chuckle as I placed my forearm against the door. I arched over her, bathing her in my shadow. "I'm talking about you entertaining the idea of allowing some stranger to cut into you."

"I'm not *just* entertaining it," she growled. "And I know you are an archaic, stubborn old goat, but that's what a chirurgeon healer does."

A stubborn old goat? If I wasn't so frustrated, perhaps I'd find the insult amusing. But now was not the time for that. I tried to reason with her. "What if this is all some big ploy by the Goddess of Knowledge? What if there is something more sinister at play here, something we are missing?"

"She guarded the Creator's secret about me for millennia. She served *him*, not her sister. Besides, look at the place she has built, a sanctuary for male scholars. In doing so, she has gone against the empress's laws."

I gave her a skeptical look. "Do you always take people at face value?"

"Do you always think the worst of others?"

I snorted.

She tugged her chin from my hand, ducked under my arm, and started for the bathing chamber. The invisible chain between us gave a good yank, our newly mended bond toying with my emotions. I knew she felt it too.

I rubbed my hand over my face, forced a breath of air to and from my lungs, and then stalked after her. She was a walking red cape, and I was the bull, eternally damned to chase after her.

The bathing room was a fair size, consisting of all the usual fixtures—sink, tub, shitter. You get the idea.

Immediately, my gaze went to my aggravating, seductive other half. She stood by the circular raised tub, large enough to fit three people, full of hot, steaming water.

She peeled off her tunic and dropped it onto the stone floor. Next to go were her shoes.

I leaned against the wall, watching. "Sage, we need to discuss this."

"There is nothing to discuss," she stated as she wiggled out of her pants, allowing them to pool at her feet. She stepped over them, her fingers reaching for the pitiful bit of cloth that covered her sex.

As she stripped it off, I said, "I want to find our child just as much as you do, but there are certain things I will not risk. Your safety is one of them."

Sage turned toward me, granting me a view of her sexy body. Her snow-white hair tumbled over her shoulders, framing her beautiful face and plump breasts, surrounded by my ink. Her perky, pierced nipples were hard and ready, begging for the flick of my tongue or the graze of my teeth. She had one toe pointed toward the ground, accentuating the length of her leg and the curvature of her hips. She gestured to herself. "I am a goddess, am I not?"

"You are."

"Then what do I have to fear?" she asked as she placed her hand over her crescent moon tattoo. Slowly, she trailed her hand between her breasts and down the length of her torso, luring my attention along with it, all the way down to her sex. "Besides, you can heal me when it's done."

"You are not very sneaky," I murmured, unable to pull

my eyes away from her poorly deceptive hand.

"That doesn't mean it isn't working."

She wasn't wrong.

Slowly, she stepped back until her heel thumped lightly against the tub. With her eyes on mine, she lowered herself onto the ledge. She slid her legs open, showing me her glistening sex, sleek and swollen. Ready for me.

My cock pressed against my leathers, creating a prominent bulge.

This female.

"I showed you mine," she spoke sensually. Her gaze lowered. "Now show me yours." She bit her bottom lip, her breath picking up.

"Turn around first," I directed her, my voice as wicked as the game she was playing.

She gave me a confused look before she stood and turned around.

"Bend over, Kitten. Present that pretty ass of yours," I purred.

Sage did as I asked, spreading her hands on the tub as she bent over for me. My cock throbbed even harder at the sight of her. Casually, I strolled toward her, the heels of my boots scuffing the floor as I approached. I ran my hand over her bottom, feeling her smooth skin. So soft, so supple . . .

What a shame it belonged to such a *naughty* brat.

I gave her a good spank.

"Von!" she snarled as she jerked upright, spinning toward me, fire shooting from her eyes, although the flavor of her passion on my tongue spoke otherwise. She reached for her stinging bottom, but I grabbed hold of her arm, stopping her.

"Oh no, Little Goddess," I snarled softly as I lowered my face to hers. "You go ahead and feel that wee sting, and while you do, imagine the torment I will feel while you are being cut into, while I am forced to sit there and *feel* your emotions, *feel* your suffering. What you feel now is nothing compared to what you are asking me to endure. What you have *made* me endure."

"I never forced you to endure anything. *You chose* to be with me." Her words came out in frustrated growls.

"You're right. Which means I will do everything within my power to ensure I do not lose you again." Something sinister began to lurk beneath the surface of my skin. It licked at my vision, tainting it with a black film. With a lethal calmness, I vowed to her, "I will end the realms before I let that happen."

I meant every word.

She peered into my eyes, her eyebrows weaving together. "If it were to come to that, my life over countless others, I would want you to do right by them."

"Oh, my love, when will you learn? When it comes to your safety, I will stop at nothing to protect you. I would reduce the realms to bone and blood, eviscerating it all, just to ensure no one could harm you." I let her arm go, so I could slide my hand up it, my cool rings gliding along her heated flesh. My other hand latched onto her bottom, tugging her into me. "I am a selfish, selfish god, and there is only *one* thing I want. Well, maybe two."

I could hear her heart quicken its beat.

"The first?" she asked, licking her pretty pink lips.

"You."

She breathed the word in as if it were oxygen. "And the second?"

I cupped her chin, hovering my thumb over her lips. She opened them, and I dipped it inside her wet, warm mouth. "I want this infuriating mouth to find something better to do than argue with me."

She sucked on my thumb, tongue swirling around it, cheeks hollowing, eyes locked on mine. My leather pants groaned, my straining cock pushing the seams to their limits.

"Exactly." I pulled my thumb from her mouth and smeared her saliva against her lips. I lowered my face to hers and ran my tongue along her bottom lip, slowly tasting her. A throaty growl of pleasure came from me. "Absolutely divine."

My hand settled against her neck, my thumb brushing over her pulse, feeling her blood pressure spiking the second my lips found hers. I kissed her with purpose, reminding her *whose* fist was clenching the chains wrapped around her soul.

There was *so much* I wanted from her. It didn't matter how many times I fucked her—my need to taste her, to take her, in every way possible, was unrelenting. There was a way I could have her in *more* than one way. I had never introduced this possibility to her in the past, but ever since I saw her reaction to my shadow forms when I had them crawling toward the seer, it made me wonder . . .

I turned her face to the side, kissing my way to her ear. A grin pierced my lips as I whispered in her ear, "Actually, I have one more thing I want."

"What?" she asked.

"Let me show you instead." I pulled away and glanced to my right. My shadows broke off from me. They swirled to the floor, crafting a pair of feet before they worked their way up, forming a naked version of me. To my left, I conjured another.

Sage's lips parted in surprise. "What are they?"

"They are an extension of me. I can feel their pain . . . their *pleasure*, as they can feel mine."

The one stepped behind her—sandwiching her between us. His large fingers slid around her neck, wrapping around it.

"It feels so real," she breathed.

"That's because it is. They are no different than the phantom form I sent to you."

The one to my left began to stroke his cock—an exact replica of mine.

"Do you control them?" she asked.

"Yes and no. If I want them to stop . . ." I looked to my left, and the one quit stroking. "They will. But . . ." I glanced to the one who had his hand settled around her neck. "If I give them free rein—" He tightened his hand, taking away some of her oxygen, just enough to get her attention. "They will do as they please."

The flavor of rich, dark chocolate spread across my

tongue, more intense than I had ever tasted before. It was laced with something spicy, something that had my mouth watering for more—nothing tasted as good as my mate's pleasure.

I *knew* she would like this.

I was a jealous, territorial male; however, there were some things I was willing to bend on, or at least make her think I was willing to try. The night at the inn, when I'd made good on my vows, piercing and tattooing her, when I'd pledged my life to hers and placed my band around her finger, I'd told her to strip in front of the window because I knew she would be turned on by it. Little did she know, my shadows had crawled outside, blurring her naked flesh from anyone who might be watching.

Now that she was mine, I would *never* share Sage with another.

I was the God of Death, and for anyone who tried to take, to touch, to fuck, what belonged to me, I'd live up to my title.

So yes, as I was saying . . . I was a jealous, territorial god—one who would never share his wife with another, but I'd let her play with my shadows anytime she wanted. They were a part of me, and through them, I could pleasure her in more ways than one.

The one behind her shifted his foot beside hers, pushing her leg out and widening her stance. He dragged his free hand down her body and began to rub her sensitive clit. She moaned, her arm draping around his neck as she kept her eyes on me, her breasts pressed upwards, begging for attention.

With a flick of my hand, my clothes disappeared.

Her hungry, lust-filled eyes raked down my body, pausing as they reached my hard and ready cock.

"Please," she panted, her breath slightly restricted. "I want to taste you."

My shadow released her throat. His hand pressed between her shoulders, bending her forward.

I gripped her hair in one hand and my cock in the other. "Open those pretty lips for me."

She parted them, and I pressed my crown into her warm mouth. Her wetness saturated it, and I slid further inside.

"Mmm," I groaned, the sound heady.

The shadow stroking himself walked over to us. He gripped Sage's breast as he continued to pump his length. The one standing behind her began to work his fingers inside her, and she moaned around my cock.

"Fuck, you feel so good, Kitten," I praised her as I began to thrust inside her mouth, slowly working myself deeper.

The shadow form standing behind her got down on his knees. He spread her wide, and then he slipped his tongue inside her, his fingers swirling her clit in tandem.

The flavor of apples exploded in my mouth, replenished with each stroke of my umbra twin's tongue. Like a man headed for the guillotine, receiving his last meal, I reveled in the delicious taste of her.

Pleasure building, her body trembled, her legs shook— still, she worked my length, her hand holding the base of it while she tried to take me deeper. It was as if she were in competition with herself, trying to take me farther than she ever had before.

I want to feel you down my throat, she purred through the bond. I brushed my thumb over her cheek, feeling the fullness on the other side, feeling how it heated as she admitted to me, *I want your cum inside me. All over me. I want you everywhere, Von.*

Matching the heat of her cheeks was a redness brighter than a cherry. Was she ashamed of wanting me in such a carnal way?

That simply wouldn't do.

Despite the patriarchal bullshit beliefs her society had so willfully embraced, her sexual desires were nothing to be ashamed of, and I would prove that to her.

You can tell me what you want, Little Goddess. You never have to feel ashamed with me. I'll make every one of your wishes come true. Reveal your deepest darkest secrets to me, and I'll make every one of them happen, I promised her through the bond. *Now, tell me again—what do you want?*

I want your cum, she answered, her curved tongue rubbing the underside of my shaft.

Where? Be specific. I'd break her of her shame, free her from it.

In my mouth. Down my throat, she rasped.

The shadow form that stroked himself pinched her nipple, and she let out a garbled moan. Pleasure building, both hers and mine, I knew she was close.

Come for me, and I'll give you what you want, I promised her.

A flood of her sweet arousal burst across my tongue, and she came undone, unraveling before me in pure, cataclysmic bliss.

I picked up my speed, fingers tangling in her hair. My muscles contracted and my balls tightened. I tipped my head to the ceiling, and I roared as I spasmed inside her mouth, shooting my hot cum down her throat.

Chest heaving, I looked down at her, enjoying the sight. Eyelids heavy with lust, she looked up at me with her pretty blue eyes. I rubbed her cheek with my thumb, feeling the firmness of my length on the other side. "You did so well."

Releasing my hand from her hair, I gently pulled myself from her mouth. A string of fluids—hers and mine—snapped, landing against her chin. I smeared it with a swipe of my thumb. "Now, tell me again—what was the next thing you wanted?"

Her words were carved into my mind. I just wanted to *hear* her say them again.

My umbra twin stood up behind her, grabbing hold of his length and running it against her slit. I groaned at the feel of it, my erection already starting to return, more than ready for another round with her.

"What?" she panted, chest still heaving for air.

"Tell me again." I enunciated the words, my finger curled under her chin, guiding her to stand up.

My shadow forms exchanged positions. The one now standing behind her ran his ringed fingers over her breasts, encircling the one, massaging it. I could feel the weight of her breast in my hand, as if I were the one doing it.

"Von," she resisted, leaning into my shadow form.

Oh, but I wasn't about to just let this go.

"I'll help you out. Your wish was to have my cum everywhere. I've already claimed your mouth, so the question is, what should I take next?" I ran my fingers down her torso. "Here? All over your soft skin?"

My hand slid lower.

I ran my ring finger along her slick sex, toying with her for a moment before I pushed two inside her and mused, "How about in here instead?"

Chapter 60

Sage

"Mmmm," I moaned as Von slid his fingers into my swollen center. In slow, sensual motions, he stroked me. His fingers curled, hitting that soft, erogenous part of me. I rolled my hips against his hand, grinding against it, chasing after his delicious ministrations.

Shadow hands moved to my thighs, picking me up from the floor as if I weighed nothing at all. They shifted my legs apart, spreading my thighs wide, Von's fingers still inside me. I looked down, watching the powerful muscles in his forearm flex as he drove his fingers into me, all while his shadow twin held me in place. The other one joined us, and he lowered his mouth to my breast, his teeth scraping across the sensitive flesh before he began to suck on my nipple. His tongue toyed with the piercing, heightening my pleasure.

I had no control over my body, my trust placed completely in my mate's hands, and I was living for every second of it, to find out what he and his likenesses would do to me next.

Von pulled his fingers from me, his hand swiftly replaced by his shadow's. Molten eyes on me, Von tongued his fingers, licking up my arousal, not wanting to waste a single drop. He gave me a handsome grin, one that sent my insides fluttering.

It drove me insane when he did that, the act of it so primal, so sexy.

Von groaned in pleasure. "If I could have you on tap, you are all that I would ever drink."

"Even better than bourbon?" I teased breathlessly.

"*Much* better. Nothing tastes better than you, Sage," Von answered as the shadow form removed his hand from me and took a step back. Von grabbed his length and placed it at my entrance, the girthy crown stretching me open as he slowly pushed inside.

We both moaned in pleasure. His hands wrapped around my thighs as he took me from his umbra twin. Both of them disappeared.

"Gone so soon?" I panted as Von stole the breath from my lungs, lowering me further down his cock. I slid my hands up his torso, wrapping them around his neck, my legs hooking around his waist.

"They can come back to play whenever you want," he promised.

"Good." I lowered my head against his chest, gasping for air as he sank even deeper. Because of Von's size, adjusting was a bit of a process—one that was pleasureful beyond my wildest imagination. It felt like he was evicting some part of me, forcing me to make room for him.

It was a claiming, carnal and fervent.

And I craved it every single time.

When he was as deep as my body would allow, he walked us over to the tub, stepping over the side. Water splashed as he lowered us into it. He moved to the middle of the tub where he could stand, the warm water lapping at my bottom, drifting over my feet.

Starving green eyes fixed on mine. "I love you, Sage."

"I love you too," I panted back.

"Remember that." A sinful grin played across his lips. "Because I'm going to fuck you like an animal now." His hand clasped the back of my neck, one arm supporting me as he withdrew himself, leaving just the tip in, before he slammed his hips forward, driving himself back inside.

I cried out his name, his thrusts so deliciously powerful it was like I was visiting the stars with each one. His hand on my leg turned crushing, keeping me there as he thrust and thrust *and* thrust.

Water sloshed over the sides of the tub.

I tossed my head back, relying solely on his arm wrapped behind me. He licked his way across my neck, my chest, biting and nipping at my skin, sucking on my breasts like some ravenous beast who couldn't get enough.

I moaned over and over again, not a single intelligible word leaving me.

Heat drifted across my neck, then Von's teeth pierced my flesh, slowly sinking in. The pain of his bite was gone in seconds, and my world exploded with pleasure. I was *so* close. I ran my hand over his shoulder, my nails biting into his skin, leaving behind deep scratches as he drank from me. He pulled the ichor from my veins, replenishing himself, feeding our bond.

"Look at you, *wife*, doing such a good job," he praised as he raised his head, his tongue darting out to lick my ichor from his lips.

His words and the visual of him hit me like a boulder, sending me flying over the edge into oblivion.

I cried out as I climaxed, my sex spasming around his cock. White light blinded me, sending me to a place only Von could take me. When I came back to reality, my body spent, my gaze caught on his.

"We're not done yet," he said, pulling himself out of me. My core clenched as if desperate to keep him inside. With swift hands, Von turned me around, positioning me so I knelt on the underwater ledge, meant to be a bench. His hand gripped my hip, and he slid his length back inside me in one swift thrust, leaving me sputtering.

I grabbed on to the side of the tub as his hips slammed against my bottom, sending the water between us shooting out.

"Oh! Fuck!" I groaned.

"That's the idea, love." He chuckled, his hand smacking my bottom playfully as he thrust inside me. Heat exploded as I let out a pleasure-filled moan. "You said you wanted me everywhere," Von reminded me, his hand massaging my bottom, grasping a cheek and pulling it to the side. Something cool and wet dribbled over that intimate spot. Von removed his hand, and then I heard him sucking on one of his fingers. His hand lowered back to my bottom, his hips keeping up their rhythmic thrusts.

My eyes went wide as the pad of his thumb swirled around the tightest part of me, smearing the wetness.

I bristled. I'd never done *that* before.

"Von, what are you—"

He pressed the tip of his thumb inside, cutting off my words instantly.

I gasped at the wicked intrusion.

"Trust me," he said, before he began to press his thumb further inside, exploring a very unknown part of me.

I squirmed—my body unsure what to do. It felt so strange, and yet, it felt so incredibly right.

"Give in to me, Sage," he demanded softly, rolling his hips sensually, stoking the coals of my need. "Relax." Gently, he rotated his thumb, and my nerve endings went wild. "Give in."

I stole a deep breath, doing as he asked.

"That's my good girl," he praised, his thumb slowly starting to sink deeper. I panted for air, moaning and groaning. I was half out of my mind. He gripped my bottom, his length sliding in and out of me, the sounds of our sex— wet slaps and guttural moans—bouncing around the bathroom walls.

Rapture swallowed me whole, and I climaxed for the third time that night. Von found his release at the same moment, and I could feel his hot seed lashing at my insides, drowning my sex in his essence. When he pulled out of me, the world swayed, and my body, which was fully spent, felt like it was on the verge of giving out.

Von took me in his arms, turning me around and pulling me into him. His lips found mine, his kisses tender and soft and filled with so much love it could make my pounding heart burst.

I stroked my hand along his cheek, my voice half dazed as I said, "That was incredible."

"*You're* incredible," he said, kissing me once more.

He took us to the side of the tub and sat down on the ledge, placing my body on top of his. I settled against his sturdy torso, soaking up the feel of the warm water. Von conjured a cloth and a bar of soap. He wet the cloth then lathered it. The soap had no smell to it. I knew why—Von didn't want to mask *his* scent on my skin.

A small smile touched my lips. *Territorial male.*

He placed the soap on the edge of the tub, picked up my left arm, and slid the cloth over my skin. As he did it, he asked, "How do you feel about *everything*?"

"About you sticking your thumb in my butt?" I quipped, unable to help myself.

"The intensity of your orgasm told me everything I need to know." He tacked on, "Smart-ass."

I chuckled. We both did. Then I asked, "Where did you learn to do that?"

"Do you really want to know the answer to that question?" he challenged softly.

I thought about it. The idea of him doing that with

another woman had me seeing red. I shook my head. "No, you're right. I don't."

"That's what I thought." He lowered my arm into the water and turned his attention to the other one. "I'm talking about everything Naia told us."

"I haven't really had time to think about everything yet," I answered honestly.

"You have time now."

"I don't even know where to start." Wasn't that the truth?

"Alright, I'll go first. What are your thoughts on what she said about the Creator being your father?"

"I don't know what to make of that. What do you think?" I asked, looking up at him.

He glanced down at me. "I think it's true. When she was telling us the history of your origin, I didn't detect any lies. Not only that, but I've watched you, Sage. You have an unfathomable amount of untapped power, power I believe surpasses my own. I've seen little glimpses of it, here and there." He paused. "For example, when the stone giant hurtled the slab of land at you and the others. Out of nowhere, you created a mountain, just like that. I believe you are more powerful than either of us know. So yes, I do believe you are the daughter of the Creator."

Face shifting back down, I stared at the ancient symbols etched into the wall. I sat with that for a moment. I needed to.

If I was truly the Creator's daughter, what did that mean for me? If the Mother Realm had the same hereditary monarchy laws as the Three Realms, it would make me heir to his throne—a throne overtaken by the empress, who was technically . . . my stepmother. Her ruthless laws had destroyed these lands and made so many suffer.

A heavy weight fell over my shoulders, pushing them down.

"Talk to me," Von said, dipping the cloth back into the water, warming it.

"If I'm his daughter, does that mean it is my responsibility to fix this broken world?" I asked, the words bearing even more weight the moment I freed them from my tongue.

Von lowered his cheek to the side of my head. "No, it's not your responsibility. Who your parents were does not define who you have to be." He dropped the cloth into the water and wrapped his arms around me, hugging me tightly.

I needed it.

I felt some of that pressure ease, but not all of it. My fingers intertwined with his.

"Can I be honest?" I asked, my voice small, as if the walls might judge me for what I was about to admit.

"Always."

"I feel for those who have to live in this world, I do. It is not right, what the empress is doing to them." I took a breath. "The Sage who grew up in the cottage would want to stay here and see if she could help make this world better, but . . . the Sage I am now? All I want to do is find our baby's soul and go home to the Three Realms as a family. Does that make me horrible? For wanting that?"

528

"That doesn't make you horrible at all, my love," Von answered. "Putting your needs before others is okay to do, especially in this situation. You have lost so much, and now, you just want what we once had—a second start at a family. It's okay to let that be the thing that drives you. The rest is just noise."

"Says the villain."

"Says *your husband* who wants what's best for you," he corrected me.

I grinned at that, glancing at the rings on our fingers.

We spoke for some time after that, and when Von finished washing every inch of me, he dried my skin and carried me to the bedroom. He brushed my hair, braided it, and then we crawled into bed.

Chapter 61

Sage

My *mother always had a calm, flowing way about her,*
much like a gently rolling tide, smooth and rhythmic. She
loved to laugh, and when she did, it was infectious. Soon,
you'd find yourself laughing too. Her smile was bright—so
bright, it could light up the dark. That was why she'd been
given her name. Luna.

When I was a little girl, I would sit on the floor in front
of my mother as she brushed the knots from my hair. As she
did that, she'd tell me stories. Sometimes, they were funny
ones, and we'd laugh and laugh and laugh, no matter how
many times I had heard them before. Other times, she would
tell me fables, full of warnings.

There was one in particular she didn't tell it often, but
when she did, it always stuck with me for a while. It was of
a girl whose family had left their war-torn country in hopes
of finding a better life. While the girl went down to the river

to bathe, she caught the eyes of a giant wolf who stood downstream. Frightened, she waited to see what the wolf would do, worrying it had come to devour her, but the wolf simply sat there, watching her. For the next three weeks, as the family continued their travels, the wolf would appear to the girl every so often, to the point she started to trust it. One day, she was walking through the woods, searching for food, and she heard the roar of a bear. It emerged from the trees, and then it charged at her. She started to run but tripped and fell. Seconds before the bear's massive mouth nearly clamped down on her, the wolf showed up, growling and snarling as he flew into the bear's side, knocking it away from her. It was a bloody battle between the two animals, but ultimately, the wolf won, and the bear ran off into the trees. The wolf approached the girl. "You saved my life," the girl said to it. She opened her arms to give the animal a hug, but its maw found her throat, and it snapped her neck. Then, the wolf ate her. He wasn't her savior—he had just been protecting his food source all along.

Initially, the girl's instinct had been not to trust the wolf, but with time, as it appeared to her over and over again, she'd let her guard down—something which ultimately led to her demise.

I realized now I was no different from the girl—in place of a wolf, though, it was a dragon. And instead of my life, it was my heart I had given to him. During the months we'd spent together, locked away from the world, I'd fallen deeply for the male who'd told me his name was Von, and I'd thought he had fallen for me. We vowed we would be together. On the day that I planned to give myself to him, a bird passed through the barrier at the top, flying out of it. It didn't ripple or wave like it had done before, and we realized the barrier that had kept us in was gone. Von flew us out of there. When we reached the top, he said he needed to get back to the emperor, to speak with him, to tell him he would take me as his wife. Then, he would return for me.

But he never did.

He never came back.

And I never saw him again . . . until today.

I could have done so much worse to him than just tossing my wine in his face, however wonderfully cathartic it felt. My only regrets was not grabbing a wine jug and dumping the entire thing on his head instead.

As the spectators cheered outside, Empress Avena strode in front of me, her too-pretty face twisted in anger as she snarled, "Explain everything. Now."

I dabbed at my tears, wiping them from my face. "Fine, but can we speak somewhere else?"

"Very well." Her light wrapped around us both.

We returned to the Celestial Opal Palace, and there, I told her what she wanted to know, although I left a few parts out.

Wolves came in many different forms.

Later that night, I felt exhausted, my body emotionally spent. All thanks to the bastard who had played my heart like a fiddle and then tossed it into the flames like it meant nothing to him, letting it burn to ash.

I laid on the soft, luxurious bed in the grand chambers I stayed in, an arm draped across my face, covering my eyes. Despite everything, the empress was still hopeful that I'd be able to charm Nockrythiam again. It was as if she had completely missed the part about me saying that he'd promised to come back for me, but he hadn't. The empress seemed quite intelligent, so I couldn't possibly understand where her blind faith was coming from. I couldn't shake the feeling she knew something I didn't, but what could it be?

What was I missing?

Knuckles rasped against the door.

I jerked upright and looked out the window, clocking the position of the moon. It was late, well past midnight.

I grabbed my robe off the chair and put it on as I walked over to the door and cracked it open.

A dark, brooding god stood on the other side, dressed like a regal mercenary. Leather pants wrapped around his muscular thighs, cut off by knee-high leather boots—sleek and polished, forged for combat. The neckline of his tunic was cut to a low V, granting view to the swell of thick, hard muscles waiting beneath. A cloak, pinned to his shoulders, swayed gently behind him, as if it needed to move in order to handle the immense power he exuded. Black eyes burned like coals as they lowered to mine.

"Open the door, Little Mortal," Nockrythiam said from

the other side.

I knew what I was supposed to do—the empress had made the role I was to play in this little charade loud and clear. But what I was supposed to do and what I wanted to do were two very different things, and damn it all, I was stubborn. I couldn't stand the sight of the bastard.

"Go away," I snarled, muscles firing as I tossed the door back—

Whack!

In a blur of tanned skin and silver rings, his hand slammed against the door, stopping it before it had a chance to latch. He shoved it open, and I stepped back.

Lungs heaving, my pupils turned into daggers as I stared at him. "What do you think you are doing?"

"Coming to collect you," he said, shadows pooling around him, seeping down to the floor. Somehow, he seemed even bigger than I remembered, his towering build even more imposing. He moved with confidence. Purpose. Like some ancient predator on the prowl. A merciless, unyielding black dragon coming to retrieve his treasure.

"It's a little late for that," I hissed at him with the veracity of all my angry foremothers who had been left with a broken heart because of a man.

"I needed time to think," he said, his voice hitting that rich, deep timbre. I could still remember the way his chest had rumbled when he spoke, when I'd laid my head against him each night as he ran his fingers through my hair and told me about his past, about the battles he'd fought, the armies he'd led, the things he had done for the emperor. The

good and the bad. Throughout it all, I had still fallen for him.

"What?" I asked, my feet drawing me back as he approached, keeping the distance between us. It wasn't because I feared him; it was because I feared what he would do to my heart if I let him get too close.

"I planned to return to you, but when I came back here to speak to the emperor about my intentions, he told me something—a truth I could feel with every fiber of my being, and it made me hesitant."

"Well, whatever it was, I hope it was worth losing me." My back landed against the wall. I looked from side to side, deciding where to dart to next, but Nockrythiam was quick, killing the space between us.

"If I have truly lost you, then why does your heart quicken as I draw closer to you? Just as it did when we were trapped together for all those months," he pressed, his hand clasping my chin, lifting my face to his. "And do not lie to me and say it is because you fear me. We both know that isn't true."

Venom seeped onto my tongue. I wanted to spit it at him. To yell at him. To scream. To tear my chest open and show him what he'd done to my heart. I wanted to show him all the pieces I'd had to glue together after he'd shattered it apart.

But . . . I could not.

Because even though he had hurt me in the end, the good memories overpowered the bad.

There had been a time when I wanted him more than

anything.

In truth?

I still did.

Damn it all, I was the stupid girl from the fable, and I was destined to be devoured by the dragon standing before me. So what was the point in fighting it anymore?

"Tell me then," I stated, the anger in my voice slowly beginning to fade. "Tell me what it was that the emperor told you that made you decide not to return to me."

"He told me who you really are. He told me of the threats that would come your way should the empress ever discover the truth. I never gave up on you. I just needed time to figure out how I was going to protect you, and I knew that bringing you to this castle was the last place you should be. But somehow, the empress discovered what you are to me, and she brought you here, which forced my hand."

"You are telling me a lot of things but giving me very little context." I shook my head, trying to make sense of a puzzle I had only been given a few pieces to.

"I'll tell you everything," he promised me. "But first, there is someone waiting to speak with you."

"Where are we?" I asked a short while later as we stepped into a tower, completely open all they way up to the ceiling. Twisting vines, tall trees, and lush green plants grew around us, painting the towering structure in the colors of life. Birds cooed softly from their resting places. A monarch

butterfly floated past me, before it settled on a blooming daisy.

"The Creator's Tower," Nockrythiam replied, his hand in mine as he walked us forward. He guided the wispy branches of a willow tree to the side, and we stepped through them. Under the canopy of the breathtaking tree, sitting in front of a desk carved from wood, was Emperor Alaric.

Swiftly, I bowed my head.

His laughter was soft and pleasant and heartwarming as it reached my ears. The chair lurched behind him as he stood and walked over to us. Gently, he clasped my shoulders. "You do not need to bow to me."

Looking up, I asked him, "Isn't that what I'm supposed to do?"

"No." He paused, his eyes meeting mine. "You are my daughter, which means you bow to no one."

Daughter? No. That couldn't be.

Herulf was my father.

"Sorry. You must be mistaken," I said, shaking my head in disbelief, but my words were clipped short as his eyes flashed white, and suddenly, I was seeing through them— from the day my soul rose from his anvil, to the day he saw my mother dancing in the moonlight, to the day I drew my very first breath, my mother taking me in her arms, crying tears of joy and everything that followed. Then came a memory of when he had appeared to me as a deer with a white marking on its neck, racing through the forest, drawing me toward—

I gasped, realization dawning. "You were the reason we were trapped in that hole, weren't you? You were the deer! Leading me toward it."

"I was," he answered, a mischievous twinkle in his eye. "Why?"

"I wanted you two to have that time together, away from prying eyes," he answered, his voice kind. "Away from everything and everyone. Away from her."

"You know, most parents arrange courting sessions for their children. They don't trap them in a hole in the ground for months on end with a dragon." I didn't bother to hide the sarcasm in my tone.

The emperor chuckled, the sound like rolling thunder. "Sure, sure, that's what mortal parents do, but you see, I am not a mortal, and you, my darling daughter, are half of me."

"It just occurred to me what you meant when you said you were sending me to find a princess," Nockrythiam stated, his endlessly black eyes sliding to mine.

"Alas, you found her." The emperor smiled, and it was more sublime than a dawning sun.

Gently, he took my hand and Nockrythiam's, joining them together.

We both peered down, then up at one another.

Emperor Alaric's voice was deep and resonant as he said, "She is your bonded, as you are his. Two halves of a circle, but together, you are complete. Without one, there cannot be another. Yin and yang. Black and white. Creator and Ender. Life and Death."

When I awoke that morning, I had much to think about. My dreams had gone on and on and on, revealing *almost* everything from that day forth with blurring speed.

It was like I had opened a book to my past life, the pages empty at first, but as I flipped through them, all the words started to appear until the chapters of my story were nearly all there, right before me. Or at least, most of them were. The chapters at the very end were still missing, those pages blank. A mystery.

That day, when the emperor revealed he was my father, he also told me he knew the empress was plotting something. I told him why she had brought me here and said that perhaps I could try to get closer to her and gain her trust then share the information with him and Nockrythiam. At first, neither of them wanted me to do it, worried about my safety, but with a great deal of persistence, I convinced them both. I also made my father promise me he would protect my clan and my family, which he agreed to do.

So, over the next so many months, that's exactly what I did.

I fed everything she told me to them.

Knowing how things turned out, I realized my efforts had been in vain—the empress had won the War of the Creators anyway. Which made me wonder about the information she had given me—had it been . . . wrong?

A sickening feeling washed over me as I heard a voice from the past—my voice—answer the question—

Yes.

Chapter 62

Sage

The library in Clearwell Castle was nothing, absolutely nothing, compared to the one I stood in now. This library was a palace in itself, made up of grand rooms, sprawling hallways, and towers—every square inch of it saturated with books. So many, many books. I couldn't even begin to fathom how many there must have been. Surely, it was the largest collection in the Mother Realm, if not the entire universe.

Which seemed fitting, considering its owner was the Goddess of Knowledge.

The library smelled musty and earthy, with the slightest tinge of dyed leather.

Von, Artemesia, Folkoln, Kaleb, and I followed behind Naia as she gave us a tour of the vast library. Each time she turned around to tell us what genre we'd find in this room or that tower, her eyes would twinkle with pride. After we spent the better half of the morning learning about the library, she led us up to a colossal set of oak doors, flanked by two guards.

"This is my private collection," Naia said as the guards opened the doors and we all filtered inside. "Every item is the last of its kind. You will find them nowhere else."

From wall to wall and floor to ceiling, there were custom-built shelves chock-full of ancient tomes. In the middle was a private sitting area, and to the right, a table surrounded by chairs.

Kaleb and Artemesia conversed with Naia. Earlier, we had a brief meeting in Kaleb's room, deciding we would ask Naia about the energy stones, and then leave the palace after. Naia had been sad to hear we planned to leave so soon, but she said she understood. As the three of them chatted, Folkoln found a wall to brood against. Smoke drifted off him, disintegrating into bits of nothingness. He tipped his head against the wall, lengthening his masculine neck and exposing his prominent Adam's apple. Through his black lashes, he tracked Artemesia like a hunter watching his prey.

Speaking of being watched . . .

I glanced over my shoulder.

Vivid green eyes, the color of leaves after a nourishing rain, met mine. The mountainous male stood with his heavily inked arms crossed, his muscular body clad in leather pants and a black tunic stretched firmly across the breadth of his chest. He was a demon of a god, a lethal, dark temptation, brimming with unrivaled power.

And he was *mine*.

My pulse quickened as the rapturous memories of last night returned to me. His umbra twins had been an unexpected surprise, pleasuring me as I pleasured their master. Von had been rough with me in all the best ways, and yet this morning, I felt none of it, not a lick of pain. I suspected he had used his ability to heal me. Whether he did that last night or when he'd woken me with his head between my thighs this morning, I didn't know.

Light footsteps sounded at the entrance, pulling my attention to it. A girl, carrying a tray with two teapots and six cups, walked inside. She bowed her head toward Naia and then scurried over to the sitting area. Gently, she placed the tray on the lower, oval table.

"Ah, the tea is here." Naia clasped her hands together. She walked over to one of the wingback chairs and sat down. She gestured to the cups as she said to the girl, "If you would be so kind, my dear."

"Of course," the girl replied, her voice soft. She reached for one of the nearly identical teapots. As she poured the tea, Kaleb, Artemesia, and I joined her. The smell of cinnamon, turmeric, ginger, and something else I couldn't quite detect permeated the air. I breathed it in. With it, nostalgia bloomed. It reminded me of when life was much simpler—when Ezra and I would sit across from one another, a blanket draped across our laps, and hot cups of tea in our hands. I yearned to revisit those days sometime soon, with Ezra.

Ezra . . . how I missed her.

"It smells so good," Artemesia crooned as she selected

two cups, offering me one of them. The act pulled me from my wistful thoughts.

"Thank you," I said, taking it. It was hot against my fingers. Steam danced from the golden-colored water, swirling and twirling. Artemesia and I sat down on one of the settees beside one another.

"What kind of tea is it?" Kaleb asked as he took one of the cups and sat down across from us.

"It's called dragon's delight. It's a blend of different spices, but it's the rubrum draco aroma that makes it so highly sought after," she answered.

"It comes from the red dragon tree," Von said, emerging from the shadows. I glanced at him, wondering if he had remembered something.

"Indeed, it does. There was once a time when you were quite fond of it," Naia answered, reaching forward and picking up a cup. She offered it to Von.

"I'll have to take your word for it," he said, taking it as he sat down beside me. I shifted closer, yearning for that constant contact. The pull I felt to Von was gravitational—always tugging me toward him, like the river to the ocean. The tide to the moon. My soul to his.

Naia picked up another cup, extending an arm toward Folkoln as she asked, "What about you, dear?"

"I'm not a tea drinker," he said, declining her offer as he sat beside Kaleb.

"You are missing out," she spoke in a teasing tone. She withdrew the offered cup, taking it with her as she returned to her chair. Her attention swung to me. "Now, Sage, dear,

I've been meaning to ask—have you thought about what we discussed yesterday?"

"I have. I've decided I'm going to hold off on it for now," I replied, resting my cup in my lap. Out of respect for my mate, I wouldn't put him through that, feeling my pain and suffering as I was cut into. Perhaps Von was right, perhaps sometimes, I could be too trusting.

"That's completely understandable," she answered, nodding slowly as she blew on her tea, scattering the swirls of steam.

"There's another reason why we came," Von started. "We were hoping you could tell us about this." Shadows pooled in his flattened palm, conjuring the necklace he had gotten from the giant.

"May I?" Naia asked, setting her cup down beside her on the end table.

"Of course." On the breath of his wind, he sent it over to her.

"It is a travel stone," she said as she studied it, rotating it around. "I believe around sixty-five percent of travel stones came from the Elswaina mines. Due to the stones' inactivity, the mines shut down. Now, they are nothing more than a relic, just like all the other energy stones floating around out there."

"What caused the stones to become inactive?" Folkoln inquired, tipping his head ever so slightly in that confident, superior way of his. The act was taken straight out of Von's own book, titled *Better than Thou.*

"Originally, they were tethered to Alaric. When he

died, they stopped working, like so many other things in this realm," she said, sending the stone back to Von.

His shadows swallowed it. "I thought Alaric died at the end of the War of the Creators."

"He did," Naia stated, nodding as she twisted toward the end table and picked her cup up.

"But how can that be?" Von challenged. "The giant who used this very stone to travel to the Three Realms, where we are from, did it centuries after the war ended."

"Ah, that's because my sister found a way to make them work for a brief time," she replied. "Although whatever method she used clearly was not sustainable, because they didn't last very long."

"Why did she want them to work again?" I wondered.

"Because she needed a way to send her venum stoomics out to all of the realms to look for a soul and send it back to her," Naia answered. "Their souls, due to their size, require a lot more magic to send to another realm in comparison to ones like ours, hence needing the energy stones."

"Whose soul was she trying to find?" Kaleb asked curiously, leaning forward in his seat.

But I already knew the answer—it was the same reason she had sent my soul to the Three Realms. "She's after Von."

"Correct," Naia replied, taking a small sip of her tea.

"Why?" Folkoln asked. "Why is she after him?"

"Only my sister can tell you that," Naia stated, taking a deep breath.

"I don't understand." I shook my head. "If she was after

him, why didn't she just go to the Three Realms herself? Why send giants? Why send me?"

"Before the Creator died, he tied her life force to the Mother Realm," Naia answered. "She physically cannot leave here, which is why she has to send others out to do her dirty work."

Kaleb scrubbed at his jaw. "I have a question." We all looked at him. "If the Creator was the one who originally powered the energy stones, and Sage is his daughter, shouldn't she be able to power them too?" he asked.

Collectively, our gazes all swung back to Naia.

"It's quite possible," she replied.

A small seed of hope planted itself within me—if I could power the energy stones, we might be able to find our way home.

"However, a word of caution," Naia said, her brows lifting. "Energy stones consume power at a monumental rate. It took your father many, many years before he was able to get them to work. You should train yourself and slowly build up toward powering them. If you don't, who knows what it might do to you? It could drain your soul's energy completely, something there is no returning back from."

A flavor spread across my tongue. It was bittersweet, like lemons and honey.

"I understand," I answered, sparing a glance at Von. Black lashes lowered, his eyes shifting to mine. In the depths of them, I found confirmation of what flavor I was tasting—*worry*. The bitter part stemmed from his concern, and the sweet part was because he cared for me.

Naia tapped her chin with one long finger. "Come to think of it. I believe your father had a journal somewhere where he documented how he learned to power the stones. Perhaps it would be of use to you. That is, if it still exists."

My hand slid into Von's, and I offered him a reassuring squeeze. Looking back to Naia, I asked, "Do you have any idea where we might find it?"

"I don't, but I can have some of my scholars look into it. You might have to extend your stay a day or two longer, though, to give them some time," she replied.

I glanced at everyone else, trying to read their faces. I knew we were all eager to get going and join back up with the others, but my father's journal could help me learn how to power the stones, which would be our ticket home. "What do you all think?" I asked them.

"The journal could be very beneficial to you and the rest of your group," Artemesia said, shrugging one shoulder.

Kaleb nodded.

I looked at Folkoln. "What are your thoughts?"

"If it helps us get home, it's worth the wait," he stated, dark pools shifting to Von. I followed his gaze.

"Thoughts?" I asked my mate.

"Many," he answered, but didn't expand any further. The smallest taste of lemon and honey returned, and I knew his *many* thoughts centered around me. Von was trying to decide what the safest option for me was, but that wasn't what this was about—it was about what was best for the group.

If it can help me safely power the stones, it's worth it, Von, I spoke down the river that linked our thoughts.

Von studied me, reading me as if I were a book. Then, with a hint of reluctance, he spoke out loud, "We'll stay one more day."

"Wonderful!" Naia exclaimed, standing and walking over to the table. She poured herself another cup. "Now . . ." She lifted the teapot and smiled. "Who would like more tea?"

Realizing I had yet to try it, I lifted the cup, noting it felt much lighter than before. I glanced down—

It was empty.

Did you have something to do with this? I pushed the question into Von's mind.

Yes, he answered back, face as unreadable as a blank sheet of paper.

Why?

Von's attention flicked to Naia. *She's being pushy about the tea. She couldn't have cared less if we ate the food and drink she had prepared for us this morning, but she went out of her way to offer each one of us a cup. I spoke with Folkoln—he finds it suspicious as well.*

Okay, but she's drinking it too. If it is poisoned or something, why would she do that?

Doesn't mean anything. She could have an antidote.

He wasn't wrong.

So then . . . What about Kaleb and Artemesia?

Folkoln already took care of Artemesia's cup. Kaleb can be the guinea pig.

Von, I scolded him.

He just smirked.

I sighed, watching as Kaleb stood. He extended his empty cup toward Naia. "I'll have some more."

"Wonderful," Naia exclaimed, positioning the spout over his waiting cup and filling it up. "Anyone else?" Her attention swung to me. "Sage?"

"I'm good, thanks," I said, smiling warmly. The second Naia looked away, I swung my face to Von's. I squinted at him, shooting little daggers as I demanded through the bond, *Drain his cup.*

He's already had one cup. What's the harm in—

Von! I cut him off in a harsh growl.

Alright, alright, he replied in a smooth, playful tone, eyes shifting toward Kaleb's cup.

Chapter 63

Sage

Later that night, I stood in front of the window in the bathroom, brushing my wet hair, a towel wrapped around me. I studied the full moon. It was huge, but despite its impressive size, it was the color of it that caught my eye—blood red. It lit up the desert lands, painting the dunes an eerie, ominous color.

Von's arms swept around me, pulling me into him. A smile bloomed on my lips.

He dropped his head beside mine, his heated breath tickling the shell of my ear. "For many years, I stood outside your bedroom window, watching as you'd brush your hair, wondering what it would be like to do it for you. Now that I'm on the other side, I intend to answer that question every night." Long fingers curled around my wrist, stalling my hand so he could pluck the brush from it.

I nibbled on my bottom lip then asked in a sensual tone,

"Are you sure *that's all* you wanted to do to me back then?"

"Brushing your hair was one innocent thought . . . among a thousand depraved ones," he purred, taking a step back. Playfully, he tapped my bottom with the flat of the brush. "Now let me brush your hair, wife, just so I can mess it up after."

The unexpected little swat stirred a giggle from me. "Such a gentleman you are," I teased warmly.

"If there is one thing I'm not, it is that." He gathered my hair and swept it back. He started at the ends, but I'd brushed the majority of those tangles out, so he moved the brush further up, working on the middle section.

My hair could be a real nightmare sometimes. Although my strands were thin, they were bountiful, which was a recipe for calamity. It didn't matter if I brushed it until it resembled soft silk; by the end of the day, my hair was guaranteed to be tangled.

And it had been like that for as long as I could remember.

In truth, it was something I used to be very self-conscious about when I lived in the Golden Palace, especially after I had overheard the other goddesses laughing and exchanging jokes about my hair—

What type of immortal has hair like that? At the end of every party, she looks like the king took her to a back room and had his way with her. That, or maybe he loaned her out to his friends.

Maybe someone should introduce her to a brush.

I would, but I'd be scared to lend her mine—who knows

what kind of fleas that horrible hair harbors, especially considering the God of Death shows up and takes her every time she falls ill? Who knows what he does to her.

She probably gets down on her knees for him. She's got whore hair—makes sense she would act like one. Disgusting female. The king should do all of us a favor and strap her to the tree with the white leaves in the courtyard. He's shown her nothing but patience and kindness, but she fails to bear children for him. Sometimes, one needs to know when to put a useless bitch down.

They'd gone on and on, their words like knives, cutting me where I stood. Tears pricking my eyes, I'd gathered my skirts and raced out of the room, searching the massive palace for Aurelius. When I'd finally found him, I'd thrown myself into his arms and told him what I'd heard. Soothingly, he'd stroked my hair and said he had a solution to the problem—instead of leaving my hair down, like the other goddesses wore theirs, perhaps I should wear it in braids or in an updo of some sort. That way it wouldn't get so tangled come the end of the day.

I had been hurt and saddened by his suggestion, but I had done as I always did when it came to moments like that one—I stuffed them in a box, shoved them into the furthest, deepest recesses of my mind, along with all the others, and nodded, telling myself he was right, that he knew best.

The next morning, when my lady's maid came to my room, she'd told me I would be wearing my hair different from that day forward. I'd never known the pain of my constrictive corset could be transferred to my head, but as she'd tugged and pulled on my hair, braiding it so tightly it felt like it was being plucked out of my scalp, I'd learned it could. After she was done, I'd went to the throne room, taking my spot beside Aurelius's throne. He'd given my hand a squeeze, telling me this was a wonderful improvement, and then went about his duties.

All the while, I stood there, slowly dying inside.

But now, here I was, standing in front of someone who adored me. Who loved *all* the messy parts of me—tangles and all.

Von *cared* for me.

He loved me.

Aurelius *never* had.

He'd hated me.

And now I understood the difference.

Hate made you feel small. It stole your worth and drained you of all you were.

Love made you feel big. It taught you your worth and made you feel empowered.

Hate was trauma and tears and broken bones.

Love was healing and happiness and tender touches.

Love gave you courage.

"Von," I said, my voice soft.

"Yes, my darling?" he asked, working on a section of hair.

"I need to tell you something," I whispered, my heart quickening. I was ready to tell Von what Aurelius had done to me. I was ready to say the word I had been hiding from—

Rape.

I started out slow. "Do you remember when you asked me why my hands were trembling?"

The brushing stopped for a second then slowly picked back up. "I do."

"I'm ready to tell you why."

"Alright."

I took a shaky, shaky breath, knowing I was going to need it and a thousand more. "When—"

Our door swung open, and the words on my tongue died. Footsteps rushed into our room, then into our bathroom. *Folkoln.*

"Don't you know how to knock?" Von snarled at him.

"Knocking is for those with patience. I have none. Besides, it wouldn't be the first time I've walked in on you with a—" Folkoln clamped his mouth shut. His eyes slid to mine, and he reached up to scrub at the back of his neck, offering me an apologetic grin. "Never mind."

The bond took over, painting my vision red. Now it was *my* turn to snarl at him. "Were you about to say *with another female*?"

"No, no." Folkoln shook his head. He stopped, quirked a brow, took a deep breath, and moaned, "Creator above, your jealousy makes for a tasty little meal. I wonder if your sister would taste the same."

"Von?" I asked.

"Yes, love?" he replied.

"Give me the brush." I held out my hand.

He dropped it in my palm. "Aim for his head."

"Wait. Wait," Folkoln said, raising his hands, stopping

me just before I was about to chuck it at him. "I come in peace, alright? Actually, Von, I was wondering if I could talk with you."

Von's voice was flat. "Well, speak and get it over with. I have to finish brushing Sage's hair."

He smirked. "Is that code for some kinky sex thing?"

"Folkoln!" Von and I shouted at the same time.

He chuckled, lowered his hands into his pockets, and said, "I don't think this is something Sage is going to want to hear. It's about Artemesia."

"Whatever you have to say about my sister, you can say to me," I told him, lowering the brush to my side, my arm still more than ready to fire at a moment's notice.

"You want to hear me talk about how bad I want to bone your sister?" he asked, looking genuinely surprised.

"No. No!" I shook my head, trying to forget what he just said. I turned to Von. "Before he says anything else I can't forget, maybe you should go talk with him?"

"I don't want to leave you alone," he argued softly.

"His room is just down the hallway. I'll be fine," I reassured him.

Von sighed. "I'll return shortly," he promised. His thumb and forefinger captured my chin, lifting my face to his before he gave me a deep, breath-stealing kiss. Then, he and Folkoln left the room.

I finished brushing my hair and then headed into the bedroom. A smile tugged at the corners of my mouth when I saw the silky bit of white cloth folded neatly on the bed.

A gift from Von before he left, no doubt. Always so

thoughtful, my mate.

I ran my fingers over the smooth fabric, eager to put it on. As I got dressed in the lavish nightgown barely long enough to cover my bottom, I got lost in my thoughts.

Von and I were no closer to finding our child, but I still remained hopeful. My hand fell over my stomach. I wondered . . .

What if I had been carrying them with me all this time?

In truth, a selfish part of me hoped for that so that I could experience all those firsts with them. The first kick. The first smile. The first word. The first walk. I wanted to witness all of those big milestones, and I wanted to do it with Von.

My heart brimmed with happiness at the thought, of the possibility of a future like that.

But first, we needed to find them, and then we needed to get home.

Speaking of . . . I wondered how the others were making out, wishing I had a way to reach them—

Wait.

Soren, I said, the words echoing through the chasm of my mind. When there came no reply, I tried again, louder this time. *Soren!*

A shadow mouse appeared before me. *Sage?*

How are things going? I asked.

Soren rubbed his little paws over his face. *Not great. Some lady groped Ryker and tried to buy him off Harper.* He sighed. *Harper knocked her out. Turns out, she was the mayor. So now we're trying to keep a low profile. How are things going with you?*

It's a bit of a long story, but I might be able to power the energy stones, I said. *There is a journal that might help us figure it out. The Goddess of Knowledge is going to see if she can find out where it might be.*

That's amazing, Soren squeaked. *Oh, one second— Harper wants to know what you're saying. I'll relay the message to the others.*

Alright, I'll wait, I replied, returning to the bathroom. I eyed the small glass jars full of various oils—for face, skin, and hair. But considering Von had grown suspicious of those as well, I decided not to investigate them any further. With my luck, the brooding male would probably walk in at the exact moment I pulled the stopper off, and I'd be caught red-handed. Next, I'd find myself strewn over his lap, his hand branding my bottom.

I smiled at the thought.

Something was seriously wrong with me.

Ah! Soren screeched inside my head, his small paws covering his eyes. *I did not need to see that!*

Mortified, I blinked. *You saw?* I seethed.

All of it, Soren flicked his head, as if he was trying to get the image out of his memory.

I rubbed my temple and took a deep breath, letting it out. *Sorry about that.*

It's okay, he answered.

For a minute, we stood there awkwardly.

Finally, he said, *Ryker wants to know what our plan is next.*

I have to talk to Artemesia about that. We're going to need somewhere safe to stay, as it might take me a while to figure out how to power the energy stone, especially if I don't get that journal. Also, we are going to have to get more of them, as we'll all need one to get home.

We might be able to look after that part right now, Soren replied as he scrubbed at his mouse chin. *There are a lot of energy stones here. The antique shops are full of them. Apparently, travel stones are rare, but we might be able to find some more.*

That sounds like a good plan, I answered, nodding. *But please ensure you all stay safe.*

We will. Same to you guys.

The door opened and closed. I glanced over my shoulder, finding my dark, broody mate standing there, a wicked grin on his lips as he took me in.

I better go, Soren said, and before I could say another word, he scurried back to his hole, probably afraid he'd see something else he didn't want to.

Sighing, I faced Von. "Well, how did it go?"

"Well enough," he answered, offering no more, something I was thankful for. Like Soren, I didn't want to know.

"That's good," I replied, walking toward him. I draped my arms over his neck. "Is it okay if we resume the conversation from before you left?"

He wrapped his arms around my lower back. "I would love to, but there's something we need to do first."

"What?" I asked.

"I want to go back to that room Naia took us to earlier, the private one in the library. I know she's hiding something there."

"But the room is guarded."

He winked at me. "I'll take care of them."

I blew out a breath of air, thinking it over.

"Well?" he asked, a brow raised in challenge.

"Alright," I said, nodding. "Let me change and then we can go."

The library was quiet tonight, so quiet one could hear a speck of dust land.

Earlier that day, it had been full of so many people, but now there were hardly any, most of whom were just a handful of guards patrolling the aisles.

Von and I kept to the shadows as we made our way down a narrow row of shelves.

He pressed his back against the shelving and snuck his head around the corner, looking to see if anyone was coming.

Swiftly, he jerked back, his eyes meeting mine. He flicked them toward the way we had come.

Message received.

I nodded and headed back that way, Von following behind me.

When we made it to the end of the row, I peeked around the shelf, scanning the hallway. I didn't see anyone.

I glanced back at Von, jerking my head to the left.

On silent feet, we advanced, slowly weaving toward the back of the library, where Naia's coveted private room was. When we were close to it, I placed my back against the wall and looked around the corner.

Oddly enough, there were . . . no guards.

It didn't sit well with me. It was strange for the room to be left unguarded, considering all the valuable items inside. I found it even more weird that the rest of the library had guards patrolling it, so why not Naia's most treasured room?

Well? Von mouthed the word, raising a brow, the one with the slit in it.

"No one is there," I whispered back, my words barely audible.

He gave a small nod, his sleek black hair glinting in the dull candlelight. The feather he usually wore—*my* feather—wasn't in his hair tonight. Although he didn't always wear it, I felt proud when he did. The same could be said for his eyes and the vibrancy of the green in them.

At some point, I'd become just as possessive over my mate as he was over me.

Focus, dumbass, I scolded myself.

My attention shifted back to the room. I debated what to do.

What if it was protected in another way, or what if—

Von slipped his hand in mine and pulled me around the corner, straight for the room.

"Von, wait," I whispered as he rushed up to the double doors, dragging me with him.

"We don't have time," he urged. "Someone's coming."

"What?" I breathed, glancing over my shoulder to see if I could detect movement behind us, but my inferior mortal-acting ears heard nothing.

Von opened the door and pulled me inside. That's when I noticed it, my feather wasn't the only thing he wasn't wearing tonight. His wedding ring was also missing.

The bond gave a desperate tug—*away* from him.

My eyes widened—

"You're not Von," I hissed, rearing back.

"No, I'm not," he said, turning to face me. "Hello, Moonbeam. It's *so good* to see you."

Chapter 64

Von

A muscle squirmed in my cheek, desperate to escape the clench of my molar-combusting jaw. Surprise, surprise, Folkoln was a moron—a moron who had just wasted twenty minutes of time I could have been spending with Sage. Or *in* her.

When Kaleb—who seemed completely fine post-tea—and Artemesia showed up at Folkoln's door, a bottle of wine in each of their hands, asking if we wanted to join them for a round of cards, Folkoln quickly forgot about his blue balls. He invited them in and happily said he would, his tongue nearly falling out of his mouth as Artemesia walked by him.

The bond was doing a number on my brother, but it seemed to have absolutely no power over her. Although, that wasn't uncommon. It did typically seem to hit males harder. And for some reason, it was really taking a round out of Folkoln. I didn't know if I had ever heard of someone sensing the presence of their bonded long before they laid eyes on them, but that was exactly what had happened with Folkoln. When we'd first arrived here, he'd sensed something pulling on him. I wondered if it was something to do with the fact he could feel emotions; perhaps it made him more sensitive to the bond. It was a theory, nonetheless.

As the three of them went over to a small, round table, I spotted my chance to leave. I told them to have a good night, and I made my way back toward Sage's and my room. Sage had been just about to open up to me about something—I wanted to get back to her so she could. I didn't know what she was about to tell me. Regardless, I would support her through it, whatever it was.

I reached for the handle, stopping when urgent footsteps sounded to my left.

"Von," Sage said as she came running down the hallway, straight for me, eyes wide with fear. A cape flailed out behind her. She was dressed in pants and a tunic.

Where had she gone? And why?

I raced for her, every protective nerve ending within me lighting up. I took her in my arms, eyes skimming the hallway behind her. Seeing no threat, I asked her, "What's going on?"

"Something's wrong," she spoke frantically, pulling back from me. "Come on. I'll show you."

"Sage, wait," I said as she spun and began to race down the hallway. Swiftly, I followed her, my long legs catching up to hers. "Where are we going?"

"To the room Naia took us to earlier," she answered as we rushed ahead.

"Why?" We took a swift left.

"You wouldn't believe me if I told you!" she exclaimed, quickening her pace. "It's something you have to see for yourself."

"Sage, wait," I beseeched her, grabbing hold of her arm while I pressed down on the backs of my bootheels, bringing us both to an abrupt stop. I spun her toward me. That was when it hit me—her scent. Something was off about it—she no longer smelled of me, and considering I'd been a damn dog about marking her every chance I got, that struck me as—

Her faced twisted in anger, and a glint of silver flashed as she withdrew her arm from her cape and swung it toward me.

Pain exploded in my neck as a metal dagger sunk beneath my skin, sliding along my iron bones. My nerves screamed in agony as I took a few stumbling steps back, wondering what the hell she had just done.

"Fuck," I snarled, my hand curling around the handle of the dagger. Wincing, I pulled that fucker out then studied the blade. There wasn't a speck of blood to be found.

I growled at that truth, at the imposter standing before me.

I grabbed her by the throat and shoved her against the wall, the stone cracking on impact. Pressing the blade to her throat, I demanded, "Who the fuck are you?"

"Von, please," she whimpered, her hands desperately trying to pry mine off. "You are hurting me."

"You are *not* my mate," I roared at her.

The throbbing sensation in my neck began to dull, my

nerves no longer screaming as they once were. But it wasn't because the wound was healing—this felt different. It felt like a foot going numb.

"Please, don't do this," the female pleaded with me in my mate's voice. "What if I'm pregnant? Stress isn't good for *the baby*." A wicked grin spread across her lips. Whoever this imposter was knew exactly what they were doing.

But I wasn't falling for it.

The strange feeling in my neck began to spread, crawling down the length of my arm, until it reached my fingers. I knew what this was—poison, and it was working fast.

"What was on the blade?" I hissed, trying my best to keep the imposter pinned against the wall, but my strength was beginning to fail me.

"Something that's going to make you very weary," the female said, tipping her head to the side. "But before it knocks you out, I want you to hear the truth come from my tongue, so you can suffer just as *you made me suffer*."

My hand slid from her neck, the knife clattering against the floor. I willed myself to lift my arms, to move, to do something, but the toxin was taking hold. I stumbled backwards, my head swaying. I collapsed against the wall, sliding down it.

The female walked toward me, her gait more masculine than feminine. She dropped into a crouched position, her arm falling over her bent knee. "Tell me, *Blood King*. Did Sage ever confide in you about what Aurelius did to her while you were napping in the Spirit Realm?"

Granite filled my stomach.

"Did she tell you how he chained her to his bed? I guess she put up quite the fight, to the point that he dislocated her arm." The imposter's lips curled into a masochistic grin. "But the second he pried those sweet, sweet lips of hers apart and he forced his ichor down her throat, her legs fell open in welcoming invitation."

I felt like I could vomit. I couldn't stomach what I was being told.

"He knew she didn't want it, and he said that made it even more satisfying when he stuffed his cock into her, giving her no time to adjust. He said it was like she turned into a mindless doll, disassociating from her body. He told me he became disgusted by her for doing that, so he made sure she'd feel the sting of him when she returned from wherever she had gone. He told me the sheets were stained with so much of her blood, the maids had to throw them out after."

No. No!

Fire burned through me, scorching my insides.

I was wild with anger.

Anger so intense, I had *never* felt the likes of it before.

It was blinding. Deafening. And it demanded retribution.

Blood for blood.

Thinking of that happening to Sage, of her choice being stripped away and that fucker forcing himself on her after he drugged her—it made me wish Aurelius was alive so I could cut his cock off and force it down his throat. It made me want to hunt down every rapist, end their miserable existences, and lay their corpses at my mate's feet in offering.

But most importantly, I would find Sage first. Because in all of this, *she was who mattered the most*. Not my anger or need for revenge. *Her.*

I would take her in my arms and tell her how *strong* she was, how strong she *continued* to be.

I would tell her how proud I was of her for *fighting*.

How proud I was of her for *surviving*.

She was a *warrior*.

Although she might not have physical scars to show for the battle she had endured, I saw her hidden wounds. I would do everything within my power to comfort her, to take care of her.

Tears stabbed at my eyes. I blinked them away.

Urgency filled me—I needed to get to her.

SAGE! I roared her name through the bond.

Silence was my only reply.

Fuck. FUCK!

I tried to clench my fists, tried to do something—anything—but my body would not comply.

Folkoln could, though.

FOLKOLN! I shouted down the line linking our thoughts.

Nothing.

"I wonder—" The imposter looked at her hand then used a finger to hook the neckline of her tunic. She pulled the shirt open, looking down at her breasts. "When I get my body back, perhaps the empress will let me have some fun with Sage." She looked back up at me and licked her lips. "Rumor has it, she tastes like apples."

That was when I realized who was standing before me.

"I'm going to destroy you, Nicholas," I promised him, my words slurred.

"Eh, probably not before Aurelius and I destroy her first." Nicholas grinned. "In every way you can imagine."

Internally, I roared, but externally, my eyelids were beginning to close. I tried to fight them, warring with the poison, a raging tempest dragging me under.

He smacked my cheek. "Wait, wait, before you go night-night, I have one last thing to tell you." He leaned in, whispering in my ear, "Did you know you have a son?"

A . . . son?

I fought to keep my eyes open. I fought so damn hard.

The poison was just too strong.

Nicholas pulled back, but it was Sage's smiling face that followed me into the darkness.

Chapter 65

Sage

"Aurelius," I snarled at the lie standing before me.

Every cell within my body blared in warning, my flight-or-fight instincts screaming at me, demanding I do something. But I wouldn't run, no. I wouldn't turn my back on the vulture wearing my husband's hide, which meant I needed to fight. I just needed to find the opportune moment to strike.

I stroked my power, pulling it to the surface, just beneath my skin.

"Is that how you greet your husband?" Aurelius scoffed, his voice sounding *too* much like Von's. I hated it.

"You are *not* my husband," I grated from between clenched teeth.

His nostrils flared, but he kept his temper bridled, at least for the time being.

Aurelius raised his hand in front of his face, surveying

the long, tattooed fingers. "Amazing, isn't it? The stygian forgemaster—Victor—he is rather talented, isn't he? He made this vessel to look exactly like the Blood King's."

Of course, Victor was involved in this, which meant the empress must have been too.

Did that mean . . . Was she here? Lead filled my stomach, weighing it down like an undigested meal, one I had just barely been able to swallow.

Aurelius dropped his hand, sliding it into his pocket. He tipped his head from side to side. "But as impressive as his forging is, I'm looking forward to getting back into my own body when *we*"—his eyes flashed pointedly at mine—"return to the palace."

We?

"I'm not going anywhere with you," I seethed venomously.

"We'll see about that."

Footsteps sounded, coming from the hallway, toward us. Not daring to take my eyes off Aurelius, I maneuvered to the side, away from the door, closer to the window.

The Goddess of Knowledge stepped into the room. A flick of her wrist had the door slamming shut behind her, locking the three of us inside. Her eyes joined with mine, her expression full of sadness and regret. I *knew* that look. It was the same one Soren had worn—it was the look of a betrayer.

She started, "Sage, I am sorry for—"

"Save your useless apologies," I cut her off, my voice a sharpened blade, ready to slaughter. "What did you get in return?"

"An exemption from the empress's laws that means my people won't have to live in fear anymore." She let out a breath, her chest falling along with the strength in her voice. "I had to do what was best for my people."

"You are a fool to trust her, just as I was a fool to trust you," I growled.

"Perhaps I am," she answered honestly, softly. *Truthfully*.

I didn't respond. There was nothing left to say. Von had been right. I *never* should have trusted her.

Von, I whispered through our bond, *where are you?*

My mate did not answer.

Von! I shouted on our private channel, desperation seeping into my voice.

Again, nothing.

"Where is Von?" I demanded, my gaze shifting between Aurelius and Naia.

"Nicholas should have the Blood King dealt with by now," Aurelius answered with nothing but confidence.

Nicholas.

A sickly feeling washed over me.

He was the reason I lost my family. Now, he was here, in the same palace as my sister and my brother. I'd be damned if he stole any more of my loved ones from me. I knew Von could handle himself, but I didn't know how Artemesia and Kaleb would fare against the sadistic god.

"What about the others?" I growled at Naia, concern lashing the words from my mouth.

Aurelius's eyes narrowed, swinging to Naia. "You

didn't say anything about there being *others*."

"I don't know what she's talking about," Naia lied. She tilted her head to the side, gaze shifting to mine. "What do you mean by *others*?"

Damn it. Apparently, Naia hadn't sold *all* of us out, and I'd just let a vital piece of information slip.

"Nemtuk and Imari," my tongue swiftly supplied, before I could give it further thought.

"And they are?" Aurelius asked, his tone bored.

"My guides," I said, hoping it was enough, praying to the Creator it was.

"Oh, *them*," Naia cut in, nodding her head, playing the part. "I saw no need to involve them in all of this, and so I had some wine sent to their room. The wine was laced with something to make them sleep. I imagine they will all be out for a while. Since I betrayed you, I'll pay what you owe them when they wake, and then I'll send them on their way." She shrugged, as if it was the least she could do. She raised her brows, looking at Aurelius. "Unless you want them?"

He glanced at us both, his expression flat, unreadable, then before he scoffed. "I couldn't be bothered."

Relief flooded my veins—he was buying our story, which meant Artemesia, Kaleb, and Folkoln were safe-*ish*—heavy on the ish—for now.

My thoughts returned to my mate. I tried the bond again. *Von?*

A deep yawning *silence* was all that answered—stretching on and on and on.

I didn't understand what could have been blocking me

from reaching him. Von had been suspicious about the tea, but we hadn't drunk it. My brow furrowed—maybe we didn't need to drink it . . . maybe the aroma was enough, something we had *all* breathed in.

"Well, as wonderful as this dusty palace is," Aurelius said, voice full of sarcasm as his gaze shifted around the room, "I'd quite like to return to the palace." His eyes— Von's eyes—slid to mine. "Shall we?"

"I'm not going anywhere with you!" I roared. My powers erupted from me, marrying with the stone surrounding us. With a warrior's cry on my lips, I gave a mighty heave, and the granite and limestone ceiling above him collapsed.

I didn't wait to see if my plan worked, knowing even if it had, it wouldn't be enough to keep him down for long. I dashed for the window and drove my shoulder through it.

Glass shattered, slicing my skin open as I launched to the other side.

Gravity grabbed me, its mighty hands pulling me toward the ground dozens of feet below. I picked up speed, falling faster and faster.

I fumbled for my powers, looking for the best option to break my fall.

Earth? Water? Fire?

Wind pressed against my back, and just the feel of it— of falling—called upon some instinctual part of me, and my wings erupted from my back. But this time, my skeleton wing, it was . . . it was fully covered in beautiful white feathers. *A perfect set.*

"Holy shit, I have wings," I exclaimed, tears misting my eyes. "I have *wings!*"

Focus, dumbass. You're about to be Sage splatter! my internal critic seethed.

Right.

Gritting my teeth, I twisted my body so my back was toward the sky. I pushed my wings out, unaccustomed to the heavy feel of them. I tried to remember all Von had taught me about flying. With his teachings returning to me, I looked for a current. Finding one, my wings caught it and instantly I began to lift—my body no longer falling freely.

I was flying! I was—

Thwishhhhh.

I twirled around, my bident emerging from my hand. I swung it just in time, hitting the arrow off course before it had a chance to bite. Pupils turning into slits, I eyed . . .

Myself.

Standing in a window, nocking another arrow, a wicked smile on my doppelgänger's face. Chills ran the length of my spine, my blood to running cold—although the lips were mine, there was only one person who had a smile as cruel as that.

Nicholas.

Aurelius might have stolen my worth, but Nicholas stole my life, my baby, the future that *should have* been mine. He had stolen from me and Von, and for that . . .

I would kill him.

"Nicholas!" I yelled as I fired my bident at the same time he released his arrow. Our weapons collided, but mine came out the victor—splitting his in two and continuing its deadly path.

At the last possible second, Nicholas jerked behind the wall, out of view, and my bident flew through the window, biting into the wall on the other side of the room.

That was the first moment I was afforded the chance to see that I had a chunk of glass in my arm. Wincing, I plucked the jagged shard out, dipped in my ichor, and tossed it. It fell to the sand.

In my periphery, a blur of onyx—

I spun toward *him*—my eyes met my mate's, but they were not truly his. My movement was far from graceful, as I had yet to adapt to the feel of my wings.

"Aurelius," I snarled at the imposter. Densely packed water molecules blasted from my hand, conjuring my azure sword. With my free hand, I reached out, calling upon my bident. Obliging, it answered my call, landing in my hand.

"I forgot about how much of a selfish bitch you are," Aurelius sneered, brushing the dust from his shoulder. He eyed my wings but said nothing about them. "You know this is not a fight you will win, Aurelia."

Thwishhhh.

"You have no idea what I'm capable of." I swung my arm, my bident deflecting Nicholas's arrow before it found purchase—my eyes never straying from Aurelius's.

"On the contrary, I do. I know you better than you know yourself. You are a weak, useless goddess." His voice—*Von's* voice—turned mocking. "And to think, I gave you everything you could ever want. My patience, my kindness. My *love*. I gave you a position beside my throne, gowns spun of the finest gold, and what did you do? You gave *my* heart to the enemy. You betrayed me, led me on for centuries, even when I gave you a second chance." He shook his head in disgust. "You are the one who broke us. An unloyal, useless whore. You are *worthless*."

"You're right," I started. "The Aurelia you knew was weak, but the Sage who stands before you now, *she is strong*." I pointed my sword toward him. "And you're about to meet her." I launched at him, and an animalistic growl emitted from me, coming straight from my heart—

The *roar* of a lion.

Aurelius conjured his flame swords, half a sun crowning each pommel—one with a hooked blade, the other straight as an arrow. His wings stroked down, propelling him toward me at a blurring speed, faster than fire moving through a forest.

Our swords sung as they crossed each other—fire against water.

Sun against moon.

Abuser against survivor.

Narcissist against warrior.

This battle wasn't just for me, it was for those who were *like* me. For anyone who had ever been made to believe they were worthless. For anyone who had been beaten down and told they weren't enough. For anyone who'd had their bodily autonomy taken from them, who hadn't been given the chance to say *no*.

This fight was for us all, and so was this—

I jabbed my bident, aiming low. It was a distraction. Aurelius took the bait, sweeping his curved blade to the side, shoving my bident outwards. For a brief second, it left him exposed, and I took full advantage of it—

I punted him right in the cock.

"Fuck!" he howled, his blade releasing mine as his wings carried him twenty feet back. He tossed his one blade. Sunlight glinted off it as it fell to the ground. Scowling in pain, he leaned forward—his breathing labored as he cradled his squashed sex.

I tilted my head to the side, sarcasm drenching my words. "Considering Von's size, I bet that *really* hurt."

Aurelius snarled at me, nothing but hatred sparking between us.

He thrust his hand outward, and fire blasted from his palm. I answered with my own, my flame barreling into his.

We charged again, straight through our fire.

Our swords clashed, this way and that, as we fired blow after blow after blow. In a stroke of luck, my sword caught the side of his face, slashing a bloody groove. Droplets of red sprayed into the air, drenching the tip of my blade.

Surpassing the loud clamor of our swords, a mighty voice rang out from above. "Enough!"

The empress.

A bolt of lightning blasted from the heavens, throttling between us. Like a kerosene fed fire, it exploded, causing a tidal wave of air to blast us backwards.

I spiraled around and around, my wings desperately trying to correct my path.

Thwishhhh.

I tried to right myself, swinging my blade toward where I *thought* the arrow was coming from, but I was a breath too late—

Pain exploded as the arrow embedded in my side.

I groaned in agony.

Wings catching on a current, I used it to lower myself to the ground. I landed in the sand, my wings falling beside me as if all the strength had been drained out of them. My bident was starting to dematerialize . . . and so was my sword.

My brows wove together. *Something* was wrong.

A strange numbness, prickling like pins and needles, began to spread throughout my legs, my arms. My weapons became too cumbersome. I dropped them beside me. When they hit the sand, they disappeared completely.

My left leg gave out, and I dropped to my knees.

What was happening?

Glancing down, I eyed the arrow—it had to be poisoned. That had to be what this was.

I wrapped my hand around the shaft, gritting my teeth as I just barely managed to pull it out. Sloppily, I tossed it to the side. Silver ichor poured out from the wound. I placed my hand over it, trying to stop the bleeding. Warm liquid spread between my fingers.

Footsteps approached—two sets.

Weakly, I lifted my head, my eyelids growing heavy.

"It would seem it's a good thing you didn't die after all," the empress said with a smile as she and Aurelius approached me. Light glinted off the chains and diamonds that swayed from her antlers as she moved. Her light, airy robes, adorned with intricate embroidery, swooshed behind her. The soft green fabric pooled in the sand as she crouched before me. She lifted my weary head, forcing me to look at her. My body was too weak to fight back.

With a cruel smile on her painted lips and a malevolent twinkle in her lilac eyes, she said, "You're going to help us."

"I'll never help you," I slurred.

"You don't need to be compliant," she countered. She swept her nails down the side of my cheek—not enough to break the skin, but enough to cause some discomfort. "Come now, don't make such a horrid face. It's not all that bad. Perhaps I'll even let you meet your son this time."

"My . . . son?" I fumbled the words.

"Mhm." The empress smiled with her gleaming white teeth. She leaned in, whispering in my ear, "His name is Shadow."

Acknowledgements

First and foremost, a massive thank you to my readers. I know I said it before, but I'll say it again, without you none of this would be possible. And Von's ego wouldn't be so thoroughly fed. So thank you! Thank you! Thank you! From both of us. Apples for you all. <3

Thank you to my mama, for being my biggest fan and the calm to my chaos. Thank you for listening to me, for providing endless support, and always being there for me. Thank you for passing down those analytical genes of yours—they really help with fleshing out characters.

Thank you to Sara Flanagan, my bestie who I've never had the privilege of hugging in person—someday, my friend, someday. Thank you for standing by me, through the good, the bad, and the ugly. If I started to thank you for all that you've done for me over the past few years, I'd need a novel. So, thank you, for *all* of it. (P.S. to the top, bb!)

To my person, Helyn Wilson, who has been with me since week 12 . . . of LIFE. Thank you for being the sister I never had growing up and for enriching my life in so many ways. Thank you for being *a good one*—for cheering me on, for celebrating my wins, and just being there for me. And a super special thank you to your parents, for blessing us all with such a wonderful human.

To Auntie Candice, Angela van Liempt, A.J. Vrana, Kath, Thea Green, and my fam jam, thank you all for your support, your endless love, and for being so amazing! The world can be a tough one sometimes, but you all restore my faith in it.

To the Bunnery girls, Vee and Ky, I quite simply adore you two. You both deserve the world, and then some. <3 Love you both.

To my beta readers, my street team members, and my ARC team, thank you all for your support and for stepping up when I needed you! Thank you for being the best cheerleaders and for helping me get this book into the world! It wouldn't be what it is now if it weren't for all of you.

To my editors, Jessica, Vanessa, and Alexa, thank you all for putting up with my strange writing quirks. Thank you for meticulously polishing *Between Soul and Vessel* and getting it to where it needed to be. I'm so lucky to have such an amazing team!

To my formatter, Amy, my artists, Whitney and Steve, and my cover designer, Gigi, thank you all for applying your incredible talents to this book. It's been an honor working with you all and I can't wait to see what magic you create in the future.

To Tanner, my best friend, and my husband, thank you for showing up for me everyday, for being the best partner a girl could ask for and for having such a good heart. You make life easy. You make it fun. I'm so thankful we get to walk this path together.

And last but certainly not least, a special thank you to Sleep Token for consuming me so thoroughly it made choosing the title for this book an easy one.

About the Author

Jaclyn Kot is a prairie girl, an avid reader, occasional Netflix binger and a total foodie. She is a proud mama of many chickens, two fabulous kitties and a good doggo. She lives on a farm in Saskatchewan, Canada with her husband.

She writes high fantasy fiction and likes her fantasy served with plot twists, a side of spice and morally grey males with a palate for strong-willed females.

It is her hope that readers will fall in love with Sage and Von's story just as much as she has.

Looking for the latest information on the Between Life and Death Series or wanting to connect with Jaclyn? You can here:

www.instagram.com/jaclyn.kot/

www.tiktok.com/@jaclyn.kot

www.jaclynkotbooks.com